Forty-eight Guns for the General

EDDIE IROH

	Keys to Signs	
* Short Stories	† Poetry ‡ Plays	§ Autobiograph Biography

48

Forty-Eight
Guns for the General

EDDIE IROH

HEINEMANN

LONDON · IBADAN · NAIROBI · LUSAKA

To My Friend
ROBERT SYKES

Heinemann Educational Books Ltd
48 Charles Street, London W1X 8AH
P.M.B. 5205 Ibadan . P.O. Box 45314 Nairobi
P.O. Box 3966 Lusaka

EDINBURGH MELBOURNE TORONTO AUCKLAND
KINGSTON SINGAPORE HONG KONG KUALA LUMPUR
NEW DELHI

ISBN 0 435 90189 3

Set in 9 on 10 pt Times Monotype
Printed in Great Britain by Butler and Tanner Ltd
Frome and London

CONTENTS

Glossary of military abbreviations and other terms

* Please note that on the first appearance in the text the entries to this Glossary are asterisked.

ACK	Acknowledge
ADC	Aide-de-Camp
AHQ	Army Headquarters
Air HQ	Air (Force) Headquarters
Ammo	Ammunition
AP	Air (Force) Police
Arty	Artillery
ASAP	As soon as possible
ASO	Air (Force) Staff Officer
AWOL	Away Without Official Leave
B.A.	Biafra Army
B.A.F.	Biafra Air Force
BDE	(Army) Brigade
CCC	Charles Chukwuemeka Chumah
CDO/CODO	Commando
CGS	Chief of General Staff
C-in-C	Commander-in-Chief
CO	Commanding Officer
COAS	Chief of Air Staff
COMD(S)	Commander(s)
COOP	Co-operate/Co-operation
COS	Chief of Staff
COSA	Chief of Staff, Army
Def-Ops	Defence Operations
D-HOUR	Deployment Hour
DHQ	Defence Headquarters (Biafran)
DMGS	Dennis Memorial Grammar School one of the oldest Secondary Schools in Onitsha
DMI	Directorate of Military Intelligence
EES	Estimated Enemy Strength
EN	Enemy
ENYIMBA	A traditional Ibo war-song
GOC	General Officer Commanding
H-Hour/H-HR	Hit-Hour – hour of attack
HMG	Heavy Machine Gun

HQ Main	Literally Main Headquarters (of a Unit), as distinct from field command or Tactical Headquarters
INT	Intelligence
Intrep	Intelligence Report
Jnx	Junction
Kinkana	A crude, potent home-made gin
MIL OPS	Military Operations
MOR	Mortar (bombs, guns)
NATO	North Atlantic Treaty Organisation
NCO	Non-Commissioned Officer
OFFR	Officer
Ogbunigwe	Literally 'mass-killer', a fearfully effective home-made mine devised by Biafran research engineers
OP IMMEDIATE	Operation Immediate, i. e. requiring the most immediate action or attention
OPS	Operations
OSHA	Onitsha, the fifth largest town in the former Eastern Nigeria
RaP	Research and Production (the Biafran scientific and armaments agency which originated among other weapons, the *Ogbunigwe* mine (q.v.)
Recce	Reconnaissance
RoB	Republic of Benin, proclaimed by the Biafran régime after its forces invaded and temporarily occupied the Mid-Western State of Nigeria in late 1967
RPT	Repeat
RV	Rendezvous (see page 154)
SDECE	Service de Documentation Extérieure et de Contre-Espionage – the French Secret Service
SF	Strike Force
SHQ	Supreme Headquarters (Nigerian Army)
SIS	Secret Intelligence Service (British)
Sitrep	Situation Report (see also Intrep)
SLR	Self-loading Rifle
STF	Special Task Force
Tac (HQ)	Tactical (Headquarters)
TPS	Troops
TRG	Training
2 i/c	Also 'Two I see' – Second-in-Command
WEF	With effect from

AUTHOR'S NOTE

Since this book, though a work of fiction, deals with a theme from recent history, I have tried, to the best of my ability, to establish the known dates and sequence of major events in the period covered by *Forty-Eight Guns for the General*.

In doing so, it has been necessary to seek information, check dates, and cross-check technical military terms and jargon with informed sources on the subject. I am pleased to express here my gratitude for the help given to me in this regard, over the twenty-four months that this book has taken to write, by Peter Emekwue, Kaodi Ogbonna, Godwin Ikenga and Emeka Olisa – all young former army officers who gave their assistance most cheerfully and often at very inconvenient hours. A few others who, for various reasons, would prefer to be anonymous, have been no less helpful, and equally merit my thanks.

I am deeply grateful to many other people who have given me indirect but very valuable assistance in writing *Forty-Eight Guns for the General*. But I must record my very great thanks to Miss Veralyn Roberts, Chris Okoro and Bonny Esinulo.

I am equally thankful to Sean and Jenny Lewis who, for several days, spent most of their free time painstakingly going through the final typescript for me.

Three more people who deserve my special thanks and deep gratitude are Miss Rachel Ego Onodugo and Esther and Edna Njoku who, as temporary part-time secretaries, devoted themselves almost full-time to typing and retyping my unflattering scrawl. Their contribution to the completion of this book was valuable.

Enugu, April 1975   *EDDIE IROH*

PROLOGUE

It was not like the night before, nor one of those other inauspicious nights.

The time was fifteen minutes to three o'clock and the darkness was complete. The sky was cloudlessly clear and the tropical air made the nostrils tingle. The elements' conspiracy of silence was not breached by the insistent chirps of field crickets and muffled rustle of leaves. It was a perfect night for a clandestine operation.

A few minutes back, everything and everyone had been cleared from the tarmac.

Dozens of crates of goods classified as 'essential supplies', and several other cases of undisclosed wares had been trundled into waiting military trucks in one brisk and precise movement.

The handful of ground personnel, who usually lingered on after the post-arrival chores, had been given a sudden air-raid alarm to get them out of the way. Usually nervous and tense from fear of possible raids on the new airstrip which, they knew, was a prime military target, they had relaxed that morning in the euphoria generated by the twin good omens of pitch darkness and perfect stillness.

On a deserted bay of the airstrip, some three hundred yards from the runway, a black Mercedes saloon merged with the tarmac-black darkness. The bay was known as Finger Eight, the lot used exclusively by top military-government officials.

Inside the car, Captain Michel's icy calm began to melt. His palms nervously traced the diameter of the steering wheel. He took a brief, anxious look at the illuminated watch strapped to his left wrist, felt for the tiny knob and began to wind it, twisting furiously, wishing he could give time and events a hastening prod.

A few seconds later, and as if his action had triggered it off by remote control, the sharp, angry burst of a Bofors anti-aircraft gun rent the air, rudely breaching the black serenity of the night. For a second a flash lit up the runway, silhouetting the giant aircraft perching like an enormous black eagle.

For Captain Michel the blast signalled the 'All-Clear'. It restored his calm.

The right offside door of the car opened noiselessly and Michel came out slowly. He was a cautious man. He put his right foot on the door frame, heaved himself up several inches taller and reconnoitred his surroundings. The dark, still night stared back at him.

1

Back behind the steering wheel, he gunned the powerful engine, engaged the gear with slow deliberation and slid off, very slowly, towards the waiting aircraft. His blacked-out head-lamps gave out two strips of light that shone no brighter than pencil torches.

Some fifty yards from the aircraft, Captain Michel stopped the car and climbed out. With the natural confidence of one who knew his surroundings even in the darkness, he walked quickly towards the Super Constellation buried in the blackness of the dark runway.

From the aircraft's cockpit, the pilot snapped on an interior light, spilling an arc of bright glow around the nose of the giant aeroplane. Headphones tight across his dark crew-cut, the pilot leant towards his window and gave Michel a lop-sided grin and slow wink.

Pilot Wilmer, though a veteran of the midnight runs, never failed to experience moments of tension and anxiety on this strange strip in the middle of a tropical jungle. But the appearance of the familiar, confident Michel seemed to relax him.

The captain winked back at the pilot, thrust both hands forward above his head and gave the cockpit crew an extravagant thumbs-up.

Pilot Wilmer nodded Michel on, inclining his head slightly over his left shoulder in the direction of the main gangway.

Michel took the stairs two at a time.

The huge aircraft had been stripped bare of all but six seats, to make room for the crates and cases. On the remaining seats sat six white men in civvies.

"I'm Michel," he extended an open palm to the first white man. "Michel Debré?" the man enquired, his face dead as a waxwork.

The others laughed briefly.

"No thanks," Michel smiled. "Just Captain Michel. The surname might twist your tongue."

The first white man rose on cramped feet, shook the hand firmly, rather forcefully. "The name is Rudolf. Colonel Jacques Rudolf." The English bore a French accent that was beginning to wear thin at the edges.

Rudolf introduced the other five men, surnames first. Later he was to learn to his amusement that most Africans introduced themselves forenames first.

"Did you have a good flight, sir?"

"Rather bumpy. Pretty old ship this." It was the second white man who answered. His English, Michel noted, had a native twang to it.

Led by Michel, the six men came down the gangway, each holding a bulging knapsack. Each one winked his thanks to Wilmer and his co-pilot and followed Michel to the waiting car.

Not far from the runway, across a narrow stretch of bush, was an

2

uncompleted single-storey building that served as control tower for the airstrip, from which a man in military uniform watched the ground proceedings through a pair of binoculars. The building was in total darkness and expertly camouflaged from hostile eyes with thick green palm-fronds that, in day time, married harmoniously with the surrounding vegetation.

From his position on the balcony overlooking the runway, and in the glow thrown by the Constellation's cockpit light, the man in uniform could easily make out the figures of the black man and the six white men.

He pushed the binoculars from his face and, without turning his head, snapped his fingers several times over his right shoulder.

Another man walked across the darkened room and joined him on the balcony.

"Now!" the first man said tersely.

The second man went back quickly across the room to a rear window, opened it, pushed aside the curtain of palm-fronds, picked up a torch-light from the window sill and thrust it through the opening. He snapped the torch-light on and off. He did it three times.

The flash blinked at the gunners crouched behind the battery of Bofors some two hundred yards inside the bush.

A gunner took an instant hold of his nerves and adjusted his grip on the heavy gun. He released three shots in quick succession.

It was the 'All-Clear'.

A neat row of hurricane lamps with red globes appeared on both edges of the runway, straight as a ramrod, for nearly one mile.

The man with the binoculars soon appeared on the glowing runway too, to set the Super Constellation on its way.

For a brief moment he thought grimly what a clear, sitting target the precious, precarious jungle airstrip made for a hostile plane at that time. It had happened before. Not once, not twice, but almost every night since the test-landings began one week previously. A distant whine, a frantic fusillade from the anti-aircraft guns, a bomb or two, though no direct hit yet. But he knew that one day a plane would be wrecked, many people wounded, a few killed, including, perhaps, a ground control man with bats in his hands.

The thought filled him with sudden apprehension. But he rallied in the same instant. "Not tonight," he told himself hopefully.

With the mute, arcane language spoken with eloquence between all flight crews and ground control staff, the man and Wilmer had the engines revving in noisy unison soon after.

The man knew little about the big black car parked a few hundred yards from the roaring aircraft. He needed not to know, as his commander would put it.

All he knew was that it was a state car. He could link the presence of the car with the elaborate precautions against the presence of ground personnel on the airstrip soon after the unloading of cargoes.

He was not unduly bothered by this lack of information. He was getting to live with operations carried out on a no-need-to-know basis.

In any case, he thought with complacent resignation, whatever was going on must be on the orders of Defence Operations. And they knew best.

The big car did not move until the aircraft had safely peeled off the runway and headed back for Lisbon.

Then, with its black window-curtains drawn, it drove on to the runway, heading south. For a brief minute the departing Constellation was directly above the Mercedes, a huge fighter aircraft giving escort.

PHASE ONE:

End of a Bad Week

CHAPTER ONE

IT WAS THE first week of October.

Mangoes, oranges, pawpaws and sour pears – loyal trees all – hung green and drooping with their seasonal burden. The rainy season was beginning, reluctantly it seemed that year, to give way to the dry. It had not been a good week for the General, his officers and men.

In a large room at the Defence Headquarters, two army officers faced each other across a desk crammed with maps and situation reports.

"I see, sir," Major Chime Dimkpa agreed, not quite seeing, and proceeded to put through the call.

Colonel Charles Chumah sat back in his soft swivel chair and lit a cigarette. "Listen carefully, Uche," the Colonel told the Chief of Military Propaganda as soon as Dimkpa handed him the handset. "I want a special lead on the military news this evening."

"That's easy, Charles. We're just about to up-date the seven o'clock bulletin," the propagandist told the Colonel.

"Good then. Get all this in, verbatim." Chumah cleared his throat to indicate the beginning of his dictation. "A high military spokesman from Defence Headquarters has confirmed that our forces have made significant advances in the northern sector of the war.

"In a war bulletin issued this afternoon, the spokesman said that our forces at the strategic junction of Opi, forty miles north of Enugu, today smashed through an enemy concentration north-west of the junction and are clearing the last pockets of enemy resistance as they continue the drive towards the enemy Brigade Headquarters in Makurdi!"

He punctuated the dictation again with another brief clearing of the throat.

"Are you following?"

"I'm all right."

"Good. In the university town of Nsukka, forty-five miles from here, all has remained quiet after our gallant forces routed the last remnants of the enemy troops bottled up there for three days.

"In the other sectors of the war, our gallant forces have been inching forward on all fronts."

"All correct?" Chumah asked, indicating the end of the dictation.

"OK, Charles."

"Right. Read it all back to me, please."

The propaganda man did.

"Very good," Chumah was pleased. "I want that on the seven o'clock newscast."

"Sure."

It was Colonel Charles Chumah's first action since he was appointed the Commander of 'V' – for Vengeance – Brigade a few hours earlier. His orders were clear: maintain a high public morale while mobilising forces to defend the capital city to the last man.

Before this appointment and his promotion to full Colonel, Charles Chukwuemeka Chumah was Principal Staff Officer at Army Headquarters.

Aged thirty-five years, he was tall, trim and not exactly good-looking; rather pleasantly ugly. His upper lip was weighed down with a heavy patch of hair which tended to lend his face a permanently severe mien that did not improve his looks.

Charles Chumah was a career soldier. He was intensely proud of his khaki greens and fiercely loyal to the leadership. His total dedication to *the cause*, even if sometimes overly zealous, was a qualification that held his stock high in the High Command.

Born on banana leaves behind a thatch hut in his native Iketu village in the former Eastern Nigeria, Charles Chumah rose from a background that was not nearly so fortunate as his military career had been. His parents had lived from hand to mouth while poverty followed them like a faithful dog all their lives.

Charles scraped through his education with communal help and contributions from his local Roman Catholic priest who hoped young Charles would take to the priesthood. But he wanted to be a soldier, and although he was older than the average school-leaver when he finished his secondary education, the tall and strongly built village boy was a natural choice for the army.

Trained at Sandhurst in true British tradition, along with the General, Charles Chumah had, as he often complained, been a ceremonial soldier until the Congo crisis of the early sixties shot him into active service on the United Nations peace-keeping force commanded by his GOC*, Major-General Johnson Aguiyi-Ironsi.

The Congo assignment seemed to have changed Charles Chumah, the ceremonial soldier. It had made a fighting soldier out of him.

"You're a soldier when you join the army, and a fighter when you have fought a war," he was to tell his subordinates later.

The Congo transformed Chumah in another way. He discovered a flair for military politics and the ideological nuances of military conflict. A man of intense emotions who hated and loved, when he did, with consummate passion, Charles Chumah came out of the strife-torn re-

*See Glossary

8

public with two passionate hates: white diplomats and white mercenaries.

He had hoped that the General would appoint him to the coveted job of Chief of Military Propaganda, but the signal came naming him as Commander of 'V' Brigade. Chumah was not unhappy. He always loved an opportunity for a fight.

The glad news in the seven o'clock broadcast massaged the city with euphoria. A new glow of optimism seemed to light up the dark night with the brightness of a full moon.

By the time the news was repeated in summary at nine o'clock, more than half of the quarter of a million people that inhabited the capital city were already snoring peacefully.

But they did not sleep for long.

Thirty minutes after the news summary, the fragile, artificial calm of the city snapped as the dark, quiet night was rent asunder by a heavy artillery barrage. Artillery bombs from 105 mm and 106 mm batteries began raining on the northern skirts of the city. Their crashing explosions reverberated in the night, violently shaking windows and throwing a confused, rattled city astir.

For about fifteen minutes the crash-landing continued, mostly at the foot of the hills, some three miles shy of the high-density areas of the town.

Colonel Chumah and his deputies were at the Signals Office waiting for the late-night situation reports from the northern command headquarters when the bombardment began. Chumah stiffened momentarily, violently threw away a barely lit cigarette and grabbed his braided cap and leather-encased swagger stick.

"Well, I'm damned!" His teeth were clenched in consuming fury. He charged onto the front porch and halted in a riot of thoughts, just in time to see the black veil of darkness that masked the city lift to flash a momentary lurid glare, followed by a trembling explosion. The ground vibrated under his boots.

He turned to notice Major Chime Dimkpa beside him. For a full minute both men gazed silently at each other in the faint glow of light from the signals room, not saying a word, different thoughts in each one's mind.

"It looks like things are moving nearer than we thought, Chime," Chumah managed to say. "I must dash over right away and see the General." He spoke rapidly. "We've got to move much faster, if possible now. In the meantime, there are a few things you can do."

He proceeded to give a chain of orders, and ended: "The reinforcements have already been alerted. All you will do now is see they are ready to move as soon as I get back from State House."

9

Colonel Chumah had barely uttered the last syllable when a distant pair of lights flashed across the porch from the left flank, forcing him and Dimkpa to blink several times and shield their eyes. He shifted his weight to the left foot, leaned sideways to get a clear look.

Only a select number of vehicles were allowed access into the Defence Headquarters premises, and what Chumah saw looked like a convoy of vehicles. He stepped clear of the beam of light and peered harder down the northern approach road.

A speedy entry into the Defence Headquarters was precluded by a network of speed-breakers that formed part of the area's security perimeter. But the laden seven-ton truck in front was noisily bumping down the uneven road with unusual, impatient speed.

Through the darkness it beamed a bright undulating tunnel that ended at the spot where the new commander and his second-in-command were standing, blinking and shading their eyes expectantly. Several more trucks and a couple of Land-Rovers followed in a long, tumbling convoy.

Chumah began to stride quickly towards the first truck as it cleared the last bump and eased up for the last plain stretch of tarmac. The driver suddenly spotted the shining gold braid and red band of a senior officer's cap and jolted the lorry to a stop with a violent screech of brakes and tyres.

Colonel Chumah walked up to the truck and surveyed the silent, mournful convoy of wounded troops and hastily evacuated military stores. It was the vanguard convoy that usually preceded a retreating army.

The Tactical Headquarters of his new brigade had withdrawn into the city he was to defend even before he had got to the battlefront.

CHAPTER TWO

THREE MAIN APPROACHES gave access to the General's sprawling foothill capital city.

A vital north-westerly artery meandered through the Miliken Hill range and led on to a strategic junction, the Ninth Mile Corner, where it split into a T, to the gateway city of Onitsha on the west and the warfronts of Nsukka to the north. A north-easterly road led to Ogoja, a ding-dong battlefront some one hundred miles away. The third approach, a southerly route, led to the safe cities of the southern heartland.

The northerly outlets were both vital and easily vulnerable to artillery and infantry action from the Nsukka sector. A severing of the north-westerly artery would puncture the only supply route to the troops' forward lines and seal off the sole avenue for evacuating to the western country if need be. A blocked north-easterly outlet would similarly cut off a one thousand man force fighting an inconclusive battle on the Ogoja front, near the northern border, as well as excise a sizable arable portion of the country.

Thus the General's orders on this score had been uncompromising from the first shot. Each hour of bitter fighting had been followed by a fresh exhortation, punctuated with strident cries of "TROOPS MUST, REPEAT MUST, SAFEGUARD VITAL ROUTES AT ALL COST".

The troops' long and bloody effort had thus been concentrated on keeping the vital routes open.

The enemy advance on the city had however quickened in tempo and ferocity shortly after seven o'clock that Sunday evening.

From behind its dark, jagged edges, a company of enemy troops had stormed the heights of Okpatu Hill in a blaze of small-arms fire that swept the few remaining troops of the General's disorganised forces from their last entrenched lines around the hill.

The vantage peak was secured by the advancing troops and they were able to move up their artillery batteries for the opening barrage on the capital city.

Seven days before, the enemy had achieved the same peak in a pyrrhic victory that soon proved short-lived after the General's forces had made an equally costly counter-attack and recaptured it, though not before their enemy had let loose a couple of artillery shells on the city centre.

Today the enemy seemed to have secured it firmly, as they began to consolidate, with a row of artillery guns and Saladins ranging up for action on the city that lay just ten miles across the dark green carpet of tree tops.

When, in the evening, shells began crashing on the skirts of the city some seven miles behind them, the General's forces panicked with mortal fear of encirclement. Hastily the Tactical Headquarters of the Brigade was evacuated as the general atmosphere along the forward positions hung heavy with imminent disaster.

Behind them the thunder of artillery continued to pound the city's northern outskirts. One shell hit a government industrial laboratory near the foot of the hills and sent it erupting in a fury of smoke and fire. Another whined further in and exploded behind a row of residential houses.

The opening barrage lasted thirty minutes. Then the Federals, by now poised to pounce, began an intense and indiscriminate bombardment of the city.

Shells hammered furiously. Even in the dark night, clouds of smoke could be seen looming over parts of the city in small, obscene mushrooms.

Under the canopy of artillery fire, the Federals fanned out into a three-pronged advance on the city. Two columns of infantry supported by a lavish battery of artillery and Saladin armoured cars struck out in two directions on the left and right flanks of a central assault force.

Before long the right flank column had the strategic Ninth Mile Corner under concentrated mortar fire. Almost at the same time, the left column advanced on the north-easterly route, and placed a solid bar of small-arms and artillery fire across the vital route at a point some nine miles from the imperilled city, as artillery and Saladin cannons thundered along the northern arc of the city.

Underneath the rumble and thunder of artillery a fierce infantry battle raged like a wild bush fire.

With no supplies or reinforcements coming through, the General's forces slowly began to despair of holding out for much longer in the face of mounting casualties. But they went on, dredging up some hope from the promises of relief made by Defence Operations in response to several distress signals.

Soon after midnight a radio message reached the harassed men from Colonel Chumah's command headquarters: the new commander, with reinforcements of men and ammunition, was setting off for the besieged Ninth Mile Corner.

The city itself held on, panicked but intact, through the initial wave of bombardment.

For a brief moment the din of exploding bombs lifted, only to let in the distant bursts of machine guns and the fierce, hope-shattering chatter of small arms coming from way up the hill at the Ninth Mile junction. Ground fighting had rolled to the city's door-step.

The town reacted to its peril in one terrified movement.

In a few minutes about two-thirds of the city's population were jammed into the southern route, now the only outlet from the bombarded city. The swarm of people jostled and shoved in utter confusion, buffeted by fear of the rolling danger. Screams and yells blanketed the air and sealed off the rumble of artillery and rattle of machine-gun fire.

Everyone on two feet carried a little luggage of hastily assembled valuables – only a pathetic proportion of each man's belongings.

Mothers strapped sleeping children on their backs, their little heads jerking from side to side to the frantic movement of the fleeing women.

Possession of a motor vehicle was no special advantage that sad Sunday night.

A convoy of private cars, trucks, and mammy wagons driven on horns, with personal effects flung hastily on their roofs, jolted and honked frantically to avoid collision with the swarm of refugees.

One truck lost its brakes, went straight into a smaller van in front of it, and set off a chain reaction that ran like shock waves down the snaking convoy of fleeing vehicles.

For nearly one mile down the route, the convoy was held up, unmoving, and across the narrow bridge it contracted into a bottle-neck of men and machines. Voices cursed angrily, heads bobbed frenziedly, arms flailed desperately, and kids fell and were trampled upon in a blind scramble to flee first.

Even then, only a few in the deluge of people knew where they were fleeing to. Most were heading for nowhere, in opposite directions from their home towns. The compelling urge was to get away, far away, from the bombarded city. Like pebbles carried by a massive flood down a steep terrain, they flowed, furiously, blindly and oblivious of destination, under the gauntlet of thundering artillery. By morning thousands would be washed up on unfamiliar roadsides, cold, hungry, and forlorn, but far away from the deafening thunder of war.

Back in the city the next wave of evacuees surged out from all estuaries. Soon they reached the southern confluence of the city and flowed into the mainstream of the wailing, screaming, stumbling and fleeing population.

The waves continued for over two hours.

His meeting with the General had been tense and overhung by mutual apprehension. But the General had not flown into a rage as Chumah had feared.

"If we lose the capital city," the General had told Chumah finally as the shells crashed in the far distance of the city centres, "we lose our credibility. But I've confidence in your ability, Charles," he had added. "On with it. While I keep vigil." He had sounded lonely and apprehensive, like the captain of a vessel menaced by a storm. And Chumah had sworn in a fit of emotion, "I'll defend this city with everything I have or die in the attempt. I assure you of that, sir."

The General had patted his shoulder in the same sad and sombre fashion with a silence that eloquently spoke his prayer. Chumah had dashed off after a hurried salute, this time not to his comfortable office at DHQ,* but to the barracks where he knew Major Chime Dimkpa was marshalling the counter-assault force.

The sight of the fleeing city had struck Chumah with a deep and depressing blow. Emotion welled up inside him and tears flooded his eyes. He felt personally affronted by the attack on the city. Its timing couldn't have been more designed to ruin his personal credibility.

*See Glossary

13

From the heavily guarded entrance to the barracks Chumah could breathe the tense, charged air of anxious mobilisation for battle. Dimkpa was by the car, saluting before the Land-Rover door could open.

"How's it going, Chime?"

"Fine, so far, sir."

"Good. The C-in-C* says to give them hell right there up the hills," he pointed his swagger stick to the hill ranges, "for daring to disrupt our civilian life." He lowered the stick and hit the side of his thigh with it. "I've sworn to him I'll do it or else. . . . I've more reasons than one for doing just that."

"I'm with you, sir. . . ."

"I'm heartened."

"And so are the boys. They're itching to attack."

"That's the right morale. Where are the battalion commanders?" Chumah enquired, starting to walk towards the rows of infantry.

"Right there in the front row."

"Good. That's as it should be. Tonight, Chime, we shall be in the front line, too; we are going to *lead* the boys into action. We're going to be right there in the front line, with the boys *following* us." Chumah had slowed his walk to dramatise the import of his remark. He quickened his stride again.

"It is clear to me, sir," Dimkpa assured the Colonel.

"Now I'll have a word with the troops first, then the officers."

"OK, sir."

An RSM's voice shrieked in a call to arms as the Colonel walked towards the troops. He waved the salute aside. "Forget the ceremonies tonight, boys. There is a war on," he said. "Tonight," he said in a voice loud and gravely penetrating, "we are mates. We are equals. We're surrounded and *all* our lives are threatened. Yours, mine, your families', mine. And we are going to fight as equals, brave and gallant equals. Tonight, right there in the trenches, I'll be with you; not behind you, with my own machine-gun!"

The troops cheered briefly.

"As you move up that hill," his swagger stick took in the arching range of hills, looming gloomily and menacingly in the dark night, "remember this: at least two thousand of your comrades in arms are trapped there. All their hopes rest on your courage and bravery. They're probably running out of ammo* now. Towards them a vicious vandal force is rolling unhindered. And behind them, as I speak to you now, your fathers and mothers, sisters, wives and children are fleeing in confusion to unknown destinations. Only you can stop them.

"You are going to get in there, knowing that as you set the enemy

*See Glossary

14

running away under fire, you are sending your family running back to the city, safe and secure."

He got another round of applause.

"CCC*!" someone cheered.

"Above all," Chumah ended, "remember you're the Commander-in-Chief's proud force. You are his last line of defence. And the C-in-C is waiting now. Waiting for good news from you!"

The final round of cheers was long and loud.

But not loud enough to drown the thunder and clatter coming from beyond the hill.

Somehow Chumah found an eerie reassurance in the continuing thunder. He knew time was not on his side, but he reckoned that as long as there was the sound of battle up there, there remained a chance that someone was still able to engage the advancing enemy. There was a vestige of hope that he would take position before the city was critically swarmed.

At twelve midnight, after a final signal to the beleaguered brigade, Colonel Charles Chumah's Vengeance Brigade prepared for battle.

CHAPTER THREE

COLONEL CHARLES CHUMAH's counter-attack force swung into action at thirty minutes past midnight.

There were none of the ritual preliminaries of counter-artillery bombardment. In any case the General's arsenal, which had been virtually emptied for the night's action, held a total of six artillery pieces, captured from a surprise, but short-lived, incursion into the west bank of the Niger River. And Chumah was quick to see the feeble drop his tiny artillery force would constitute in the ocean of enemy heavy-arms fire.

Chumah's forces formed up into three units of about a battalion strength each.

From outside the barracks, one unit led by a captain headed towards the north-easterly flank. Another, smaller, but heavily armed assault squad under the command of Major Dimkpa struck out for the north-westerly road that meandered through Miliken Hill. Colonel Chumah took command of a larger unit. The tiny artillery detachment he left behind, at the foot of the hills.

*See Glossary

Chumah's last order to his unit commanders had been to advance along as parallel a line as was possible in the vast arc of the enemy advance.

"Make constant use of your radio," he had told them, "and let me know your exact positions every few minutes."

Colonel Charles Chumah knew he was setting off with few advantages and innumerable disadvantages.

Among the more serious of his disadvantages was that the brigade, though heavily armed by the rebels' standards, had severely limited ammunition. There was no artillery to rattle about.

Behind him he was leaving no reinforcements that could be called in at any stage, however critical; he was putting everyone in the trenches.

He was outnumbered three to one, and for every rifle he could produce, his opponents would probably produce two.

The civilian base had been disrupted after all the unrestrained attempts made to hold it together.

Charles Chumah's immediate move was to make maximum use of his countable advantages, among which was the terrain. He knew the lay of the land around the city.

He concentrated on the terrain.

Thus, the point he chose to advance from was the most unlikely of battlefronts. The Iva Valley was a vast ravine, lush with green tropical forest that disfigured the scenic hill ranges which enfolded the city in their semi-circular embrace. Enemy reconnaissance had long concluded it was impassable, as indeed it seemed. But Colonel Charles Chumah knew better.

Into the valley, which was in a strategic position to the left of the enemy's right flank and to the right of his central column, Colonel Chumah poured in one thousand and fifty of his men.

At one hour past midnight Chumah halted the advance of his two other columns. They had advanced six miles from the city on their different fronts. Each was roughly three miles from contact with the enemy. His own column continued to march down the valley.

Thirty minutes later this column was exactly one mile from the nearest enemy forward line. The sound of small-arms fire now had a close metallic clatter.

"Sergeant," he whispered to the signals man behind him. "Get me Captain Duru and after him Major Dimkpa. Quick!"

"Yessah!"

In a minute the Colonel was speaking to Duru, his voice barely above a whisper. "What is your estimated position from the enemy's forward line?"

"I make it two to three miles, sir," the Captain crackled on the radio.

"Good. You are to advance to a position approximately one mile behind the One Brigade unit now engaging the enemy. Understand? One mile. Then halt, take up an ambush position and wait for further orders."

To Dimkpa he gave similar orders.

Then Chumah called up Lieutenant-Colonel Eno Duke.

Duke, commander of the ill-fated One Brigade was slipping his last clip of ammunition into a machine gun, as everything around him seemed to be whistling and exploding, when the call came. The last signal an hour before had told him fresh reinforcement was on the way. Since then his main Brigade HQ had been overrun, his brigade major killed and his ammunition was down to the last clip. He had absorbed heavy casulaties and though he knew he had given as much as he received, he had begun to realise that every second he survived was a bonus.

"Eno," Chumah called. "I'm here."

"Thanks. At last," was all he could say.

"Now listen. I'm positioned approximately a mile on your right flank. Below you and the junction there is about a battalion. Right?

"You will now radio all your flank units. We have about a battalion approximately a mile behind each of your three units."

"On all three flanks?"

"Exactly. Your boys will immediately begin a fast but deliberately disorderly retreat towards the city. But remember, just a mile behind you are our fresh troops."

"OK, sir, but the vandals are rather close."

"Yes I know. . . ."

"And they are certain to advance in hot pursuit along our abandoned lines. . . ."

"That's the idea, Eno," Chumah snapped impatiently. "I know you have been under fire long enough, but for Christ's sake use your head. Or better still, do as I tell you and leave the rest to me! Over and out!"

Several minutes passed. Chumah and his men lay buried in the silent bottom of the dense valley.

Then the sound of gunfire began to close in on them from the left flank. The enemy was hard on Eno Duke's tail.

At fifteen minutes to 2 a.m., Chumah sent a final message to his flank columns:

"Close in on the vandals. But hold your fire."

He waited another fifteen minutes.

The enemy right flank had done just what Chumah expected it would in the face of the retreating rebel forces. It shot like a spear after a fleeing enemy.

Advancing with all speed, it took the first, the second and then the third rebel trenches.

Soon a blood-spattered Ninth Mile Junction was seven hundred yards behind it. No artillery was called in to back up the swift advance. None was considered necessary. The enemy continued in merry pursuit. The artillery battery remained on the northern axis seven miles from the junction.

Meanwhile Chumah had split the column in the valley into three companies. Two lay in wait in its dense no-man's land. The third he took and began treading the armpit of the valley.

At the northern end of Iva Valley lay a steep ascent that might have once held a waterfall. Advancing in a single line, Chumah's men ascended swiftly and emerged onto a plain. The plain led through a maze of bushes and shrubs straight to Ninth Mile Junction.

Led by Colonel Chumah, his innocuous swagger stick long since replaced by a Madsen automatic rifle, the men began to crawl and crouch into the abandoned trenches and bunkers that ringed the now quiet junction. There they waited.

Down the highway that led through the meandering hills into the city, the enemy pursuit force was beginning to realise how dangerously they had stretched their lines without consolidation or cover-up action by the other flanks.

The prized and costly junction was over a mile behind them when Colonel Chumah's personal force of one company appeared from the quiet bush to occupy the empty trenches. But the thought of victory, in the form of the capital city just over the hill, was magnetic, beckoning like a ripe, drooping pawpaw. And the little energy and supplies that the swift dash had taken left the troops bulging with strength and ammunition for a coup-de-grâce.

Slowly but steadily caution began to overcome zeal, and the major eading the unit decided to slow down the march.

He couldn't have chosen a more unfortunate spot to order the halt. It was in the jaws of a rebel ambush party.

"Halt the men for a while," he told his platoon commanders. "Time to reorganise and call in reinforcements."

"Reinforcements?" a captain was incredulous. "We don't need reinforcements to get in there and finish the rebels, sir!"

"It sounds a bit too easy, Audu," the Major said softly.

"May be not easy, sir, but possible – tonight!"

"Possible with a lone brigade and no reinforcements?"

"How many troops do you think the rebels have, sir?" the Captain asked the Major. "It's a simple question of entering the town and linking up with our troops from the left flank. They have probably entered the town already." The Captain was confident, almost cocky.

"They haven't done any such thing. The assault on the capital will be a co-ordinated thing. So the Commander said. By the way, get me the Commander. We should report our progress and position. No further movement. And that's the last order."

"Last order be damned," someone muttered into his neck. "We are going to miss a chance of smashing those bastards ahead of schedule and getting into the town first." he grumbled.

"We will do fatigue for the other flanks when we arrive later," another added regretfully.

The atmosphere was relaxed as the Major tried to get through to his HQ. The argument had been divisive, but an exultant confidence died hard.

At that very point, on one side of the tarmac, in a long line deep inside the bush, Major Dimkpa, tense behind a machine gun, crouched with half of his battalion. On the other side another half itched and waited for their retreating colleagues of One Brigade to get clear of the firing line of the ambush party.

It was not difficult to distinguish friends from foes in the pitch-darkness. Only the enemy could afford the security of steel helmets.

Major Chime Dimkpa had followed with amusement, the enemy's brief debate, and had held his fire and let it go on. It helped him relax.

Then he heard the officer's last word, as he strolled over to call his Headquarters.

Dimkpa wiped his palm on the thigh of his trousers, took a grip on his trigger and shouted: "Fire!" The cry was drowned by the violent fusillade that blew out from the right side of the tarmac. The fire swept the enemy in a sudden wave that levelled almost a quarter of the massed troops. The Major lay on the tarmac, shredded by machine gun fire, a mutilated signals man sprawled across him, and a field radio set lay alongside them. A large body of the bitten troops stampeded blindly into one another in a desperate dash to the left side of the road to take quick cover and return the fire.

Dimkpa's forces, having delivered their deadly volley, quickly fell flat on their faces in fore-knowledge of what was to come.

The left side party of another five hundred men opened up on the stricken troops then running, limping and skipping into cover. It was point blank range. Several dark silhouettes folded up in quick succession as a shower of bullets sliced through men and the midnight darkness. The screams and yells were louder than the chatter of guns.

Dimkpa's side fired another burst while the left side flattened itself in safety. The two sides alternated in short, fierce bursts, bouncing their quarry from side to side in a blazing alley of automatic fire.

In front of the surviving enemy lay the city, now near, now far and unattainable. Behind them lay the road from which they had made the ill-fated dash. They began a hasty retreat, running as fast as they had advanced, and leaving at least two thirds of their comrades dead, dying or injured along the stretch of Major Dimkpa's ambush parties.

As the survivors broke into a run for life, Dimkpa grabbed his rifle, leapt weightlessly into the air and jumped onto the road in hot pursuit. Flat on his belly on the blood-spattered tarmac he swept the heels of the retreating forces with a long burst of gunfire. "Go at them boys!" he cried, waving his left and then his right flanks out of the bush. The ambushers swarmed out from both sides of the road, fell into position beside the Major and opened up with long bursts.

"Advance! Fire!" Dimkpa was running now, crouching, ducking and firing endlessly.

It was a one-sided affair, as the completely disorganised troops raced away from this bitter frying pan, to reorganise in the strong defensive trenches of the junction.

But there at the junction Colonel Chumah's fire smouldered, waiting to be ignited.

Half a mile to the junction, Dimkpa halted the ambushers. "OK, boys," he called, out of breath. "The Colonel himself will take over from the junction."

"*Who* will take over from where, sir?" asked an incredulous lieutenant at his elbow.

"Yes. Colonel Chumah. CCC himself. Ninth Mile Junction." Dimkpa hadn't regained his breath.

"That man must be the devil himself!"

"A damned disrespectful thing to say of your Commander, but I think you are right," Dimkpa took off his peaked battle cap and ran a hand over his head. "What's our casualties like Lieutenant?"

"Light, sir."

"How light?"

"About three dead, seven wounded. Mostly from our own cross fire."

"Too bad. Still, nothing is won without a sacrifice," Dimkpa said grimly, and began to mop his brow with the cloth-cap.

Colonel Chumah's own ambush squad had listened with thumping hearts to the sound of the battle down the road. For minutes they had sat anxiously on the top of the dug-out trenches, their rifles between their knees, while they waited with chilling anxiety for the success of the Major's attack.

Their spirits rose rapidly as the frantic clatter of footfalls drifted towards the junction, and overwhelmed the growing sputter of small-arms fire.

Chumah could picture the enemy retreating desperately to the safety of their erstwhile trenches around the junction. At his order the anxious roops began to creep back into their trenches. Tension gripped their rigger fingers as the dazed enemy drew nearer with each footfall.

Chumah waited for the survivors to fall into the ring formation of his roops around the junction.

Then he let out an earth-shaking yell: "Fire!" He was the first to obey his orders with a furious burst from his sub-machine gun.

Blazing lead flew from the wide arc like fiery arrows. After a couple of bursts Chumah plucked a hand grenade from his belt band, pulled the pin with his clenched teeth and hurled it smack into the middle of the confused and stampeding enemy troops. Rifles leapt up in the dark night air as their owners jerked and crumbled under the blazing hail of lead and shrapnel.

Colonel Chumah's ambush was as brief as it was decisive. Enemy survivors totalled twenty prisoners of war. In the sudden silence, the triumphant ambushers hurrahed out from their trenches to reap a harvest of arms, ammunition and equipment.

On this dark, grim, triumphant morning, Chumah's rare smile was noticeable even in the darkness. Good, simultaneous progress had also been reported by his other flanks on the north-eastern route.

Now he ordered Major Dimkpa and his forces to proceed to the junction and reorganise. Captain Duru was to fan out in a long westerly direction to link up with the two units the Colonel had left behind in the valley. After the link-up they were to wait for fresh orders.

Chumah clambered out of his dug-out and surveyed the coveted junction, bought with so much of the blood of his comrades and a large measure of his personal credibility.

In the faint light of the clear morning sky, he could see the lifeless forms and figures that littered the now quiet junction. He walked over the dead invaders and felt his way across the tarmac, to the row of captured Federals.

He inspected the dejected men closely in the vague light of the bright sky.

"Any officers among you lot?" he barked. Two lieutenants stepped forward timidly from the ranks of the downcast prisoners.

"Rank?"

"Lieutenants, sir."

"Where's your CO*?"

"Killed down there, sir," the officer pointed towards the city in the direction of Dimkpa's ambush.

"What's your unit?" Chumah the old interrogator was on familiar terrain.

"First Brigade, Vengeance Division, sir."

*See Glossary

"Vengeance Division," Chumah repeated the phrase with a slow smile. "Interesting. Very interesting indeed. At least we have something in common," he muttered. "Murdering bastards!" he scowled suddenly.

"Where's your Tac HQ*?"

"Okpatu, behind the hills, about nine miles from here, sir!"

"And your Main?"

"Opi Junction."

"Always say, sir, you bastard, will you?"

"Yes, sir!" The dejected pair stood to, hands stiffly at their sides.

"Now tell me the present locations of your so-called Vengeance Units. And don't tell me anything I can guess!" he added with quiet menace.

The Lieutenants told him at length, not daring to lie. They knew the hopelessness of it.

Chumah mentally filtered the intelligence from the frightened splutter of details. He calculated that the ambushes on the right flank had blunted the enemy assault. Neither the Federal left flank, now being decimated on the north-eastern route from the city, nor its right flank, already decimated at the junction, was in contact with the central assault force waiting in the hills. The successful ambushes had put a wedge between the two flanks and isolated them from the central column.

'God damn you bastards," Chumah cursed. "Now you can have the junction and the city if you can!"

"What do we do with the prisoners, sir?" one of his aides enquired from behind him. "Radio HQ for transport?"

"I'll tell you what to do, if I must. Take all twenty of them behind the trenches. And shoot them. All of them." Chumah spat out the words like bullets.

"Yes, sir." The officer turned on his heel without question.

"And shoot them with their own rifles!"

"Yes, sir!" And turned to proceed with his orders.

"Sergeant Duke," Chumah called calmly. "Get me Defence Operations on the wireless." The change of subject was made without fuss.

"The vandals say this is a civil war," Chumah reminded himself. "So be it. Geneva Conventions say nothing about *uncivil* war, do they?" He lit a cigarette, throwing a glow of light around his slit trench.

"In any case," he continued to himself, "Conventions are drafted by politicians for politicians who fight their wars sitting behind desks. Not soldiers who have to face the thunder, blood, and bitterness of the battlefront. Politicians of course would not know a damn thing about vengeful commanders and Vengeance divisions. To hell with Geneva Conventions. The General is the politician. He can worry about Conventions. I'm in the battlefield, and here I'm the C-in-C."

*See Glossary

22

Chumah snatched the set as Defence Operations interrupted his grim soliloquy.

The Battle of Ninth Mile Corner was over. The aggrieved Colonel Charles Chumah became a hero over-night, his sins of overzealous propaganda and miscalculation now remitted by his gallant act of having "wiped out the vandals".

In no time his march on the junction became an epic tale of ruthless, magnificent heroism and inimitable gallantry, to be told and re-told in numerous corners of the country and many foxholes of the battlefronts.

And even when he eventually lost the capital city his folk-hero image went marching on.

CHAPTER FOUR

MONDAY THE SECOND of October. The dawn of a new day. But it was like the dusk of the old, dull and grey over the deserted city.

Over the hill ranges gun-smoke still drifted up to the low ceiling of cloud. A fragile quietness overhung the night's battlefronts.

In the city itself, a ghostly quiet prevailed. From miles away one could hear an occasional sound of life as a military Land-Rover tore through the deserted streets.

The advance of the General's victorious troops continued. Okpatu Hill was behind Colonel Chumah and his forces by breakfast time on Monday morning.

At nine o'clock he was back at Defence Headquarters for a meeting with the General at ten. Chumah knew he had only gained a breathing space, not a decisive victory.

The enemy, he knew, would call in massive reinforcements in the face of this humiliation. Chumah knew too, that he had nothing to counter such an eventuality. The city thus remained in danger.

The best move, he decided, was to use the breathing space to evacuate the city officially, and prepare the ground for a long, bitter battle for it. There was no alternative.

In the afternoon lorries loaded with government property and truckloads of personal effects began rolling out of the city in a long, depressing convoy. In the city centre, shops and offices were boarded up and the litter of evacuation dotted the streets.

Later in the day, a long convoy of half-tracks with mounted heavy machine guns was seen grinding noisily and confidently down one of the city's main highways.

At the roundabout the convoy wheeled right, ground and clattered past the level crossing and headed for the railway station, to be evacuated by a special night train under cover of darkness.

The vast military machine of the new State was being quickly dismantled and dispersed to new locations.

But State House, the General's residence and command post, remained intact, reflecting the General's stubborn confidence in the ultimate survival of the city. Defence Headquarters itself had evacuated certain essential equipment, files and stores, but the military nerve-centre churned and hummed as feverishly as before.

At noon of the third day of October, all was still quiet on the fronts

By evening, a handful of refugees had started trickling back into the city to collect abandoned relatives and belongings. Lured by tales of reigning quiet from the latest evacuees, several hundreds had slipped in for that brief, vital moment.

Dusk settled on the bleak, ghost city on this Tuesday night like a huge vulture. Electricity had long since been cut off as engineers and technicians fled. Water had dried up more than a week before. The city stank of unattended sewage in the open drains.

Only one building in the whole city glowed, with power supplied from a stand-by generator: State House, the General's headquarters. This night it stood out like a lighthouse across a dark sea, the only thing alive in a dead, bleak city.

The site of State House was selected by a political premier with a deep love for nature, an eye for scenic beauty and an intuitive concern for personal security. The elegant mansion lay some four miles north-east of the centre of the city, high on the top of the table of grassland facing the ranging arc of hills several miles across. From its south portico the General had in the peaceful past ritually enjoyed the scenic panorama of the sprawling city, at night a vast and twinkling field of little fallen stars. As he stood there, like a black colossus, all else at his heels below, it had always given him a physical feeling of over-lordship, rekindled his spiritual flame.

Tonight, standing there, a tall, brooding silhouette against his glowing background, he surveyed a grimly unscenic vista: a vast grotesque ghost town, a bleak, black and bottomless sea of tranquillity, inhabited by a deathly silence and over-powering stench.

He felt alone and deserted. He rocked on his heels and surveyed the scene once again, listening and half hoping for a reassuring sound from somewhere. But only the black silence of the city kept hooting at him like a night owl.

Hands behind its back in a characteristic pose, the silhouette strode quietly into the warm, lighted room and began gradually to face up to an inevitable decision.

State House was to be evacuated by Wednesday the fourth.

The news hit the staff at DHQ with the suddenness of a hidden bomb.

It was good and bad news. It brought relief from concern over the General's adamant refusal to evacuate a site that had virtually become a sitting duck. Again it signalled the end of a defiant optimism about the fate of the capital city. But still there was room for optimism. State House was to move to a small town merely thirty miles south of the capital. There it would perch, like a threatened eagle waiting on a neighbouring branch for the proper atmosphere to hop back into its nest.

Colonel Chumah returned to his office at DHQ on Wednesday morning, tired and irritable after a sleepless night at the northern front. He read the directive on the evacuation of State House with some relief.

"About time, too," he muttered to himself, as he drew a blank sheet of paper to draft a top-secret report for the General. The grim report took less than half a page.

CHAPTER FIVE

IT BEGAN AT four o'clock on the evening of the fourth. It might have been anger at the humiliation and brutality of the ambushes that interrupted their drive into the city. It might have been part of the tactics, based on the suspicion that the rebel capital was more heavily fortified than anyone could have imagined before the Monday counter-attack. It might have been both.

When the enemy resumed their drive to capture the capital on Wednesday afternoon, the city and its environs shuddered and trembled under an unprecedented thunder of shelling.

Soon Chumah's forces began to quiver under the barrage. They had long yielded all the ground they had recaptured two days before and conceded victory to their opponents in the fight for a large slice of the northern tip of the prized capital territory. By six o'clock they were precariously installed in a hastily improvised network of trenches spanning the northern perimeter of the city, at the base of the hills. The Federals had occupied the vantage hill-tops, consolidating them with nests of machine-guns and batteries of artillery and mortar.

Chumah's position lay below the hills at the end of the slopes which rose sharply above, bare to the enemy gunsights and open for artillery and small arms to fire down on the rebel troops, for whom it was futile to fire back.

During a brief respite from the Federal shelling Chumah called in his precious six-piece artillery in a desperate bid to counter, if only psychologically, the enemy barrage that was slowly crippling the morale of his troops.

The guns shelled a few miserable rounds, in spasms and on no chosen target. But the effort only succeeded in rousing the bees.

Like a toothless man laughing last in public, Chumah's deformity was bared. The enemy batteries responded with a thirty-minute drumming that sent Chumah's lines shivering once more.

Another thirty minutes of fireplay followed. Heavy machine-guns from high on the hills beat down a deadly, rhythmic staccato. Several of Chumah's men in the open trenches writhed and thrashed about in death or injury. The casualties mounted by the dozen.

After that, the enemy again began another round of furious shelling using artillery and mortar bombs like a battering ram at the gates of the city. A thunderclap of small-arms fire clashed acrimoniously with the continuing rumble of artillery guns, and Ferret turrets poured a steady fiery tom-tom.

The air over Chumah's lines was filled with the whistle of bullets and the cry of fragments. The earth around him seemed to be erupting and throwing up showers of mud and dirt over his men.

Pinned down in their trenches by the enemy's heavy fire and unable to take proper aim, Chumah began to appraise his men's dilemma.

One step backward would bring his forces right into the heart of the city and the battle for the capital would be as good as lost. He had absorbed heavy casualties and could not ask the General for reinforcements. You don't ask for a chair when you see the head of the family sitting on a mat.

He guessed the only choice was to face the enemy with what he had and try to hold on to his position for as long as possible.

He looked up at the sputtering hills and considered the enemy's vital positions along the ranges. He caught the attention of his second-in command, and motioned him over to his trench. Major Dimkpa began to run to Chumah, crouching and ducking.

From the hill-top a lone machine-gunner spotted the moving figure of Dimkpa and began to sweep his trail with bursts of fire.

"Somebody give cover!" Chumah cried.

"Yes, sir," Dimkpa panted.

"Now, I want someone, a chap with guts who can get up the side of the hill and take out that machine-gun nest. It is causing us problems." Chumah began, his field-glasses still peering from behind the parapet at the Federal gun positions. Dimkpa followed the Colonel's gaze with his own binoculars, to the cluster that shrouded the machine-gun nest. It looked as uninviting as a hangman's noose.

"Do you want me to do it, sir?" the voice carried no enthusiasm.

"My God, no, Chime. I want somebody else you can send."

"Corporal James will be all right, sir, but I'd rather not order him. I'd rather not order anyone . . ."

"What would you rather do then? Go yourself?"

"No, as you said. I would rather ask for a volunteer."

"Right then. A volunteer," the Commander agreed.

"I want permission to promote whoever goes two ranks *before* the mission, sir."

"Three if you like. Four if he succeeds. . . . I don't give a bloody toss. As long as he gets those bastards out of the way."

Dimkpa went back to his gun, this time crawling on all fours.

It was James, promoted to sergeant a few minutes back for knocking off a Federal gun, who volunteered. "You don't have to if you don't want to, James," the Major explained to him, amidst the plague of gunfire and explosions.

"I want to, sir."

"You sure? I'm not ordering you, you know?"

"I know, sir. But I'd love to knock out those vandal guns. They killed Jupo here." Jupo was James's trench mate a few minutes before.

"OK. Good Luck. Here . . ." Dimkpa knelt down in the trench beside the volunteer, prised a ball-point pen from the top of his boot and began to inscribe a tiny star on the shoulder straps of his khaki. "You are now a lieutenant of our gallant army," he intoned. Inwardly he felt for a brief moment like a priest administering extreme unction.

"Thank you, sir!"

Lieutenant James's effort soon proved fatal. A sniper got him halfway on his climb to the Federal gun position.

With James died the rebels' last hope of holding on to their position. The gun nest continued to rain lead on their lines, making their position untenable.

The ramming and battering of the city proper became intense by the afternoon. From above the lines enemy mortars began coughing angrily. The trench lines erupted and spewed their contents about.

The firing built up swiftly to a rattling, exploding crescendo. Under

27

the steel blanket of shell and mortar bombs the enemy infantry began their advance down the hill.

Miliken Hill seemed suddenly to erupt like a volcano. Down its slopes and dense, narrow valleys, troops rolled like molten lava, all guns blazing in a furious, decisive charge on the rebel trenches.

But the trenches were now empty.

Demoralised and worn by the fury and weight of the blitz from the hill-tops, Chumah had come to the conclusion that the best method of defence when faced by an overwhelming force was retreat. It was a slow, painful decision, followed by speedy action.

He had not felt unduly ignominious about it. Almost every General who lost a stronghold or a battle in history, he told himself, did so after vowing he would rather die than budge. But they invariably did . . . alive.

But to his disorganised and demoralised forces, retreat had not meant a tactical withdrawal, a chance for reorganisation and counter-attack. It was a release from the leash of an imperilled trench.

Beaten by their enemy's overwhelming fire-power and massive strength, the General's troops fled, unchecked and uncheckable.

There was still enough left behind in the city by fleeing refugees swept off their feet by a sudden violent deluge. It was a natural redoubt for a hungry, beaten, lawless army in retreat. Without delay, they wheeled round and attacked the shops and houses.

For what seemed eternity the shopping district of the city was the seat of an unchecked reign of looting and drinking. Shots rang out wildly in the empty air. Doors and windows splintered under the crash of rifle butts. The city's largest supermarket was the command post of the rulers of terror.

Down the hill the human lava was still rolling steadily towards the heart of the city. Shells were now crying over rooftops and the ground was trembling to its marrow. In spite of their inebriated state, Chumah's deserting army was not asleep to the approaching danger. Having crammed themselves with all the food and beer their stomachs could hold, they turned to the vital contingency of acquiring a new identity.

The men's-wear departments of the big shops had their most riotous and impecunious customers ever. Each deserter fitted himself out with fresh civilian clothes and then trampled upon what he did not need.

Before long the rag-tag troops were a blaze of bright colours. And about the streets and corners, sodden khaki uniforms and peaked caps formed litter of no more consequence than the paper wrappings and empty bottles in the looted shops.

In time, the town was several tons lighter, as every man set out on the long, drunken trek home, through every bush track and footpath that led south out of the city; every man for himself.

For a few skilled drivers it was a quick flight. They commandeered the half tracks and armoured personnel carriers that formed the backbone of their mechanised units, disarmed them of the heavy machine-guns, and drove them from the crumbling city. It scarcely mattered that none had enough fuel to see it beyond the southern environs of the city. It would take them past the bridge, and that was safety enough.

A cautious probe halfway into the city having led to no contact with the rebels, the Federals slowed down their infantry and stepped up their shelling.

Once ambushed, twice wary.

They stuck to their heavy guns, as several hundreds of shells man-handled the city, tearing through roofs and razing empty homes.

By early night the shelling stopped. The bleak and silent city smouldered in dark agony. For several hundred yards away further south, the black, mourning face of the capital was lit with the bitter smile of a burning fuel dump.

Along their forward lines, once the last trenches of the General's forces, the enemy infantry listened to the silence as a virtual unilateral truce temporarily prevailed. Their advance patrol had been gone a long time. Better wait for a situation report before the next move, they decided. They must know as accurately as possible the positions of the enemy who must now be digging in for a bitter last stand inside their capital city.

Nothing happened for hours.

The silence crept in, closer, audibly.

The fright that follows late night began to creep in too.

A breeze whispered in the trees and crickets gnawed the grass.

The tension of a long wait began to grip the lines. A few got edgy. A glow-worm on the grass looked like a streaking fire-bomb. A tense trooper swerved instinctively.

No sign of the patrol.

And no firing had been heard inside the city.

No life from the city.

No war.

No peace.

Exasperation broke out like a plague.

"Let's get the hell out of here and get a move on."

"To hell with the patrols."

CHAPTER SIX

By MIDNIGHT OF Wednesday Colonel Charles Chumah and the remnants of his forces were exactly twelve miles south of the capital city. His brigade had been reduced by death and desertion to a little over three companies.

The city lay securely in the hands of the enemy.

The three companies, Chumah thought, were just about enough to guard the main southern route. The enemy, he reckoned, would be consolidating their gains for the next fortnight or so. That diminished the probability of their advancing beyond the city itself. Time enough for the troops in training to pass out and reinforce the battered 'V' Brigade.

He hoped he was right. For if the enemy had the faintest idea of his forces, they would certainly pounce for the *coup de grâce*, he told himself.

The rest of the night was a waking nightmare for Colonel Chumah. The commander and proud hero of Monday morning smoked and brooded in the silence of his new command headquarters, the abandoned staff rooms of a shell-torn school. He felt very little pride, racked by his thoughts and saddened by defeat.

It was not the physical discomfort of his new surroundings that robbed his eyes of sleep. Nor the mental agony inflicted by the disaster itself. It was the thought of facing the General the next morning.

He had failed his Commander-in-Chief. Failed the nation. And he knew too well the price of failure in this struggle. He knew even better the nature of the struggle. A struggle with a difference, where the achievement expected of you was always in inverse porportion to the strength and size of your enemy and the weakness of your own forces. It was the accepted rule of the bitter game. It was a *peoples'* struggle for survival. You did not count weapons, men and material.

You relied on your wishes, called determination: "No power in black Africa can defeat a determined people." It was based on a Maoist theory —how to beat a bigger army with scanty weapons and fewer men.

But even in his present near-state of doom, Colonel Chumah did not want to change the rule, he would not want to; he was one of the makers of the rule. The triumph of the rule would make history, enshrine their names on the scroll of history, like the Chinese. It would reverse the decadent belief that God was always in alliance with the Big Battalions. It would bring God back to the side of the Small Battalion, the under-dog. It was possible . . . with determination.

He went on, cradling his head in his palms, his mind a tormented jumble of thoughts and anguished reflections.

He was like that when dawn mercifully came to the rescue. He washed, breakfasted on black coffee and cigarettes, and went to his temporary situation room one hundred yards across the lawn.

He had not been there five minutes when the signal from Defence Operations came. It was marked OP IMMEDIATE* in bold red ink. With steady fingers, he unfolded the green-lined sheets of quarto paper slowly, unhurriedly, as if he already knew the contents. A glowing cigarette burnt away unaided between his lips as he read ...

OP IMMEDIATE

OPS/60/67

FROM: DEFOPS*
TO: CGS* mim GOC mim
INFO: COMDS* V BRIGADE mim DELTA BRIGADE (.)

TEXT
C-IN-C FOR CGS GOC(.) I HAVE FOLLOWED THE SUDDEN COLLAPSE OF V BDE*(.) THE ENEMY HAS TAKEN CONTROL OF THE CITY AREA WITHOUT A FIGHT(.) MAY SOON CROSS AND THREATEN SOUTH(.)

YOU MUST TAKE DESPERATE MEASURES TO STEM TIDE OF DISASTER(.) YOU MUST ALERT TPS* AND INFO THEM SITUATION DIFFICULT BUT NOT IMPOSSIBLE(.) YOU MUST BE READY TO MAKE TPS AVAILABLE FROM TRG* DEPOTS AND MOVE THEM AROUND AS SITUATION DEMANDS UTMOST FLEXIBILITY(.) IT IS NOT MY INTENTION TO ABANDON STRUGGLE SO GLORIOUSLY WAGED UNTO POINT OF VICTORY(.)

THE ENEMY HAS ONCE AGAIN OVER-REACHED HIMSELF(.) WE BURST HIM TO PIECES NOW AND FOR EVER(.) THIS COULD BE OUR FINEST MOMENT PROVIDED WE DO NOT PANIC(.)

MY ORDERS ARE THAT EVERY AVAILABLE MAN MUST FIGHT THE ENEMY EVERY INCH OF THE WAY(.) WE MUST TOGETHER BLOT OUT THE SHAME OF V BDE(.) ENEMY BID IS DESIGNED TO FRUSTRATE DIPLOMATIC RECOGNITION BY MID-DECEMBER(.) YOU MUST NOT ALLOW HIM TO SUCCEED(.) MY FAITH REMAINS UNSHAKEN(.) MY FAITH AND THE FAITH OF THE ENTIRE NATION RESTS ON YOUR REACTIONS TO THIS SIGNAL(.)

*See Glossary

MEANWHILE I AM GOING FULL SPEED AHEAD WITH THE FINAL STAGES OF THE SECOND PHASE OF THE STRUGGLE(.) I SHALL INFO YOU IN THE NEAR FUTURE ABOUT RADICAL MEASURES BEING IMPLEMENTED RIGHT NOW TO STRENGTHEN OUR ARMED FORCES(.) I REPEAT FOR NOW YOU MUST TAKE DESPERATE STEPS TO STEM TIDE OF DISASTER(.) ENDS MSG(.)

Second Phase. Radical Measures.

The phrases sounded exotic and full of hope. Curiosity pounded Chumah's imagination.

Second Phase. Radical Measures. Final Stages . . . In spite of himself, he smiled hopefully.

But the sadness of the truth was to wait for many months.

For as he folded the signal, Colonel Chumah heard the sound of a jeep pulling up outside on the lawn.

He put the paper in his breast pocket, picked up his cap and swagger stick and went outside.

He met the Provost Marshal at the door. There were a dozen armed Military Policemen behind him.

"I arrest you in the name of the General Commander-in-Chief," he told Chumah without emotion.

Colonel Chumah made only one request before they took him away: "Could you ask someone at Army Headquarters to see that my family is evacuated to Port Harcourt where my younger brother will look after them?"

PHASE TWO:

White Deaths in a Black Jungle

CHAPTER SEVEN

THE BIG CAR sped along the airstrip and soon was on the broad tarmac road from which the airstrip was carved out at its finest stretch.

The only sound for miles was the deep, throaty purr of its powerful engine. Through the windscreen, misty with early morning dew, the white men caught their first glimpse of this extraordinary country whose problems had dominated their lives for nearly four weeks.

It wasn't much of a sight; a dull lit tunnel hewed through the mountain of darkness by the two streams of light from the car's almost painted-out head-lamps.

One of the two white men squeezed in the front passenger seat beside Michel struggled into his breast pocket with great effort and produced a packet of king-sized Portuguese cigarettes and a red cylindrical lighter. Gravely, almost matter-of-factly, he stuck one cigarette into his mouth, leaned backwards over the seat, passed the open pack around to his comrades in the back seat, returned to give one to the other on his left and finally reached across to extend the packet to Michel at the wheel.

"Smoke?" he asked. Even the monosyllabic query was spoken with a detectable French accent.

"No thanks."

The white man snapped on the red lighter and did the rounds again. Soon the interior of the car was foggy with tobacco smoke.

Major Dan Marc, the big Belgian, curled up in a fit of violent coughing.

Leaning forward from the back seat, Johann, the South African with a British passport and an English accent, gave Michel a tap on the shoulder.

"May we?" he asked, indicating the black-out curtains and rolled up windows as Michel took his eyes from the road and briefly turned his head. "It's getting a bit foggy in here."

"Oh, sure", Michel said. "It is OK to bring them down now. Draw the blinds and roll the windows. Sorry, but it was necessary at the airport. Precaution, you know."

"Never mind, old chap," Johann told him.

A gust of early morning breeze flushed the car as the blinds parted and the windows slid into the bowels of the car doors. On both sides of the road tall trees, rangy, ghostly silhouettes against the clear skies above the pitch darkness, raced frantically backwards as the car tore along the flat open road.

"That's fine now," someone sighed, exhaling a pall of smoke that could have come from a factory chimney.

"C'est parfait," another agreed.

"Comprenez-vous français?" one white man asked Michel in a low conspiratorial whisper.

"Un peu."

"Ah, ha, you're being modest, hey?"

"Pas exactement, mon Major. I can't speak it as well as you do," Michel insisted modestly.

"But you speak it well enough, very good indeed."

"Thank you, sir."

"You've got yourself an assistant, Jacques. Captain Michel here speaks French," he said to the unsmiling man in the corner of the back seat.

"Does he?" Jacques Rudolf asked from the back seat. "That's fine."

Colonel Jacques Rudolf was really pleased as he relaxed into his corner once more.

Michel's right foot came down hard on the throttle pedal, and the huge car heaved furiously through the night, its tyres playing a rubbery alto on the broad, level tarmac as the exhaust rose to a throaty baritone.

The pitch began to falter as the car came up the hill, turned right at the roundabout and soon lowered in a rhythmic diminuendo that brought the car finally to a halt on a grassy lawn outside a row of caravans fenced in with palm fronds. The drive had taken just a little over an hour.

"Here we are," Michel told them in French.

"Where are we, Michel?" the Colonel spoke again.

"Umuahia, mon Colonel. Our temporary capital city."

Michel came out, followed by the white men. The night was still a crow's wing. Not a glow blighted the pitch darkness for miles around, as the town lay completely invisible inside a blackout tent.

From the breast pocket of his shirt, Michel brought out a ring of keys.

"This way," he told the white men, and began to lead the way through an entrance in the high fence, towards the caravans.

The next night's flight brought in another party of six white men, this time from Libreville. Again, Michel was there to pick them up in his black car.

Subsequent flights continued to bring in parties of six each night, mostly from Lisbon, but occasionally from Libreville or the tiny Atlantic island of Sao Thome. No two parties arrived on the same night or flight.

Nor were any two groups housed together in the city. Nor met any other outside its small group of six men, recruited together and briefed together.

36

By the eighth day Michel had ferried in a total of four dozen white men and settled them in, in caravans carefully situated in widely separated areas in the low density zone of the town. A small number were camped in a deserted, spacious college premises at Umudike, some six miles south-east of the city, a smaller number were quartered in government-owned bungalows nearby.

Each settlement was enclosed by a thick fence of tall, fresh palm fronds that provided privacy and camouflage from enemy aircraft during bomb-raids.

Colonel Jacques Rudolf and his men lived two to a caravan. They found to their delight that the homes on wheels were reasonably comfortable, with refrigerators that were generously filled with food and liquor, and frequently replenished by Michel. Food was fresh and varied as were the drinks.

Michel even provided a variety of games—chess, a pack of cards and Scrabble.

Often the parties busied themselves trading and bartering reminiscences and future expectations. There was a great deal of talk about such disparate countries as the Congo and Algeria. Then there was Biafra, the matter of the moment.

The exercise of memories ebbed and flowed like the tide; from the sparkling blue sea to the muddy, murky banks; from war to wine and women; from the sublime to the iniquitous.

No one, not even Michel, their only link with their hosts, made any contact with them after their arrival.

The thought of Captain Michel set Colonel Jacques Rudolf wondering about the young officer. He put his feet on the table, beside his loaded automatic pistol, a glass of whisky and iced soda in one palm, a cigarette between his lips, and pondered on the young man.

He was certainly not a day older than twenty-seven, Rudolf thought, and already a captain! Soldier, linguist, chauffeur! A remarkable man. Ought to be watched; ought to be useful, Rudolf decided.

He rose and walked slowly to the door of the caravan. He stopped, leaned heavily on the side of the door and watched the rain falling in feeble droplets from a clear, bright and sunny sky.

He remembered a similar day in Katanga when it was drizzling and shining outside his tent in the five Commando Camp just outside Elizabethville. His Simba guide, bodyguard, and interpreter, Picolo, had told him it was a bad omen that warned that the terrible *dawa*, the feti-shes of the Simbas, were about to take a fatal look at the foreign white soldiers. Three of his comrades had been killed in a counter-attack by the ANC that week. He wondered if the omen held here. He hoped not.

Colonel Rudolf spat the stub of his cigarette into the rain, thoughtfully watched it gasp a final wisp of smoke as the rain soaked it dead. He gulped down the bottom of his glass and returned to his cabin. He put the glass down on the table and picked up his pistol. He examined it in his palm, as if it had just been issued to him from the armoury.

At the butt of the weapon he found the tiny horizontal lines he had chiselled across its spine with the aid of spent shells. Each line represented the countries to which his adventurous career had taken him. He thumbed his way up the spine of the butt, across each sign: Indo-China, Algeria, Katanga, the Yemen. He found his pen-knife and sawed a fresh line above the top one. "Biafra," he said aloud.

"Biafra," he said the exotic word aloud again. Here was his last post. He knew it had to be.

Colonel Jacques Rudolf had long come to the conclusion that the time had come for him to lay down his rifle, not in surrender but in the contentment of retirement. At fifty-two years little of his youthful vigour remained. The weight of two decades of danger and risk was beginning to strain his burly shoulders. He had survived Cao-Bang and Vietminh prison camps. He had weathered the biting Algerian desert, left after the suppression of the Generals' Revolt to fight with Moise Tshombe's doomed rebel forces in Katanga. Service with the forces of the Iman el Badr in the Yemen had quickly followed the failure of his Katanga stint but had produced even less rewards.

He had fought for money for over two decades, had had little success and less money.

Jacques Rudolf needed a rest. But he knew, too, that he needed a financial break more than he needed rest. There had to be something to retire on. A soft cushion for a comfortable retirement.

And he knew that one last adventure would provide in arrears the pension for over twenty years of relentless, dangerous pursuits.

He had no idea where from or when. But he was certain in his mind.

And now, Biafra! This was *it*. The valedictory war. The final honour tattoo for a soldier of fortune.

Slowly, Rudolf put the pistol back in his hip pocket and went into his inner room for his siesta.

CHAPTER EIGHT

WHEN MORNING CAME, someone had brought a suitcase of neatly laundered uniforms and other personal items of military wear to Rudolf's cabin. An accompanying note written in French and signed by Michel told the Colonel that the white men would be meeting the General at 10.00 hours and that the Captain would personally call for them at 09.45 hours.

At 09.30 Jacques Rudolf was ready and filled with anticipation. His burly figure barred the door of the caravan as he leaned on the side of it, a half-smoked cigarette between his nicotine-stained fingers, and sipped his first morning glass of whisky. It was neat, hot stuff.

Chain-smoking and raw whisky had torn the ceiling from the roof of his mouth and left his tongue with the permanent taste of wet shoe leather.

He was a tall man, nearly six feet, with light hair, a ragged, rugged face that wore two light creases of middle age and a mask of permanent coldness. His mouth was a thin-lipped slit that twisted, crooked and snarled more easily than smiled. It seldom opened in genuine laughter. There might be the twisted, sinister grin, an elusive shadow of a smile, but never a really mirthy laugh from Jacques Rudolf's belly. His forehead was the only part of his face that reacted to situations, folding into three ridges in grave moments. Otherwise the face was an impassive waxwork that loyally hid a scheming, ruthless and deeply mercenary mind.

He was not a big man like Major Dan Marc, but his broad shoulders and wide chest on narrow hips gave him a burly, menacing appearance.

Rudolf was dressed in green and olive camouflage uniform that had the pattern of the skin of a newly ecdysed cobra. His French automatic pistol was thrust deep inside the band of his belted, close-fitting trousers the legs of which were neatly tucked into the top of ankle-length black, shiny jackboots. His shirt sleeves were rolled up to the arms, just below the shoulder. On either shoulder a black epaulet, with an eagle and two pips woven into it in gold fabric, sat with what seemed accustomed confidence. On his head a red beret, trimmed off with black leather and pressed down to a proud, rakish slant over his left eyebrow, sat equally confidently. On the high side of the slanted beret, just above his right ear, perched the dragon-head emblem of the Légionnaire Française. Altogether the Colonel cut an elegant figure.

The beret and the pistol were no ordinary trappings of an ordinary soldier. Like his tiny personal pennant, they were more than testimonials: they were symbols of Rudolf's independence. It did not matter what country it was; what uniforms and colours its army wore; what personal weapons its officers were issued with, or what codes and regulations were mandatory, Jacques Rudolf always carried and used his personalised red and green emblem, his automatic pistol and, somewhat inappropriately for his chosen career, the Légionnaires' standard, *Honneur et Fidélité*.

From the fiercely disciplined and bizarre ranks of the Légionnaires, Jacques Rudolf had migrated, with his small trove of mementos, into an even more bizarre, unorganised, unorganisable but powerful army of adventurers whose career knew no territorial or moral boundaries or political ideologies, was blind to colour lines, owed no loyalties or allegiance to anyone, and was motivated by a single ideal—that life was a fight and you *fought to live*, not to die.

Standing there waiting for Michel that bright and cool morning, he looked like a figure drawn out of an officer's honour line in the grand days of French Indo-China. *Sans* the black and yellow Rising Sun crest at the top of his left and right arms.

"Military promptness," he muttered to himself with cynical surprise, as he heard the sound of Michel's car.

"Johann," he called. Major Schmuts answered from the inner cabin. "Are you ready? Looks like Michel is here," he announced, tugging his belt into place.

The party led by Jacques Rudolf was the first to arrive.

Their destination, Rudolf realised with surprise, was only a few minutes' drive from their caravan camp.

The car paused briefly at the heavily guarded entrance to the new State Lodge.

It was a simple but elegant single-storey building which was still fresh with signs of a somewhat hasty re-decoration, although its occupant had moved in a fortnight before.

The original state capital having fallen irretrievably, if only temporarily, it was believed, into the enemy's grip, the General had deferred hopes of an immediate return to his seat of government. The small, dusty, traders' town of Umuahia had had the sudden honour of being designated provisional capital and command headquarters.

State House had then been moved from its precarious perch a mere thirty miles from the fallen city, to the relatively secure hinterland town, a further sixty miles down south. But it was its mobile, military body that moved; its national political soul remained in the occupied city.

Thus the new command post was named *Lodge*, a transit camp offering temporary lodging to the Chief, while he waited for his eventual, triumphant return to the *House* in the capital city.

The high and heavy iron gates flew open to let in the car. A sergeant stepped out from the rank of guards to wave the car on through the gate, was presently stunned by the sight of the white passengers in brilliant army uniform complete with officers' badges of rank, and managed to stutter out a call to present arms. Startled heels clicked in disharmony and open palms clattered on the butts of hastily, awkwardly sloped arms.

The car slowed to a crawl, turned into the courtyard, and stopped. Michel hurried out from behind the wheel, walked round to the right back door, opened and held it. He stood beside it, stiff to attention and trim in his own camouflage uniform. His right hand flew up and vibrated momentarily, his palm above his right brow, as if shading his eyes from the morning sun, and then the hand came slashing through the air, down to his right side as Colonel Jacques Rudolf slowly, stiffly, and with dignity, emerged from the back seat and touched the rim of his beret in acknowledgement.

The other five men followed the Colonel and, led by Michel, began walking across the courtyard. Through a paved narrow path across the well-kept lawns, Michel led the way to the rear side of the building.

The premises gave out a strong odour of fresh paint and caused Rudolf to slow down and light a fresh cigarette. He was expectant and not unhappy.

Soon they rounded the rear corner of the house and entered a small unlit room that seemed to lead to nowhere. Then from behind him his white followers noticed Michel's height shortening with every step as he began an unexpected descent into the basement of the building.

Rudolf had taken a few steps down before he guessed where they were heading to. As a youthful zealot in the Hitler Youth in Berlin many years before, he had heard vivid, picturesque descriptions of the *Fuehrerbunker*.

A bright row of lights lined the low concrete ceiling above their heads and down the narrow tunnel that ended abruptly at a steel door above which a naked red bulb glowed.

At the steel door Michel rapped out a coded signal with his bare knuckles.

It was the General's personal Aide-de-Camp who opened the steel door from inside an anteroom, saluted briskly, and mutely let the men in. In the right wall of the anteroom was a second steel door above which another bare bulb, this time a green one, burned. The General was in his command bunker.

"Paddy," Michel called the ADC* as soon as the first door was closed behind them. "You know the set-up. The other parties will be here in a few minutes. They will wait for a while, along with these gentlemen, while the Colonel sees the Chief. The other people should be here in about thirty minutes."

"OK, Michel," said the ADC, a tall, fair-skinned captain.

"Any new instructions from the C-in-C, by the way?"

"None."

"Has he seen the GOC, as scheduled?"

*See Glossary

41

"He has. It was a brief meeting."

"And stormy?"

"Apparently."

The ADC returned to his chair, behind a small, neat, almost bare table, and picked up the handset of a green internal telephone. He put it to his left ear and stiffened to attention at the faint click of an answering sound.

"Michel and the Christian Brothers, sir!" he shook the words into the mouthpiece.

A faint murmur.

"Yes, sir!"

Another faint click.

The ADC relaxed, put down the hand-set and came out from behind his table.

"The C-in-C will see the Colonel straightaway, Michel," the ADC announced. "But first," he turned to Colonel Rudolf, "you'll have to leave your weapon with me, sir."

Rudolf hesitated for a second, then shrugged his concession. He pulled the pistol out, weighed it affectionately in his palm and deposited it with eloquent reluctance on the ADC's table. He put his half-smoked cigarette in the ADC's ash-tray and crushed it dead with his thumb.

The ADC went over to the second steel door, put two firm palms on the handle, threw a final enquiring glance at Michel and the Colonel, and began pulling the handle with both hands, towards himself, straining every nerve to open the powerfully sprung door. The door began to inch grudgingly towards the ADC, yielding a steadily widening gap. Michel motioned to the Colonel.

Colonel Jacques Rudolf took a step through the opened door, his burly figure barring the narrow entrance, and came to ramrod attention to salute his new employer.

It was a powerfully executed salute. Left hand stiff, fist clenched with the thumb downwards at his side, his right hand sprang up as if released from a spring; midway between his hip and chest it bent at the elbow, the palm flew open, level with the right ear, the fingers and thumb arched tautly towards his back; the hand shivered for a split second, and returned with a whistling slash through the air, back at the side once more. It was a style that was soon to be the trade-mark of the forces under Colonel Jacques Rudolf's command.

The door sprang shut as Michel, following Rudolf closely behind, disappeared into the room.

"The General will see the Colonel alone, first, then the rest of you when the other parties arrive." The ADC's tone was polite but protective.

*　　*　　*

The meeting was brief and, apparently, cordial. It had lasted a little over fifteen minutes.

There had not been much to discuss, beyond formal pleasantries and the General's sombre emphasis on the critical nature of the military situation and his country's hope in the salvationary mission of the white brothers.

Like two eminent chiefs, they had met in summit to put their initials in ratification of an accord reached by the experts a few weeks before.

Except that the details of the accord were not so much worked out as dictated by the white party, represented by the Chief of Recruitment Operations, a Frenchman with the parsimonious code name of 'Roger', a battle-torn face and feet heavy with lead and shrapnel. He was, like Rudolf and most men of his profession, ex-many trouble spots: ex-Indo-China, one of the few to survive from the crack paratroop regiment of the Legion, ex-Algeria, ex-Katanga and ex-Yemen.

Age and partial disability had relegated him to the less active but lucrative role of the quiet recruitment officer. He was a shrewd, heartlessly efficient mercenary and a ruthless bargainer who played for the highest financial stakes and prayed for the lowest danger.

In the General's case, Roger had played from the strongly advantageous position of the gambler who knew his opponent's desperation and his own monopoly power.

Each white soldier was to receive one thousand dollars a month, to be paid either in French francs or American dollars, into bank accounts in Zurich. In addition, a field allowance of one hundred pounds a week in local currency would be paid to each white soldier.

Every fortnight a special flight from Lisbon would air-lift food supplies and liquor into the enclave for the men, and every month a mercenary pilot would hand over a teller to satisfy the white men that their black brothers had indeed been keeping faith.

A personal insurance clause provided for twenty thousand dollars in the event of death on the battlefront, and ten thousand in the case of injury leading to permanent or partial disability. The contract was for eighteen months in the first instance, with six months' pay in advance.

Roger had earlier promised to recruit a total of one hundred soldiers and had indeed collected six months' advance pay for that number. But on the day of reckoning he had produced only a list of fifty soldiers. Over the past week only forty-eight had arrived.

The General's desperate, pressed emissaries had had little choice, and a telexed reply to their urgent enquiry had produced the predictable response of most desperate men: if you cannot get what you want, you take what you can get. It was the logic of despair, but there was hardly any alternative for a desperate client.

But above all, and to the further advantage of the other party's strong bargaining position, the General's emissaries had operated from a virtual prison built by their insistence upon complete secrecy. Thus to disguise the mercenary element, they preferred, in all open discussions, to refer to the mercenaries as a volunteer force of *Christian Brothers*, motivated by an altruistic concern for the human tragedy of Christian Biafra, willing to help actively at no professional fee. The white men were to be an anonymous, faceless force, forbidden to feature or participate in any activity that would give publicity to their active involvement in the fighting.

From the onset Jacques Rudolf had been on the ascendancy, next only to Roger, the chief of operations. And when Roger had signed the contract and limped onto a plane back to Paris, Rudolf was next to no one.

Before he flew into the jungle airstrip nine days before, Major Jacques Rudolf had, to his infinitely pleasant surprise, received a telexed message through the General's Lisbon outpost, acceding to his request, or rather, one of his two conditions for bringing his men into the war: promotion to a higher rank, thus formalising his supremacy over a force which, Roger had said, included six other majors.

He was a Colonel of the Biafran People's Army even before he set foot on Biafran soil.

It was quite an ascent for the former sergeant of the French Legion. With a higher allowance and appropriate paraphernalia to go with it, it was a short, effortless battle from the down-trodden ranks of NCOs* in terrorist Algeria, the Iman's camps of Yemen and the secessionist tents of Katanga.

And now, Colonel of the People's Army, Jacques Rudolf, carried himself with a distinctive air, a suitable senior officer's dignity that was second nature to the best that the Ecole Militaire had produced.

His obscure background and mixed, shady parentage were now behind him. He had been born a German of French mother and German father, had joined the Hitler Youth at an early age, believed in Hitler and fought with the Nazis against the French. But it was with customary artfulness that he escaped from a French prison camp, melted into the civilian ranks as the end of Nazism dawned, and, after the liberation of Paris, re-emerged as a persecuted anti-Nazi emigré. The Legion had later recruited him with open arms.

Now Colonel Rudolf would be responsible to the General himself. He was to be in overall charge of the Christian Brothers: their movement, deployment and their discipline.

Within his own tactical concepts and plans, and subject only to the

*See Glossary

44

General's overall strategic aims, Colonel Rudolf had control over the Christian Brothers' military activities.

Above all, Rudolf would sit on the Joint Planning Staff, the General's highest military panel.

Colonel Rudolf had hoped for a free hand.

Colonel Rudolf got an even freer hand.

He emerged from the meeting with a visibly different frame and mien, stiffer now with the force of his new powers.

The ADC's tiny room was cramped with white men in military uniform, foggy with tobacco smoke and buzzing with the sprinkle of half a dozen foreign languages of a miniature international force.

It was a bizarre mélange of mercenary fighters, homogeneous and homoplastic at the same time. Severally, they were as incongruous as they were jointly alien to the people they had come to fight for.

They might behave alike, live alike and fight alike in a profession that placed high premium on money and survival. But their origin and background could not be more disparate.

There were racist South Africans with Dutch blood who were there for the joy of making money killing kaffirs.

There were fascist Portuguese paratroopers who habitually grinned away their ignorance of every language except theirs and a smattering of English, and who seemed to relish with quiet cynicism the irony of their involvement in the civil war of an independent black nation.

There was no mistaking the ex-French Légionnaires who spoke English with diffident assurance. They exuded a superior air generated by their pioneer role in the lucrative anachronism of mercenary warfare.

Less superior in deportment were deserted Belgian gendarmes in their first adventure outside their motherland.

There was at least one erstwhile Luftwaffe pilot with an ancient ostrich's neck, a scrawny face and a faded knowledge of only North Africa.

You could not miss the cockney accent of the ex-Royal Marine, who kept on making references to the colonials as if he were on a punitive imperial expedition.

But there was another group, too: two tiny, mysterious cells within the team. They had been *seconded* by an equally mysterious, almost clandestine hand, infiltrated into the mercenary team and for all practical purposes were indistinguishable from the rest.

Excluding the seven *seconded* men, they were all male vultures of different plumage, from one polygamous family, congregated at the latest scene of death. And now they perched together for the moment. This was where the action was.

A tiny number Rudolf had met or known for a reasonable time; like the five men who arrived with him.

Maintaining a proper air of dignity, he went from man to man, shaking hands, patronisingly patting backs, and cracking unsmiling jokes in a strict order of degree of familiarity.

He spent a longer time talking to Kapitan Hans Heinz. The two shared common nostalgia not for Germany but for Katanga where Heinz ran arms shuttles between Brussels and Elizabethville for Tshombe while Rudolf fought with the forces of the French mercenary Michel de Clary.

"Tremble, Major Derek Tremble," the next man said, extending a hand.

Rudolf gave the man a close, brief look. He took the hand limply and shook it bonelessly, without warmth.

"Encore les Anglais?" Rudolf had wanted to smother the offensive query under his breath, but his proximity to Tremble and his belated effort to stem the flow of his resentment betrayed his words to the Englishman who understood and spoke excellent French.

Tremble looked back at the Colonel from deep, narrowing eyes. The man next to the English Major was another Englishman, the ex-Marine, who lacked neither knowledge of the French language nor patriotic fervour.

The two Englishmen exchanged glances.

Major Derek Tremble had reason to feel apprehensive.

Major Derek Tremble was, indeed, a mercenary of some mystery, secretly *seconded* by London.

CHAPTER NINE

PORT HARCOURT WAS a white man's city in the black man's heartland, hacked out of dense mangrove swamps. It was named after a white man and lived in after his fashion.

In the military context, it was also a paradox. Although it perched on the banks of the Atlantic delta, a few nautical miles from the farthest enemy base, Port Harcourt was a *safe* city. Not a single enemy patrol boat was within shelling distance of the coastline.

In the three weeks following the capture of the capital, and the imminent threat to a string of smaller neighbouring towns in the north, the delta city had been bulging at the seams with the daily influx of refugees and uprooted hinterland dwellers.

Pre-war Port Harcourt had a heterogeneity that was deeply steeped in its oil wells and its immense industrial power. Foreign oil prospectors in white straw hats and native technicians in metal helmets had prospered together like a successful black and white minstrel ensemble, transforming the former fisherman's murky station into the economic and social metropolis of the breakaway country. And it had a robust, bustling night-life that out-glowed the rest in the territory. Neon-lit names like the Lido, the Bradford Arms and El Khany, nightly spelt out the city's multi-national character.

But the war had changed it a bit. It had reverted it to a homogeneous African city. The few hardy foreigners who had wanted to guard their huge investments and wait out the war had had their minds changed for them by stories of brutal treatment given to British nationals up in the capital.

The whites had all left. But the red-light district they created glowed on, not even resting for a night to commemorate their exodus.

So too glittered the native girls they had picked up, washed and brushed and at great expense propelled into the sophisticated world of gold bangles, stiletto heels, chilled champagne and cold turkey dinners.

The Lido still resounded with the blare of jukebox music, and El Khany glowed in multi-coloured benignity over its reduced but still exclusive clientèle. The Bradford Arms faithfully held its doors open for the usual late, late-night crowd. Liquor still flowed like the waters of the nearby lagoon.

It was an ideal city for the Christian Brothers.

The Bradford Arms was like a beehive that evening, the first weekend after the meeting with the General. The clamour of hilarious common-sense alternated with the hum of bemused nonsense; the clangour of clinking glasses and the merry jangle of slot machines sharply pierced through the languid drone of a soft, live band.

The green military car pulled up in front of the building. Four white men spilled out of the car.

All four of them were armed with pistols prominently displayed on their persons. One even had his weapon stuck inside the front fly of his trousers, right down to the hilt of his penis.

Slowly, with swaggering strides, they began to walk away from the car, almost abreast, as soon as the young black officer behind the wheel had joined them to lead the way across the street into the night club.

The din in the Bradford Arms faltered a pitch at the entry of the armed white strangers.

The young officer-escort seemed to know his way around the clubhouse. He led the white soldiers past the main, crowded ground-floor lounge, into the equally teeming open-air terrace, and took the flight of stairs that led to the sparsely populated first floor. The chairs were soft as the blue lights, the room air-conditioned; even a television set was blinking through an out-dated Western.

Before long two other cars pulled up outside the club building, disgorging two more parties of four each. The eight men joined their comrades upstairs in due course.

A curious crowd began to join the foreigners, at first warily, diffidently, and soon, warmed by the apparent friendliness and the euphoria that enfolded the lounge, confidently and merrily.

These were *our* Christian Brothers.

"We've come to kill the vandals," one had declared, to loud cheers.

They were the defenders of those God had abandoned. The help to the helpless. The saviours who would turn the scale of the one-sided war.

"Give each of them a drink and send me the bill," a fat, satisfied man ordered the waiter.

"No, not a drink," Kapitan Heinz waved away the offer. "I want a woman! Give me a woman."

"Ah, you can always have a woman when you want," the fat man assured the Christian Brother. "Have a drink first," he insisted. "It is a good appetiser for a woman." The room roared in approval.

The drinks came. Georges Denault lifted his glass to his face, "Here's to Biafra!" he toasted.

"Excuse me, sir," a middle-aged man, sober but timid with incredulity, touched Amilo Relli's shoulder.

"Yes?" Relli turned to his caller.

"Is it true you are our soldiers?"

"Yes, that is true," the soldier of fortune told the enquirer.

"You mean you people will fight for the Biafran Army?"

"Yes, why not? We like your people."

"You will fight for us against the vandals?"

"Sure. We hate the vandals. Don't we, Johann?" Amilo turned to Schmuts at his side.

"Yeah," agreed the South African.

"God bless you all, sir!" the man prayed, and left satisfied.

Kapitan Heinz's only regret was that the woman he duly got stole eighty-five dollars from his wallet while he was asleep the next morning.

CHAPTER TEN

CALABAR. The name of the town, they claimed, was an acronym for Come And Live And Be At Rest.

But this apocryphal nomenclature had long become woven into the authentic fabric of local lore.

To the natives, Calabar was nothing if not the haven to live in and rest; a cool, invigorating oasis in a desert of toil and turmoil. They even nicknamed it the Canaan City.

To live in Calabar did not connote the shallow, existential toil and sweat that life was largely made up of for the dwellers of other cities. It was not the tear-eyed, blistered-palm, daily duel with poverty and hardship.

To the Efik man of Calabar, living meant something more. To him, life was made up of *living*. And living meant giving, taking, appreciating. It meant love and loving. It meant resting; a state of joy and contentment, abhorrent to worries and anaesthetic to pain, poverty and misery. *Living* in Calabar meant endless excitement and contentment that liberated the mind from the bitter concentration camp of daily hardship.

Though their Ibo neighbours to the south-west were scorned as amateur practitioners of the fine art of *living*, theirs was accepted as the vernacular expression that came closest to the Efiks' concept of living. They called it *ibi ndu*—living life.

Unlike Port Harcourt, Calabar offered not a foreign-scented, Anglo-Arab-American-flavoured style of living. Here was an indigenous living, uniquely native, with a character all its own. It was nobly, charmingly primitive; uncontaminated by sophistication and immune to alien scientific and technological corruption.

It was to be seen in her women—warm, welcoming, generous, scantily clad, robust, puberal beauties. In her wine, song and dance that transformed the winers, singers and dancers into mirthy, writhing, gyrating and graceful patterns of gaiety. In its *Ekpo* masquerade that drove the hearts out of juveniles and joy and gladness into stouter hearts.

Calabar might not boast Port Harcourt's neon-lit glow, but the moonlight was there, generously beaming its more congenial light to bathe the jagged skyline in grotesque splendour.

But now, the wine man comes no more.

The pulsating, happy rhythm of the wooden gong and the throaty chorus of the men have been drowned by the harsh, strange thunder of naval guns.

49

The gay, graceful, dancing figures have scurried away, giving place to images of gloom as refugees without destination squat on the outskirts of the Canaan City, covered in wrappers against the morning chill, waiting without hope.

The Federals' sea-borne assault on the city that dawn of Monday, October 16, had emptied the suddenly embattled city and cast a pall of gloom over it.

By the morning of Tuesday, while the Christian Brothers were still relishing their weekend in Port Harcourt, the legendary folk city of life and living had become a blazing, bloody battleground.

Tuesday morning in Umuahia, nearly a hundred miles away, in contrast, wore a bright, sunny, almost cheerful air.

Colonel Jacques Rudolf was in his caravan command post. His face was a wax model of concentration as he studied the sheets of maps that covered his desk.

Rudolf had not joined his lesser comrades in the excursion to Port Harcourt. He had been busy with other things. And over the weekend he had briefed himself on the military situation as revealed in piles of signals, situation reports and acres of operational maps.

He had also tried to settle himself in physically, comfortably and suitably. Before Major Johann Schmuts went off to Port Harcourt, Rudolf had had him move out to share quarters in a nearby bungalow with a Belgian artillery captain. The Colonel needed all of the caravan, a huge, coach-sized two-berth house on wheels, as both command post and living quarters.

He had also ordered a telephone installed in double-quick time, and obtained the General's agreement to have extensions run to the caravan from the General's personal, secure line, the Defence Operations and the Joint Planning Staff lines.

Power, Colonel Rudolf had told himself with a secret smile, sometimes ran through a telephone cable. Now it was at his finger-tips, so to speak. The thought did not fail to elate him. He did not want some desk captain censoring his requests and proposals to the General.

In the meantime, his shrewd mind had gone quickly to work.

Colonel Rudolf had had a definite impression after his meeting with the General that the big man needed the Christian Brothers more than the Christian Brothers had imagined. They were not just white soldiers fighting with his native troops. The Christian Brothers, Rudolf was in no doubt, were to the General what a floating raft was to a drowning man.

Rudolf shifted the top map and ran a left fore-finger along a meandering line that traced the overland route from Umuahia to Calabar. He took a soft red pencil from behind his right ear and drew a circle around

50

the beleaguered city. He ran the finger northwards and did the same around Enugu. He laid the pencil down with a clang, leaned from the desk and began to light a cigarette.

"Bloody bastards," he hissed with sinister compassion. "They're in a bloody tight corner!"

He pocketed his lighter and began to pace the caravan room.

He thought it was not difficult now to see why the General was desperate for them and only too willing to give them a free hand.

The fall of his capital was more a political blow than a military setback, Rudolf knew. The city in itself was of marginal military importance, though it did presage a serious threat to the militarily more important hinterland. And the General, he reasoned, obviously harboured reservations about his officers' competence to prevent such a threat from materialising.

The General, Rudolf calculated, had lost confidence in his officers. And the speedy collapse of Calabar over the weekend could only harden the loss of confidence. That was it.

Put side by side with the tales of charges of treachery and sabotage against some of the General's top military leaders, which Rudolf had heard over the weekend, the secret summary trials and execution of some culprits, Rudolf thought he could see a clear picture of a deep crisis of confidence.

Outside the gate of his fenced camp, Rudolf's batman, Chiko, a sergeant with one missing right finger, an unwilling concession to the enemy at the battle of Ninth Mile Corner, stood armed guard.

Rudolf's first move after his meeting with the General and the confirmation of his command of the Christian Brothers had been to bar all officers and men of the General's armed forces from access into his headquarters unless at his specific request.

The only exceptions were, of course, his batman and Michel, the French-speaking Captain, whom he had designated his personal assistant and link with the outside formations and commands.

The despatch-rider stopped at the gate and handed the previous night's situation report from the Calabar front to Chiko who quickly snatched it at the sight of the OP IMMEDIATE stamped in bold red ink across its top and took it straight to the Colonel.

Rudolf ripped it open and began to read, his brow folding with each line.

The enemy had made a headlong push overnight of more than three miles. Now pressing beyond the south-western skirts of Calabar itself, they had already over-run the rebels' first and second defensive positions. The General's retreating forces were now wedged into a three-mile stretch of rubber plantation beyond which lay the unbridged Cross River. One more thrust from the enemy would lead to a disorganised withdrawal across the river; without river-craft this would mean mass annihilation from enemy guns and the muddy river.

Rudolf shrugged, put the report aside. He went over to the built-in wine cabinet, poured himself a glass of whisky, hitched himself onto the edge of his map-covered table, and began to drink.

He decided quickly against a swift response to the situation. Any move now, he told himself, would be a panic move. And that could destroy the foundation he was trying to lay; the end of the whole damn job. He wasn't growing any younger, he reminded himself, nor were there many civil wars going on nowadays. Nor, if there were, had he much enthusiasm for them; after here.

Retirement, next to physical survival, had become the craving closest to Jacques Rudolf's ageing heart recently. Before Biafra he had resisted the despair of unemployment. He had concluded that in the unlikely absence of suitable employment, he might strive for a less adventurous but equally lucrative role like 'Roger' had. But he had known, too, that he possessed neither Roger's powerful connection with the clandestine arms of the government in Paris, nor his semi-official status.

Well, Biafra was his *own* post, his last post. It was his route to the nest of retirement and rest. The pay was good. His future lay in his own hands.

Yes, he needed to case the joint, as it were, and see how best to move . . . not let anybody rush him into panic action with panic signals. If they were wedged in, then they were in a good fighting position. A good soldier was at his best when there was no rear ground to fall back to.

A river behind you.

The enemy before you.

What do you do?

Fight back!

He thought it would be a good laugh to send back a signal along those lines to the panic-stricken Chief of Defence Operations, Colonel whatever-his-name-was.

Panicky bastard. First day on the job, and he began his morning with a panic report. OP IMMEDIATE!

"Bloody hell," he swore aloud, banged his glass down on the table and resumed his pacing.

The situation, he told himself, was not bad. In fact it suited him. He would bide his time, temporise, give the General's chaps a long rope to compound their incompetence in a few more routs and blunders. Then he would move in and strike for a spectacular victory . . . and so legitimise the General's confidence in him and his men. That was it in bare outline. The details he would work out later.

Through the window he saw Major Georges Denault coming through the fence gate.

52

"Bonjour, Jacques."

"Bonjour, Georges. And how's your new bungalow?" Rudolf had hitched himself back on the edge of his table.

"It's not bad. Not bad at all. Got more room than a caravan, too." Denault took a seat on the built-in settee that doubled as a bed at night time.

"Very good," Rudolf said with satisfaction.

"And I can hardly recognise your own quarters now," Denault was looking at the battery of telephones, piles of sitreps* and maps.

"Yes, yes," Rudolf said. "I've been touching it up a bit. Just to get things going."

Rudolf picked up the signal from Calabar. "Read that," he said. He handed Major Denault the piece of paper. "Apparently I'm not going to get a chance to find my feet."

Georges Denault gave him back the sheet of paper. "Pretty bad situation that," he said in a subdued tone.

"I agree, in a way."

"What are you going to do?"

"Nothing. Nothing yet," Rudolf said firmly. "I've got to get things organised. Work out logistics and all that. I don't want to be rushed."

"But, Jacques . . ."

"What?" Rudolf sounded impatient. "Are you prepared to move to the battle-front now yourself?" the Colonel asked the Major.

"I'm a soldier. Under orders . . ."

Rudolf's response was a short, cynical laugh.

"You're fresh from a weekend, Georges, aren't you?" he asked and laughed again. "My dear Georges, this is not the French against the Germans. This is a black man's war!"

The red telephone jangled harshly. Rudolf stopped pacing his cabin. It was the first time any of the three phones had rung in the three days they had been installed.

The black instrument was the open line, the red secure line dually served Defence Operations (two long rings) and Joint Planning Staff (three short rings).

The Red jangled a second time.

Rudolf lifted the handset and put it to his left ear.

"Yes," he said curtly. From behind his right ear he produced his red pencil, pushed aside a sheaf of reports and found a scribbling block.

"Yes, I have the sitrep. Pretty bad, I agree."

His forehead recorded displeasure. He lifted himself a few inches and hitched himself back on to the edge of his table.

"That sounds like an order, Colonel," he snapped into the mouthpiece.

*See Glossary

"Have you discussed it with the General? You haven't? Well, I'll have a word with him myself. Good morning." He put the handset down with a noisy clatter and began to curse obscenely in French.

Rubbish, he thought angrily. If the General did not subject him to the superintendence of the Chief of General Staff and the General Officer Commanding his army, why should he let himself be given orders by a desk colonel?

He took an angry gulp of his drink, nearly spilling the liquid over his face.

"Who was that?" Georges enquired.

"Def-Ops. Defence Operations. They want my men at the Calabar front today. Imagine that! Today! Now! Bastards!"

Major Denault said nothing, just crossed and uncrossed his legs.

"Well, I've got to work out my own ideas first," Rudolf said and went back to his table's edge.

CHAPTER ELEVEN

COLONEL JACQUES RUDOLF's *own ideas* were conceived during several waking hours of the night. It was a careful assembly of obvious facts and obscure implications that came naturally to an artful schemer.

Forty-seven mercenary soldiers, plus himself, less than a half of one company, he told himself, did not constitute a significant force for him, a Colonel, to command. With a tiny posse like that he would just be leading another unit, a glorified platoon, to be deployed, at someone else's will, under the existing formations, in any battle-front. Thus, he feared, the power and privilege of command would easily slip from his grip. He did not see that as the best way to wield the free hand the General had given him.

Surely, the General didn't intend him to command a white force under his native officers, did he? "Within your own tactical concepts . . ." he remembered the General's phrase clearly.

He could foresee the difficulties that would face him and his men if he should be stupid enough to rest on the oars of the assurance that he had overall command of the Christian Brothers. Full stop. He could visualise with horror the loop-holes and fox-holes into which he and his team would fall if he should let them be absorbed into existing formations.

First, he would end up commanding a platoon of forty-seven soldiers, his hands and feet tied.

Under pressure from the fronts, absorption would become almost

54

inevitable. A simple phone call from the General: move your men to Calabar, to Enugu, or wherever.

Black officers, he remembered from his Congo days, were notoriously inept. And he would not have them ordering him about.

But on the other hand, he could not see the General giving him command of an existing brigade or division. It would cause rancour and friction, and possibly mutiny from the native officers who would naturally be superseded by him and his men, and probably endanger the General's position.

He was not anxious to endanger the General's position. Not as long as it was not necessary. Not as long as there was mutual confidence.

He had to have his own force. A large force, too, strong and effective, not a tiny, miserable posse. A powerful force, entirely his, moulded in his own image.

Among the black natives, he went on silently, former colonial subjects all, the white soldiers were clearly an élite group. They should, therefore, naturally lead an élite force. He would build them such a befitting force; entirely officered by them.

That would ensure them a stable employment while this job lasted. And that should, in its turn, make the boys happy, and keep them loyal to his command.

But, above all, command of an independent force would be compatible with the freedom of action the General ceded to him. He shouldn't have any difficulty obtaining the General's approval for his plan.

And, he calculated finally, sitting on the Joint Planning Staff, the highest military policy-making body in the land, with an élite division behind him (not just as a commander of a tiny platoon under some inept native) would give him a voice. It would give him power.

Yes, power, as some Chinese sage had said, comes from the barrel of an automatic rifle. The Americans and Russians, he remembered, now claim power comes from the silos of an inter-continental ballistic missile site. Maybe it did; but that was inappropriate in dark, Black Africa. What do they know about ICBMs and megatonnage? It is still the barrel of the rifle.

Maybe in darkest Africa it would even come from the sharpened edge of a machete, or the poisoned tip of an assagai; but in the circumstances here, it was the rifle, he concluded with firmness.

Colonel Rudolf was sitting at his table, and poring over fresh maps and reports while he waited for Major Georges Denault and Captain Amilo Relli whom he had asked over for a drink earlier on.

He examined his wrist-watch. Nine-thirty. He glanced through the morning's signals from Calabar. It wasn't any brighter than the previous day's, though no worse; sort of ding-dong, like an even tug-of-war.

He had decided against opening a discussion of the Calabar front with the General as he had promised to Defence Operations the morning before.

He was not going to work at the instance of some faceless colonel commanding a desk. He would call the General when he needed to or wanted. In his own time. On his own initiative. He did not want to appear to have been prompted by the call from Defence Operations or the frantic signals.

He wasn't going to let anyone get a toe-hold on the direct line of communication he had established between himself and the General.

He would call the General in his own time, he repeated to himself.

Or the General could call him.

He did. Just before a quarter to ten.

Rudolf looked at the shrieking green telephone with visible surprise. He reached across the table and picked up the handset.

"Good morning, mon Général," he said without waiting, spurting a stream of grey smoke into the mouthpiece.

"Yes, mon Général," he answered after listening for a brief moment. "I've been following Calabar very closely. As a matter of fact I've just read the last night's sitreps." He listened intently to the voice, slow and sombre, but firm.

"Yes, mon Général. You're absolutely right. But we, here," he glanced around the small room and noticed that Captain Relli and Major Denault had slipped unobtrusively into the caravan.

"We here," he repeated, "are taking a close look at the overall situation."

His French accent was now more perceptible as he picked his words with courteous care. "I do not wish to look at the war in terms of fronts, in isolation, so to speak, mon Général." That should impress a man with broad vision like the General, Rudolf thought.

"Surely, mon Général. Right now we are meeting to take a final look at the fronts. I assure you we are examining the military situation as closely as you would wish it done. Perhaps more closely than anyone has in the past. Except of course your good self, mon Général." The big man would not be totally above the reach of the soothing palm of flattery extended by a white soldier, surely?

"And the result of this," he continued, picking his words, "should be reaching you in concrete form in a matter of days."

Rudolf listened for a brief while, gave a slight nod and said: "Good, mon Général. I knew you would agree. I will get my ideas over soonest. Yes, mon Général, I appreciate that. And I assure you I'm no less aware of the urgency at the fronts. Good-bye, mon Général."

Rudolf laid the handset to rest and turned to Relli and Denault.

"The General. Nothing much. Just getting as fidgety as his staff, I think," Rudolf told them.

"I don't blame them, really," Denault began in a slow, sympathetic tone. "A man from the Calabar area says the enemy are pounding them with a sledgehammer. Heavy guns and all that."

"They want to get hold of a few heavy guns real quick," Amilo Relli added.

"Well, there you are, Georges," Rudolf said quickly. "We are soldiers, not weapons. We've got to look at things closely first and see where we can best fit in." Rudolf continued. "And I intend to do this in an atmosphere free from pressures, internal or external." The last word was aimed at Denault who acknowledged it with a perceptible nod.

Rudolf's shrewdness appeared to be growing with the job. So far he had kept the General, if not his staff, in good humour while the fronts blazed and everyone else around the General screamed despair.

Now he wanted to take care of his flanks and rear, tend to his comrades who were the base of his power. He needed their support and loyalty.

He didn't want a revolt of the mercenaries against his command any more than he wanted a mutiny against the General by his own officers and men. But after two less than agreeable conversations with Georges, Colonel Rudolf was becoming increasingly apprehensive about the French Major's dissentient, puzzling approach to their job.

Though he could not know it, there was ample cause for Rudolf to worry. Major Georges Denault was the leader of the *seconded* French Six.

Georges Denault was aged forty-six, a stocky man of slight physical proportions but demonic energy who used himself unsparingly in battle.

He and five other French Officers had been secretly recruited and infiltrated into the mercenary team that Roger was then assembling in Lisbon, by an anonymous, invisible arm of the Quai d'Orsay in Paris.

The recruitment and infiltration of the six into the mercenary group had been so skilfully arranged that neither Georges Denault nor any of his five other comrades had been able to spot the identity of their recruiting organisation.

All that he remembered was that after the initial contact, giving him what was in effect an order, a call-up, he got a message from a man called Henri to meet him in a Paris restaurant one evening.

Later in the night he had been introduced to the five younger men who were being seconded along with him.

His brief, for what it had been worth, had been *bref* to the point of parsimony: you will do all that is possible within your scope to support and sustain the resistance of the General's forces, while the French

Government weighs the events and considers its options with a view to possible substantial covert or overt assistance in the future.

Their briefing officer, a plain-clothes, sad faced colonel in the Para-troops Corps, had remarked that their sponsors would not be averse to the seconded soldiers discreetly influencing the pace of the mercenary team in fighting for the rebels. He got the impression afterwards that the official idea was not so much their supporting the resistance as influencing the notoriously dilatory mercenaries to abandon their traditional tactics and push ahead.

In retrospect now, Denault thought that the invisible men of Quai d'Orsay were not only invisible but afflicted with a myopic mind. Probably the men had not consulted and communicated effectively with their agent Henri, who was obviously an ex-mercenary.

Henri must know Rudolf at first hand. Rudolf played for the maximum stakes and prayed for the minimum risks. And with Jacques Rudolf in ascendancy, Denault could not see how Quai d'Orsay foresaw his minuscule team playing any effectively influential role.

Almost certainly Quai d'Orsay had kept the number to the barest minimum in order to avoid the attention that a larger group might draw to their own identity. Similarly Jacques, and not Denault, was put in command of the whole outfit to cover up effectively the role of the French Six. That might have been a sensible idea for a man operating from Paris. But on the spot, Denault saw it as the greatest hindrance to the performance of his team's discreet task.

CHAPTER TWELVE

BY AFTERNOON, RUDOLF had, alone, worked out the last tiny bits o details of his plan for forming a division.

Most of his unit commanders were ex-Katanga or ex-Congo veterans though they fought at a later stage of the war there, after he had left Many had taken part in one *revolt* or another.

The first name was Major Johann Schmuts. His South African origin was a consideration that over-rode everything else. And in the Congo he had been a protégé of fellow South African Mike Hoare, the 'mad colonel of 5 Commando fame.

Next was Hans Heinz, Rudolf's fellow German, ex-Luftwaffe fighter bomber pilot and lately operator of Tshombe's arms shuttle between Brussels and Elizabethville.

Heinz was getting past his peak, being on the wrong side of fifty; he was an air, not an infantry man. But Rudolf felt he needed him for a start, after recalling his record of frequent acts of mindless savagery.

Then there was Amilo Relli, at thirty-six, young and a captain. The meditative and quietly ruthless former Italian marine and mercenary was well known to Rudolf. They were on the night flight from Lisbon but had spent nine months together in Katanga six years before.

The deceptively comical Italian was a thin man, with a thinner face, on either side of which his wide ears flew out like a small car with both rear doors open. Relli had returned to the Congo after his first stint, fought and escaped with Jean Schramme after the collapse of the Mercenaries' Revolt against Mobutu.

So did Major Dan Marc, Schramme's fellow Belgian. The big bulky Major with a puffy face had single-handedly wiped out a platoon of ANC troops in early '67. With three other mercenaries Marc had held up a bank in Goma, when they were not paid by Mobutu, escaped through the fingers of the Congolese gendarmes, crawled through the cordon of border troops and reappeared in the mercenary haunts of Paris where Roger quickly tapped him for the Biafran stint.

There was Major Bill Ball, the tall, rangy Welshman who carried a South African passport and an English manner. He was a dubious hero from the third Battle of Katanga, escaping intact on January 21, 1963, along a trail strewn with the limbs of a sizeable proportion of the population of Kolwezi, the last bastion of the Tshombe mercenaries.

Finally there was Major Denault, ex-OAS from Rudolf's Algerian days. He took part in the revolt of the Generals and was the only one without Congo experience.

Rudolf wondered whether he hadn't more than a shade of second thought about Major Georges Denault. He was showing dangerous signs of dissent and over-zealousness. Rudolf could think of no quality more unbecoming of a soldier of fortune than over-eagerness for battle.

Eagerness for war was understandable, but over-eagerness for battle was another matter; it was an illness, a potentially fatal illness.

But he needed Georges on the team. Not solely because he was a senior officer and a Frenchman from his adopted native land. But Denault had survived Algeria, and to have survived Algeria was, in his view, the greatest credential for a mercenary career.

He hoped that Georges would soon learn that it was not a white man's war. Germany against France or even France against the Algerians. It was not fought with sophisticated weapons, nor according to the Geneva Convention.

The white man provided food and shelter for his civilian adversaries and his prisoners of war. He did not chop his enemy's head off, drink his blood, ritually gore his heart out and eat it alive to render his own heart stouter.

At any rate, he decided, he had to have Georges on the command team. The alternative would be that damned British Major, Derek Tremble, the only high-ranking officer he excluded. He would keep Tremble out if he could manage it. The British were responsible for all his problems in the Congo. You never knew what side they were fighting on or what end they held their rifle.

CHAPTER THIRTEEN

COLONEL JACQUES RUDOLF and the six selected Christian Brothers met for their secret session on Sunday. It was midnight and very quiet.

The cabin offered only small room, barely big enough for the seven of them. Outside, nothing stirred; the town huddled beneath an air-raid blackout. Sergeant Chiko, slumped on a chair, a rifle between his knees, dozed on sentry duty outside the gate.

Inside the cramped cabin a bare bulb shone, but with the curtains drawn, not even a glow flickered through the dense fence of green palm fronds.

"Well, gentlemen," Rudolf began, perched in his favourite position on the edge of his table, "I have decided to form a new unit, *our* own unit."

It was a firm declaration. He had not called them to harvest their brains. He summoned them to fertilise their minds, if they needed fertilising.

He searched the faces of his select half dozen and got a scattering of nods of approval. He pushed his buttocks further on to the top of the table, raised a booted foot and planted it firmly on the seat of the chair below his table. He felt a measure of confidence.

Then suddenly, Rudolf lowered his voice, dropped into a confidential, rusty rumble.

He skinned his scheme bare to the boniest detail and explained why they must have a separate, autonomous unit.

He glanced at Major Georges Denault, sitting in a corner, legs doubly crossed and arms folded over his middle, his face expressionless. But the corners of his eyes narrowed to a shade of query.

"Any questions, Georges?" Rudolf asked.

"I was just wondering," he cleared his throat, "what happens on the fronts while we train our troops. I guess this is going to take weeks, up to ten or twelve."

"Ah, there, there," Rudolf chuckled darkly, "I do indeed hope *something* happens at the front." He looked Georges Denault straight in the face and added, "*Something* really critical, I mean.

"A critical situation at the front," he went on to elaborate, "would suit my purpose, our purpose" – he remembered to correct quickly – "most admirably.

"It would be a situation beyond the ability of the General's officers to cope with.

"Then we move in.

"And let me tell you, Georges, we came here to earn a living and help the General. In that order. Not to score a quick victory."

Denault did not react visibly.

"And if you are fighting to make a living, you fight to stay alive, my dear Georges.

"A good soldier fights to fight another day."

"Just one further point you could clarify for me, Jacques," Denault said, amidst the silent anger he felt surrounded him in the cabin. "In the meantime, while we train our troops and form the unit, how do we keep our hands in? You've got to realise the General expects some action from us on the fronts. We don't want to be thrown out for inaction before we can get a shot in, do we?" Surely Jacques hadn't all the answers?

Rudolf skirted the question and gave Denault an epigram in response.

"Georges," he said in a deliberate, decisive tone, "someone, a fellow countryman of yours, I think, I'm not quite sure now. He said: 'a good general fights where and when he likes', or something like that. I think the General must be aware of that remark."

Rudolf picked up a green folder with a bulge of papers and diagrams, extracted six copies and handed a copy to each of his colleagues. He picked up his glass, put it to his lips and studied them over its brim.

"That," he declared a trifle proudly, "is the outline of 5 Commando. It has its ancestors in the Congo, you'll remember. It will have six Strike Forces, each named after you, their commanders." Rudolf read off the names of the six Strike Forces.

"Now there we are," he straightened up. "Recruitment begins tomorrow. I propose to see the General tonight for the necessary orders."

"Tonight?" asked Major Ball, unfolding his full lofty height.

"Tonight," repeated Rudolf firmly. "The General never sleeps. So I'm told."

The cabin of the caravan was steaming like an oven as the noon-time sun glared viciously overhead.

61

A little earlier it had been drizzling, that end-of-season rain that dripped down in glistening strips of silver. But it had not lasted more than fifteen minutes. Now for all the heat you would think it had not rained a drop for months, Rudolf thought.

He had found the switch just beside the small shelves above the short curtains and snapped it on. The air-conditioner shivered and purred into a steady hum.

Rudolf was alone, drinking whisky and waiting for Major Georges Denault who had asked to have a private meeting with him; Rudolf waited, and thought about the major.

He thought about the Frenchman and began to shake his head.

He was still shaking his head when Denault pushed open the wire-mesh gate that kept out mosquitoes and pests. He entered the cabin.

"Now Georges, mon vieux," Rudolf began as soon as the major was seated in a corner of the cabin, "what's on your mind?" His tone was genial.

"We've been together before and friends for long. But we don't seem to be hitting it off in Biafra, do we? It's a shame, a bloody shame, isn't it?" He tut-tutted several times. With Georges alone he could speak in French, and felt more confident, even talkative.

"We were together in Algeria, Jacques," Denault acknowledged. "Well, here, it's different," he sighed. He looked Rudolf straight in the eyes. He thought he saw a tiny curl of smoke rising from the man's cold blue eyes.

Algeria, Rudolf told himself, had been the OAS's war, the French's war, as the Congo later was to be the Belgians' war.

But Biafra, Rudolf believed, was, as Georges had said, a different war. Though they believed it was different for different reasons.

This, as far as Colonel Jacques Hemult Rudolf was concerned, was his own war, with him in command. Calling the tune. Calling the shots, literally.

He was not going to allow the futile sentiments of old friendship and loyalty to throw a monkey wrench into his carefully wrought scheme, only half of which he had disclosed the night before.

"Well let's put it this way, I feel like getting into the battlefront and giving these poor people a helping hand," Georges said finally. "I believe that's why I left my farm and family to come out here. Most ordinary Frenchmen at home feel that way, and I'm an ordinary Frenchman at heart. In fact most of the French boys biting their nails here and drinking gallons of whisky every hour are ordinary Frenchmen, deep down in their hearts."

"You are sure most of them feel the same way as you do?"

"I am positive!" Denault declared.

62

"All right, Georges," Rudolf said after a while. "Find out all the boys who would rather fight now than train the Division. Let me know by tomorrow morning." Just as well to weed out every latent spanner in all latent cogs in the works of the 5 Commando machine, he thought.

"You can have it this evening, if you want."

"Right. This evening, then. What time?"

"Six-thirty."

"Six-thirty," Rudolf agreed. "For now, I agree to your relinquishing command of your Strike Force. No hard feelings. Believe me." He hoped his tone carried conviction.

"Good-bye." Georges saluted. Rudolf drew a clean sheet and began to scribble.

Soon he was through with his writing. Georges, he thought, couldn't possibly be sufficiently envious of his position to want to rebel against it by opting for the front, thus dividing the team. That was out of the question. Georges wasn't that sort of jealous creature. But he couldn't have subverted his leadership more effectively if he had openly mutinied against his command. If Georges should succeed in battle, Rudolf could imagine no action more positively calculated to divide the mercenary front.

But that would be only *if* Georges should succeed at the front. If he should succeed . . .

Georges Denault, one-time comrade and old friend he might have been. But Georges Denault might have to be eliminated.

Major Denault walked the short distance to his bungalow at a slow, thoughtful pace.

He doubted that he had tackled Jacques Rudolf as tactfully and discreetly as Paris would like.

But he wondered if tact and discretion were not hopelessly blunt weapons for dealing with a determined, ruthless mercenary leader like Jacques. Once again he regretted the hopelessness of his small team's position inside the callous fold of Rudolf's larger group.

For a brief moment he wondered on whose side Roger was. If Roger was playing along with Quai d'Orsay's under-cover hand, Henri, surely he would have briefed their sponsors adequately on Ruthless Rudolf. He would have warned them of the hopelessness of six men effectively influencing the operations of a group led by Rudolf, the archetypal mercenary gambling for his survival.

Maybe, he concluded desperately, Roger was not on *anyone's* side. Roger was *pro* no one. He was *pro*-Roger. Playing both sides against the middle, taking his fat cut, limping off and damning the result.

He might not have been tactful. All the discretion that was possible in the circumstances had been his election to talk to Jacques privately, alone.

But he had deliberately abandoned tact because the circumstances dictated so. Tact here would have been tantamount to the dilatory tactics of Rudolf.

But what he got, the consent to take out his men to the fronts, was perhaps the best bargain in the circumstances.

He hoped desperately that he had not aroused Rudolf's suspicion. He didn't think he had. The choice of only *six* men to operate effectively inside a larger group might have been unbelievably short-sighted, but Quai d'Orsay were no fools. By choosing him, an ex-O.A.S. officer and known participant in the *putsch*, to lead the team within a team, Paris displayed a masterhand that had all potentially suspicious eyes gazing the other way.

The last thing Rudolf would suspect was the notion of Major Georges Denault leading a French-government-sponsored under-cover team. Denault had little doubt about that.

CHAPTER FOURTEEN

A FRAGILE TRUCE hung uneasily over the Calabar battlefront on the afternoon of Tuesday. To call it the Calabar front was, of course, a misnomer, since the battle lines ranged just a few miles from the Cross River, over forty miles from the Canaan City itself.

Across the rubber plantation, now charred and defoliated by the withering bombardment of artillery and cross-firing of small arms, both forces poised gun-sight to gun-sight in their humid trenches, trying to get their breath back after the bloody but indecisive sparring session of that morning.

A few miles behind the General's forces, the Cross River, still swollen from the generosity of the season's rain, deep and perilous with no bridge spanning it, had become a greater incentive to fight than mere victory.

Above the parapet of a dug-out trench, two lines from the forward position, Major Chime Dimkpa, capless and unshaven, peered out like a tortoise from the security of his shell.

From the floor of the trench he picked up a dog-eared map and spread it on the parapet. He ran a finger along his men's defensive positions and studied with a sinking heart their narrow, precarious fall-back position. A few miles behind his rearmost lines, the Cross River snaked down like a black, deadly dragon.

Brigade Major Chime Dimkpa had assumed command of the Calabar forces only a few hours after his commander was wounded in the morning operation. Two days before he had felt strangely new to the rank of major when he was once more promoted from the rank of captain to which he had been demoted after the fiasco of the capital. In an odd way he had felt he was lucky to be simply demoted when his commander, Colonel Charles Chumah, had been imprisoned, his future uncertain.

Although they had not always agreed on their approach to the war—he didn't see why they should—Dimkpa admired his former commander immensely.

Colonel Chumah was a resourceful, daring planner and a fearless, if ruthless, forward-line commander. Chumah's imprisonment, Dimkpa always thought, had been a great mistake by those who were only notionally aware of the enemy's tremendous fire-power and over-whelming numerical strength.

Chumah's success at the Ninth Mile Corner had been almost an impossible achievement, and was in a paradoxical way the cause of his downfall, the Major had always believed. The High Command had felt, perhaps, that if Chumah could achieve what he did at Ninth Mile with what little he had, they could not see why he could not repeat the miracle in the more vital defence of the capital city. Perhaps, Dimkpa had since then wondered, Chumah would not have fallen from command if he had been beaten outright at the Ninth Mile.

Dimkpa had plunged into Calabar with a desperate zeal reminiscent of Ninth Mile where he himself had led the main assault force. Calabar had been unlike Ninth Mile in several ways; only two days before he had been reinstated to his former rank. And now here he was, acting as the brigade commander.

Major Dimkpa folded back the map and thought quickly. Raising his hand over his head he snapped his fingers several times and soon had the eye of two of his boys. He waved them over.

"I want the commanders of 'R' and 'D' Battalions, quickly."

"Yessah," the boys scurried away to different locations.

The two captains were young. Like most of the other young officers, one was a second-year university student and the other, a sixth former, who now encamped as a soldier in the school where a few months back he had been a student.

Dimkpa liked them. He would not call them career soldiers like him-self, but they fought well in difficult circumstances. He was slightly older than them and out-ranked them, but he treated them as friends.

"I don't think we would be wise to wait for the enemy to attack first again," he began as soon as the two officers slipped into the trench beside him.

65

"Our position is still precarious. We can't afford to be too defensive," he told the two young men.

"Then we attack, sir?" asked Captain Offor.

"We attack," Dimkpa confirmed.

"Attack?" Captain Ude's tone was slightly incredulous.

"Yes."

"When?"

"Tonight. H-hour* is seven o'clock. Enemy's supper time. Catch them while they are supping. It worked the last time the Commander tried it."

"They might be wiser this time."

"They never are. The vandals' strength lies in their heavy armour and number. Not their brain power." Dimkpa said contemptuously.

"Then I'll have to have some reinforcements, sir," said the captain. "Especially for 'E' Company. They haven't recovered from the bloody nose they got yesterday."

"I doubt that we can get any reinforcements today," Dimkpa said in a regretful tone.

"And if we do, it will be too late for the attack. Actually what we are trying to do is buy time before something happens. Otherwise we'll be on the banks or at the bottom of that river soon after the enemy's next move," he held a crooked thumb over his shoulder in the direction of the Cross River.

"Our advantage lies in a night attack, boys." He felt a certain amusement at his use of *boys*, for they were all boys in a sense. And he detested the undertone of condescension that it carried when older, senior commanders addressed younger, junior officers.

"Our advantage lies in a night attack," he repeated, omitting the offensive word. "You must know by now that the vandal at night is like a bat in daytime. Catch him when he is at his meal and you have him at double disadvantage—blind and guns down."

Major Dimkpa could see that two of his three commanders were not exactly boiling over with enthusiasm for the proposed attack. He didn't blame them. He couldn't. They had absorbed so much punishment during the morning operation.

He admired their courage and would have gladly let them have breathing space. But his instinct was firm that an attack that night would pre-empt a dawn assault by the enemy.

The two captains remained quiet for a time. Major Dimkpa looked from one to the other.

"You are not growing cold feet are you? It would not be like you. You have been doing marvellously well under impossible circumstances. Keep up the gallant spirit."

*See Glossary

66

"No, not cold feet, sir," Captain Ude rallied. "Just that my boys are rather weary. I wish they could have a break, you know, they're not getting reinforcements, and that's not too good for morale."

"Besides we are low on ammunition," Captain Offor added. "I don't think any of my boys has more than ten rounds."

"Where's C.O. Bravo Battalion? Let me hear his own woes."

Captain Ude returned with the Bravo Battalion's Lieutenant Deze a few minutes later.

Lieutenant Deze was like his new commander in one respect. They were both tragic beneficiaries from the enemy's morning offensive. A few hours before he had been wearing a second lieutenant's lone pip. But the noon had seen a second pip and battalion command thrust upon his shoulders by the sniper's bullet that plucked the captain commanding his assault battalion from the hillock from where he had been directing fire against the enemy's forward troops. Deze had assumed command of Bravo under fire.

He was tall, lanky and visibly full of fight. Like most of the rest he was in school before the outbreak of war. But now he had shed all traces of the student that he had been less than six months before and was carefully grooming the unwilling shadow of a moustache, the trademark of a fighting soldier.

He fell into the trench beside Offor, panting from a tense crouch and run through the defence lines.

"We attack at seven," Deze was told directly he hit the trench.

"Tomorrow morning sir?"

"Tonight, Bravo leads the assault."

"As usual," Deze said grimly.

"As usual."

"Are we getting any reinforcements, sir?"

"I'm afraid not. I'm still waiting to hear from Umuahia. But we can't wait for them now."

"What about ammo, sir? We should need many rounds."

"You'll get a few, not many, Deze. You'll get the little reserve we have."

"Only a few, for a night attack, sir?"

"That's right. And you're the only one who's getting any at all. Ranger and Dragon Battalions are not. They'll depend on you."

"Depend on me, sir? We can't possibly . . ."

"They will depend on what you capture from the enemy in this operation," the Commander explained.

"Well, let's hope we capture something, sir."

"You will. You'll hit the enemy at seven. He'll be at supper then. Not even the most zealous vandal will hold a gun in one hand and a spoon in the other." Dimkpa looked at the teenage lieutenant briefly.

67

"So you surprise him; wipe him out and go for his weapons. Surprise is the thing. There won't be mortars or anything like that. Hand-to-hand fighting if necessary."

"Then we pass on to Ranger and Dragon?"

"That's the idea. They'll then join battle for a deeper penetration assault to counter and squash enemy's reinforcement."

"In that case, sir, can 'R' and 'D' lend us at least fifty rifles? I have three hundred and fifty men in Bravo and only one fifty of them armed."

"One fifty will have to do. We have to have a fall-back position, in case your first wave misfires. And that is perhaps more important than the assault itself."

"Twenty-five rifles from me will leave me with one hundred and nine armed men in the Ranger Battalion, sir," Ude complained politely.

"I'll have roughly the same in Dragon; perhaps less, sir," Offor added.

"Well, there you are, Bravo. Hang on to what you have. You will get a few more rounds of ammo, as I said. But not to worry. The first attack won't be much problem, I hope. Then we can take care of the enemy's counter-wave with their own weapons." Dimkpa didn't need to say so, but it was the last order.

The three young officers began to crouch and run back to their units.

The commanding officer of Bravo Battalion returned with greater apprehension than the other two, for his troops held the most forward lines, almost within breathing distance of the enemy.

"We attack tonight," he whispered to his NCOs as he thudded into his foxhole and they surged around to find out the latest.

"We attack tonight," he repeated.

The word passed the length of the lines like ammunition ration.

"When, sir?" a voice murmured.

"Tonight, seven o'clock."

"Oh, God . . ."

"Never mind. You'll be all right. The enemy will be eating."

"We can take care of them. They shouldn't be more than a platoon."

"Then we need fresh ammunition belts for the HMG*, sir."

"Yes, I know. I've told the Commander. He says he will try."

"*Try?* For a night operation?"

"Yes, *try*. He'll only give us what he has," the lieutenant's tone was reproachful. "You've got to realise he's not to blame. *Nobody* is to blame. We just don't have anything. Simple. So fight with what you have and capture what the enemy has. That's the idea."

"I don't like night attacks, sir."

"I don't like any attacks at all, Ike. Nobody does. But there's a war on."

*See Glossary

68

We're fighting for our lives, for our parents, for our new nation. That's why we have to fight in the night. Fight every time, with anything; with bolt-action rifles; with machetes; with bare hands if necessary." His voice was rising beyond a whisper. He tried to check himself but was carried away.

He might argue with the Brigade Commander and press for ammunition and reinforcements. But he knew where his duty was when the decision had been made and the order given. Like now.

"That's why," he went on, "we have to attack the enemy at seven in the evening when he is eating and attack him on a Friday afternoon when he is at prayers. It is our only way out."

"Hail Biafra!" Someone raised a low cheer.

"Sh-sh-sh!" An anxious voice hushed the cheerer.

From behind the clump of trees, a hundred and fifty yards or so in front of them, came a sudden volley of small-arms fire.

Several heads on either side of Deze hurtled back behind the safety of the parapet. The young officer held his position, for a moment defying the outburst. Bullets whined past both ears, to bury themselves in the bleeding trunks of rubber trees.

Lieutenant Deze's startled batman at his left elbow frantically tugged at his commander's sleeve and shouted, "Down!"

Then the batman rose back on to the parapet, picked up his rifle and shifted the bolt of his Mark IV and took aim.

Lieutenant Deze raised his head at the click of the bolt and whispered urgently: "Don't!" He put a firm hand on the breech of the rifle. The batman looked at him, appalled.

"But I can see them well now, sir!" he protested.

"Yes, I know. But only the enemy can afford to do that."

"Do what, sir?"

"Fire at will like that. We can't. We need every single bullet we have for seven o'clock."

It was six o'clock when Major Chime Dimkpa took the lone dug-out canoe across to the western bank of the Cross River where a staff car picked him up to his main Brigade Headquarters in an abandoned school house, six miles beyond the river, to scrounge for supplies for the evening operation.

When last he left the headquarters he had been Brigade Major. Now as Commander of the Brigade he didn't feel any different, except that the rear troops and men of the Headquarters Company saluted with a notably brisker movement.

After the fall of the capital and demotion, he was only too well aware of the fluctuating fortunes of war and of those who fought it to be stirred

69

into self-consciousness by what might easily be a probationary *up* before the next *down*.

First he went to the signals hut and asked for any messages from Defence Operations or Defence Headquarters. There had been none all day, he was told. The long-expected ammunition vehicle had not arrived, either.

He crossed the grass lawn, over to the bigger, former schoolmaster's quarters that was the commander's office and sat at his command desk for the first time. He surveyed the riot of maps and papers, and realised he had really nothing to do in this dry, dusty, spartan room that held only two chairs, a desk and another chair behind it.

He rose and went over to study the maps that plastered the four walls. With the tip of a paper-knife he prised out a red pin from the shaded area that showed the hotly contested plantation and replaced it in a fresh spot several inches above its former position, thus recording the bitter victory of one mile recaptured in that morning's encounter at the cost of ninety-four lives. It was perhaps the longest mile in his military experience.

"A tribute to the commander and those dead," he said in a bitter tone, as he examined the new, costly spot in which the pin rested. "At least they haven't died entirely for nothing!"

The crunch of heels on the gravelly forecourt caused him to turn sharply. From the window he could see a signals man charging across the court, towards the office building, a slip of paper in his hand.

Major Dimkpa went to meet the courier at the door and had the paper in his hands before the man could complete his salute and presentation routine.

The signal was not only belated; it was bad. It said that the brigade should expect no reinforcements in men or ammunition for now. The enemy, the slip of paper said tersely, was threatening to open a third front, having burst out of the capital and advanced westwards towards Onitsha. It was as terse and abrupt as that.

The Major's face fell. His mind sauntered slowly over the progress of the war in which he had taken part from the moment the first nervous shots were fired on that fateful dawn on July sixth.

Once again, he thought, the priority was changing. Soon it would be Onitsha. Everyone to the defence of Onitsha. A couple of months before it was Nsukka. A few weeks ago, Enugu. A few days back, Calabar. He wondered what the next priority would be. Port Harcourt, perhaps?

CHAPTER FIFTEEN

As MAJOR DIMKPA's command car was tumbling down the rough earth road back to the battlefront, Colonel Jacques Rudolf was meeting again with Major Georges Denault in his caravan command post.

Georges had kept his promise and brought along the five other French Christian Brothers.

"Well, here you are, gentlemen," Rudolf began in French as soon as the six men were seated.

"*I'm* deploying you to the Calabar front with immediate effect." He ignored Denault's appalled stare and fixed his gaze on the faces of the other five officers. They were all young; three captains and two lieutenants.

"You'll be under the command of Major Georges Denault here, who will report directly to me, daily. You leave first light tomorrow. I'll get Def-Ops to signal the Calabar command. I'll also inform the General this night."

It was a brief, arrogant order, and Rudolf had had no wish to make it otherwise.

Georges licked his lower lip and looked at Rudolf. He had a strong urge to tell the Colonel just what a despicable, clever, cunning bastard he was. But he overcame the emotion, mollified in part by the actual fact that he was at last getting into action, no matter at whose bidding.

At seven-thirty Captain Michel called on Rudolf. The energetic, enigmatic black officer was facing the Christian Brother alone for the first time.

Rudolf did not know much about Michel. He did not bother to know much about Michel, either. For Rudolf had not much besides contempt for any of the native officers.

One of Rudolf's devious qualities was his ability to mask contempt behind a genial front. With the General it worked admirably smoothly and spurred Rudolf to greater lengths of pretended amiability, bordering on sycophancy. Sometimes his submission to the General hurt his inner pride. But he consoled himself easily. It was a means to an end.

As for Michel, he knew he spoke excellent and rapid French, an invaluable quality in a native officer, hence his choice as the Colonel's personal aide.

But what would the native do as his personal assistant in an exclusively white officer corps, Rudolf had wondered soon after the choice? His job as Commander was not such that he would share its intimate details with a native soldier.

But Georges Denault's *mutiny* had suddenly presented Rudolf with an answer. Michel, too, could be used as a means to an end.

"Well, Michel, I haven't seen you for a while now, eh?" Rudolf began in French, in the paternalistic tone in which he conducted his conversation with those natives he came in contact with.

"I have been busy handing over at the Def-Ops, sir."

"It is all over now, then, is it?"

"Not quite, sir. Maybe by tomorrow morning."

"Tomorrow morning?"

"Yes, mon Colonel."

"Sure it will be?"

"I believe it will, sir."

"Good. You are going to the Calabar front tomorrow evening," Rudolf announced abruptly.

"With Major Georges, sir?"

"How do you know?"

"Oh, I was at the Def-Ops when your message came through for Commander Calabar, sir."

"Oh, well. Not *with* him. On your own, Michel. Smoke?" He extended the packet.

"Thanks, mon Colonel."

Rudolf leaned forward and snapped his lighter under the young man's chin and lit the cigarette, darting stealthy glances at the young man's face in the process.

Rudolf lit one for himself, blew out a shaft of smoke and leaned back on his seat with satisfaction.

Michel Michael Migan Delema was twenty-four when his mother brought him back with her to her native Ibo homeland three years before.

The return of the woman had marked the final collapse of twenty-five years of marriage to Monsieur Migan Delema, an itinerant Togolese merchant who had met Michael's mother, Ezidiya, during a successful business trip to the Ibo heartland.

The marriage of the two different nationals with only a smattering of pidgin English between them, had begun to flounder three years after the birth of Michael. Ezidiya had not followed up the birth of young Michael with another child, and Monsieur Migan Delema, a true African family head who was not insensitive to the precariousness of a lone male child, had not masked his displeasure.

The widening rift began to show itself in clear contours; notably,

Migan junior became Michael to his mother and Michel to his father. Madame Ezidiya Delema began to give the young boy a crash course in her native Igbo language, and began to refer frequently to Nigeria, her homeland.

And when she had to leave Togoland, twenty-one years later, and return to her homeland, Migan Delema senior lost his precarious, lone son; Migan junior had elected to follow his beloved, maltreated mother. But he had made the parting with a gesture of compromise—he chose to be called Michel, rather than Michael; though he was later to be forced to drop his surname during the crisis, for fear of being closely identified as a foreigner and a risky element in his new sensitive homeland.

He was in his last year at university, appropriately reading for a degree in French, when the war broke out and interrupted his studies.

Captain Michel had been delighted at his choice as Colonel Rudolf's personal aide. Perhaps because of his Francophone ancestry, he was excited at the thought of working, fighting and living with this French colonel who was to lead the team of Christian Brothers who would bring the war to a quick, victorious end.

Naïvely, he had thought that with his partly foreign ancestry he was in a sense a Christian Brother, too. A black Christian Brother. A *foreign* soldier.

Thus, he had seen the opportunity of serving Colonel Rudolf as a unique privilege, to be guarded by loyalty to the Colonel and devout obedience of his orders and wishes. Many captains in the Army, Michel had thought, would give away a pip to be close to the Commander of the special white soldiers.

'Now listen, Michel." He leaned forward and began to speak in a confidential tone.

"I like you," he managed to make the claim sound credible to the native officer.

"That's why I want you to work with me. I was impressed directly I saw you at the airport. You work hard, the way I believe all your good countrymen should."

"Thank you, mon Colonel. I am flattered."

You ought to be, you bastard, Rudolf smiled, but said aloud: "I'm going to trust you, Michel. I believe I can."

"Absolument, mon Colonel." His tone was humble.

"I may be wrong in what I'm going to say, so don't let it out to anyone."

"You can rely on me, mon Colonel."

"It's about Georges. Major Denault," Rudolf began and stopped to examine his listener's countenance. Reassured, he continued.

"I don't think I quite trust him. I never have. I don't think he is

73

reliable. He has been complaining a great deal in the past few days. And he was beginning to get on everyone's nerves."

"What about, sir."

"About everything. The conditions here. Our contract and whatever. He is not satisfied with the pay. He finds living conditions terrible, the weather intolerable and all that," Rudolf lied glibly.

"That's regrettable, sir."

"That's what I told him, too, Michel. I have tried to make him realise we are here on a mission. A mission of mercy, kind of. To help save a lot of people who are threatened by war and suffering, and that we have to make a small sacrifice to do so; but he doesn't seem to realise it."

"Hence you're deploying him, sir?"

"Precisely."

"Pity he should feel like this in the midst of suffering."

"I tried to point out to him the mindlessness of such an attitude. Same as those other chaps with him. Five of them. They are Frenchmen, you see, Michel, my dear. They are hard-core fortune-fighters who would check their pay against every burst they fire." Rudolf shook his head in what looked to Michel like genuine dismay.

"Don't you think you ought to inform the General, mon Colonel?"

Not the General, you fool, Rudolf cursed silently. I'm in command here.

Aloud he said: "No, not the General. I think it will upset him because he has so much faith and confidence in us. And he sees us as a team, not as individual nationals."

Michel nodded in agreement.

Rudolf said again, "No, I don't think I should upset the General with the selfishness of six soldiers. I can deal with that. They will go to Calabar and we'll keep an eye on them and see how they get on in actual combat."

"Then, I'll keep an eye on them, mon Colonel?"

"For the moment, yes, Michel. You will keep a close watch on Georges. You may have to do more than that, but this will do for now."

"I'll be glad to do whatever you wish, mon Colonel."

"Very good, Michel. You know it's in your country's interest."

"I realise that very well, mon Colonel."

"I shall issue you with special orders and special responsibilities as my personal representative. That will cover your activities in the Calabar command. You will report to me in person here as regularly as you think necessary." Rudolf looked up at the face of the eager young captain.

"All right?" he asked.

"Perfectly understood, mon Colonel."

74

Rudolf rose slowly, went over to the cabinet and poured out two glasses of whisky.

Rudolf did not call the General until midnight. The big man ought to know that he, too, stayed up and worked late, Rudolf had said to himself. It should please him.

He thought the General would like to know that he was despatching six of his *best men* to the Calabar front, first light in the morning. They would be leaving in a few hours, should be at the front by 0600 hours.

No, he assured the General. It certainly would not affect his training programme. Hell, sorry, but he had made damned sure it would not.

Yes, Major Georges Denault, a very able and eager officer, would lead the task force. Oh, did the General remember Denault? From that brief meeting? Oh dear, mon Général had an enviable memory.

Oh, yes. How very gracious of mon Général. The Colonel would be extremely honoured to come over for a drink and informal chat with the General. But there just wasn't a spare second. Dashing about and charging around getting this division together; Calabar still causing anxiety; though he was certain he would plug the leak there in a couple of days.

Well, never mind, mon Général. There will be plenty of time in the near future; when our troops are marching forward against the enemies on all fronts. Then the Colonel would love to nip over to toast Major Denault's speedy march.

"Bon nuit, mon Général."

The Colonel put down the handset of the Green hot line, lit a cigarette and blew lazy smoke rings.

Now, he thought, casting his mind back to re-examine the trail over the past twenty-four hours, there was reason for some satisfaction with his good beginning.

By the time he woke up in the morning, he knew with an odd relief, Georges would be off to Calabar, and off his back.

Before he went finally to bed, Rudolf made a terse note on the top blank copy of his scribbling pad:

"Maj. TREMBLE to take over trg. and comd. of Georges' Strike Force."

CHAPTER SIXTEEN

AT TEN MINUTES to seven the Calabar front was like chinaware flung from a high rooftop.

The sky growled and grumbled intermittently. The moon, twice the size of the pale, yellow crescent of a week before, now cast only a foggy, dull light from behind a fast-flowing storm of bleak clouds.

On Major Chime Dimkpa's side of the battle line, tension gathered and built up a more convincing threat than the sky above. His troops began to stir quietly for action. Hands spoke louder than words as unit commanders and NCO's passed on precious rations of ammunition and motioned and signalled their men into position, in silent readiness for the meal-time assault.

The disappearance of the moon and the sudden darkness seemed to complement the preparations, at the same time providing the shadow of a good omen.

Lieutenant Deze, whose Bravo Battalion was to spearhead the attack, tensed in his trench. He peered closely at his illuminated wrist watch and listened to the disgruntled sky. Five minutes to H-hour.

He twisted over in his foxhole, took one final look on both sides at his equally tense troops.

He could see them all, or silhouettes of them, as they squatted or crouched on both flanks. One hundred and fifty armed men in all. Just a little over a full company. One hundred bolt-action Mark IVs. The rest, Cetme automatic rifles captured from the enemy. Twenty-five rounds of ammunition each. One Heavy Machine-Gun. That was all.

Deze reached for his steel helmet, a booty from the day's operation. He put it on his close-shaved head, pushed it down and felt its elastic bands grip his head firmly just above the temples.

The young officer knew he needed no further orders to move. The leader of a suicide battalion, he had been told countless times, was his own commander-in-chief when in action.

In fact tonight, he thought, he was everyone else's commander-in-chief. He would be issuing the orders to the other battalions. His success in the first wave of assault would be a signal to the commanders of the other two battalions to move.

At five minutes to seven, too, some five hundred yards away, across the expanse of darkness and rubber trees, the first of the enemy forces were filing into a clearing for supper.

They came in shifts, one group eating its meal and returning to relieve the next. Some lingered on; others, a larger number, preferred to put their guns aside and eat their meals in their trenches.

From two large bowls in the open back of a supply Land-Rover, an agile-fisted kitchen private was doling out the night's meal to his handful of assistants who passed the plates down the line of troops.

"Rice and beans again tonight!" a private grumbled.

"Sharrap!" rapped a Sergeant. "What did you eat when you were at school?"

"Well, what do prisoners eat?"

"Prisoners? You should ask what the rebels eat."

"Pounded yam with chicken soup," someone else teased, and chuckled down a spoonful of food.

"Nonsense!" snapped the Sergeant. "The rebel prisoner we caught yesterday said they ate only once every day."

"Yes, pounded yam and chicken once a day. Still better than rice and beans," insisted the disgruntled private.

"You forgot to mention our lumps of meat," the private's companion nudged him in the darkness.

"Two tiny lumps, just like in the prisons."

"Say, have you been in prison before?"

"Do I have to have been in there to know what they eat?"

"How else?"

"Oh, yes. I remember now. I have been in prison for a few hours. To see your elder brother when he was jailed for rape."

"Damn your mother, you bastard," the victim of the verbal assault cursed, throwing a bone at the private.

"Sharrap all of you!" the Sergeant ordered again. "Now you eat quickly and get back to your positions".

"What about beer, Sarge?"

"You can drink your piss."

"You don't have to," someone said. "When we smash the rebels and get to Arochuku, there will be beer in the shops."

"And women hiding in the bushes."

"*Walahi!*"

"I left one in Calabar. I hope I find her when I get a pass."

"Did you?"

"Sorry for you."

"Pity you."

"Why? Are you all jealous?"

"You won't find her. Your commander must have commandeered her by now."

"Sorry to disappoint you, then. My commander was killed before we left. He was buried alive by the rebel Red Devil in St Patrick's School."

"Buried *alive*? Then he will rise and find your precious woman!"

"He was buried, full stop."

"Oh, well, someone else will get your woman."

"Blast you. If he does, I will get another in Arochuku."

The Sergeant had been listening with quiet interest and munching away, for once not yelling for silence.

"Offsah!" Someone with X-ray eyes had peered through the darkness and recognised the angry bulk that was one of their officers.

The man stood and frowned into the darkness at the hilarious nonsense going on as usual at meal-time.

"Will you men eat up and take up your positions!" he barked.

"Yes suuh!" the Sergeant answered through a mouthful of food.

"And don't you be such bloody fools. The rebels attacked you in just these circumstances ten days ago!"

Memory flooded back to the men in a chilling wave. The men eyed their rifles apprehensively. The clatter of spoons and metal plates rose frenziedly.

Lieutenant Deze, several yards ahead of his assault squad had halted on his belly and waited for nearly five minutes, listening to his victims' light-hearted mealtime chatter.

Bravo had fanned out left and right of him and advanced in a long painful crawl in a file parallel to their enemies' own forward line.

The angry Major's warning to his leisurely troops was the order for Deze to pounce.

He crawled back quickly to his men, rose to his knees and found his way behind the lone HMG between two rubber trees.

He laid two firm hands on the gun, heaved the barrel down to the level of the trenchful of diners a mere fifty yards away—and pressed the trigger.

"Fire!" he yelled at the same time.

His men leapt from behind trees and opened fire.

The enemy officer's warning had been too late.

So was his departure.

Deze's first fierce burst caught the Major in the middle of the back as he turned to leave his men. He stiffened violently and then crumbled over the bonnet of the Land-Rover.

A night attack being a shot in the dark, Bravo Battalion kept up their firing, but dared not move forward.

Deze began to nose his heavy gun up and down and swivel it from side to side. Cetmes sputtered and Mark IVs exploded.

From the enemy trenches yells and anguished screams and groans replied.

But Deze and his men knew they could not sustain their firing for more than a few minutes.

Deze knew that with the more powerful HMG, he held the balance between success and bloody retreat.

He calculated that if the boys ran out of ammunition before they charged the lines, the HMG could keep up cover before Ranger and Dragon moved in.

He swivelled the gun in a wider arc and swept the enemy trenches with fire.

In the distance, the enemy's forward lines groaned and screamed. Deze and Bravo could hear some wild, faint spasms of firing. It seemed to be growing fainter and wilder.

He guessed the enemy was firing in confused retreat.

"Charge!" he yelled, and abandoning the machine gun simultaneously with his order, he ripped his pistol from his waistband and led a heedless charge on the enemy trenches.

Right from the first trenches Bravo began to trip over hastily abandoned rifles, ammunition pouches and litters of plates and spoons.

"Ike," Deze called a Sergeant, reaching for the walkie-talkie held out by his batman. "Get some men to gather all enemy weapons and ammunition. And start issuing them immediately!"

"Yessah!"

"I'll get the Commander to send in 'R' and 'D' after the vandals."

Deze moved over to the shelter of the Land-Rover, knelt down, flicked the switch on the walkie-talkie and began to call his tense and expectant commander.

The signal from Defence Operations reached Major Chime Dimkpa in the trench just before Deze called to report the success of the first wave of assault. Dimkpa sank into his foxhole and read the piece of paper with the help of one of his officer's cigarette lighter.

It said curtly that a special reinforcement of six Christian Brothers was joining his Brigade first light Wednesday morning. Ends message.

The signal mystified and filled Dimkpa with annoyance.

He had asked for an urgent reinforcement of men and ammunition of at least fully-kitted company strength. Now all he had in his hand, nearly twenty-four hours later, was a tardy piece of paper announcing the arrival of six miserable, mysterious *Christian Brothers*.

Whoever were the Christian Brothers, the Major wondered agonisedly. Army chaplains, perhaps? They had better carry a rifle and a box of ammunition each. They would need them.

His quiet agony was mercifully interrupted by the call from the Bravo forward line, re-tuning his mind to the wavelength of the firing ahead of him. He crouched over to the communication trench and began to listen to the Bravo commander.

By midnight Major Dimkpa's three battalions were three miles forward of their pre-attack positions. Ranger and Dragon, having moved in after the first wave, had sustained the tempo with the help of the enemy weapons and ammunition they had shared out, and added some two miles to one gained initially by Bravo.

But by midnight the advance had been stymied as the surprised enemy seemed to have gathered their wits.

A few mortars began to thud here and there and occasional screams and curses warned Dimkpa and his commanders of mounting casualties.

Dimkpa ordered a general halt. They were now over a dozen miles away from the river. That was not too bad, the Major thought. Behind the river, Arochuku, the next strategic target of the enemy was another dozen or more secure miles away. Some twenty-four miles plus an un-bridged river for the enemy to tackle. Atani I was their immediate rear location, and Atani II held their present forward locations. Not too bad at all for a night operation, Dimkpa thought once more.

The sporadic mortar fire continued to come. Dimkpa calculated that a counter-attack then was not likely, and began to consolidate for a morning action.

He ordered seven machine guns, four of which had belonged to the enemy a few hours before, to be kept in selected strategic positions and in full cry during the rest of the night. He could afford to do it; Bravo had captured 8,500 rounds of HMG ammunition alone.

Dimkpa was still nagged by the mystery of the Christian Brothers. But he was mollified by his small success of the night, his first achievement as Brigade Commander.

At 0200 hours he left for his rear location to wait for morning and the Christian Brothers, whoever they were.

But at exactly that time an urgent INTERCEPT message was waiting for Major Dimkpa on his table in the commander's office.

CHAPTER SEVENTEEN

FROM: CO
TO: COMDS 108 BN(.) 109 BN(.) 110 BN(.)
INFO: COMD AIR FORCE 'RAKE' SQN(.)
INFO: AHQ(.) SHQ(.)

FOLLOWING SURPRISE REBEL AMBUSH THIS NIGHT YOU WILL PREPARE IMMEDIATELY FOR THE FOLLOWING COUNTER ACTION(.)
BETWEEN ATANI I AND ATANI II 108 BN WILL DROP 7000 MOR BOMBS(.) BETWEEN ATANI II AND ODORIKPE 109 BN

WILL DROP 7000 MOR BOMBS(.) AND BETWEEN ODORIKPE
AND AROCHUKU 110 BN WILL DROP 7000 MOR BOMBS(.)
TPS WILL REORG AT AROCHUKWU FOR FINAL PUSH TO
UMUAHIA(.) AIR FORCE WILL PROVIDE SUPPORT(.)
H-HOUR 0700 WEDNESDAY(.)
ALL ACK*(.) ENDS MSG(.)

A copy of the message was also on Colonel Rudolf's desk when he
entered the caravan sitting room, still in his dressing gown, for his first
whisky of the day.

The message had been delivered by courier as soon as the duty officer
at Intercepts Unit gave his sleepy-eyed clearance to the crucial signal.

The time stamp on the form read "01.15 hours". It showed also that
Defence Operations had immediately signalled the Commander at
Calabar front, and sent a copy "for info", as a matter of routine, to
Colonel Rudolf, as commander of the six men who were going to the
threatened front in the morning.

Rudolf's forehead furrowed into severe creases as he read down the
message. Twenty-one thousand mortar bombs on one battlefront.
Followed by a brigade attack under air cover.

He pulled out a chair and sat down at his table.

Now this was *something*, indeed. This was something like the drastic
development he had predicted. This was the hard stroke that he always
knew was bound to fall, to break the back of the General's last trusted
commanders and create the vacuum that he and the Christian Brothers
would fill, beginning a long, secure and lucrative reign.

And now, Georges Denault was at the Calabar front!

With slow-burning anger, Rudolf put the message down on the table
and picked up the Red telephone.

He was on to Defence Operations at a flick.

"The Colonel, please," Rudolf's voice was thick and low. "I've been
looking at this intercept on Calabar," Rudolf said, successfully putting
anxiety into his voice as soon as the Chief of Defence Operations was
on the line.

"Well as you know, Major Denault and five of my other officers are
there right now. Yes, a good thing too. They couldn't have gone at a
better time.

"But tell me a few things. What's the strength of your men at
Calabar?"

Rudolf drew up a chair, sat down, picked up his red pencil and tore off
the top doodled-up sheet of his scribbling pad.

"One brigade," he repeated after the Colonel at the other end of the
*See Glossary

line, noting the statistics on his pad, "three hundred and eighty-four of them armed, plus a hundred enemy captured rifles, you say?" He put an asterisk beside the latter figure.

"That's about four hundred and eighty-four armed men in all, isn't it? Good."

He ran a line across the middle of the sheet of paper.

"And what's the estimated enemy strength?" he asked.

"EES* c. 2,000," he wrote. "Almost a full brigade."

"That's of course far more than your, I mean our own strength? OK. Thank you, Colonel."

Two thousand troops against four hundred and eighty-four armed troops. Rough odds of five to one. Surely they wouldn't have a snow-flake's chance in blazing hell. A walk-over.

Sans Georges Denault.

He knew Georges was no genius. But he knew, too, he was a hardy fighter and great improviser. If a misguided one.

Denault would have a few other advantages, Rudolf reasoned. He had the brains that the native officers certainly hadn't.

He had the good luck of being forewarned of the impending attack. The enemy had lost the element of surprise.

Like all misguided men, Georges would be fighting like a wounded devil to justify the wisdom of his going to the front.

If Jacques Rudolf needed any persuasion to go ahead with the elimination of Georges Denault, it was not that morning.

The intercepted message kept Major Chime Dimkpa awake for the rest of the night.

It was an unwelcome addition to the unresolved mystery of the six Christian Brothers.

He had had a copy made of the intercept by the signals typist, scribbled a footnote to it, directing the three battalions to proceed immediately with the task of digging in and further consolidating their gains in readiness for the dawn counter-attack by the enemy. He would be at the front before the enemy's H-hour.

Over his desk in the commander's austere office, he had cat-napped. He had risen again, red-eyed, but with his mind tuned to alert by the developments he had to grapple with that morning, he had washed his face, had black coffee sent over from the officers' mess across the lawn and was drinking it thoughtfully when the mud-covered Land-Rover pulled up outside his office at 0601 hours.

Dimkpa leant back in his chair at the sound of the vehicle, to get a clear view through the narrow window.

*See Glossary

82

The cup of coffee on its journey to his lips came crashing down on the table top, spilling its hot, black contents on the tattered blotter.

Dimkpa gaped, eyes wide with incredulity, as six white men, all dressed in the Army's camouflage uniform, complete with the respected Rising Sun emblem, alighted from different sides of the Land-Rover, fully kitted and apparently ready for combat.

Dimkpa's surprise deepened as he saw one of the white men, a major's brass eagle on his shoulders, walk round the nose of the car, acknowledge the smart salute of the other white soldiers and look enquiringly at the driver of the car who pointed at the door of the commander's office.

Outside on the grass lawns, at the gates and in front of several little huts that served one strategic purpose or another, about two dozen men of the HQ Company stared, totally lost in the strange, unexpected arrival.

Sentries stood at ease, but with eyes riveted in an amazement that their faces spoke more distinctly than words.

For a brief second the white man read the black man's face, and felt like a Protestant envoy on arrival at the Holy See.

He tried to muster his composure and break the ice before it sent a chill down either of their spines.

He clicked his heels and gave a brief, brisk salute.

"Major Dimkpa?"

"Yes?" The curt reply sounded almost unfriendly. But the white man's patently unimposing demeanour began almost as quickly to impress Dimkpa.

The white man was completely relaxed, at ease, Dimkpa noted.

He pushed his chair from the table, rose to his feet and walked out from behind the table.

"I'm Major Georges Denault," the white man told Dimkpa. "My men and I"—he nodded over his shoulder towards the door—"have come to join your command."

"You're the Christian Brothers?"

"That's right. And we are your friends, Major. We are *under* your command." He put emphasis on the preposition. "Feel free to use our services as you think best. That's why we are here."

Chime Dimkpa began to feel some scepticism. When he had read the words *Christian Brothers* from the signal, his over-exercised mind had not had the slightest suspicion that he was going to have six white soldiers on his hands. Six white mercenaries innocuously christened Christian Brothers.

What a misnomer! If he remembered well his tales of mercenaries, from newspaper reports when he was a cadet at Sandhurst, from several angry denunciations by Colonel Chumah, who had been in the Congo, he should be ordering them to be locked up at once, at least on the pretext of awaiting further clearance. But there was an attack coming in less than an hour. And time was not waiting.

Under my command, Dimkpa repeated the phrase silently. He had not yet heard of a mercenary who let himself be commanded by a native officer. They were always the commanders, the bosses, who gave orders and retired to the safety of their camps to wait for the next week's pay.

There must be a well-wrought and cleverly concealed booby trap somewhere, Dimkpa thought, giving the man a closer look.

He shrugged his shoulders reluctantly.

"I must confess I wasn't expecting you gentlemen," Dimkpa told the white Major.

"Still," he shrugged again, "here you are."

He walked over to his table and picked up the intercept.

"You've walked into it," he looked up from the piece of paper and looked at Denault.

"There's an attack coming in the next fifty-five minutes." He looked at his watch, and extended the paper to the other man.

"An attack," Denault, accepted the paper and began to read.

"A counter-attack, to be more precise."

"I see. You must have given them hell to ask for this massive retaliation," Georges said, looking up from the paper.

"Yes, I'm afraid so. It was a pleasant little dinner-time surprise. Bastard vandals," Dimkpa cursed uncharacteristically.

Denault handed back the message to Dimkpa.

"I can understand the fury behind 21,000 mortar bombs, then," he said, shaking his head a little sadly.

"I know," Dimkpa agreed. "A woman scorned has no fury like an enemy humiliated," he misquoted flippantly.

"And how many mortar bombs can you muster?"

"Not one. Just two 105 and 106 artillery pieces. About six shells each. That's all my heavy equipment," he answered sombrely.

"We had about six amoured personnel carriers. Three have been knocked out by the enemy. Three are immobilised by shortage of fuel. We have had the HMGs dismounted and used in the lines. No point making them sitting ducks for vandal mortar and artillery."

"Well, for what it's worth we each have two-inch mortars and quite a handful of grenades."

"That's great news," Dimkpa looked at the man with a fresh eye. "Great news indeed," he said. "In this war, on our side of this war, little things are great news. Your mortars will be the first this brigade has had."

"I think we had better be going. Where are your other men?"

"Waiting outside."

"Seven minutes past six. Let's go."

On the evening of the same day, another officer was to join Major Chime Dimkpa on the Calabar front. His name was Michel.

CHAPTER EIGHTEEN

COLONEL JACQUES RUDOLF took several cautious minutes before he emerged from the concrete-topped air-raid shelter just behind his caravan.

He patted a spray of sand and dust from his body and neck and replaced his beret.

Captain Michel followed closely behind him.

Rudolf halted just outside the staired entrance to the bunker and scanned the now quiet sky.

"Pity you have no answer to this nuisance," he said to Michel without turning.

"Those HMGs are like rubber slings against MiG jets. And with the Calabar airport secure in his hands the enemy has got a forward staging base for this kind of raid."

"It is a sad thing, mon Colonel," Michel agreed.

"I don't know what the General can do about it, though."

"It seems he is trying to do something, sir," Michel said in a quiet confiding tone. "We hear France has promised Mirage fighters."

"Do you believe that sort of fairy tale, Michel? Surely not?"

Michel hesitated, licked his lips and answered. "We believe everything here, mon Colonel. As long as there is hope in it."

"And you see hope in this French rumour, do you?" Rudolf had turned and was looking at the hesitant Captain.

"It is not just a rumour, mon Colonel. It is a rumour of promise," the Captain answered, surprised at his own conviction.

"And you see hope in it, do you?"

"It seems to encourage hope, sir," Michel replied, unyielding.

"It is a bad hope, Michel, my dear. A very bad hope."

"A bad hope is probably better than despair, sir," Michel insisted, wondering for a brief while what his French Commander had against the French.

The Colonel peered into the face of the usually docile young Captain.

"Listen, my dear Michel." The white Colonel put a patronising palm on the black man's shoulder. "A bad hope is as bad as despair; perhaps worse. Make no mistake about it. A bad hope is despair that is avoiding the evil day."

"Yes, sir," the young man agreed, preferring to defer to the white master.

"And a bad hope is the child of a false promise," Rudolf added.

"Yes, sir."

"And a Frenchman's promise is a false promise," Rudolf ended.

At this the young Captain looked up at his Commander, nodded in feeble agreement but hesitated.

"Even General de Gaulle's promise, sir?"

"General de Gaulle is a great man, Michel. I like him. But General de Gaulle is a Frenchman. A true Frenchman. The most dangerous Frenchman is a true Frenchman, Michel.

"And so, my dear Michel, is Major Georges Denault!" Rudolf had been working himself up to this climactic declaration. He spat out the words, withdrew his hand from the Captain's shoulder and left for his cabin.

The two had been talking about Major Georges before the skies shrieked nearly three hours before.

Michel had arrived in the morning from the Calabar front for his third personal report to the Colonel since he left five weeks before.

The first time around he had given Rudolf a graphic account of the miracle Georges wrought with the troops during the enemy's counter-offensive.

Morale, he told the Colonel, had shot up like a tracer bullet the moment Georges and his five comrades joined the front line a few minutes before the enemy's H-hour. The sight of the white men, with the Brigade's first mortars which, added to the substantial caches of ammunition captured from the operation of the night before, had en-livened and emboldened a worn-out and fretful force.

Ten minutes before 7 a.m. Denault had had his six mortar guns positioned in selected strategic positions, under the personal command of each of his French colleagues and himself.

Gambling on the enemy's calculation that the rebel forces could ill-afford a mortar gun, Georges had opened up a six-pronged mortar barrage shortly before 7 o'clock. Having pilfered both the advantage and initiative from the enemy by throwing in a weapon he least reckoned on, Georges had clung to his guns, moved three to more forward locations, and was able to throw in twenty shells before the dreaded H-hour.

By H-hour Major Georges had moved Dimkpa's forces forward, into the no-man's land between the enemy's forces and the rebels' bombarded stronghold. He had duly made contact with the opposing forces on the enemy's own grounds and was engaging him in a bitter fire fight soon after 7 a.m.

The dreaded twenty-one-thousand mortar shells were thudding largely into empty trenches behind Georges and his men as they battled on the enemy's doorsteps.

Rudolf had listened to Michel's verbal report with a secret, grudging admiration for the resourceful French Major.

"But you do realise that was a suicidal risk, don't you, Michel?" he had asked at last.

Michel was not quite sure he agreed with his Colonel. He felt an impulse to ask him what he would have done if he were in Georges' place, but yielded to the quick realisation that he dared not challenge the boss.

"He was risking the life of the whole Brigade, Michel," Rudolf answered his own question as Michel kept silent.

"All the men and equipment," he went on. "I still do not trust Major Georges, Michel," he had told him that day.

Michel's second report was undramatic. Troops on both sides held their grounds and gains, exchanged only sporadic fire and frequent abuse.

But Michel's third visit today, less than twenty-four hours before Christmas Day, seemed pregnant. He had barely begun when the air raid drove both men into the shelter, which had seemed hardly an auspicious place to continue a report.

Colonel Rudolf scanned the sky a final time before he entered his caravan. Michel followed at a discreet pace.

Rudolf sat down on the chair, leaned back and lit a cigarette.

"Now, back to Calabar," he began, motioning Michel over to the seat beside him.

"What did you say the recce* reported?" he asked the young man.

"A heavy enemy build-up in men and arms, sir."

Rudolf exhaled luxuriously and asked again.

"And Major Georges knows this, does he?"

"Yes, sir."

"And what does he think?"

"The Major is convinced there will be a major attack soon after the Christmas lull, mon Colonel."

"Have you any idea of his counter-plans?"

"Not exactly, mon Colonel."

"What do you mean not exactly?"

"I mean there's no doubt that Major Georges is planning a counter-action, but I don't know the details. The Major does not believe in talking about his plans, he says."

*See Glossary

"Secretive as the devil, Georges is, Michel. Shows you he has something to hide." Rudolf could hardly see a better opportunity for insinuation.

"Perhaps, mon Colonel."

"Not perhaps, Captain," Rudolf was suddenly offended by the lack of conviction in Michel's voice. "I'm certain. He has even proved it. And I think now you should waste no further time in doing what I told you earlier on."

"I remember, mon Colonel." Michel remembered clearly, for Rudolf's final order came reeling through his memory ". . . Georges is the enemy behind you. Worse than the enemy in front of you behind a machine gun. Don't hesitate to eliminate him . . ."

"Or else Georges will do more dangerous things when the enemy attacks next time," Rudolf added. The Captain nodded.

"As you wish, mon Colonel."

"You understand the details, of course, and that you must employ the utmost discretion."

"I have the details, mon Colonel. I understand."

"But before then, Michel, I'm going to have a final word with Georges. We must make everything look natural."

"When, sir?"

"Tell him to report here as soon as you get back to Calabar, will you? And unless you have my orders to the contrary, which I seriously doubt now, you should proceed with the details of your original instructions. Good afternoon, Michel."

"I see you're still taking this war too close to your heart, Georges," Rudolf began as soon as Major Denault arrived on Christmas morning.

"I'll tell you what my little nigger sentry said the other day."

"He said the Ibos have a saying that in war, it's the chap whose head you see that you shoot at!

"The Federals have been seeing your head too often, Georges. A damn sight too often! I see you want to be a hero. But Georges, heroes draw no higher wages than cowards."

"You are wasting my time, Jacques," Denault moved to leave. "I'm satisfied with doing the job I'm paid to do."

"Conscience and morals don't come into war, Georges. But if you must be a hero, the good hero is a living hero."

"I suppose you will call yourself a good soldier, Jacques?" Georges taunted, standing up and straightening his beret.

"Sure, Georges, why not? A good soldier fights to fight another day."

Good-bye, Georges, the Colonel thought. It is hard but I don't think I'll ever set eyes on you alive again.

88

CHAPTER NINETEEN

CAPTAIN MICHEL WAS sprawled at the foot of a rubber tree, his body leaning heavily on its bullet-pocked trunk. Between his feet, his right hand caressed the barrel of a captured Cetme automatic rifle.

Captain Jules, hot and sticky, his lips cracked from the fury of the harmattan, sat in a similar position on the near side of the tree on Michel's left.

Jules was one of Georges' five comrades.

Both men seemed physically weary but relaxed as they lit the cigarettes that Jules had provided.

The Major was expected back from Umuahia any minute. Michel had seemed more nervous, edgy, if no less pompous, today, than ever. Jules had noted this and had decided it was time he talked to him.

About eight hundred yards from them, on both sides of the still heated battle lines, the sporadic clatter of machine guns reminded them that there was no Christmas for the men of war. The sound of the firing was carried across with fierce shrillness by the harmattan wind.

Jules thought about Michel. The Frenchmen found it easy to get along with the young black captain of uncertain ancestry who, with his natural fluency in the French language, was a charming person, although he often got a bit pompous about his job as the Commander's special representative. He had also found Michel a bit furtive.

"Merci," Michel said, handing back the Frenchman's lighter and packet of cigarettes.

"It's terrible weather, this harmattan, isn't it, Michel?" Jules began, feeling his way, and finding it painful to move his lips.

"It is," Michel agreed. "But rather nice early in the morning. A bit like Paris in Spring."

"You been to Paris?" Jules looked at him with surprise.

"Yes. For a brief holiday."

"Did you like Paris?"

"Very nice. Beautiful city. Lovely food." Michel exhaled a curl of smoke and abruptly brought the conversation back to the weather. He did not want to be corrupted by memories of a country he loved very much, and whose national he had been assigned to eliminate.

"It could be worse. It's bound to get worse," he said.

"What?"

"The weather."

"Oh, the harmattan."

"Yes. It'll get worse towards the end of January," Michel forecast.

"I hope we can stand it," Jules said apprehensively. It was bad enough with him unable to move his lips easily.

"Is it possible for you to leave, under your contract, Jules?" Michel asked innocently.

"Oh, I don't even know if I can. Maybe if one is badly wounded. Certainly not because of an unbearable harmattan, I suppose," he grinned.

"What are the conditions of your service like?" Michel looked briefly at the Frenchman. "I mean what's the pay like?"

"I guess I know that. A hundred pounds a week here. A thousand dollars in Europe every month."

"That's good money, Jules."

"Not good money, Michel," the Frenchman said, eagerly, seeing the chance to work in his proposed dialogue with Michel.

"It's not good money," he repeated for emphasis. "It is blood money," he turned to meet Michel's eyes. "Blood money isn't good money."

The black man's face held genuine amazement.

"Are you surprised at a mercenary talking the way I do?" Jules asked challenging Michel's unspoken mind.

"No, no. I mean," Michel stammered, "no, you kind of sound re assuring," he said honestly.

"How much do you get, yourself?"

"Fifty pounds a month nominally. But actually I only get a small field allowance. The rest is supposed to be held for me and from that my dependants could draw an allowance."

"Now that's good money, Michel. That's good money. You're a professional soldier?"

"I *want* to be a professional soldier. I was reading French at the university before the war. But now I think I would rather continue to be a soldier after the war is won," Michel confided.

"Why? Any special reasons?"

"I don't know really. I suppose I want to continue to defend the fatherland. It's being won at such great cost."

"Would you be prepared to fight for another country, in another army just for the money, Michel?"

Michel thought for a while, his head in his palms, and cigarette smoke drifting from his fingers up his forehead.

"I have never thought about it, frankly. But to do that I suppose I have to feel strongly enough for the people concerned."

"I get what you mean, Michel. But suppose your government wished you to do so?"

"Well, that would be an order . . . to be obeyed."

90

"Of course, yes," Jules agreed.

"And if I happen to feel some compassion for the cause of the people concerned, you know, fighting the racists in South Africa, for example, I would feel happier doing it," Michel added.

Both men threw away the dead stubs of their cigarettes.

"But why do you ask? I'm intrigued."

Michel pulled his rifle nearer, covered the muzzle with both palms and rested his chin on it.

"Because . . . because—oh forget it." Jules fidgeted with his lighter, nervously lit another cigarette and threw his head back on the tree trunk, exhaling lazily.

He was not quite certain now that his suspicion about the young captain was right.

"Go on, tell me," Michel urged. "We are friends. You should trust me."

"I'm going to," Jules said, giving in.

"Go ahead."

"Michel, I believe you are here on some kind of mission. To spy on us maybe," he blurted out before he could check himself. And having crossed the Rubicon, he continued heedlessly.

"Maybe Major Georges doesn't suspect this, but I do," Jules said. "I don't know exactly why, but I imagine you report back to Colonel Rudolf regularly. Am I right so far?"

"I don't think I know what you are talking about, Jules," Michel denied, "but it sounds fantastic enough to interest me; go on. I find it gripping."

"You know I don't believe you. But before you go on with Rudolf's wishes, before you make any regrettable mistakes, you ought to realise one thing."

"Tell me."

"That the six of us here in the Calabar front are the only genuine friends you have among the forty-eight of us."

"How do I believe you? The Colonel says the same thing about himself and the other forty-one men in the training camp." Michel's tone was casual, as if he never made his earlier denial.

"I don't know how to prove it. But the truth is, and I'm letting out a secret because I consider it necessary to do so. We are *not* mercenaries. We are not fighting for your money. We are here because the French Government want us to help you."

Michel remained quiet for sometime, his face immobile above the muzzle of his rifle, his mind a riot.

"And how did you team up with the Colonel, then?" he asked at last.

"It was the only way. We had to come in covertly, or France would be accused of interference and all that sort of political rubbish. We had to come under their cover."

"Do our people know it?"

"No. The French Government didn't believe you would resist the temptation to use French assistance for propaganda," Jules explained.

"Does the Colonel know it?"

"I believe he doesn't. He might suspect something, but again he might conclude we are just being idealistic and foolish. He is no doubt hurt by our operations. It clashes with his scheming."

"His scheming?" Michel was puzzled.

"Yes. He wants the longest possible route to victory, Michel. It pays him more that way," Jules said, straining his voice for emhasis. "And I'll tell you something else, Michel. When Colonel Rudolf has trained his division, he will be running your army! I shared a bungalow for a brief while with one of his chief assistants, Major Dan Marc."

Michel was horrified. He shifted nervously on the grass.

"You suspect so, do you?"

"I don't. I *know* so."

"You won't tell the Major about this conversation, will you, Jules?" he asked anxiously.

"Only if you don't report it back to your Colonel, Michel."

"Fair is fair."

"Then it's a deal."

"A deal it is."

"Oh, just one thing."

"Yes?"

"I shall not be seeing the Colonel. Not again. I'm going to go straight to Defence Operations. I shall want to report to them about this matter. Certainly not about the French Government. But bits of the conversation," Michel was hurrying to his feet.

"Bits of it, that's all right. As long as you use discretion, and stop your people from being misled by Jacques Rudolf. Where're you going?"

"Back to Umuahia. To get at Def-Ops and to the General this evening. I should be there around 5 p.m." He looked at his watch. "I'm afraid they've made many mistakes already."

"Why not wait a bit for the Major? He should be returning about now," Captain Jules looked at his own wrist watch and began to rise to his feet. 2 p.m.

"I'd rather not. I'll probably run into him on the way. In any case, I don't think I need to see the Major now."

"Good luck, Michel," Jules touched the tip of his fingers to the rim of his beret and turned away towards the front-lines where he could see troops of the rear trenches passing ammunition and exchanging cigarettes.

92

He shook his head sympathetically. He couldn't believe it was Christmas day.

The Joint Planning Staff had been meeting all afternoon in a secret outpost on the skirts of Umuahia. The General had presided as usual.

Colonel Jaques Rudolf had received his sudden summons to the meeting with some anger. But fortified with a lavish Christmas lunch and rich Portuguese wine flown in specially for the festive day, he had recovered his mood quickly enough to participate in the deliberations with his customary aplomb.

It was a quarter to five when the meeting ended.

Rudolf's white Mercedes was soon nosing onto the main highway that led to the left, back to his caravan camp six miles away, and right to Arochuku and the Calabar sector.

Rudolf's driver suddenly braked on the threshold of the highway as a military Land-Rover, thumping furiously down the road to the city, swept past in a spiralling trail of dust and dried leaves.

The Mercedes waited a few seconds for the dust to settle and eased onto the highway, heading for the city. The Land-Rover was nearly a hundred yards away and keeping up its furious pace.

Nearer the city's main check-point, it began to slow down at the first speed-breaker.

The steel bars were beginning to ease upwards at the approach of the military vehicle when Rudolf's Mercedes slowed down to some five yards behind Captain Michel.

Rudolf suddenly leaned forward from the back seat, gripped the driver's seat in front of him with both hands as his eyes caught the skull and crossbones emblem just above the military number plate of the Land-Rover in front of them.

"That's Michel," he mumbled anxiously. "Follow him, driver," he said aloud to the man behind the wheel. "Follow the Land-Rover."

"Yessah," came the reply and the huge car responded too, heaving forward, past the check-point and the saluting guards and was soon hovering a few yards from the tail of Michel's vehicle.

In spite of Christmas Day, the town remained as bleak as Michel knew it twenty-four hours before.

As he negotiated the roundabout at the confluence of highways into the city, he saw again the wreckage of coaches in the rail yard. A diesel engine, or what was left of it, still smouldered stubbornly. The tortured telephone and power lines leant grotesquely in the silent yard.

Michel shook his head sadly. The Colonel, he thought, would probably be sleeping off his Christmas whisky and dreaming up fresh accusations against Major Georges and his boys.

No. Michel remembered. The Colonel would be waiting for news of the Major's death.

To hell with Colonel Rudolf, he cursed silently, and took the right turn to the heavily guarded stretch of road that led to State Lodge and Defence Operations.

Behind Michel, Colonel Rudolf's Mercedes slowed down at the road-turn. Rudolf leant forward again, calm as never before, and tapped the driver on the shoulder.

"Get in front of that Land-Rover and stop it. Quickly!" he ordered in a cold voice.

The car shot forward, horns blaring in flagrant breach of the 'noise-less zone' warning posted about the road.

Michel slowed down and began to edge the van towards the side of the road, making way for the car behind.

As the car drew up he looked out to his right. He saw the unmistakable burly features of the white man in the back seat of the car. Colonel Rudolf! The Captain's heart leapt.

In shocked confusion, Michel's feet shuffled between accelerator and brake pedals, found the brake pedal as the white car sped up ahead of him, beamed the red warning lights and stopped.

Chiko was out in a flash, opening the rear door and saluting stiffly.

Rudolf came out and went to the side of the Land-Rover, face to face with Michel.

"What's happened, Michel?" he asked in French, his tone calm and apparently unsuspecting. Beads of cold sweat trembled on the young Captain's face; his fingers rattled on the steering wheel, rattling Rudolf's suspicion.

Without waiting for his answer now, the Christian Brother went round the nose of the vehicle, opened the front door and climbed into the passenger seat beside Michel. He looked at the Captain's trembling face suspiciously and nodded his head over his shoulder in the direction of the caravan camp.

But Michel had recovered his composure when they reached the gate of Rudolf's camp. He parked the vehicle clear of the road, close to the high fence, and came down. He looked back down the road but saw no sign of the white car. He went through the gate followed by a wary Rudolf.

Michel bit his lower lip in self-recrimination as he passed through the gate. Jules's words rang through his mind like a tape recording: "When Colonel Rudolf has trained his Division, he will be running your army." Why had he forgotten to use his rear-view mirror as he drove into the city? he asked himself.

Rudolf fumbled in his pocket for his bunch of keys, went past Michel up to the door of the caravan and began to select the caravan key.

Michel looked at the burly back with hatred.

He took one step backward and placed his now calm fingers on the butt of the automatic pistol in his hip pocket.

He pulled.

Rudolf had deliberately baited the Captain, and had missed no single twitch of Michel's fingers. His suspicion aroused, he had in fact simulated an air of unsuspecting casualness for Michel to take advantage of.

As Michel pulled the pistol clear of his pocket, Rudolf's left foot lashed out viciously backward, missed the gun but caught the Captain flush on the groin. Michel doubled up and let out a groan.

Rudolf bounded round in a flash but found the gun still wavering at him as Michel held his groin with his free hand.

Rudolf was not going to have a shot fired in his camp, within shooting distance of State Lodge and the General. So he quickly feigned surrender and threw both hands above his head.

Michel, grimacing with pain and rage and edging menacingly towards the white man, still stooped from the pain in his groin.

"Now I know all about you, Colonel Rudolf!" he panted. "I know why you want me to kill an innocent man. I'm . . ." he ran out of breath and began to pant heavily.

Fear at Michel's words brought out the brawling OAS Sergeant that hid behind the impassive mask of Colonel Jacques Rudolf. His waxen face splintered in venomous anger that seemed to send tiny curls of smoke spiralling from his narrowing eyes.

Heedlessly he grabbed for Michel's gun hand, gripped the Captain's right hand with his left, shifted clear of the caravan door behind him, tilted backwards and flung Michel over his head in a swift, perfect judo throw.

Michel lay in a gasping heap, his pistol resting at his feet.

Rudolf charged at him again, but seeing the automatic, he stopped to retrieve and secure it first.

With dazed eyes, Michel summoned all the strength in his left foot and kicked out viciously at the pink face that hovered over his feet.

He caught Rudolf smack on the neck and seared a purple bruise above the collar of the Colonel's camouflage uniform shirt. Rudolf fell sideways, plunging his head into the bristly grass.

Michel wobbled on to his knees hurriedly before Rudolf could regain his balance and pounced on his white master.

He landed two quick but feeble punches on the spot where he had stamped with his boot. Standing astride a kicking Rudolf he yanked the Colonel up on his feet, swung him sideways and caught him flush on the pelvis with a more powerful punch.

95

Rudolf bent, feigned a crumbling fall, and had Michel hovering over him, gathering strength for a coup de grâce.

Suddenly Rudolf snapped like a sprung plank.

The back of his head shot swiftly upwards and stopped with an ugly thud at Michel's chin.

The Captain flew backwards, landed in an almost lifeless sprawl before his Commander.

"Goddamn you fucking black bastard," Rudolf panted, hovering briefly over the fallen Michel.

Rudolf hurried to the caravan door, opened it and dragged Michel's unconscious body into the cabin.

He made straight for his table, picked up his telephone and in a moment was speaking to Major Johann Schmuts at the training camp.

"Johann, I want you and Hans here. Straightaway! Emergency!" He slammed back the receiver without waiting for a response.

Rudolf heard the sound of the Mercedes drawing up outside almost as soon as he put down the handset. He drew up the collar of his shirt over his ugly blotch and went over to his cabinet and began to pull out a bottle of Vat 69.

By seven o'clock he, Major Johann Schmuts and Kapitan Hans Heinz had arrived at the 5 Commando training camp with Michel in the Mercedes.

Rudolf had dismissed his driver for the night, told Chiko, the sentry to go for an early supper and return later to guard the caravan as he would be spending the night at the training base.

"I can't deal with this bastard here. Better at the camp," Rudolf had told Johann and Hans after the briefest of explanations.

They had then spirited a now conscious but dazed Michel into the back seat, between Rudolf and Heinz, with Johann at the wheel.

At the camp they had driven straight to the single-storeyed building at the far end of the vast training base, now being renovated for Rudolf's eventual use.

There they interrogated Captain Michel all through the night. By midnight they had tortured out of him just about everything he knew from Captain Jules.

At the end, free from the grinding pain, Captain Michel wept, not from the pain of his torture but for breaking the deal he made with Captain Jules. He was lumped into a corner of the room, his face a blotch of blood and tears, as the three men deliberated the import of Michel's disclosures.

The revelation about the French Government being behind George and his group intrigued Rudolf.

At last, he told himself, there was a greater reason than any to eliminate not only Georges but the whole gang of de Gaulle's men.

On the morning of Boxing Day Johann Schmuts and Hans Heinz met with Rudolf over breakfast in the Commander's temporary quarters.

"I want Captain Jules brought here and put away. That's the first step," Rudolf said, putting down an empty cup of coffee and reaching for his cigarettes.

"I can't do it myself, Jacques," Johann said. "For obvious reasons."

"Yes, I know. I think Hans will go down. OK, Hans?"

"Sure, I'll bring him back. I'd love to," he grimaced.

"Tell Georges we want Jules to handle special mortar instruction here," Rudolf directed. "Tell him it's only for two days. I don't want him to get curious."

"That's it," Johann agreed. "And meanwhile I'll find a replacement for him," he proposed.

"I want the replacement to go along with Hans in the morning," said Rudolf.

"What about Michel?" Heinz asked.

"Tell Georges we've reassigned Michel," Rudolf told him. "He will be in the training base."

"Right."

"Now, Jules's replacement has of course one task," Rudolf's tone was grave.

"He will eliminate Georges and the rest of his crowd—before the New Year. Before the next enemy offensive."

Heinz and Schmuts nodded slowly.

"That's his sole task. After which he returns here. That should see the end of de Gaulle's little adventure."

"In that case," Johann Schmuts began, clearing his throat uncertainly. "I mean, to make sure the next man doesn't pull a Michel on us, why not two men? I can spare them. One can go in as Michel's replacement."

"Thanks, Johann. That's a fine idea," Rudolf agreed. "I don't want to know who they are. But make sure they are smart and reliable; and brief them properly."

"I'm thinking of Captain Belgar and Lieutenant Coullar. They're good boys."

"Frenchmen again?" Rudolf's fingers crept to the blue and purple bruise on his neck.

"Hell, no. They're Belgian."

"On your way, then. I'm going back to Umuahia." Rudolf began to rise to his feet. "Michel remains in the guard room. And keep everything as quiet as possible. I think I should be moving down here by the New Year."

CHAPTER TWENTY

MAJOR GEORGES DENAULT was pleasantly surprised at Jacques Rudolf's apparent change of heart. Maybe, he thought, that Christmas morning *confrontation* had awakened him to the urgency of the war.

Now he had an extra man, and invaluable relief for the brave but battered young lieutenant who had so ably commanded Bravo Battalion.

He was sorry they took away his able deputy Jules. But if the two new men together proved as good as Jules, then it would have been a worthwhile swap. Their job was to join the fight and fight hard; he didn't mind if the replacements were Germans or Belgians.

Now he and Major Dimkpa, with whom he got on exceedingly well, could put their heads together and face up to the enemy's anticipated New Year present.

At 7 p.m. on the evening of the third night before the New Year, Major Georges Denault, the new men, the other four Frenchmen, and Major Chime Dimkpa and his three battalion commanders held a review group and discussed the expected January offensive.

It was, ironically, Major Georges who thought up the idea. A raid behind the lines on the enemy's ammunition dump which the reconnaissance patrol had reported on exhaustively.

"That will be a damned daring move, Georges," Dimkpa warned without really seeming to discourage the raid. "We will have to reckon with the moonlight which will deny us the necessary cover for that sort of thing."

"The moon won't be out until a little after midnight at this time," Georges reckoned.

"Maybe not," Dimkpa agreed. "But it's a long journey away. How early can we set off to beat the moon?"

"We could strike about midnight if we set off nine or ten o'clock. I'll lead the boys myself," Georges replied quietly.

"You'll need a recce man as guide."

"Yes, of course. You'll assign the best man, Chime, please."

"Sure."

"I will go along with you if you wish, sir," Captain Belgar volunteered, addressing Georges, his gentle voice masking deep excitement with casual enthusiasm.

"We haven't done much since we arrived, have we, Coullar boy?"

In the darkness Belgar's elbow found the rib of Lieutenant Coullar at his side and nudged him gently.

"Not really, I will like to go, too," Coullar offered. He did not sound suspiciously enthusiastic. Georges' four French comrades also volunteered.

"Now that's eight of us," Georges noted. "A bit too many, but never mind. An operation like this is best carried out by volunteers."

"When do you move, then?" Dimkpa asked. "I mean what day?"

"When?" Georges asked himself aloud. "I haven't decided."

"Why not tonight?" Belgar's voice quietly stole into the void of silence. "New Year is not too far away, sir."

"Tonight is all right by me," said Coullar casually.

The Frenchmen, two captains and two young lieutenants, did not mind when.

"Tonight, then," Major Georges ruled finally.

"I'll keep the boys on alert," Dimkpa promised.

"And you'll prepare us some very good kits, Chime."

"Of course, straightaway."

Less than three hours later, three miles behind the enemy lines, Major Georges Denault, his four comrades and patrolman Ujor were lying dead among the rubble of a blown Federal ammunition dump. They had been shot in the back in a moment of tension and confusion by Captain Ernst Belgar and Lieutenant Pierre Coullar.

CHAPTER TWENTY-ONE

IT WAS NOT Colonel Jacques Rudolf's skill in covering the trail that quickly threw the scent of suspicion off the killers of Major Denault and his men. It was the propaganda of triumph practised with great enthusiasm by both parties to the war.

At the Calabar sector, Major Chime Dimkpa and his troops were shocked anew when their transistor radio confirmed the sad news brought home earlier by Belgar and Coullar, that they were the only survivors of an enemy ambush behind the lines.

In the Defence Operations HQ, the big Zenith transistor radio on the Colonel's cluttered desk was, as usual at this time of the day, tuned to the Federal Radio Station. It was blaring with a liveliness that did undue credit to the run-down batteries inside it.

The newscaster's voice bore a triumphant resonance as he kicked off the seven o'clock newscast with the dramatic leader:

In a major offensive launched at the Calabar sector yesterday, our gallant forces last night killed five white mercenary soldiers fighting

alongside the rebel troops. A military spokesman in Army Headquarters told our correspondent that the white soldiers of fortune were
leading the rag-tag rebel troops when they were attacked and wiped
out by a company of our gallant forces . . .

The Chief of Defence Operations clicked the set dead and agitatedly
reached for the telephone.

"Morning, Colonel," he greeted, as Rudolf came on with a sleepy
hello. "Any direct signals from Calabar front to you, Colonel?" he
asked, trying to keep worry from his voice.

"Not yet," he heard Rudolf reply. "Have you?"

"No, no. But Lagos radio had something on a few minutes ago about
heavy fighting there," he said trying to sound routine.

"Heavy fighting?" repeated Rudolf, his interest aroused.

"Something like that," the Chief said with deliberate imprecision.

"Any details?"

"Not much. It seems there were heavy casualties, though."

"On both sides?"

"Mm-huh."

"Well, tell me all about it; you listened in, didn't you?"

"Yes I did. Look, I'll send you a monitored text. I'm sending one to
the General, too."

"Is it as bad as that?"

"Rather so, I'm afraid."

Georges Denault and his French collaborators were dead. Rudolf had
no doubt about that. He didn't need to ask further questions.

He replaced the handset, tightened the cord around his dressing gown
and went back into his bedroom.

Colonel Jacques Rudolf did not give further thought to the Calabar front
until about noon when the General rang up to offer his sympathy on the
death of the Colonel's colleagues.

"Very kind of you, mon Général," Rudolf said when the General had
spoken. "It is a high casualty to absorb," Rudolf intoned in a borrowed,
sombre voice. "But I assure mon Général that we shall not be deflected
from our commitment to your gallant forces. We always reckon with
the occasional sacrifice. It is an inevitable part of the job." He tossed his
dead cigarette into the ashtray and put a foot up on the nearby coffee
table.

"It's very gallant of you to say so, Colonel. I'm heartened," he heard
the General say. "I shall of course instruct the proper reparations to be
made without delay in accordance with the provisions of the contract.

"Thank you, mon Général."

"Once more, accept my sincere sympathy, Colonel."

"Thank you again, mon Général."

Rudolf put the Green handset to rest, allowed himself a wink and went over to his liquor cabinet. He smiled at the smooth success of these initial moves in his grand design.

The Vat 69 was empty.

He pulled out a bottle of Cutty Sark.

For two weeks the harmattan mist and a heavy gloom hung over the green arms of the forest on the Calabar front. The troops, depressed and demoralised, squatted in their trenches like a house bereaved.

Their 'Major Georges', around whom, in their fantasy, they had long built a myth of invincibility, had been killed in an enemy ambush. So said the surviving white men, now recuperating at their commando training camp from the shock of their miraculous escape.

The broom of sadness and gloom seemed to sweep their bereavement anew each day that passed.

In Umuahia Colonel Rudolf read the crystal ball: the death of the Frenchmen in action, it told him, would call a temporary halt to fresh urgings for his men's early deployment.

There would have to be a respectful allowance for a period of mourning. At least a fortnight. Time enough to round off the training of the crack 5 Commando Division. After which would begin the period of sharpening their fighting teeth.

Then he would be ready.

The next day Rudolf moved his command post over to the training base at Etiti, the new headquarters of his division.

Now he was on his own.

Major Denault's fatal foray into the enemy's rear location did set the enemy's plans back.

But only for a fortnight.

Major Dimkpa's troops were still in their trench of gloom when the offensive opened two weeks after the New Year with a fury and swiftness that underscored the enemy's feeling of injury at the stab in his rear.

By the 16th of January Dimkpa's Brigade was teetering on the banks of the Cross River.

Dimkpa had quickly calculated that safety from total rout lay across the muddy river. He ordered a speedy but orderly retreat across the river.

"No number of miles held is worth a single life that could be evacuated now when we can," he told his battalion commanders.

By night time they were digging new trenches along their own banks of the river, now a wide safety belt between them and their enemy.

Rudolf would say that their weakness and incompetence had been unmasked.

Johann Schmuts would add that their soft underbelly had been exposed.

Georges Denault's death had worked to Jacques Rudolf's advantage just as he had reckoned.

The Christian Brothers would soon try to grab hope from the jaws of despair.

PHASE THREE:

White Brothers of Black Soldiers

CHAPTER TWENTY-TWO

IT WAS NOT the same Land-Rover, with its open back and weather-worn tarpaulin covers.

This one was gleaming green, with an immaculate interior and a red crest bearing a lone star beneath its military number plate.

He could see, as it drew nearer the gate, that it was his old command Land-Rover.

But he was not sure it was his old driver behind the steering wheel.

It was the same officer, though, the Provost Marshal. He would recognise him a mile off. A polished brass eagle now glistened on his shoulders in place of three rubber-stamped pips of eleven months before.

None of his armed military policemen seemed to be in sight this morning. He was alone but for the driver, who was now backing the car into the parking area outside the guarded entrance.

The Provost Marshal strode to the gate of the detention camp, a heavily guarded, remote building at the rear of a huge re-training garrison in the middle of nowhere. Its seclusion had been perfected with tall concrete fences doubly secured with barbed wires.

The Major spoke briefly with the sentries and showed them a piece of paper he held in his palm.

They let him through the gate without ado.

Colonel Charles Chumah withdrew from the barred window and turned to the dim cubby-hole that had been his home for the past eleven months, as the Major crossed the small compound to the second sentry party at the door of the tiny house.

The room was empty but for a few civilian clothes hanging from a nail drilled into the wall, a narrow iron bed and cotton mattress, a handful of paperbacks on military derring-do piled on the floor near the bed, empty packets of cigarettes and matches. It smelled of stale tobacco smoke and tired air.

Even before the guards unlocked the door to the room to let in the Major, Colonel Chumah began to pack the books and fold his shirts. The Provost Marshal, he told himself, certainly wasn't calling this morning with his former command car to tell him it was Saturday morning, and that he would spend another eleven months in jail.

The Provost Marshal's polite demeanour spoke even before the man himself. It was not the gruff, grudging courtesy of the day of arrest.

"The General Commander-in-Chief has ordered your immediate release, sir," he told the Colonel, accompanying the proclamation with a stiff-armed, rigid-fingered salute. Colonel Chumah listened hard to hear the Major add the crucial phrase—'and reinstatement'—but the Major had apparently spoken all his brief.

The Major brought his hand smartly to his side with a whistling slash. He looked at the Colonel.

The Colonel, he noted, was different now. His face was now hidden behind a thick growth of beard. He'd lost some weight, too, though none of his purposeful air of inner strength and authority.

"I'm delighted," Colonel Chumah said. "You can see I'm ready." He turned and took one ironically nostalgic look at the room that had given him shelter, albeit an impersonal one, for nearly a year.

"I'm pleased to see you are in good health, sir," the Major noted respectfully, taking the bundle of books from the Colonel.

"Thank you. And I notice you have been promoted. I'm glad. It shows you ve been working hard."

"Thank you, sir."

"Let's go. I can't wait to get back into things," the Colonel said.

"So, how's it going. How are things?" Chumah asked the Provost Marshal as they rode in the back of the command car.

"So, so, sir. Nothing yet to fire a twenty-one-gun salute about." His voice was sad, the Colonel noted.

"How's Major Dimkpa making out? Chime Dimkpa, you must know him?"

"I do, indeed, sir."

"Is he still alive?"

"Last time I heard of him, he was OK, sir, but that was then. You know what this business is like. You live by days. Every day is a bonus."

"Yeah, that is war."

The Provost Marshal had met Colonel Charles Chumah only a couple of times before that morning eleven months ago when he arrested him on orders and took him away to the detention camp, and this morning when he had the pleasure of executing his release. He would not have said he knew the Colonel well.

But in the eleven months between, he had come to feel he had known the man from childhood. The Colonel's reputation, built around the fiery drive that manifested itself in ruthless bravery, and his abiding loathing for white men, whom he saw as enemies of the republic, had become legendary folk tales.

CCC, as he was popularly known, had become a cry that sometimes reverberated as strongly as the name of the General. Officers and men who had fought under his command regarded his bravery and stout heart with an esteem that no other commander had engendered in fifteen months of war.

106

The Colonel, the Provost Marshal had no doubt, was still the most popular commander in the army. If CCC could not hold the capital City, nobody, absolutely nobody else, could have. He knew this very well.

In eleven months, the absence of the sheer force of his fierce leadership seemed to have taken the heart and morale out of the army.

For a while, when the Frenchman, Georges, and his men were in the fighting lines, the wind seemed to have changed, and morale soared.

The Calabar front had withstood some ferocious attacks and even replied with some daring counters of their own, made small but spectacular gains, and captured much-needed weapons.

But only for a while.

For morale and hope both suffered dramatic reverses soon after the death of the French Five. They had been an unusual breed of mercenary soldiers, probably the best breed there ever was.

With the death of the Frenchmen, a new clamour for the release of CCC had begun. The Frenchmen had come nearest to the troops' ideal of Charles Chumah's bravery and leadership.

Within their own 5 Commando the ranks were becoming noticeably restive as their number dramatically plummeted after each suicidally ambitious operation.

The recent Aba counter-attack, Shadrack recalled, had provided a sharp stab of pain. It was illusory in its conception and unbearable in its heavy casualty. Nearly one thousand 5 Commando infantrymen had died at the now notorious Ugba Junction, under Colonel Rudolf and his men. Twice that number had been injured. Yet not one Christian Brother had suffered a bullet graze.

Only the High Command knew how much the Christian Brothers had cost the country in scarce foreign exchange. But the Provost Marshal knew the particular case of a few days before when one of the Christian Brothers collected a total of twenty-five thousand dollars from friendly sources in Europe, on behalf of the State, for the purchase of Zodiac armoured canoes for a purported amphibious operation. Intelligence reports were now beginning to speculate that the mercenary banked the money in Zurich and flew back into the enclave.

Not even the fall of Aba, the legendary warrior city which the General himself had once called the 'heart of our resistance', and the mercenaries' inept performance there, had shaken the big man's confidence in the Christian Brothers.

The last resort had been to strive for the release of Colonel Chumah, the only man they know who could do something to stem the flow of disaster.

The Provost Marshal looked out of the window at the tall grasses and taller trees. The car had entered the tarmac and was speeding along a road pot-holed by cannon and rockets from high-flying MiG fighters.

The road had been the scene of recent heavy troop movement and an equally heavy air action. The junction ahead of them now had been a temporary rendezvous for bloody but unbowed units retreating from various points of the fighting to regroup for fresh deployment.

The once small Añara Junction, now overnight the nerve centre of massive troop and civilian movement, was despondent as the command car rode in.

A white relief truck bearing a bold Red Cross sign clattered and trundled past.

Forlorn civilian refugees hungrily gaped at the food from the roadsides.

Shadrack fumbled in the pocket of his tunic and brought out a fresh packet of cigarettes, broke it open and offered it to the Colonel.

"The army will be pleased to see you back sir. The boys need you badly."

"Same here. I'll be damned pleased to be with them again. But they'll have to wait for a couple of days," he said vaguely.

"Wait a couple of days, sir?"

"That's right. I've got to get to Port Harcourt directly I finish with the Defence Operations his morning."

"Port Harcourt!" a horrified exclamation escaped the Provost Marshal before he could check himself.

CHAPTER TWENTY-THREE

"IT'S VERY GOOD to see you again, Charles," the Chief of Def-Ops said, settling into his chair behind a vast table topped with telephones, situation reports, maps, diagrams and pens and pencils.

"Same here, Eme," Colonel Chumah replied.

The Provost Marshal had delivered him there and made his disappearance. The two were alone now in the big office and the Chief of Def-Ops had buzzed his assistants that he would receive no callers for the next hour.

The Chief of Defence Operations was a tall, fair-skinned career soldier in his early thirties. After a training stint in the United States before the war he had affected the close-cropped, crew-cut hair-style popular among American soldiers. He smiled easily and wore a halo of perpetual unflappability. Though they were both colonels, Chumah was his senior in the pecking order.

The Chief of Defence Operations lifted his eyes from a sheaf of situation summaries and looked at the man before him.

The Chief of Defence Operations put the papers together carefully and pushed them to a corner beside his braided cap and slim polished baton. He shifted in his chair nervously.

"Now, Charles," he began, not quite certain how to continue. "I . . . I suppose . . . I think we better get back to where we were eleven months ago."

The Chief's voice rumbled sombrely for nearly thirty minutes. He had missed out nothing. But he had decided to skip Port Harcourt for the time being. He had also skilfully skated over the matter of the Christian Brothers.

On the other hand, the Chief of Def-Ops thought, picking up and examining afresh the green message sheet lying face down at his elbow, the Colonel was going to join the 5 Commando soon. So might he not as well get on with it?

"Now, Charles, your orders," the Chief said. "The General has directed that you assume, with immediate effect, the deputy command of 5 Commando under Colonel Jacques Rudolf." The Chief looked up from the message form.

Chumah uncrossed his legs, took the cigarette from his lips, and glared across the desk.

The Chief did not meet his eyes. He scanned the message form again. "Colonel Rudolf is being informed this noon," he added finally, and put aside the green paper.

"Listen, Eme," Chumah was jabbing the stub of cigarette at the Chief of Defence Operations. "Do you mean that the General wants me to join what you call the Christian Brothers?"

The Provost Marshal had told him about the white adventurers.

"That's the order, Charles."

"Join mercenaries and fight alongside them, you mean that?"

"I suppose it means the same thing as the contents of the message, Charles," Eme said, without meeting Chumah's eyes.

"Then I must demand an urgent meeting with the General."

"Is it necessary, really?"

"Absolutely. I must have a word with him."

"I doubt the chances of a meeting, Charles. The General has been very busy lately." The Chief's eyes met Chumah's briefly. "Besides, Charles, the subject of the Christian Brothers is not one he'll readily discuss just now. He thinks we ought to give them a chance to carry out their offensive plans . . ."

"You sound as if these chaps have just arrived here and are trying to find their feet. But I gather they have been here for nearly one year. One very costly year!

"Do you, for one moment, reckon a that soldier of fortune fighting for money will plan an offensive to win you a war and thus terminate his employment?"

"Now take it easy, Charles," the Chief said. "I understand your feelings very well."

"I'm not accepting the General's orders," he announced bluntly. "I'm not prepared to fight alongside mercenaries who are making money at the expense of the lives of the people who are contributing the money. They will prolong the war as long as they can. And I'm not sure I want to help them do that." Chumah broke off to light a fresh cigarette.

The Chief made no reply.

"Let me repeat what you'll tell the General," Chuma resumed. "Tell him I refuse to be led by a white mercenary commander. I'm a senior member of the High Command, not an under-officer!"

"But that, as you know, Charles, amounts to disobeying orders," he tried not to sound threatening. "Not my orders, hell, you are my senior in the hierarchy, but the General's orders. And he may not like it. I should stick to the old rule, Charles. Obey before protest."

"I don't expect the General to like it. But neither do I like his orders."

"I doubt that I can tell him that, Charles. Maybe I should try to wangle a meeting after all. But most of us would hate to see you back in detention, Charles. Truly."

"Back in detention, yes," Chumah replied. "Frankly I would prefer that to being commanded by your Christian Brothers."

"I told you earlier on Charles, that I understood your sentiments," the Chief replied. "It's genuine. But why don't we say you'll think it over for a day or two? That would sound reasonable," the Chief suggested quietly.

"I shall indeed let you know if I do change my mind. In the meantime, I shall get down to Port Harcourt and look up my family. They are staying with my brother. I've got to see them first before I think of going off to be commanded by mercenaries."

The moment the Chief of Defence Operations had dreaded most and avoided longest had descended without warning. His palms gripped the arms of his chair firmly as Colonel Chumah rose from his.

"Wait a moment, Charles," the Chief held up a trembling hand.

Chumah sat back into his chair.

"You . . . you . . . can't go to Port Harcourt, I'm afraid," the Chief began shakily.

"I can't what? Another arrest?"

"Not an arrest, Charles, but . . ." the Chief rubbed his eyes and his face uncomfortably.

"Port Harcourt," he said with difficulty, "fell five months ago. I couldn't tell you that at the beginning . . . "

"Five months ago?"

"Yes."

"And where is my family? Where did they evacuate to?" Chumah asked in strangely calm voice, rising to his feet at the same time. He fixed an enquiring gaze at the Chief, who was slumped back deflatedly, avoiding Chumah's eyes.

The continued silence began to forewarn Chumah of an unpleasant answer. His heart raced in panic.

"Where were they evacuated to then, Eme?" he repeated.

"We're still trying to locate them, Charles . . ."

"Locate them? What the devil do you mean?"

"Now sit down, Charles. Sit down and take it easy. Listen to me," he pleaded desperately. "I tell you, Charles, it's not easy."

"I can listen just as well standing," Chumah snapped. "Forget about taking it easy. Just tell me where in the devil you say you're trying to locate my wife and child."

"It is like this . . ."

"You know what the terrain there is like. Only two approaches to the city, a virtual cul-de-sac. The enemy burst out along the Aba road, a few miles to the city, cut off that outlet into the town and threatened the other, Owerri road. With a situation like that only a few people managed to evacuate the city. Most of them are still bottled up in there."

"You only *hope* they are, don't you? The vandals have almost certainly massacred them for sport! My God, why are you all so naïve?"

"We believe your family will be found as soon as we clear the town of the enemy," the Chief said without much truth.

He didn't mention the reports that confirmed the mutilation of his wife, child and younger brother by irate natives soon after the enemy's entry.

The Chief stopped, expecting the ultimate explosion that would submerge the room in the debris of Chumah's famous wrath. He held his breath and waited for it.

For three minutes that seemed like three hours, nothing happened. The Chief could hear his own heart thumping loudly in the reigning silence.

Slowly he raised his eyes at the man standing, frozen before his desk.

Tears were rolling down Colonel Charles Chumah's face, falling in droplets on to his beard. His clenched fists were rigid beside his body.

111

Chumah's lips moved. He licked them and raised his eyes at the Chief of Defence Operations.

"Who lost Port Harcourt, Eme?" It was a thick, subdued tone that didn't seem to come from the powerful man the Chief knew.

"It was an emergency unit assembled from all divisions," he answered vaguely.

"Yes but who manned the main positions?"

"The Commando, Colonel Rudolf."

"Thank you," Chumah said. He fished out an over-used handkerchief and dabbed the tears from his face.

"Now you can tell the General I'm accepting his posting to 5 Commando," Chumah said unexpectedly. "And send a signal to Colonel Rudolf that I look forward to joining him." He pocketed the handkerchief, brought out the pack of cigarettes and began to light one.

"I'm reporting to 5 Commando first light tomorrow. Now that I've got no family to look after, I suppose I've got time on my hands." His voice was bitter.

"Charles for God's sake don't take it that way, you . . ."

"Thanks for your sympathy, Eme. It's appreciated."

He was out of the door before the Chief could put in another word.

CHAPTER TWENTY-FOUR

THE GREEN MESSAGE form lay on the desk beneath Colonel Jacques Rudolf's chin.

                                                      201500
                                                      910/110
FROM: DEFOPS
TO: COMD 5CODO* DIV
INFO: CGS(.) GOC(.)
C-IN-C FOR COMD(.)
UNDERSTAND YOU HAVE BEEN RESTING ON YOUR OARS(.)
THERE HAVE BEEN NO RECENT IMPROVEMENTS FROM
YOUR AXIS(.) AND NO LESS IN AMMO DEMAND(.)YOU MUST
RPT* MUST WAKE UP AND CATCH UP WITH YOUR
PLANNED OFFENSIVE PROGRAMME(.) SITUATION DOES
NOT WARRANT PRESENT INACTION(.) ENDS MSG(.)
  *See Glossary

The blurred date stamp showed the previous day's date.

For reasons of personal tactics the Chief of Defence Operations had left his copy of the dramatic signal locked in his top drawer when he met with Colonel Charles Chumah earlier in the morning and had thus not disclosed the fact that at last even the General was becoming impatient with the Christian Brothers.

Rudolf had received the signal late on the evening of the day shown on the stamp.

While Colonel Chumah was at Defence Operations that morning, Rudolf had summoned his Strike Force Commanders for group action later on in the evening.

They weren't looking like soldiers that night.

Johann Schmuts and Derek Tremble were the first to arrive, both in fancy casual shirts and slacks that were shiny from repeated ironing.

The Commander's office was a large room in the middle of a big, long, storeyed block in the heart of the vast compound. When the school was not a military camp, it had been the fifth form classroom.

Jacques Rudolf held up the green message form to the men seated before him.

Major Dan Marc looked bulkier than ever in open-necked cotton. His chest forced itself out of the shirt front and his hairy, tattooed arms wore a two-tone colour of tan from the wrist up to his upper arm where a cream-white skin showed beneath the sleeves.

Captain Amilo Relli was as quiet and meditative as ever.

Kapitan Hans Heinz, his neck thin and scrawny, looked a little less drunk than when Rudolf saw him earlier in the afternoon. He gave an impression of marginal presence of mind, at best of impatient interest in whatever it was that his commander had to say. Heinz had reason to worry. Without a plane to fly, Hans had recently become the prison guard of the 5 Commando.

Between the commander's quarters and the command office was the former school library block, now Heinz's office. Behind a bare topped desk at which he sat drunkenly most days, two very precious prisoners sat incommunicado in a dark store room. They were Captain Michel and Captain Jules.

Any few minutes Heinz turned his drooping eyes from them gave him cause to worry. If Michel had a chance to chat with just one of the guards, Heinz knew what would happen to their whole mission.

Major Derek Tremble's eyes met Jacques Rudolf's over the rim of the green paper. The undercover agent from the British SIS* quickly removed his. Rudolf's cold blue eyes always struck Tremble with suspicion.

*See Glossary

That man was as cold and cunning as the devil, Derek Tremble thought uncomfortably.

"The General," Rudolf began briefly, putting down the paper and reaching for his packet of cigarettes, "appears to be getting worried." He read out the General's signal.

"What the hell does he mean, resting on our oars?" Johann Schmuts asked, frowning.

"Resting on our oars doesn't really worry me," Rudolf said, picking up the paper again.

"The General is possibly under some pressure, Jacques," Bill Ball suggested.

"Maybe, maybe not," Rudolf answered, non-commitally. "If he is, it only makes things difficult for him. I shan't have us pushed around."

"Meanwhile," Rudolf continued, "I'm looking at the general military situation. I think we ought to make a push for Onitsha." He looked up at his comrades.

No one said anything. Jacques was the leader who did not act without reckoning with their interests first and fully. If he said Onitsha, it was not without reasons they would find congenial.

"Hans and I are going to work out the plan," Jacques told them. "But briefly, you can see it's like this."

He went into some detail about his thinking so far. His commanders seemed to harbour no objections. In any case, after nearly a year Rudolf's leadership had been established beyond challenge.

"From our point of view," Rudolf continued, "Onitsha is a more congenial objective than any other. The enemy's supply route is erratic, having been punctured severely by the guerilla task forces. Reports show their supplies are the least heavily built up of all the fronts."

"And how soon will this be, Commander?" Major Tremble asked in a quiet, formal tone that marked his uneasy, mutually suspicious relationship with Jacques Rudolf, and at the same time masked his acute personal curiosity.

"We can't be sure now," Rudolf told him without meeting his glance. "But I expect in about three or four weeks. It needs careful planning and Hans and I are going to get down to that pretty soon." He looked at Heinz who nodded impatiently.

"Johann," Rudolf called. "You will give me a summary tomorrow of all combat-strength Strike Forces. And also ammunition strength, transport, etc. It's going to be a big thing. Our biggest battle. Probably our last."

An urgent knock at the bolted door cracked the intervening silence. All eyes turned from Rudolf to the door. Schmuts went over and opened it a crack.

114

"What's that, Chiko? We're in a meeting can't you see, you fool?" the South African shouted angrily.

"Sorry, sah! . . . but . . . sah!" Chiko waved an envelope frantically through the opening.

Schmuts opened the door wider. Chiko came in quickly, holding forward the reason for his intrusion. He saluted and handed the envelope to Rudolf, burly and immobile as the desk behind which he sat.

"Sentry at the main gate just got this from the despatch rider from Umuahia, sah," Chiko said. "He says it's urgentest," he concluded breathlessly and turned to leave as quickly as he had barged in.

Rudolf turned the envelope and examined the three blotches of security sealing wax along the flap.

FROM: DEF-OPS
TO: COMD FIVE CODO

COLONEL CHARLES CHUMAH(.)
C-IN-C DIRECTS THAT ABOVE OFFR* REPORTS TO YOU AS TWO I SEE 5 CODO WEF* TOMORROW 0700 HOURS(.) ACK(.)

It was signed by the Chief of Def-Ops.

"Yes. Almost certainly our last battle." Rudolf repeated calmly as if he had been talking about Onitsha throughout the time Chiko interrupted him with the paper in his hand. He passed the message to Major Ball nearest to him at the left corner of the desk and said, "You read that and pass it on. The General seems to be driving rather hard."

Hans Heinz on Rudolf's right read the message, pursed his thin lips viciously and returned the slip of paper to the Colonel.

"I see this as the first step towards change of command, Jacques. I can smell it," Heinz said without cheer.

"That's what the General may think, Hans, but he will be wrong. Dead wrong," Rudolf assured him and the others.

"By God! I'm not going to take orders from a bloody kaffir," Johann Schmuts swore softly.

In about six hours Colonel Charles Chukwuemeka Chumah would report at 5 Commando headquarters.

*See Glossary

115

CHAPTER TWENTY-FIVE

IT WAS NOT only Kapitan Hans Heinz who was anxious to get back to his room that night.

So was Major Derek Tremble.

In the past months he had worked late nights trying to keep his reports up to the fast pace at which the walls seemed to be tumbling down around them. He had to report each development every night after the day's operations, so as to catch the next night's flight, while he awaited the next dramatic turn of events.

A lean Portuguese captain and he shared the former science master's quarters. They were far at the back of the compound where most of the Christian Brothers lived in an expatriate community of caravans and small camouflaged bungalows. The Captain had sometimes expressed mild envy at the frequency with which Derek Tremble wrote letters to his wife.

"I wish I could do that," Henrique had said once to Tremble. "But I'm not even married."

"It isn't as much fun as you think, Henrique," Tremble had replied. "More a labour than pleasure. But you can say it's necessary. If she didn't get my letter each day she would think I'd been knocked off by a mortar bomb or something."

"Don't sell me that crap. You English are old-fashioned enough to be in love with your wives," Henrique had accused.

Derek Tremble had laughed both at the accusation and, in his case, the ironic fallacy of it.

For although he was married, and did in fact address a letter each night to a Mrs Barbara Tremble at 188 Bride Lane, London, his estranged wife, whose name was Catherine, lived in another flat in Manchester with their three-year-old daughter and baby son, and had not read a line from Derek in one year. Nor had she the merest suspicion that he was in an obscure corner of Africa, knee-deep in the mud of war and intelligence operations.

Derek Tremble's letters usually went by the daily courier to the airstrip where, along with mail from the other Christian Brothers and foreign relief workers, they were taken aboard the night flight to Lisbon. There, the General's men would pick them up, procure Portuguese postage stamps and despatch.

At the Bride Lane address, a cipher clerk whose name was Miss Barbara Salmons, would pick up the letter from Tremble. It was the only one that arrived with a Portuguese postage stamp. Salazar's Death's Head, she called it to her philatelist boyfriend. Miss Salmons would quickly decode the letter, reproduce six copies in neat double-spaced typescript, and deliver it in a sealed and waxed envelope to another office, an electronically guarded basement room in another part of London.

That was OOPS—Overseas Operations Section of the British SIS*. And from OOPS Tremble knew his report would eventually land on the table of his Chief, a faceless, anonymous bureaucrat-cum-super-spy, known internally as 'C', after the first holder of the post, a man called Cummings.

The circuitous maze of corridors and basement offices his intelligence reports followed often reminded Derek Tremble of the air of weird mystery that surrounded his positive vetting for his current assignment.

Derek Tremble knew the routine. But he was not quite so certain what the reports were eventually used for. Almost certainly, he had concluded long ago, though, they provided day-to-day intelligence for British defence strategists.

He could guess that they were finally used in determining the supply of arms to the Federals. For he recalled that his brief had emphasised the need to include in his reports advance forecasts of strategic plans, volume and quality of rebel fire-power and the involvement of any foreign personnel.

If that was the end to which his reports served, Tremble thought, Rudolf's four weeks' estimate should leave London whatever time they needed to do whatever it was they wanted.

He assembled his standard lined blue sheets and began to think out a summary of the night's meeting.

Captain Michel had been in Rudolf's jail-house for nine months. It was within the Commander's authority to lock him away, or anyone else for that matter, if he had strong security or disciplinary reasons to do so. And the fact that a white captain was detained along with Michel made Rudolf's action all the more unquestionable, and indeed plausible.

Colonel Rudolf had specifically directed that the two prisoners should not be tortured, but be well fed and looked after. He was anxious to avoid the maltreatment that could lead to discontent and probably cause their detention to attract attention. He would avoid having to have them shot if he could help it. It helped the image of a tough, dedicated, but humane commander. Hans Heinz had the worrisome job of executing the Commander's wishes in this regard.

Kapitan Heinz's position on the mercenary team was as incongruous as the presence of the mercenaries in the war itself.

*See Glossary.

A former Luftwaffe pilot who later flew shuttles for Moïse Tshombe in the Congo, where he met and made friends with Jacques Rudolf, Hans Heinz was not a young soldier. He was fifty-five. He was also an asthmatic who continued flying combat missions against medical advice, often proffering the rather powerful argument that there was nothing else he could do to earn a living if he couldn't fly. At other times he would boast that he was probably the only asthmatic who flew combat aircraft.

After his weekend excursion to Port Harcourt, and before Rudolf finalised the formation of the 5 Commando Division, Hans Heinz had flown a couple of missions in the General's surviving combat aircraft, an aged B25. After one particularly close call over a densely forested battle-front, Heinz's plane had its fuselage blown open by ground fire one afternoon, a week after his arrival.

That was the end of Heinz's air war.

He refused to fly the creaking French helicopters used on occasions of despair for raids on deteriorating battlefronts by the General's Air Force.

Despite repeated promises of French Mirage fighter-bombers, which he called a combat pilot's dream, Hans Heinz never saw a combat aircraft on the ground again.

Not that he was unhappy about it.

When Jacques Rudolf named him a Strike Force Commander it was because Rudolf wanted to keep his ageing fellow-countryman around, both so that he would not be retrenched by the General, and because Heinz would be of great use to him in the management and administration of the Division.

As a matter of fact, the effective command of the Strike Force that bore his name was taken over by a lean, fierce-tempered veteran of Salazar's colonial army named Captain Henrique Martinez.

Hans Heinz soon became the administrative officer, chief security officer, quarter-master; the divisional factotum.

But none of his jobs was more important than sitting at his desk daily and making sure that absolutely no one made contact with the two prisoners behind the locked doors, without his close censorship.

Once every week he would change the three guards who stood as firm and immobile as the pillars outside the building that once served as the school library and storeroom.

He would bring in a fresh trio of guards each week, brief them with the single, strict injunction—"guard this building and allow no one in without my express approval".

At the end of each day, Heinz would personally give the prisoners their supper, check the bolts on the windows of his main office, lock the doors with double, heavy padlocks and pocket the keys.

It had been a smooth, uneventful arrangement for the previous nine months.

But recently Heinz began to realise that he was fast exhausting the services of the one hundred and twenty men of the Headquarters Company who did the guard duties in the Division Headquarters. One hundred and eight men of the Company had done a week's guard duty in groups of three for nine months. He had preferred not to involve combat troops on rest and recreation in this specifically camp duty. Nor did he ever recall past guards, however good, for a repeat performance. They could easily develop familiarity with the prisoners and, consequently, a dangerous sympathy for them.

Soon he struck on what seemed to him a sensible, simple compromise; he began to extend the duty for each trio from a week to a fortnight. It worked well for the first two fortnights.

The current shift was due to end duty at six a.m. on Sunday morning, an hour before Colonel Chumah assumed duty.

That morning Captain Hans Heinz replaced the outgoing guards with three young privates from the list of twelve remaining men of the Headquarters Company.

One of the new guards who innocently took position outside Heinz's office that morning was a dark, lanky nineteen-year-old rifleman named Sampson Udoka, alias Cetme Sammy, because of the havoc he was reputed to have wreaked on enemy units with captured Cetme rifles.

When Cetme Sammy joined the army ten months earlier he had volunteered for the Commando because his cousin was a Captain in the Division.

"B.A.*" he had been told by veterans who had reasons to be cynical, stood for *Brother Army*.

He had chosen to be where his relation was.

Captain Michel was his aunt Ezidiya's only son, his first cousin.

*See Glossary

CHAPTER TWENTY-SIX

SUNDAY MORNING 0600 hours.
"CCC IS BACK(.) HAIL BIAFRA(.)"

The enthusiastic message flashed through the signals network of all the formations and spread like a call for ceasefire. A ripple of cheers ran through the despondent frontline locations.

Though in the 5 Commando where he was due to arrive in sixty minutes, no one knew him, except by his folk-hero reputation. And of course Sergeant Chiko, now Colonel Rudolf's batman.

Colonel Jacques Rudolf was up unusually early on Sunday morning. By 6.30 a.m. he was already on his way to his ground floor command office in the former classroom block.

He had slept little after the late meeting, and would perhaps admit it only to himself that the thought of Colonel Charles Chumah had not been sleep-inducing.

He was dressed in his full battle camouflage uniform, starched and creased to razor-edge sharpness. His red beret was aslant and rakish on his head. His pistol rested in the band of his trousers behind his wide clothbelt.

Rudolf put out the stub of his third cigarette of the morning, and drew himself closer to the edge of the table.

With one hand he reached for a ball-point pen and with another a green message form with the skull and crossbone emblem of the 5 Commando. He began to write quickly.

TOP SECRET
OF IMMEDIATE
TO: ALL SF* COMDS
FROM: COMD 5 CODO

IN VIEW OF PRESENT EMERGENCY THE FOLLOWING SPECIAL DIRECTIVES TAKE IMMEDIATE EFFECT.
  I. IF YOU HAVE REASON TO SUSPECT THAT A NATIVE, CIVILIAN OR MILITARY, IS HOSTILE, OBSTRUCTING MIL OPS*, IS AIDING THE ENEMY DIRECTLY OR INDIRECTLY;

*See Glossary

II. IF ANY COMBAT TROOPS REFUSE ORDERS AND/OR ARE
    RELUCTANT TO FIGHT;
    YOU SHOULD SHOOT THEM. AND SHOOT TO KILL.
    READ, STUDY AND DESTROY.

He quickly pushed the paper aside, drew another blank message sheet
and scribbled a brief memo in German for Kapitan Hans Heinz's eyes
only.

The note asked Hans to increase the Commander's personal bodyguard detail from one to six with immediate effect.

Finally, Rudolf read both messages over, called Chiko and handed
him both papers for immediate delivery to Kapitan Heinz, who would
implement.

Colonel Rudolf was ready for the arrival of Colonel Chumah.

Colonel Charles Chumah's green command car arrived at the main
gate at precisely 7 a.m. At the sight of the military number plate and lone
star, the metal bars rose swiftly.

The capless guard at the gate lowered the bar again and hurriedly
threw his shoulders back in salute. Chumah looked back and gave a brief,
stern acknowledgement.

As the command car rode slowly through the compound, the Colonel
surveyed the vast compound with admiration.

Everything was spick and span. The lawns bristled with tree trunks
sunk halfway into the ground in neat rows, carefully erected artificial
hillocks and other impedimenta for obstacle training that contrived to
lend the camp a sort of rugged, martial beauty.

Beyond the training grounds, everything was lush and green. All
buildings had been carefully hidden in a camouflage of fresh palmfronds
woven together like giant fans.

In the forecourt of the main single-storeyed block, just a few yards
from the twin flag posts and the white saluting dais, even a white stone
statue of the Madonna, patroness of the former school, was covered in a
green shroud.

Only the saluting dais, which rested between the two flag-staffs, atop
which the 5 Commando emblem of Death's Head and the national
Rising Sun flag fluttered in the morning breeze, was white and bare.

Sergeant Chiko and five new guards were sitting on a row of benches
outside Rudolf's office, rifles between their knees, when Colonel Chumah's
command car reached the end of the driveway.

Chiko raised his chin from his chest, drew his rifle closer and peered
through the tendrils of palm fronds that enclosed the corridor and
blocked his view.

121

He stood up quickly from his chair, gathered a fistful of the fronds and pushed them aside to obtain a better view. He blinked a couple of times.

The once familiar face was at first glance almost unrecognisable behind its lush beard.

But there was no mistaking the firmly set, stern lips and sparkling eyes of Chiko's former Brigade Commander. And when the Colonel's tall, trim figure towered to its full height as he alighted and stood beside the green command car and mentally probed his way into the building, Sergeant Chiko was pushed by an uncontrollable surge of emotion.

He threw his Cetme rifle aside and dashed onto the driveway. The stocky little sergeant came to a halt in front of Colonel Charles Chumah. He stamped the ground with vigour, threw his chest out and delivered the stoutest salute Colonel Chumah had received for many months.

"I'm Sergeant Chiko, sah," Rudolf's batman announced with a smile of joy. "I was under your command in 'V' Brigade, Ninth Mile, sah."

Chumah nodded slightly.

"Ninth Mile, eh?" he asked at last.

"Yes, sah," he nodded vigorously.

"What unit?"

"Lieutenant Ude's platoon, sah, C Company."

The Colonel nodded. "Good to see you, Chiko."

"This way, sah," said a happy Chiko, leading the way.

He tapped gently on Rudolf's door, heard a murmur of assent, pushed it open and announced Colonel Charles Chumah.

Colonel Jacques Rudolf was sitting behind his desk as Colonel Charles Chumah entered his office.

Rudolf ran his eyes up and down the tall, dark figure in smart green khaki uniform. The corners of his mouth twitched with distaste as he took in the full colonel's eagle and two pips studded on Charles Chumah's shoulders.

He had somehow half-hoped that the fellow was a lieutenant-colonel.

So he was a bloody full colonel.

The black bastard.

Two captains in one bloody boat.

Two chefs cooking one broth.

The black devil!

Colonel Chumah strode confidently towards the huge desk.

"Colonel Rudolf, I believe? I'm Colonel Charles Chumah reporting for assignment."

The last phrase tasted sour in his mouth. *Reporting for assignment!* Reporting himself to a white mercenary adventurer in his own army!

122

Chumah held his feelings in check as he met the cold eyes of Jacques Rudolf.

The white soldier rose reluctantly, almost condescendingly, and pushed his chair back noisily. He held out a tanned hand, and shook Colonel Chumah's across the table.

It was a cold handshake.

"Welcome to Five Commando," he said perfunctorily.

Colonel Chumah nodded faintly.

He had had no illusions about his liking Jacques Rudolf and his gang of foreign soldiers.

Now he was certain he hated the man. The cold and complacently callous face of the mercenary veteran aroused a deep loathing in the black Colonel.

For nearly three minutes, neither spoke to the other. Neither had anything to say to the other, nor wished to. A tense silence filled and dominated the room.

That evening Rudolf met for several hours with Schmuts and Heinz.

Together they reviewed their logistical strength for the proposed operation in Onitsha. 5 Commando still had some six thousand combat-ready troops. The ammunition position was given a particularly close look.

Hans was preparing a high priority requisition for light ammunition, heavy artillery pieces, bazookas, mortars and rockets.

From a purely logistical point of view there seemed to be little cause for worry, Rudolf judged at the end.

But they re-examined their plans against the presence of Colonel Charles Chumah.

Obviously the man, they acknowledged, was a powerful influence, a senior officer; a full colonel.

His actual presence in the 5 Commando Division now added a new dimension, an extraneous complexion, to their plans for Onitsha. Rudolf's fears told him that this new dimension could, if unchecked, upset his careful calculations.

He had sensed from that first, cold confrontation with the fellow that he could not easily push Chumah around. That he could no more easily trip him than he could a horse.

For the first time since his arrival nearly one year ago, Colonel Jacques Rudolf had begun to feel vulnerable.

It had been this fear of vulnerability that masked itself behind an attitude of contempt and condescension towards Chumah.

Now he was desperately aware what Onitsha meant to him as the commander of a crack division, pitching his strategic and tactical skill against the reputedly brilliant black Colonel.

Rudolf would of course not consider bringing Chumah into the detailed planning of Onitsha. That would be an invitation to a subversive influence, for he saw Chumah now playing a kind of Rudolf to his Denault.

Jacques Rudolf was moody by morning, and for several days afterwards. Outwardly he bore his familiar waxen visage of mysterious calm.

With Colonel Chumah he grew colder, quietly more suspicious, and no less contemptuous.

He avoided meeting him whenever he could, preferring to deal with him through memos and minutes handed through Sergeant Chiko and the other guards.

As he planned Onitsha every day with Johann Schmuts and Hans Heinz, and occasionally some of the key Strike Force commanders like Bill Ball and Dan Marc, Rudolf hoped his inner fears would abate with his progress.

But they did not. Rather they seemed to keep pace.

Each step in the planning seemed to bring him fresh fears and fantasies of failure.

Rudolf also began to worry about his men. For Onitsha to succeed, he would need from them something he had not encouraged in them before —practical leadership of the troops, physical involvement in battle. "Get out there and fight!" had never been his favourite battle cry.

They had been for long fighting to fight another day. Old practices died hard. And they died even harder when such practices were conducive to personal survival in a bloody, brutal war.

So far they had come out of each battle with their heads intact when many lost theirs. And they had kept their pay, too. They had lost nothing. Remote-control leadership had paid off handsomely. Up till now.

There were endless reasons for worry . . .

If Michel should get half a word across to Chumah!

If Chumah should know what that perfidious son of an unmarried mother knew . . . !

Rudolf shuddered and bit his lips fiercely.

But the thought of Hans's presence, and efficiency in matters of security, calmed his panic. He knew he couldn't now take Michel and Jules behind the house and just shoot them. He would be infinitely pleased to do that, of course, but he had long ago formally reported to Defence Operations that the men were locked up indefinitely for serious security reasons. Any capital action by him against them now was out of the question. It would require the General's assent, probably after a tell-all court martial.

Court martial! Hell!

Since the death of Georges Denault and the detention of the two captains nine months ago, Jacques Rudolf had never felt any threat to his person or position.

Nor to those of his men who were singularly loyal, fiercely dedicated to him and his leadership.

He had fought several battles, or had had several battles fought; and though he had not won a single vitory he had still retained the confidence of the General, mainly by convincing him that he was in the throes of one decisive operation that would change the course of the war. He had impressed upon him that their setbacks were only temporary and would in fact turn out to be advantageous to the big operation he had on the drawing board. The enemy were like fish swarming into a vast net, heedlessly, blindly, not knowing that the fisherman was poised to close the net in on them when they had flooded in in good enough numbers.

Of course he had no such master plan.

But his bluff had paid off before the General.

Until now.

His solid base had seemed impregnable.

Until now.

The signal from the General had begun to create doubts in his mind about his confidence in his impregnability. It had opened his eyes to a deadly range of heavy guns trained on his strong position.

His men and the Onitsha Operation.

Colonel Chumah.

Captain Michel. And Jules.

And there was that enigmatic British Major Tremble. . ..

Something had to be done, he had no doubt.

Suppose Onitsha should fail?

Suppose Colonel Chumah moved against him?

What would happen if the reins of power should finally slip from him?

Rudolf shook his head several times . . . The General would be surprised out of his wits. 5 Commando would turn its full blazing fury against . . . him . . . ! It was not a bluff, he was sure. He couldn't afford to bluff in this case.

He would turn the heat fully on the General and extract a reasonable enough prize to take care of him for his retirement. He was getting sick and tired of this warrior life anyway.

Finally Rudolf came to the judgement that he was not the only vulnerable person on the scene; not by any calculation.

The General was, too. He was perhaps more vulnerable, more mortally vulnerable. And he would select the man's most vulnerable artery and extract the highest prize.

He calculated that he had about eighteen thousand dollars to his name

125

in Zurich in salary and his division commander's allowances. The weekly local allowance was worthless currency. The Biafran stint hadn't in fact been as lucrative as it had once promised.

And if it wasn't going to run its full course then he would get the most he could. By whatever means, it didn't matter. It might be even more rewarding than an eighteen-month stint.

That was it. Contingency plan number one.

The worry lines on his face softened and even the shadow of a smile hovered at the corners of his mouth.

CHAPTER TWENTY-SEVEN

"CLEAR OUT QUICKLY, you fools!"

"Get under cover!"

"Oh, Christ, who's that bastard in white mufti . . . Get out of there!"

A fierce air raid was on.

It exploded over the Commando Headquarters area at 10 a.m.

The twin MiG fighter-bombers streaked over the tree-tops in a blaze of cannon fire and a trail of jet smoke.

Three Strike Force commanders, Major Ball, Major Tremble and Major Marc, had been taking the troops through an intensive obstacle exercise when the sky above was torn open by the violent staccato of cannon fire.

Soon they were frantically shouting the men into the shelter of the empty halls and classrooms and corridors of the main storeyed block.

The three officers themselves dived under the stone stairway of the building which led on to the driveway beyond which was the training ground.

Jacques Rudolf remained mysteriously cool, calm, almost aloof, in his office in the ground floor of the big building. His composure was fortified by the knowledge that his ground-floor office beneath the stone and reinforced concrete deck of the storeyed building provided enough shelter from all but the most powerful bombs.

In any case, he did not think it would do his tough commander's image much good to be seen scurrying across the premises like a scared hare to dive into the concrete bunker specially provided for him at the back of his living quarters.

A volley of cannon crackled close to the outside walls of his office rattling the glass windows. His desk trembled and the floor vibrated under

126

his feet as one bomb exploded right in the middle of the training ground a few hundred yards away, gouging a smoking crater seven feet deep.

Rudolf winced faintly at the terrific explosion but remained calm. His hands were placed flat on the top of his desk, an unlit cigarette between his fingers.

Though his countenance told nothing, the raid surprised and dismayed him deeply.

It was the first raid on the cleverly, carefully camouflaged Headquarters complex. Everything, from the pan roofs to the whitewashed walls on the compound, had been diligently shrouded in dense, green palm fronds that merged almost undetectably with its lush jungle neighbourhood. From time to time withered or dried fronds had been removed and replaced with fresh greens. Even the vast training ground was covered with palm fronds on particularly brilliant afternoons.

A fresh fusillade of cannon rattled the zinc roof and much of Rudolf's composure, cutting across his thoughts with the sharpness of flying shrapnel.

He heard the offending aircraft scream and whine over the building. Through the glass windows he saw a lone MiG aircraft shoot across the horizon over the towering treetops and bank steeply, probably to take a fresh aim.

Further down the humid heart of the jungle he could hear the frantic chatter of the anti-aircraft battery which had been emplaced there, far away from the Headquarters proper, to divert the attention of hostile aircraft from the strategic installations in the compound at moments like this.

Rudolf reached across the table for his cigarette lighter. Thoughtfully he touched the flame to the cigarette and watched the smoke curl and swirl upwards.

Again he thought about the on-going raid.

The timing bothered him. One week now to Onitsha.

Right in the middle of the crucial build-up and sharpening of his strike forces.

He shuddered inwardly.

If it was mere coincidence it was the most curious he had ever experienced.

The Headquarters, he repeated to himself, had never been raided before now.

Then why now?

Why at this materially strategic moment?

Again, he had witnessed the jets zoom in, take their bearings and without any noticeable difficulty, without the preambles of prior reconnaissance runs, open fire right on target over the compound.

As if they knew the area like the back of their hands. As if they had been doing it every day of their raiding lives.

As if they had a map of the area.

From where he was he could feel that the northern part of the compound had received the most concentrated pounding and strafing.

That was where the ammunitions dumps were located.

Strange.

A very strange coincidence.

He could not of course be certain about what had been hit so far, since the raid was still continuing with ferocious intensity. Conceivably they might hit some vital targets, like the armoury. Not that it would matter much, for he had taken the intuitive precaution of not moving his full requisition down from Umuahia until a few hours before Onitsha.

Still . . .

He did not believe in coincidences. No man in his position did.

The more Rudolf wondered about the possible intelligence behind the sudden raid, the wider his mind wandered in search of a culprit. And the further, it seemed, an explanation fled.

One thing he was sure of was that it was not coincidence.

Then what was it?

Enemy aware of his build-up?

Thus, his plans?

If so, then wasn't Onitsha out of the bag?

If true, how did the enemy know?

Who told him?

It couldn't be! he insisted to himself.

His vital, decisive battle, his crucial secret plan, hawked to the enemy like a morning paper!

It couldn't be!

He couldn't see how it could be so.

He knew he had not let on the minutest detail of Onitsha to that despicable, potential subverter, Chumah. And even if Chumah knew from other sources—what other sources?—he would not be so loathsome as to collaborate with the enemy. The man was a notorious enemy hater; his so-called heroism had its foundation in the graves of dozens of enemy massacred, many in cold blood, Rudolf thought scornfully.

Chumah was not in the Headquarters today. He had gone off yesterday for a three-day tour of inspection of troop locations.

God! Another coincidence?

What was behind Chumah's disappearance to the front? Ah, but he had encouraged Chumah to make the inspection tour. He had been glad of a chance to get him out of the way for a while, while he put the

128

sharpening touches to his plans. He had even suggested three days instead of Chumah's two . . .

Nor could Rudolf imagine any of his commanders in the know, discreetly or indiscreetly, subverting, sabotaging his plans, *their* plans; their hope for a return to the General's good books and continuance on his payroll. Not even that devious-looking Britisher Derek Tremble . . .

Major Tremble?

Tremble. Derek Tremble. English. "C'est encore les Anglais?" His subconscious mind repeated the question he had asked himself nearly a year ago.

He remembered Tremble's uncomfortable stammer at their meeting as he enquired how long the commander thought it would take to plan and prepare for Onitsha.

Three to four weeks, he had replied innocently.

Three to four weeks.

Now . . . three weeks later!

One week to Onitsha!

Remarkable, rather than coincidental.

Remarkably circumstantial!

Had he been tactless at that midnight meeting?

Had he been indiscreet?

Immersed in his thoughts, Rudolf had become oblivious of the thunder and rattle outside. A clacking clash of cannon and anti-aircraft fire shoved the thought of a possibly traitorous Tremble from the surface of his mind for a moment.

Later, he considered that Tremble was a Strike Force Commander whose future was involved in the fate of the Christian Brothers. In the fate of the 5 Commando Division. In Onitsha. Surely any advantage given to the enemy would place the Division, as a whole, at a disadvantage. Place the Christian Brothers at a dangerous disadvantage.

Every one of them.

Including the Britisher.

In any case, how could Tremble reach the enemy even if he succeeded in stealing a stack of secret plans for Onitsha, manual of build-up, preparations and an aerial map of the Headquarters?

How could he make contact? That would require a third man. Who would be his middle-man in this kind of situation?

No.

It is not possible, Rudolf decided finally.

Not even his feverishly suspicious imagination could hold a justifiably accusing finger at Tremble, an active, if seemingly enigmatic, Strike Force commander who performed no worse in the field than the others in the Division.

But with all the possibilities closely examined, exhaustively scrutinised and tossed into the bin of improbabilities, a question mark still towered like a dark, mysterious ghost in Rudolf's subconscious mind.

So, what would be done?

The General's signal, he well knew, was a badly camouflaged ultimatum. If Onitsha failed, that would be their end, no doubt.

And Onitsha was already failing before he had fired the first shot.

The strength behind his confidence in the Onitsha Operation was the enemy's poor supply lines and weak ammunition strength there.

Now the enemy was almost certainly on the alert. Had probably been for three weeks.

He could not, he knew, apropos of nothing, just turn round on the General with his own ultimatum. He wouldn't get the troops on his side hat way. He would still need to go on with Onitsha. It would be a suitable cover for preparing for the last resort . . . the actual last battle. Onitsha would have to be a sword-edged operation!

A two-edged move, he decided.

One edge would lash out at the enemy in Onitsha, striking out with fury and venom, in the half-hope that he might still strike a blow for success and their continued stay in the service of the General.

The other edge, equally sharpened and glistening, would be held in reserve . . . a fall-back position. If the first edge should be blunted on the stone wall of stiff enemy resistance or any unforeseen eventuality like sabotage by Chumah, then . . . he would not risk the second edge in a desperate final lurch at the enemy.

He would turn around and lash out . . . at the General.

CHAPTER TWENTY-EIGHT

FROM THE DEPTHS of the jungle the anti-aircraft guns chattered acrimoniously, echoing across the vast, still compound, carried on the swift wings of the morning breeze.

Soon the MiGs were over the Headquarters again, whining viciously, streaking and strafing indiscriminately across the complex of buildings and facilities.

The raid lasted ninety minutes, coming in three thirty-minute-long waves of bombing and strafing.

Kapitan Hans Heinz sat tensely at his desk through the first fifteen minutes.

He was deeply afraid to release his prisoners to the shelter of the big, log-topped bunker behind the building. There were two bunkers out there, the strong concrete one for the Captain and a much larger, wooden one beside it.

If Heinz should let them out into the shelter, it would be the first time he had allowed the prisoners into the open. Then anything could happen in the pandemonium of an air raid.

Air raids provided cover for desperate deserters on the battlefront, Heinz knew. He had witnessed a whole platoon de-camp under the improbable umbrella of showering cannon and falling bombs.

But the three guards outside hadn't Heinz's nerves or responsibility. They were beginning to fret now with panic.

Now the MiGs were sweeping in twin formation across the training ground. Clear of the ground and over the tree-tops, they banked simultaneously, brilliantly, and began to fly in a wide arc that roped in the little house outside which the guards stood on trembling feet.

Hostile aircraft had an odd way of seeming to be heading directly for you each time you looked at them. The three kids broke simultaneously. They charged together into the room, where Hans Heinz sat, peering out worriedly through the window and considering his options.

"Sah!" they yelled in unanimous fear. "The planes are coming over here now! They are going to strafe us!"

Heinz sprang from his seat, confused and worried the more. He looked quickly at the door behind which Michel and Jules were. Without much time for delay, Heinz fished out the single key from his breast pocket and unlocked the prisoners' room.

"Out, you two!" he snarled. "There's an air raid on!" As if they didn't know it.

Jules came out first, rather unhurriedly. An equally calm Michel followed. Their eyes blinked and smarted from the brightness of daylight.

Cetme Sammy's jaw fell to his chest. His eyes widened and the balls popped out. The fear of strafing and death fled from him with the speed of a jet fighter. His hands hung limply, almost lifelessly at his sides, barely supporting the barrel of his Cetme rifle.

Kapitan Hans Heinz had his back to them as he hurried to lock the door and get the hell out of the building. For in reality, deep down, no one in the room held a greater fear of air raids than the former Luftwaffe pilot.

For many seconds Cetme Sammy seemed unable to get his tongue to move.

"Dede!" he hissed the native name of affection and respect which he used for Michel. "What are you doing here?" he verbalised in their native vernacular. He had an impulse to dash at him and embrace him.

Michel gestured him to silence with a finger across his own lips.

Just then Heinz fixed the lock and turned round to the guards and prisoners.

"Over to the back of the house!" he yelled as cannon barked overhead. The three guards fell behind the prisoners, Cetme Sammy directly behind his cousin. He couldn't bring himself to prod Michel with the barrel of the rifle.

He stared at his cousin's back with intense compassion. He seemed taller in his leanness. His light-blue mufti clung to his body with dirt and sweat.

Cetme Sammy wondered what his cousin's offence might have been. He had been standing sentry outside the building for several days now without knowing his relation was the prisoner he had been guarding with Heinz's orders to shoot and shoot to kill if the necessity arose.

He considered that if there had been an attempted breakout or something like that on any of the dark nights he had done guard duty, he could easily have been the one to shoot his first cousin; his dear Dede; his aunt Ezidiya's only son. Fate was sometimes as cruel as that.

The six of them darted out of the building almost together, Heinz leading the way. Behind the house, Heinz tried to think quickly.

All six of them couldn't get into his concrete bunker. And he would not risk cramping into that bigger, fragile, one with the lot of them.

Three to a bunker, then, he decided quickly.

He had his pistol. A guard and himself could take care of one prisoner. The other two guards would look after the other.

The Kapitan gestured one guard to his side, grabbed the wrist of Jules nearest to him, and shoved him pitilessly towards the concrete bunker.

"You two take this one down the other shelter," he told Sammy and his mate, nodding hurriedly towards prisoner Michel. "If he gets troublesome, shoot him," he ordered finally and darted down the steps of his concrete shelter behind Jules and a guard.

A sudden sweep and sputter from overhead sent the parties stumbling into their different shelters.

Cetme Sammy thought he saw the hand of fate in all this. His mate, Private Etuk, the second guard, was an Efik from Calabar who understood or spoke no word of Sammy's Igbo tongue.

Fate, he thought, could sometimes be as kind as it was cruel.

They had scarcely reached the grimy bottom of the bunker when Cetme Sammy began questioning his relation anxiously.

"Dede, tell me. What did you do?" he spoke in his native tongue. A terrified Etuk, snuggling close to the wall of the bunker with his back to the two relations, threw them only a brief casual glance.

Michel looked at Etuk worriedly and once more gestured his young cousin to silence.

"Don't worry, Dede," Sammy managed a grin. "He doesn't understand one word of Igbo," he assured Michel.

"Are you sure about that?"

"Yes, Dede."

"Sam, quickly, do you have a pencil and scrap of paper?" Michel enquired of his cousin, ignoring his anxious questioning. "There's no time to tell you anything now. The raid may be over soon. Just find me a pencil or pen and paper." He sounded weary and looked distraught, but there was a touch of relief in his voice.

Outside, a bomb exploded, rattling the wooden deck of the bunker and showering them with ugly confetti of sand and the dried powder of worm-eaten wood, and sending vibrations of fear down Etuk's spine.

Cetme Sammy laid his rifle on the wall of the bunker and fished frantically in his pocket for the ball-point pen the guards commonly used to record their attendance in the duty roster provided by the strict disciplinarian Kapitan Heinz.

In the back pocket of his camouflage trousers was the letter he had received in the morning's mail from his mother in which she had incidentally enquired when last Sammy heard about her nephew.

He handed the pencil and envelope to Michel without a word.

Michel accepted them gratefully as if he had just been handed the key to the prison door.

He brought out the white, lined sheets of letter which had been written up on one side. The back was blank. He straightened the sheet, squatted on his heels and placed the paper on his knees.

"Do you know Colonel Chumah, the new 2i/c?"* Michel asked, looking up at his young cousin?

"I do, Dede," Sammy said, emphasising with a vigorous nod.

"Good. You must find him after the raid and make sure he gets this note, do you hear, Sam?"

"Yes, Dede, but . . ."

"It is not important to me that I'm detained. But it is very essential that he knows why I'm detained. You understand me, Sammy?"

"I do, Dede, but the only thing is, the 2i/c is now away to 11 Division, Nnewi."

"Do you know when he is expected back at Headquarters?"

"I think he will be away for three days from yesterday."

"Then you must get this down to him. It's probably the best place to give it to him. Go on AWOL* if necessary. But take off your uniform; get some civilian clothes on and go to Nnewi as soon as you can get

*See Glossary

away. And don't bother to come back to the 5 Commando. It won't be necessary after he has read this note. Do you understand me, Sam?"

"Yes, Dede."

"Very good."

Michel began to scribble on the back of the sheet on his knee. He wrote furiously, desperately praying the air raid would not be over before he finished.

CHAPTER TWENTY-NINE

OPERATION SWORD: that was the code name Colonel Jacques Rudolf consequently gave to his bid to recapture Onitsha.

A two-edged move.

The day before, he had met with his key Strike Force commanders shortly after the surprise raid on his HQ. Together they had carried out a solemn post-mortem, assessed the damage done to the Headquarters complex and agreed it was extensive.

The signals block had been bombed out, the staff of six buried in the debris before they could run out for cover. Thirty-seven other soldiers, mostly other ranks, had been killed in the raid. The figure included Private Etuk, the guard, who was ripped apart, about thirty minutes after the raid was over, by a delayed-action rocket buried on the edge of the drive-way.

The armoury had been set ablaze by a rocket and gutted by the ensuing fire. So were most of the huts used as living quarters by the few young native officers. Several of the Christian Brothers' quarters had been strafed, too, though without loss of life.

Only Major Bill Ball had sustained a graze on his left arm, which he now had bandaged and carried in a sling.

The damage was, indeed, considerable.

Onitsha had assumed a greater and different dimension, Rudolf told them. With success now in some doubt, he reasoned, their move would have to be double-edged. He did not see any future for them here if Onitsha failed. Their future was in their own hands now.

Or in their trigger fingers.

For a start they had decided to postpone troop movements until a few hours to H-hour.

Ball, Schmuts and Heinz had agreed with him in general, though they had a few reservations when it came to details.

How would they acquire the extra supplies needed for a double-edged operation? No use depending on spoils from Onitsha itself. Heinz's original requisition, already approved and awaiting collection in Umuahia, had been strictly based on the logistical requirements for a single major assault. So . . . ?

How would they get the troops on their side in the second-phase move against the General, their Commander-in-Chief?

Where would Colonel Chumah, the new second-in-command, fit in in these moves? Especially in the second move?

Since their departure for the Onitsha operations might well mean the beginning of the homeward journey, what would happen to Captain Michel and Captain Jules who had been successfully kept silent so far?

There were dozens of questions to be answered to ensure a fail-safe move, the key men had pointed out.

But Colonel Jacques Rudolf had a four-word answer.

"Leave everything to me," he had said with confidence.

As soon as his officers left, Rudolf got down to sharpening the second edge of the sword, which, he admitted to himself, had been a bit blunted by the close scrutiny of his Strike Force commanders.

On a blank sheet of paper he wrote out an elaborate message to the General.

TOP SECRET
TOP PRIORITY

5 CDO HQ MAIN
5 CDO/R/108

FROM: COMD 5 CODO
TO: C-IN-C
INFO DEF OPS
RE OPS SWORD (.)

FOLLOWING INTREPS* CONFIRMED BY RECCE REPORTS OF SURPRISE EN* BUILD-UP OF MEN AND AMMO BY BOATS ACROSS RIVER INTO OBJECTIVE(.) AND FOLLOWING SURPRISE EN AIR ACTION ON 5 CDO HQ TODAY DESTROYING DIV ARMOURY AND CONTENTS(.) REQUEST URGENTEST DOUBLE SUPPLIES OF AMMO AND EQUIPMENT ETC. REQUESTED ORIGINALLY ON MSG NO 5 CDO/R/107 NOW AWAITING COLLECTION(.) ASSURE YOU OUR DETERMINATION TO RECAPTURE OBJECTIVE WITHOUT FAILURE(.) THEREFORE COUNT ON URGENTEST COOP* IN AMMO AND

*See Glossary

135

OTHER SUPPLIES(.) TPS VERY KEEN(.) MORALE VERY HIGH(.)
ENDS MSG(.)

In several earlier messages in the past three weeks Jacques Rudolf had
assured Def-Ops and the General of his awareness of the enormous importance of his Onitsha operation. He had in turn been reassured that
Onitsha was being accorded the highest logistical priority and that every
item required to ensure success would be given on request.

So he had no doubts about the fate of the signal he drafted.

When it had been typed on the proper green message form, he put the
date stamp and his initials on it and sealed it himself.

It was delivered by hand of a special courier the same afternoon.

The other questions raised by his commanders were still very much on
his mind when he left his office unusually early that afternoon, as soon as
his signal was on its way to Umuahia, to think out the next move.

The count-down had begun.

The sword was seven days away.

CHAPTER THIRTY

5 A.M. SIX DAYS TO the Sword.

Cetme Sammy woke up very early from a brief nap in the guards' hut
where he and his mates took turns off-duty.

He did not wash. But he combed his hair with a broken plastic comb
he carried in his uniform pocket. His worn brown trousers and a faded
green shirt were all the civilian clothes he owned. He had no shoes,
sandals or slippers aside from his commando boots.

He brought out the shirt and trousers from the plastic bag which he
used as a sleeping pillow on the mat, put them on quickly. His camouflage
uniforms he folded carefully and put in the plastic bag.

From under his sleeping mat he brought out the sheet of paper on
which his cousin had written out the note for Colonel Charles Chumah.
He folded it into a tiny rectangle, held it in his palm, weighing it. The tiny
piece of paper seemed heavier than a Cetme rifle.

He thought for a minute . . . he couldn't just put it in his breast pocket,
could he? He might be searched by military policemen on the road.

Then he remembered with relief that the old, second-hand trunks
which served as his underwear had a small pocket inside their front.

He unzipped his trousers, pulled up the top of the trunks, made sure the pocket wasn't torn in the inside; carefully he slipped in the folded paper and zipped up his trousers again.

As he did so he looked down at his bare feet. Dede had said he should get into some civilian clothes, but he had no shoes; only the army boots. He would have to travel bare foot, he decided.

He glanced round the room. There were a few worthless bits of personal effect, the usual soldier's gear: a knapsack he had captured from a dead enemy, now filled with his spoon, fork, pen-knife and ration plates; his plastic water bottle, another spoil of war; a muddied diary with no entries; nothing much. But there was, of course, his Cetme rifle lying by his sleeping mat.

The rifle.

He looked at it with sad, apologetic eyes that seemed to be doing penance for his treachery. The Cetme rifle that gave him fame and name as a marksman. It lay there, abandoned, loaded but helpless, as if waiting for Sammy and nobody else to pick it up.

But Cetme Sammy knew he couldn't wear civilian clothes and carry a military weapon at the same time. He felt he was deserting a friend who had stood by him, protectively spurting fire and lead, in critical moments. He felt he was not Sammy without his Cetme rifle.

But my Dede, he thought, comes first.

Before he left, Sammy went to the guardroom, greeted his mates on the night shift, signed the duty register and made his excuse to buy a cigarette.

The main gate was just stirring to an active morning when he came by. The sentries all knew Sammy by name and his marksman's reputation, and regarded him with the instinctive bond of fraternity that united all guards, sentries and prison warders.

On the highway, he turned right and began an unhurried stroll down the road.

Almost a quarter of a mile down the road, well clear of the area of the Headquarters, Sammy glanced over his shoulder, saw nobody, and quickened his steps.

The best thing, he decided quickly, was to trek to Oriagu, the large civilian centre just a mile and half down the road, and wait, hopefully, for a lift on the occasional relief lorries that gave travellers free rides. Nnewi was about fifty miles away. He knew he could get there the same day. . . well before Colonel Chumah left the following morning on his return to the Headquarters.

The previous day's air raid on the Headquarters was still haunting Oriagu when Sammy arrived there. The centre, normally lively and an-archic with near-crazed artillery shell cases from the nearby psychiatric hospital, half-naked refugees, old men and women hawking palm wine, garri, salt and stockfish at inhumanly inflated prices, was eerily quiet,

137

deserted and dense with fresh green palm camouflages. The air was sombrely expectant.

The half a dozen hopeful travellers on the roadside were mostly women traders and middle-aged men clearly above the reach of the conscription squads.

Sammy crossed the deserted road and unobtrusively joined the miserable motley.

It was a full hour before the first vehicle, a military truck loaded with troops, clanged and clattered past, blazing a trail of dust, momentarily relieving the pall of tense quiet that overhung the centre.

The interlude gave Sammy something to divert his mind from his urgent mission. The troops, over a company of them, were a ragged, bare-headed force in ripped shirts. They weren't chanting as they were wont to do, but that didn't puzzle Sammy. They were probably *going* to the battlefront. That wasn't anything to chant about anymore.

Another sixty minutes later, a white lorry with huge red crosses emblazoned all over its body bumped and tumbled along.

Sammy thumbed the front of his trousers, below his navel, and felt the slight bulge of his vital burden beneath.

The relief truck drew up on the roadside, rather reluctantly, about fifty yards from the flailing and waving hands.

The travellers rushed in a bustle of bare feet for a place on the already crowded truck. Men shoved women aside, regardless of sex and proverbial weakness; women dashed towards the stationary truck, giving shove for shove and elbow for elbow.

Cetme Sammy took it easy. He must avoid any misdemeanour like furious scrambling that would draw the driver's angry attention to him and probably cost him a place on the precious truck. He walked towards the lorry, behind the scramblers, at a pace that falsified the urgency of his mission.

No one stopped them for much of the journey. The check-points, road-blocks and barricades seemed to lift at the approach of the relief vehicle, as if the bold Red Cross signs proclaimed 'open sesame'.

That was until the lorry reached Ihioma, half way to Sammy's destination.

Ihioma was the Headquarters of the Air Force.

Like the 5 Commando, the Air Force regarded itself as an élite unit. Their young, smart, dashing officers, dapper in brown-green camouflages and red berets, still lived and thrived on the reputation built by the havoc wrought on enemy targets by their B25 and B26 aircraft, both long extinct. And though it could muster no more than one helicopter, the men of the Air Force wielded their old reputation flamboyantly.

138

Their officers flew about in the best cars, which they drove like land-jets. They drank the best liquor, smoked foreign cigarettes and wore new clothes. They were loved dearly by the girls for their generosity with foreign currency.

Their Air Police, a uniformly ill-educated lot, were a remarkably tough squad who loved their additional reputation for ruthlessness. Their contempt for every other military formation was total and unremitting. They conscripted men easily and on their own initiative.

Four of them led by a surly-faced NCO, were manning the notorious Ihioma check-point just outside the Air Headquarters complex in an old girls' school, that morning.

The heavy metal bar did not rise when the Red Cross truck drove up to the check-point. A rather gruff, brusque voice ordered "Halt!"

The driver thrust his head out of his cabin window, smiled a plastic, professional smile that he usually reserved for gruff military policemen and sentries, and said the magic words: "Relief vehicle, please, Red Cross."

"Red what? And those stragglers at the back are relief, hey?" the NCO retorted with a sneer.

"I'm not carrying any stragglers, AP*," the driver began in a gentle voice that went with the professional smile. "They're people I'm giving a lift to. And they're mostly these women who go on attack-trade."

"Don't answer me like that, driver!" The NCO shouted angrily. The driver looked at him in open-mouthed surprise.

"How did I answer you? I said I was not carrying any stragglers, only women. What's wrong with my answer?"

"Sharrap!" the NCO's face was darkening. "And say 'sah', when you talk to me! By de way why aren't you in de force? Why should you be driving a relief vehicle? Your mates are fighting and you are carrying stockfish and stragglers! AP!"

"Sah!"

"Get everybody out of dat lorry, including de driver. We are commandeering dat vehicle. If any man dey inside, check him properly!"

"Yessah!"

The driver looked around helplessly at the dour faces of the other APs about the check-point.

In the back of the lorry, Cetme Sammy was stiff with worry.

The Air Police! The AP! Good God above! Whatever brought them out this morning of all mornings; this day of all days!

Now Sammy managed to turn his head, and looked around him.

He realised with horror that he was the only young man, an able, bodied man, as far as he could see, in the crowded lorry. There were a

*See Glossary

139

couple of soldiers in uniform, on AWOL or Pass, he wouldn't know. But they were in uniform. They could prove their bona-fides.

Sammy looked down at his bare feet, his faded trousers and worn civilian shirt. He *did* look like a straggler, he told himself; at best a deserter. He know that among this lot of women and middle-aged men he must stand out . . . a green blossom on a withered tree. He clenched his teeth and his fists.

"Everyone there get down, quick," the AP ordered, glancing back to see his NCO scowling his support, his gaze fixed at the lorry. "I say everyone! And you too, idle civilian," he derided, nodding at Cetme Sammy.

Sammy shuffled worriedly, and began to edge his way down the crowded tailboard.

Two other APs had joined the one at the back of the lorry, and together, briskly, very brusquely, they began to shove the men and the women into two groups.

Cetme Sammy hopped on to the ground, and as quickly as he could, joined the group of men.

"Where are you from?" a thick-looking AP was asking one of the young men in uniform.

"STF* Division."

"ST what?"

"F Division."

"F Division? Which one be F Division? Who command it?"

The soldier, an artilleryman, concluded quickly that either the AP had a coconut head, was a total illiterate, or he was luring him into a verbal assault like the one from which their driver had emerged bruised and bowed. For reasons of caution he preferred to believe the AP was doing the latter.

"I mean the Division is called STF. S for Special, T for Task, F for Force and D for Division. Its HQ main is at Arochuku. I'm in R for Ranger B for Battalion. T for Task Brigade commanded by Major Dimkpa. Ranger Battalion is commanded by Captain Offor." The soldier explained with supreme superfluousness.

"And where are you going to?"

"I'm going to Ozubulu, to see my mother. She's ill. My elder brother is dead, my sister is in Gabon, and I'm the only one who can look after her." He knew he was overdoing it, but he did not want to give the notoriously illiterate and cunning APs any chance to set a trap into which he would be caught, and his mission frustrated.

"And you?" the AP jabbed a finger at no one in particular. Cetme Sammy thought it was his turn and mentally tightened up to face the music. But the AP ignored him.

*See Glossary

"I mean you!" he shouted at a frail young man. Cetme Sammy began to worry. The AP just suddenly seemed to be taking his time coming round to him. That was bad enough . . .

Cetme Sammy trembled, and waited his turn. The AP seemed to be deliberately, tortuously building up to a climactic confrontation with him; their prize catch; the soldier in civilian clothes without a pass! He wished, belatedly, he had asked Dede to write him a pass.

CHAPTER THIRTY-ONE

12 NOON.

Five days to Operation Sword.

Colonel Chumah's command Land-Rover slowed down perfunctorily at the Ihioma check-point, but quickly gathered speed again as the heavy bar rose, followed by a stampede of booted feet as the guards saluted the Colonel. Chumah returned a brisk acknowledgement, without turning his gaze which was fixed straight ahead of him, over the shoulder of the driver.

At that very moment, less than a quarter of a mile down the road, on the Air Headquarters training ground, Cetme Sammy was standing on the muddy bottom of a six-foot deep punishment pit. The hair on his head looked as if it had been gnawed by a not too hungry rat. The orderly who was ordered to shave Sammy couldn't have given anyone a hair-cut before.

Sammy had been relieved of his green shirt and brown trousers and now stood half-naked in his precious second-hand trunks and a tattered, threadbare green T-shirt provided by his captors after they had de-civilianised him. He was to spend six hours in the pit every day from six to twelve noon as his punishment for 'having dodged the force' for over a year and for lying to APs that he was a commando.

Yesterday they had not given him a dog's chance in a slaughter house. Not that he expected it.

When one AP gruffly hurled Cetme Sammy out of the pit, the sun was already overhead. Sammy knew it was noon, and the end of his mission.

Colonel Chumah, he knew, must be on his way back to the 5 Commando HQ. He was making his second appearance before the Training Sergeant.

"I swear I'm a soldier with the commandos, HQ Camp Company. But one of our officers sent me on a message, that's why I don't have a pass.

Please, sah, I'm telling you the truth. Believe me!" At the end of his plea tiny little stars started to swim before his eyes as the Sergeant's ugly stick rattled his skull with even greater force.

"You will stop lying to me or I'll lock you up for ever!" he threatened his stick lingering over Sammy's hurting head.

"But I'm not lying, sah," Sammy insisted tearfully.

"What kind of message? And where's your pass?"

"It's . . . it's a private message, sah, and the Captain asked me to sneak out and get back quietly the same yesterday, sah. I swear, sah."

"What's the message all about, I want to know!" the Sergeant demanded.

"It's . . ." Sammy took a mental grip on himself and hesitated. He almost let his hand feel his tiny pocket for the slip of paper that weighed like a bomb. He checked himself again. Should he buy his freedom with the Colonel's message? He thought not.

"I say what is the message about, and where's a pass from your off sah?" There was a note of cruel triumph in the Sergeant's voice. "You see? I told you, you are a liar!"

"I'm not lying, sah. Only it's a private message," Sammy's voice was cracked and weary with the pain of his failure.

"What's the offsah's name?"

Sammy hesitated again. "I've forgotten his name, sah. He has just been posted to the Div, sah," he lied brilliantly.

"AP!" the Sergeant called. An Air Policeman stirred at the Sergeant' side.

"Take that idle civilian liar away and lock him up for six days. After that I think he will be ready to tell the truth."

Alone now in the guardroom, a poorly ventilated furnace that might have been meant as a storeroom in the teachers' quarters, he brought out the sheet of paper that Michel gave to him.

In deference to his Dede and the superior officer to whom it was addressed, he had never read its contents. But now, thrown into a dungeon and his mission frustrated, he felt no guilt as he unfolded the paper and began to read with the help of the stream of light from the cannon perforated roof.

Dear Sir,

I'm Capt Michel, formerly personal assistant to Col. Jacques Rudolf Comd 5 Cdo. I'm in detention along with the only surviving member of the French military assistance team, Capt. Jules, because I'm one of two people alive today who know what the mercenaries are up to. The other person is Capt. Jules here with me.

There's little time to tell you much. But it is important you know

142

that Col. Rudolf organised the murder of the 5 French Christian Brothers (real, genuine fighters), because they were frustrating his plans. And his plans? He has formed the 5 Commando as a personal force, a personal weapon, to influence the course of the war, prolong it, and naturally, as a professional mercenary no longer in his youth, make money.

It is perhaps too late for him to shoot both of us out of hand now. He may yet try to, but that doesn't matter. What matters is that you know that Rudolf's plan is to go on losing, and if the net closes in on him, turn on the General with the 5 Commando probably to get his last huge cut of money and ask for a safe passage. Jules heard them discuss this in detail one drunken night.

Nobody else in the country knows this. I never had a chance to tell anyone. Only you can now save this grave situation. From here I know little that is happening outside, so I hope it is not too late.

Long live the Republic.

Michel, Capt.

With tears swelling up in his eyes, Sammy folded the paper, its import weighing down on him more than ever before; he slumped to the floor and sobbed bitterly.

Cetme Sammy was still sitting on the hard floor, his red eyes out of their sockets and his heart in his hands, when Colonel Chumah's command car returned to 5 Commando Headquarters at about 1.15 p.m.

It drove up to Rudolf's office, where Sergeant Chiko told the Colonel that the commander had gone to lunch.

The car drove Chumah back to his own house, a neat, two-roomed apartment he had rented inside the village just across the road from the Headquarters. For reasons of personal security, privacy and a wish to avoid the daily ordeal of living in a whole bungalow without a wife and child to fill it, he had chosen this village hideout.

Later in the evening he met with Rudolf in a tense and uneasy debriefing session that lasted only a few minutes.

"So, how's the Eleven Division area?" Rudolf asked casually.

"All quiet," Chumah replied laconically. He loathed every minute he had to talk with this savage adventurer that thrived on war and blood, in his commander and deputy, master and servant, position.

"Any reports?"

"From me?"

"Anyone, recce, DMI*, you know, don't you?"

"Only a couple of guesses that enemy might be building up."

*See Glossary

"Didn't you go into details, I mean . . . ?"

"I couldn't. You realise I have not the damnedest idea what the he[l] the 5 Commando is up to. All I know is you plan to recapture Onitsh[a] Full stop. I wanted, purely on my own, to familiarise myself with th[e] locations and positions of my divisional area. You wanted me to look i[n] on the morale of the troops manning the main strategic locations. Fine. [I] did that."

Rudolf's fingers toyed with a lighter and he lit a cigarette. He didn'[t] offer one to Colonel Chumah.

"All right, all right. What's morale like, then?"

"I should say moderately high. But that doesn't mean much. Th[e] front's been quiet and there's been no gauge for morale for some time now. Morale is almost always high on a quiet front. Naturally the reporte[d] build-up does bother them."

"I see."

There wasn't much else to discuss.

Chumah's excursion to the frontlines had been encouraged mainly a[s] an opportunity to divert him from the Headquarters while the two edge[s] of the Sword took shape. His trip or report had no relevance to the con[-] tent of the operation. Probably, too, it did varnish the façade of harmony.

But for Colonel Chumah, it had been a much-needed escape from th[e] tension and frustration of the Division, with its complacent complemen[t] of white mercenaries, to think out his own plans and moves.

If anyone imagined he was taking things lying down, he had though[t], before he left for the 11 Division, he was dead wrong.

When he got back to his village hideout that evening, he locked hi[s] front door, sat down with a cigarette and began to digest the idea tha[t] had taken shape in his mind over the past three days.

CHAPTER THIRTY-TWO

ALTHOUGH COLONEL CHARLES CHUMAH did not know, and could no[t] have known it, the Sword was dangling four days away.

The lack of cordial communication between him and Colonel Jacque[s] Rudolf did not bother Colonel Chumah at all. Indeed, he was glad o[f] this state of cold war.

Left out of the mainstream of the affairs and plans of the 5 Command[o] Division, he was able to take it uncharacteristically calmly because i[t] gave him time and freedom to work out his own plans. Isolation gave him room to consider the entire, risk-fraught ramifications of a scheme that was being constantly shaped and trimmed by his subconscious. He believed that the best-laid plans of war and battles were ground over a long time by the subconscious mind of planners.

He had time to look around, feel the pulse of the men in the trenches, and to think. His thoughts turned to Major Chime Dimkpa. Other surviving officers and men of the Ninth Mile Corner campaign would be scattered in the various locations of the war. But Chime would be able to locate them and mobilise them if need be.

He could go to his location. Why not? Neither he nor the 5 Commando were in need of each other badly right now.

CHAPTER THIRTY-THREE

MIDDAY, THREE DAYS to the Sword.

Brilliant sunshine streamed down. A gentle wind ruffled palm-leaves and shuffled the elephant grass that was as tall as the banana trees.

As his command-rover tumbled down the earth road of the active locations, Colonel Chumah's ears strained for the inevitable sound of firing, of action. But all was quiet.

His being an unscheduled trip with no one forewarned, he had not been surprised to find Major Dimkpa away at the locations when he called at the Brigade Headquarters. Chumah had expected there would be an operation going on. But the nearer he got to the front lines, the quieter it seemed to become.

The trees, defoliated and withered from the heavy artillery duel that preceded Dimkpa's retreat to the western banks of the river, had re-acquired fresh green blossoms in the dying rainy season.

The only enduring vestiges of the bitter action of the past months were the litter of odds and ends, spent artillery shells and broken ammunition boxes. Even the battered roadside mud huts of villagers, now refugees in faraway camps, were invisible beneath a dense growth of grass that had long taken over tenancy.

The Land-Rover bumped, tumbled and purred throatily through the still eternity of the wild bushes. The active locations remained inactive.

But here and there were indications of proximity to the front lines: the trickle of men in threadbare, dyed-green baft uniforms, many of them barefoot and bareheaded; a water tank hitched to a Land-Rover standing under the shelter of a clump of tall banana trees.

A little down the road, in a small roadside clearing, Major Dimkpa was leaning on a stationary Land-Rover, his back to the road, talking with deep concentration to Captain Ude when Chumah's car bumped and purred into sight.

Chime Dimkpa turned, noted the command star on the red plate and braced himself for a sudden call by the Commander of his STF Division.

He picked up his stick and cap from the bonnet of the car, put on the latter quickly and slipped the former under his armpit.

The thick, black beard had him wondering for a while, until Colonel Charles Chumah's gleaming-ivory teeth flashed in the happy-boy smile he strictly reserved for people he liked and respected, who were very few indeed.

Major Chime Dimkpa's delight was tinged with emotion, explicit in the powerful, stiff-armed and vibrating salute he delivered to his former commander.

Captain Ude's voice rang out to the Major's guards in a piercing drill sergeant's call, as he too, saluted:

"Guards, present arms!"

The men that recognised the former commander raised a spontaneous ovation that further breached the quiet jungle.

"Hail the hero of the Ninth Mile!"

"Yeeeh!"

"Hail CCC!"

"Yeeeh!"

"Hail Biafra!"

"Yeeeh!"

The few that wore caps raised them to their hero.

The Colonel was deeply touched. The brief, warm-hearted welcome was a tremendous redress from the distress of dealing with foreign mercenaries.

He stretched a firm hand, shook Major Dimkpa's and patted his shoulder with the other.

"And how are you, my dear Chime?"

"Very well, sir. I'm happy to see you again. As they say back home, sir, you will live long; Captain Ude and I were just talking about you a few seconds ago."

"Thank you, Chime. And how are you?"

He shook Captain Ude's hand. "Another veteran of the Ninth Mile, eh?" He patted the Captain's shoulder.

"Yes, sir. Captain Gideon Ude."

"Oh, yes, of course, I remember you now. You were a second lieutenant then, weren't you?"

146

"That's right, sir."

"I'm glad to see you both together again. It's good for the Brigade."

"Thank you, sir."

"How's your area, Chime?" His tone was suddenly business-like. "Any operations going?"

"Not from this side, sir. It's been all quiet in the southern front," Chime said with a smile. "So quiet both sides take turns bathing in the river every day."

"A kind of tacit truce, eh?"

"Something like that, sir."

"You think our boys are weary? You know, fed up?"

"Not at all, sir; I wouldn't even suspect that. I rather think that both sides accept the geographical reality of the present situation. The river is a virtual truce line. Either side would have to be exceptionally suicidally-minded to attempt an amphibious crossing. Besides, the equipment is just not there."

"Unless perhaps with Angus MacDiarmid's† flat-bottomed canoes?" the Colonel asked with a wry smile.

"Anything happening soon, sir?" Chime enquired calmly.

The Colonel nodded several times for emphasis. "Very soon. Where's your mess? Let's talk there. And I could use a drink. You come along, too, Captain."

Colonel Chumah had been doing most of the talking, Major Dimkpa and Captain Ude the listening, for well over an hour.

What the Colonel intended to do had not come as a surprise to either listener—they knew, like most officers and men following the progress or the lack of it, of the 5 Commando Division, that the release of Colonel Chumah from detention was the beginning of the end of the hitherto unchallenged and seemingly unchallengeable power and influence of the Christian Brothers.

But before now it had been no more than a notion, at best a fantasy. But now, listening to the man talking with such frightening determination that seemed to scorn risks, his actual plans overawed them.

To take on the mercenaries would be practically an open challenge to the authority of the General. Success or failure in the confrontation with the Christian Brothers did not come into it—yet. The mere act of striving

†Angus MacDiarmid, a BBC correspondent who covered the war from the Nigerian side, suggested to the Federals in 1968 in a BBC 'Focus' programme, that the problem of small river crossing in the war could be solved by what he called 'small, flat-bottomed canoes'. Both Mr. MacDiarmid and the BBC were frequently attacked by Biafran media for 'partial reporting' of the war.

openly to expel their presence and influence was treason. Pure and simple.

Not that, in either man's mind, there was any doubt about the necessity of eliminating the Christian Brothers. It was not treason so to do. What *was* treason, in fact, was the mercenaries' continued stay. But treason, they knew, too, was *not* what a Captain and Major said it was. It was as those in power termed and defined it. Thus, Dimkpa reasoned, only success could justify their action and give them satisfaction—whatever their individual fate was afterwards. The most culpable treason was the one that failed to achieve its purpose; abortive treason. If they tried and failed, he thought, it would have been a worthless personal sacrifice. But if they succeeded then it would have been worth the risk. And although success may not bring victory and peace, defeat at less cost in life, money and property would be infinitely preferable to the bloody pursuit of victory on which the mercenaries had been making their fortunes.

Like the Colonel, Major Dimkpa knew he did not believe in the peace of the graveyard.

Dimkpa cleared his throat, took a drink from his glass of water and brought his fork and knife together, face down on his plate. It was a good, heavy meal of yam porridge with stockfish, prepared specially for the visiting Colonel who, Dimkpa knew, had a hearty appetite.

Dimkpa raised his eyes at the Colonel, who was now scooping up the only slice of yam he had been able to eat in the silent interval.

"I'm with you if you need me, sir." Dimkpa's tone was oddly more emphatic than the simple words conveyed.

Charles Chumah looked quickly from his plate and stared at the young Major.

"That's a courageous thing to say, Chime," he said, moved. "But you realise it's not an order? You are not the type of man I would ask whether he was sure, but this job is as good as suicide—mutiny they'll probably call it down in State Lodge. You realise that?"

"I do, indeed, sir. And if there's any courage in what I'm doing, *you* should take credit for it. Courage without inspiration sometimes dies latent."

"You know, of course, that I'm with you both, sir," Captain Ude told them. "And I know my fellow officers Captain Offor and Lieutenant Deze would be only too glad to volunteer, sir. They have always prayed for a moment like this."

"Then we have to talk about the bulk of the men, sir," Dimkpa suggested politely.

"The men, yes, Chime. I would prefer the men of the Ninth Mile Corner. You know, people I'm used to and can trust their ability. But I doubt whether there are many of them left now . . . ?"

148

"You'll be surprised, sir!" Chime Dimkpa said eagerly. "I have a full battalion manned by them alone right here in the Brigade. And several companies scattered in the Division".

"That's very good. Keep them within your reach, say you're expecting an attack or something."

"That's easy enough. I happen to double as the Division's Brigade Major. I can always get the men I want."

"Good again. I fear everything is going too well, far too well . . ."

"I don't want to ask too many questions, sir. In fact the less I know about an operation the better I usually feel, but perhaps . . ." The Colonel nodded.

"I was coming round to that," Chumah said. "First," he said, laying the edge of his right hand on the table for emphasis, "we need all the men of the Ninth Mile that you can muster."

"Any upper limit? There might be up to two battalions of them about, sir."

"I think a battalion of them will do. Maybe plus a company of re-serves. Can you manage that?"

"I think I can, sir," Chime answered modestly.

"Now the substance of it. Five Commando go into action in Onitsha as soon as possible. God knows what that means, but Jacques Rudolf wouldn't tell me precisely when.

"So, since I can't tell you when the Division moves into Onitsha, all you do is keep the men on the alert and keep your ears to the ground; you will hear the ants whisper."

"So what we are planning is entirely tied up with the mysterious operation in Onitsha?"

"It's the only way to avoid too much bloodshed."

The Colonel thought for a minute.

"Another little thing, Chime," he began. "You know what messages are like, they can be garbled sometimes . . ."

"I know, sir," Dimkpa grinned a little mischievously. "Like the cable from the businessman on holiday to his wife saying, 'Darling, having a wonderful time. Wish you were here'; and it arrived with the last *e* missing!"

The room exploded in laughter.

"Well, should my signal to you suffer the same fate as the business-man's cable, I think we had better agree on some specific rendezvous. Somewhere nearer the Eleven Division area."

"Do you suggest the HQ Main*, then?"

"No; not there. I guess there will still be a few 5 Codo men about then. I should think Air HQ* Ihioma would be a good rendezvous."

*See Glossary

149

"I think Ihioma is all right, sir. Perhaps better than any other point I can think of. And I believe they have an efficient signals network, which is important."

The Colonel rose, picking up his cap and swagger stick.

"Back to the Division today, sir?" Chime asked, rising too.

"No. I've a whole day to do this trip. But I'd like to stop off for the night at Umuahia and pick the brains of a couple of friends of mine in the government."

"Hail CCC!"

"Up the hero."

"Long live the spirit of Ninth Mile!"

"Hail the Hero of Ninth Mile!"

The cries of the troops filled his ears as he left.

CHAPTER THIRTY-FOUR

TWO DAYS TO The Sword.

Everything had been going without a hitch.

The General, to the surprise of everyone, including the unflappable Rudolf, had paid a sudden visit to the Headquarters soon after lunch time and given the boys a pep talk on their coming vital operation.

In the late afternoon Rudolf called in Sergeant Chiko.

"Chiko," he called, settling into his chair. "You know we are going on a big operation, eh?"

"No sah. Yessah," Chiko blundered, caught off guard.

"What do you mean, no sir, yes sir?"

"I mean, sah, I know we are training for a big attack, but I don't know when it will be, sah." Chiko rallied valiantly.

"Well it will be soon. Very soon."

"Yessah. I would like to go on the ops*, sah. Only . . . my finger, sah." He looked at the stub of his missing finger with sad eyes.

"Never mind, Chiko. You'll be all right. There's always something else you can do."

"Thanks, sah!"

"Like now . . . we need one thing. You know what it is!"

"Sorry, sah, I forget, sah."

"Come on, Chiko," he snapped his fingers in mock impatience. "Come on, you know it."

*See Glossary

"Let me remember, sah," Chiko temporised, putting on his thinking cap in the form of a pensive mien.

"Here, Chiko," Johann Schmuts called. The Sergeant looked at the Major. Schmuts held a wrapped slip of paper between his thumb and two fingers, put it to this lips, drew the air noisily through his teeth, drew it in further down in two short, harsh gasps and exhaled through his teeth again.

Chiko nodded vigorously. "I remember it, sah, *Wee-wee!*"

"That's the boy." Schmuts cheered.

"Hemp," Rudolf verbalised. "We need plenty of it, Chiko, for the ops. The more we have the more vandals we kill, eh?"

"Yessah!"

"And the other stuff, Biafran gin, is it?"

"Yessah. *Kinkana** no de sour," Chiko grinned knowledgeably.

"Good. Get plenty of both. Kapitan Heinz will give you all the money you need. You're off till tomorrow morning, Chiko. On your way."

The General's surprise visit seemed to spark off a flurry of individual activities, as the mercenaries put final touches to The Sword.

As they packed their knap-sacks, they discreetly slipped in their scant personal items—tooth-brushes, shaving packs, etc., discarding other bulkier items.

None of them would be convinced that if they lost in Onitsha they would not be led from there to the airstrip and home.

At ten o'clock that night Major Derek Tremble wrote his valedictory letter from 5 Commando Headquarters to Mrs Barbara Tremble. It was his briefest since he arrived in the enclave.

Beloved,

I'm writing this with a glass of whisky in my hand ... How about you?

You'll be delighted to know that Gerald, our old friend from Oxford, called on me unexpectedly here at the HQ this afternoon. (Think of that! Wasn't it really pleasant of him?)

As usual he was most concerned about our difficulties and promised that he would send some sizeable relief food for the boys before their coming outing (I hope he gets the stuff in in the next 55 hours). I must say he cheered the boys no end. You ought to know what the food situation is like out here. It's been our greatest headache wondering how to provide enough food for a two-way exercise when we couldn't get sufficient stuff for the first phase which is rather important ... But

*See Glossary

151

Gerald had a characteristic answer for our problems. (I shall turn my food stores inside out just so you have all you want, he said. Good old Gerald!) So that's settled now, I'm glad to say. You need not worry your pretty head about me and my boys.

Like I said, I shall be taking the boys along on the exercise and will not be writing you until we have successfully completed our first drill, and perhaps not at all if my good friend here (Adolf, we call him, though he doesn't sport a moustache!) carries out his threat to shoot off our right arms if our boys fail in their exercise! For then I'd be on my way to good old England for rest and recuperation—hopefully!

Don't worry, darling, I'll be all right.

Love to the kids, and to Mummy, Daddy and Tommy.

All love,

Derek.

Tremble found the tiny date-and-time stamp he was equipped with, set it to ten o'clock and the day's date and pressed it down on a careless corner on the back of the lined blue paper.

As Derek Tremble was putting his coded letter into an airmail envelope, the first convoy of artillery pieces and crew, led by a Spanish Captain, was moving under cover of the thickening darkness to the Onitsha front.

By morning all the twenty-four heavy guns would be in place.

CHAPTER THIRTY-FIVE

ONE DAY TO The Sword.

Everything else seemed to roll off from Colonel Jacques Rudolf's mind as the Sword glistened and dangled in his mind's eye, a mere twenty-two hours away. The adventurer had taken full possession of the man as soon as he woke up to the auspicious omen of a bright, sunny morning.

Breakfast was spartan and perfunctory: two cups of hot, black coffee washed down with the neat whisky that was more congenial to his palate.

Kapitan Hans Heinz was already waiting in the commander's office when Rudolf walked in. Heinz had two vital documents in a folder under his arm as he saluted. He laid the folder before the commander as soon as Rudolf settled into his chair.

Rudolf examined the papers one after the other.

What he picked up first was the manifest of the largest war material the General's Quartermaster-General had been able to muster for any single operation so far; more than several major operations put together, and two-thirds of the total fire-power of the army:

24 arty* pieces of the 105 and 106 ranges × 1800 shells
100 mor* barrels × 4600 bombs
12 anti-tank bazookas × 240 76 mm Carl Gustav bombs
7100 Madsen and Cetme assault rifles × 250,320 rounds 7·62 and 7·92 NATO*
16 HMGs × 128 belts of 300 rounds ·92 NATO (large)
21 SLRs* × 630 ·67 NATO (large)
13 MK IV bolt action rifles (for Sniper Platoon) × 360 ·92 NATO
Mines: "Ogbunigwe"*: 47 Bucket class
      36 Coffin class
      12 Miscellaneous
10,000 hand grenades.

Jacques Rudolf laid the sheet of paper face down, put a paperweight of spent cannon on it, and proceeded to read the next, longer one.

For the first time he was looking at the Order of Battle for Sword One in comprehensive form. Major Schmuts, Major Ball and Kapitan Heinz he had assigned to the job of whittling the plan to the barest details, while he himself handled Sword Two, the careful, last-resort phase which existed not on paper but in Rudolf's head.

TOP SECRET
CODENAME OPS SWORD
FM: COMD 5 CDO DIV
TO: ALL SF COMDS

Below are directives for comds re Ops Sword.

All units will strive to achieve objective within first three hours of contact with en.
H-HOUR IS 0500 HRS—60 mins of arty.
1. STRIKE FORCE BILL (SFB) LED BY Maj Bill Ball will strike through bush path (even terrain, largely grassland) and head for Highway A on the Enugu–Osha* main axis. Tps will stop just short of the Jnx* (Nkpor) and lay ambush.
Objective will be control of the vital jnx along which enemy infiltrates supplies into Osha from their rear bases in Awka and Enugu. Seizure of jnx will puncture the en supply line. SFB will then split in two. One will push the wedge in the broken route down northwards, widening gap between the enemy and his base (EES at Jnx = 1–2,000 men). Second

*See Glossary

Bill will turn on the city, destroy en at notorious Cocacola factory stronghold, dig in, in former en trenches, and hold tight. Tps must deny the en, who will soon be under fire inside the city, an escape route. (EES = 3–4,000 men).

2. With Nkpor Jnx cleared of en, STRIKE FORCE JOHANN (SFJ) will proceed along the same line as SFB, but striking south-west from jnx to take position on the banks of the Nkisi river to deny en further escape route through 57 Bde Ops area.

3. From the south-east, access roads old and new (Highways B & C) will be the main axis of attack, to be manned by two SFs each. SF Relli and SF Marc to man old road into the city (Highway B) and SF Tremble and SF Hans (led by Capt Henrique Martinez) to man access road (Highway C).

The four SFs are the weight that will crush the en now bottled in inside the city. The four SFs move in immediately rpt immediately after bombardment by arty units. SFs R & M and SFs T & H must, rpt must, destroy all en concentrations inside the city and push remnants into the river within three hrs of contact with en. RV* will be DMGS* premises.

Rudolf looked up from the paper and gave Heinz a look that was pleased and at the same time questioning.

"Ja," Hans began, speaking rapidly in German. "The heavies and supports began moving in last night after the last recce had reported no adverse enemy move.

"We have got in all the artillery pieces, mortars, mines and crew. Also signals is set up at the Tactical Headquarters. Ammo and light equipment are being loaded up at Umuahia about now. We have six big trucks including two trailers. Defence Headquarters are bringing in six more trucks and three jeeps for troops."

Rudolf nodded his pleasure.

"Ammo convoy should be back here from Umuahia before lunch time," Heinz continued smoothly as if he was reading the data from an index card. "Troops are on alert for 5 p.m. By 6 p.m. every man jack would be on board for Onitsha, in position by midnight, five hours before H-hour. Should be enough."

"Just one more thing, Hans. EES." He turned over the paper to check the figures, and looked up again at Hans. "I see we've got the enemy at 6,000 men, the higher figure."

"That's right. That covers the estimated number infiltrated over the period of the reported build-up. It was originally 4,000 or thereabouts."

"Very good. Roughly same strength as us."

*See Glossary

Chumah, Rudolf thought, had no part in Sword. He would command the rear Headquarters, whatever that meant. He had told him. Still, he would not take the chance of informing him of the troops' movement before 5 p.m., alert hour. There was too much precious time before then, too precious to let Chumah know that the operation was to kick off in twelve hours. The commander was taking no chances.

"Michel and Jules," Rudolf said aloud, and looked up at Hans.

"Oh, those. We will take them along to Onitsha. The short time between departure and H-hour could prove critical for the men to be left behind under the charge of Colonel Chumah, Jacques."

"I was thinking so, too."

Too bad, Heinz thought, no one caught that deserting coward Sammy, in spite of the all-unit alarm. He would have taken the personal delight of shooting the bastard's intestines out.

They lined up there on the training ground at 5 p.m., spick and span in their freshly ironed jungle-green camouflages, ankle-length boots, steel helmets and shining Madsen rifles, a smaller number of Cetme rifles, bayonets fixed and glistening. Their heavy knapsacks hung on their stiff backs.

All 6,600 of them. They stood in six rows of Strike Force strength each, at ramrod attention.

In a smaller, seventh row, right out front, their white officers, six Strike Force and thirty sub-unit commanders, stood at attention too, like the other ranks. At either end of the troops' rows were the tiny, scorned motley of native officers that had been field-commissioned into the fringe of the exclusive officer corps of the 5 Commando, very much against Rudolf's inclination and only after lengthy pressure from Defence Operations.

The supporting units of artillery, mortar, engineers and signals, another 500 men or so, led by five white commanders, were already in the Onitsha front, placing their guns, spading away and reconnoitering the land in readiness for their comrades of the infantry.

On the training ground, morale could still be felt at mast-top where it climbed to the previous day, following the General's visit. The disenchantment of the days before had been replaced by a new enthusiasm and hope. The men seemed all set and ready to die.

Rudolf walked down each rank of troops, like a visiting foreign dignitary inspecting a guard of honour, savouring the glory, half-wondering whether it was indeed a valedictory ceremony; a kind of last supper.

Rudolf had held a thorough briefing session with the commanders after lunch-time. All the white men who had the battle order knew what Sword One was all about.

But only Rudolf and the six Strike Force commanders, including Captain Martinez, the effective commander of the SF named after Heinz, knew of the existence of Sword Two. And only Rudolf knew the details of it. He had not felt any need to share it with even his closest comrades Heinz and Johann. It would amount to sharing command of the Division. It was his commander's special privilege. Only he would call the tune if he felt there was a need to change the music.

One thing pleased him immensely. He had successfully resisted Defence Operations' intrusion into the Sword. He had originally presented the plan as a single-edged thrust with the sole purpose of recapturing Onitsha. The fact that it contained no apparent sub-plan of action in case of a setback had been argued as evidence of single-minded determination to succeed. He was not going to consider setbacks and was not making any allowances, in theory or practice, he had stated. They had had enough of setbacks and provisions for setbacks. They were going to stand right up there and slug it out with the enemy, toe-to-toe, punch-for-punch, no towels, no padded canvas, until victory.

It was a declaration he knew must be plausible to a High Command that was desperate for one success after an unbroken chain of setbacks.

But Defence Operations had, all the same, made one modification. Or tried to. 11 Division, the unit largely responsible for the Onitsha sector, should be deployed full-scale to support the Sword and doubly ensure success. Also, Defence Operations had insisted, the Navy patrol on the safer reaches of the river Niger should be deployed with their home-made gun-boats to support the operation by endangering the tenuous enemy supply route across the river.

But Rudolf had refused to consider the idea of a mixed-man force. It would give the 11 Division Commander a route to interfere, even if marginally, with his command control of Sword. The operation, after all, was his Division's brain-child, not a Defence Operations project. Finally, Defence Operations' pressure was met with the Churchillian declaration: give the commandos the tools and they will finish the job without outside help.

Now Rudolf had the tools.

And *his* plans.

CHAPTER THIRTY-SIX

Ten p.m.

The eve of the Sword.

The 5 Commando Division Headquarters was now a sprawling, deserted fort. But two men were yet to leave the HQ.

Jacques Rudolf and Hans Heinz each had a final chore to perform.

Rudolf's was Colonel Charles Chumah. In five minutes it was over. Chumah had been handed over the empty HQ, now consisting of no more than a platoon of mostly non-able-bodied remnants of the HQ company. A skeleton staff of three manned the rear signals unit, now re-established in a ground-floor room, and the only thing ticking in the huge machinery of the former Commando powerhouse. Between them the platoon left behind could muster no more than a dozen MK IV rifles and a few rounds of ammunition. Jacques Rudolf was taking no chances behind his back.

Soon he was set to go. With the hilt of the Sword now within his grasp, the soldier of fortune would not be drawn back by a team of mules.

Chiko was waiting downstairs with the Commander's gear. So were Hans Heinz and the other five of the Commander's personal bodyguards.

Three vehicles were ready on the driveway. Rudolf's white command Mercedes stood between two Land-Rovers.

Inside the first Land-Rover Captains Jules and Michel sat on top of the tools compartment, their wrists tied together and their bodies rigid between armed guards. Another guard sat beside the driver in the front seat. Rudolf's bodyguards scrambled into the second Land-Rover as soon as the Commander and Heinz disappeared into the back seat of the white car, with Chiko in the front passenger seat.

Captain Michel was growing paler with worry. He had despaired that Colonel Chumah had received his note. Certainly Sammy had been caught . . . his note had been discovered. So now they were taking them out of the HQ to shoot them . . . He began to sob softly, shaking his head bitterly.

Twelve midnight. 5 Commando Tactical Headquarters.

The biggest assault force ever deployed, backed by the most awesome armoury ever assembled by the General's armed forces for a single objective, was being readied for action.

As was usual in the absence of Jacques Rudolf, Major Johann Schmuts was the on-the-spot commander. He was pleased with things.

Nothing seemed to be amiss. Transport, movement, timing, everything seemed to have gone like clockwork. Thanks to Heinz's Teutonic efficiency. For once he couldn't help admiring a Nazi. Soon Johann would begin to lever the huge military machine into place, ready for H-hour.

When Colonel Rudolf's command convoy finally pulled away from the HQ, it was five and half minutes after midnight and deployment hour at the Onitsha fronts.

But Rudolf knew Johann Schmuts would take care of D-hour*. He sat back in the soft upholstery and relaxed.

Another nine and half minutes later, just as Strike Force Bill was flanking right, into the bush, through the foot-track that led to Nkpor Junction, Colonel Charles Chumah got very busy.

Rudolf had told him nothing precise. But piecing his own tiny bits of private intelligence together, Chumah had a firm hunch that H-hour could not be more than a few hours away.

But how few?

He was certain he had not much time left.

Inside Rudolf's office, behind the disgustingly huge table for the first time, Charles Chumah drew a blank form and began to draft a message for Major Chime Dimkpa.

When he finished it, he read it over carefully and took it across to the make-shift signals room next door.

TOP SECRET
URGENTEST
TO: CO T BDE STF DIV
FM: CCC

THE ANT WHISPERS(.) SAYS IGNORE IHIOMA(.) RPT IGNORE IHIOMA(.) RV DIV HQ(.) RPT RV DIV HQ(.) ASAP*(.) WAITING(.) NO ACK(.)

"Get that off urgentest to STF Division. Top secret," he told the signals corporal on duty.

"Yessah."

"And corporal . . ."

"Sah!"

"Tune in on 5 Codo TAC* and monitor all messages from Onitsha sector until further notice. I want them every fifteen minutes with immediate effect."

"Yessah."

*See Glossary

158

"And this is top secret too, Corporal."
"Yessah!"

At exactly the same time, fifteen minutes past midnight, the ants were whispering to another Colonel in the Command Headquarters of the Federal army brigade occupying Onitsha town.

The Colonel was at last reading the vital message that had kept him waiting through seven almost sleepless nights.

It was from his Army Headquarters (AHQ*), copied to the Supreme Headquarters (SHQ*), and signed by the Chief of Staff Army (COSA*) himself, which meant it had the utmost priority and urgency.

SHQ/A/MSG(.) 2ND

TOP PRIORITY
TO: COMD A2
FM: COSA* AHQ*
INFO: COS* SHQ*

LATEST INTREP SAYS EXPECTED EN BID NOW APPROX 55 HRS RPT 55 HRS BACKWARDS TO TEN PM TWICE(.) RPT BACKWARDS TO TEN PM TWICE(.) NO INFO EN H-HR AS INT* SOURCE VERY SENSITIVE AND COMMUNICATION VERY INHIBITED(.) YOUR ORDERS(:) ONE(:) YOU MUST RPT MUST EXHAUST YOUR LOCAL INT SOURCES WITH A VIEW DETERMINE PRECISE EN H-HR(.) TWO(:) YOU MUST RPT MUST TAKE UNLIMITED ACTION TO FRUSTRATE EN BID QUICKEST POSSIBLE TIME(.) WARNING(:) EN IS LED BY DESPERATE FOREIGN MERCENARIES RPT FOREIGN MERCENARIES AND MAY YIELD STUBBORNLY(.) EES CIRCA 5000(.) ENDS MSG(.)

The Colonel, a slightly built, rather myopic, tough Sandhurst-trained career soldier, studied the date and time stamped on the message form and looked at his wristwatch. He smiled, showing two rows of teeth yellow from the white kola-nuts which he chewed ceaselessly.

Fifty-five hours from 10 p.m. two nights before, he felt, was still not precise enough. And at 12.15 in the middle of the night, there was little time left to exploit all his local intelligence sources, or even a few of them, as urged by SHQ.

But determining the enemy's precise H-hour, he considered, was the least of his present problems. He thought he could work that one out.

*See Glossary

He picked up his pistol from the far corner of his desk, polished his spectacles, plucked a steel helmet from a peg on the wall behind his chair, and left his office.

"We are going to deploy right now," he announced to his Brigade Major through the window even before he let himself into the narrow room where the Major, like most other key officers of the Division, had kept vigil for the message that had now come.

The young major sprang to his stockinged-feet, bestirring himself from a near-nap.

"Anything happened, sir?"

"Yes, the signal has come through."

"At last," the Major sighed, rubbing his eyes with the back of his hand.

"Yes, at last," the Colonel muttered, fishing for the paper in the breast pocket of his khaki uniform shirt, and re-reading it to refresh his memory.

The Major laced up his boots, put his steel helmet gently on his head and gave the Colonel a quizzical look.

"Did they say when, sir?"

"No. I'm to work that one out."

"Too bad, sir," the younger man clicked his tongue regretfully. "That's the vital info as far as we're concerned; and it's missing. The troops are OK, on alert for the past week, there's sufficient ammo now, but . . ." He broke off, certain that the Colonel understood what he was emphasising.

They were now walking to the Land-Rover parked in the courtyard of the HQ compound.

"Not quite as bad as that, Abdul," the Colonel sounded quietly knowledgeable.

"You don't think so, sir?"

"No, I don't. Because we have a clue. Fifty-five hours from the time and date given on the signal would be about the next five to six hours. If I know my rebels well, they are faithfully conservative in timing ops."

"Like the British, sir."

"Yes, like the British. And us."

"So?"

"So, I make their H-hour 5 or 6 a.m. But I would take a chance on the former. I'll take a further chance and take a five-minute head-start on them."

"Only five minutes, sir? That's rather . . ."

"Yes. Only that. I don't want to stretch my guesses too far; it may well turn out to be 6 a.m. And the five minutes could make a whole lot of difference in terms of ammo. I want to lay on the artillery thick and heavy, and you know what our supply route is like."

160

"Tenuous as the route to heaven, sir."

"That's it, Abdul. Besides, with foreign mercenaries leading the rebels, our calculations may be wider off the target than we can guess."

The command car was purring through the chilly, silent midnight. The Colonel relaxed in his seat and put a fresh piece of kola in his mouth, ground it slowly, savouring its stimulating liquid.

He knew he had a hectic four hours ahead of him. He had 9,000 men, including support units, to deploy. Some 3,000 men more than the figure Rudolf and his commanders estimated.

CHAPTER THIRTY-SEVEN

0400 HOURS

The four Strike Forces which would advance from the old and new access roads were massed some six miles from the city on their two main axes, Highways B and C.

Major Dan Marc and Captain Amilo Relli on Highway B and Major Derek Tremble and Captain Henrique Martinez on Highway C were in regular touch by radio with one another and knew each other's position and movement.

When they link up later at the confluence of the two highways, Dan Marc would be in overall command.

Strike Force Bill, with Major Ball in personal command, was by now deep in the bush, silent in ambush eight hundred yards from their objective, the strategic Nkpor Junction. Behind them, another eight hundred yards inside the bush, was Strike Force Johann, which Schmuts had rejoined about an hour and thirty minutes before, after Jacques Rudolf had arrived and consulted with him.

Strike Force Johann would be the second unit to swing into action, after Bill had made contact at the Junction and spaded through the access route to the Nkisi river banks.

Colonel Rudolf was settled in, with Hans Heinz, in his new tactical field command headquarters. It was the huge two-berth caravan that he had used earlier on at Umuahia, now set up on the wide lawns of an abandoned school premises, three miles behind the massed troops and nine miles from Onitsha.

In the twenty-four hours since the first convoy of artillery and other heavy equipment and supporting crew arrived, the old school compound had become a replica of the 5 Commando Main HQ. Dense green

161

fronds blanketed the walls and roofs. Several military trucks and Land-Rovers painted in the defoliated cobra-skin camouflage of the men's uniforms hulked in the shadows.

Outside Rudolf's caravan, blacked out with heavy green blinds and the thick fronds, armed tension ringed the command post. Sergeant Chiko's little figure, rifle butt firm on the ground, his right palm gripping the barrel just below the fixed bayonet, was barely discernible in the darkness from his green background. The steel helmet seemed too big for his small head, as if it was placed on a cross marking a soldier's grave.

As H-hour drew nearer, his commander had, all too abruptly, it seemed to Chiko, assumed a stern, tough mood which had quickly infected the guards. He found that no one talked with a light heart any more. Everything was now an order, snarled from the muzzle of an automatic rifle, to be carried out *immediately*; *without delay*; *straightaway*. This must be a tough operation. The toughest, the Sergeant thought.

"Halt! Who goes there? Advance to be recognised!" The way the guards were carrying on, hostile and impatient, Chiko feared, they would shoot a stammerer who stumbled in identifying himself quickly.

Inside the air-conditioned cabin itself, the air was no less charged. Rudolf bent over a broad operational map that covered the length and breadth of the table and overlapped a few inches at the edges. Both hands supported his weight on the table, over the map, as he pored silently over the criss-cross that was his objective.

Beneath the air conditioner, on the long, built-in armchair that doubled as a bunk at bedtime, Kapitan Hans Heinz sat expectantly. His thoughts strayed occasionally to Jules and Michel. He felt like a maximum-security prison warder away from his post. He hoped the guards would not go to sleep. The Tactical Headquarters was not fenced in like Headquarters Main.

At Headquarters Main, Colonel Charles Chumah was studying the first significant intercept brought in by the radio corporal. He had been up all night since Rudolf and the last of the men left the HQ.

The intercept was Strike Force Bill reporting their exact position around the junction to the artillery battery that would begin bombardment in thirty minutes.

"That is it!" Chumah told himself, and sprang from behind Rudolf's desk like a man scalded on the buttocks. He couldn't be more certain now that an attack was imminent. H-hour was at hand.

The ants were whispering again. His second message to Major Dimkpa was terse!

IGNORE RPT IGNORE ASAP AND MOVE IMMEDIATELY(.)

Jacques Rudolf glanced anxiously at his watch. It showed 0450 hours to the split second.

He had asked for 600 artillery bombs to be dropped on the city, every conceivable part of it, in the sixty minutes before the infantry moved in at 0600 hours. The first artillery should take off in 9 minutes 30 seconds from now.

Heinz looked at his watch, gave him a slow wink, and nodded his head.

The Sword was poised to swing northwards.

0455 hours.

No one could have heard the distant grunt of the multiple take off.

The first wave of 107 mm artillery bombs landed exactly five minutes to Rudolf's H-hour. Not one dozen; not two; but several scores that must have leapt from a vast battery of guns.

But they did not leap from Rudolf's guns. Rather they landed on his massed locations, on his poised army of men and machines, in a deafening, destructive series of explosions that sent tremors through both the jungles and men alike.

Three of Rudolf's artillery guns, a 105 and two 106 machines, surrounded by crew who had been counting the seconds by their breathing, were knocked out by the sudden attack. The body of a lieutenant, his tense hand raised a second before in impatient anticipation of H-hour, was scattered over the wreckage of a 106 gun, a sacrificial lamb in the opening ritual. His subordinates, seven of them, now wore uniforms dyed in crimson, and showed the surprised eyes of all men caught fatally unawares.

Nearly two companies of men of the infantry lay dead, without having fired a shot, after this first deadly shower.

Confused and incoherent in thought and action, the artillery batteries held their fire, unsure now of what H-hour was meant to be.

It was a deadly effective first strike.

It had caught Colonel Jacques Rudolf in mid-stride as he paced the cabin. The earth heaved beneath him and he felt the caravan tremble. A half-smoked cigarette fell from his fingers onto the floor of the cabin. For a split, confused second he thought that perhaps his watch was some minutes late.

When he looked up from his wrist watch, Hans Heinz was at his side, a frightful look on his face, an arm now placed on Rudolf's as he cocked his ear and listened hard, hoping he had heard wrong.

That was when the second barrage began thudding ferociously in the near distance.

A riot of thoughts and wonderings began to spurt through Rudolf's mind. The fears raised by the air-raid on his HQ one week before came charging through his mind like an assault squad. The enemy had tried to pre-empt his move! Why? For Christ's sake how? A leak? Who? Christ!

He shook himself free from the floor like one breaking out of metal clamps and burst out of the caravan, nearly taking the life out of an already terrified Chiko. Heinz was on his heels, hurtling on to the ground.

Both men looked up at the northern horizon in time to see the darkness lift, like a vast, enormous black veil, and light up with a mingle of tracers and the orange flare of exploding shells.

Huddled in one of a row of trenches on Highway C, poised but now unable to take-off, Strike Force Tremble heard the riot of whistles as bombs flew angrily overhead to explode mercifully in the far distance behind them.

Rudolf and Heinz charged through the darkness, darting silhouettes in the flare of the explosions, and burst into the radio tent.

Panicked and fretful, Rudolf did the first thing that stood up in his riotous thoughts. He wrenched the set from the trembling hands of the South African Lieutenant who commanded his Signals Unit for the operation, and began to flick the knob feverishly.

"TAC HQ calling, is that First Artillery Battery? I want your commander quickly!" he bayed.

"Luiz! What the hell is happening? What the devil are you waiting for? For Christ's sake, forget H-hour and open fire! Now!"

"Yes sir! But . . ."

"But what! For God's sake!"

"But seven of my guns have been put out of action already."

"Christ bloody almighty, Luiz! Is that all you've got? Seven bloody guns? Don't argue with me or I'll shoot your arse off . . . ! What are seven guns knocked off? Knock out seven of the enemy's guns in retaliation! Open up now! Over and out!"

Strike Force Bill was soon on the line.

"Get me your commander, quick!" the Colonel barked.

"Bill! Get a quick move on without delay! To hell with H-hour! The artillery is opening up right now! Over and out!" The Colonel was not waiting for answers.

Schmuts's radio was the next to crackle with the bark and snarl of Rudolf's voice.

"Johann! We're in trouble if we don't move quickly! Move! Move in and join Bill right away and blast the cheeky bastards! Don't wait for the access route! Join Bill and blow up a hole through the junction

164

together. You can drive on to Nkisi with your men afterwards. You're having artillery support any second from now! Over and out!"

Even before he could get Strike Force Marc on the radio next, Rudolf began to hear the heartening kick-back of his own artillery taking off. He hurried to put all the men on the move.

Soon all of them were moving exactly one hour earlier than planned. Soon, too, the artillery bombardment became a duel, if still rather one-sided.

Rudolf's batteries began to thunder vengefully over the heads of the troops on the old and new access roads, imparting some heart into the shaken men.

Under the umbrella of the criss-crossing, whining bombs, Rudolf's infantry began to advance, with different degrees of confidence.

It was an unfortunate advance.

Thirteen minutes after Bill and his forces burst onto the junction and began a bitter, bloody contact with their enemy, artillery bombs began to fall on the junction. They were screaming from behind Strike Force Bill and taking a bloody toll on both sides. Bill Ball stiffened, yelled for the radio men and began to crawl back to meet them half-way.

"Strike Force Bill calling! Artillery battery! Who the devil is behind those guns, you're shelling my men! Over!"

"Where are your men, sir? Over!"

"What the bloody hell do you mean where are my men? We're where we are supposed to be! At the junction, that's where! And for God's sake stop those damned guns! You're killing all my boys! Over and out!"

The shelling did not stop for another ten minutes during which both sides abandoned the coveted junction and crept under cover of trenches and bunkers.

By the time the artillery battery commander had re-directed his fire, Strike Force Johann had arrived to join Major Bill Ball in the resumed fight for the junction.

It was not so dark anymore. Quickly, Bill took advantage of the fresh troops of SF Johann. He halted his badly mauled forces in their trench positions and huddled with Johann Schmuts for a few minutes.

"The boys have taken a bloody nose already, Johann," he sighed. "From our own guns, believe it or not."

The South African was incredulous.

"Yes. They started shelling the junction soon after we made contact. It appears the whole set-up has gone haywire."

"What the hell is Jacques doing?"

"I don't know and I'm not going to wait to find out. I think your men should hit the enemy now. I don't expect any further shelling blunders. Meanwhile I shall regroup the boys. They're badly shaken. Then we join

165

your boys at the junction afterwards. We shall be moving in from both flanks, to try to outflank the bastards, and take the junction over their dead bodies."

Johann Schmuts considered for a brief minute. "Hmm. That's a reverse of the original plan. Or rather, of the re-reverse of it. Jacques had radioed earlier on to move in and join you and take the junction together."

"Lack of communication," Bill muttered sadly. "He didn't tell me that when he called me. We could easily have turned round and attacked your men, thinking we were being outflanked."

"I guess that's how you got the arty falling on you. The battery didn't know you had moved in. Hell of a way to begin a vital operation.

"Right, then, Bill. How soon do you rejoin us?"

"Oh, thirty minutes at the most. Good luck, Johann."

"I need it."

0600 hours.

The artillery barrage from both sides lifted simultaneously, as if by a tacit truce. . . .

Strike Forces Marc and Relli and Tremble and Hans had now linked up at the roundabout where the old and new roads merged, just a mile and half from the heart of the town. On the far right flank was the bush track that led to Bill and Johann's location. A small column led by a captain guarded that flank.

Contact with the enemy during the advance to the roundabout had been light and brief. But as the four Strike Forces now stood in three columns on the doorstep of the city, a deathlike quiet overcast the men and machines.

Already the Division had lost at least three hundred men from the enemy's unexpected artillery blitz, and some eleven heavy guns had been knocked out. Morale was no longer high.

Around the roundabout, ringed by strong defensive trenches once used by the enemy, the commanders began to deploy the men, while Major Dan Marc ordered the mortar platoons, commanded by junior white officers, into the opening action.

In a few minutes scores of mortars were coughing and spitting angrily, as bombs screamed into the city from all flanks.

The bombardment went on for ten minutes before it drew the equally angry response of the men threatened inside the city. And a deadly accurate and robust response it was. A dozen bombs seemed to land for every one that took off from Rudolf's troops. On Captain Amilo Relli's eastern flank, inside the bush, a straight line of troops in a slit trench suddenly collapsed under a hail of bombs, like a bed of flowers over which steaming water had been sprayed.

166

For nearly fifteen minutes everything around the men at the round-about seemed to be exploding with devilish venom: the ground, the trenches, the grass, the tufts of bush, all seemed to be leaping up violently.

Major Dan Marc, a few yards from Relli's right, lifted his head from the trench; grains of sand covered his helmet and neck, and beads of sweat trickled down his temple in the cold morning. In the dull brightness of the early morning he could see thick black smoke rising from the town. 'Our own batteries haven't been doing badly.' he thought with a rising heart. 'These vandals are probably getting nearly as much as they're giving,' he told himself.

Over the parapet of his trench he unfolded a map and studied it hurriedly. Just ahead of the roundabout he could see the street, Oguta Road, the map called it, which led straight as an arrow into the city centre, to the school by the second roundabout marked with a circle on the map.

The major traced the northerly tentacle of the road, and pin-pointed another circle which indicated the vital Nkpor Junction, about three miles from the school, where he knew Strike Force Bill was engaging the enemy. He calculated that if one column of his men broke through the centre of the city, they could strike down the northerly road to Nkpor, hit the enemy there from behind, release the pressure on Bill, and link up with Bill's forces to secure the northerly route completely.

To his left on the map was Iweka Road, passing through the shambles of Ochanja market and encompassing the south-westerly flank of the town up to the most vital objective on that flank—the bridgehead.

Two major routes of advance. Two columns of two Strike Forces each.

Major Dan Marc motioned over his batman, Charlie Bazooka, took the radio from him and began to order the columns into the new positions he had worked out.

The mortar bombs were still screaming and exploding with relentless ferocity. But fortunately, they were thundering with less deadly accuracy now. He was heartened. Soon he gave the order for the advance into the city proper.

0700 hours.

Bill and Johann were doing fine so far, though not without heavy losses in men and equipment.

By 7 a.m. their enemy had been dislodged from the strategic junction, yielding every bloody inch of it stubbornly. The junction was now a litter of faceless, nameless and silent soldiers from both sides. The air smelt of blood and cordite.

Fighting, however, still raged around the soft-drinks factory. Major

167

Bill Ball, dishevelled and soaked with sweat, stood behind an HMG, screaming: "Fire!" as machine-gun bullets and mortar bombs shrieked into the battered factory and angry responses leapt in furious volleys from behind the high roofs.

The infantry lines chattered and the men defending their besieged strong post chorused with equal intensity, escalating the acrimonious dialogue of beserk guns.

Northwards, beyond the junction, a smaller column from both SFs Johann and Bill, under the command of an Irish officer, Captain O'Casey, held its position against an equally small but stubborn force of enemy now severed from their main unit after the junction had been secured by Johann and Bill.

0800 hours.

At eight o'clock dead, Major Dan Marc and his slowly, warily advancing columns began to witness the advancing green steel hulk of the dreaded armoured cars and ferrets.

The Major pressed his field glasses to his eyes. He could see the roundabout in the centre of the city, at the intersection of two major roads, some three hundred yards away. The life-size statue of a political chieftain loomed from its white stone pedestal in the middle of the patch of grass. The roundabout, and the bridgehead on which Major Derek Tremble should be advancing now, were both primary objectives, the capture of which would signal the ultimate doom of the enemy in the city, Dan Marc thought.

But looking through his binoculars at his prize, the Saracen car with its cannon poking out, turrets swivelling, the roundabout suddenly seemed several miles farther away.

"Charlie!" Major Dan Marc called his batman.

"Get your bazooka and one man. I want you to take out that armoured car." He pointed ahead of him. "Take the left flank, move into that broken building and knock it off. On your way!"

The Saracen had trundled slowly out of cover now, hiding its own anxiety and wariness behind a merciless screen of firing and indiscriminate shelling.

From the old-brick school buildings to the right of the column, small arms began to clatter as Major Dan Marc's forces attempted to advance by creeping outside the Saracen's angle of fire.

Charlie Bazooka, a notable marksman who had proved his skill behind the anti-tank machine so well that he lost his own surname in the glory of his successes, continued to peck away energetically but ineffectually at the flame-spurting Saracen. He could see the nose of the little tank far away behind the huge statue, but the statue and the sand kicked up by the exploding shells kept getting in his eyes, spoiling his aim.

Major Dan Marc was now yelling at him, above the clamour of small arms fire and exploding bombs.

"Charlie! Get it now! It's turning tail! Fire!!!"

Charlie hurriedly rubbed the sand from his eyes and looked as the steel green side of the Saracen lumbered its way into a side road. He reached frantically for a shell, slammed it feverishly into the chamber and fired with little finesse or aim.

Charlie shut his eyes as the bomb went off and opened them to the uproar of his cheering mates as the Saracen's left side took in the shell from his bazooka and exploded instantaneously.

Major Dan Marc smiled slowly. The green scarf around his neck was soaked with sweat and his skin nettled. He put his fingers to his throat, loosened the cloth and adjusted his binoculars.

"Advance!" he yelled.

0900 hours.

Sunshine should have brought a glint of victory to Colonel Jacques Rudolf's cold eyes. But it did not.

He had calculated, and told the General so, that Operation Sword would take a couple of hours to sweep into the river those of the enemy who survived his initial assault.

Four hours after the attack began in earnest, the reports he had been receiving were mixed. Badly mixed.

All columns had made moderately reasonable breakthroughs, he admitted. Dan Marc had even reached the centre of the city, holding the roundabout, though he was unable to lend a much-needed hand to Johann and Bill on his right flank.

But the vital Nkisi route had not been secured. And what progress the other Strike Forces had made had been at great cost.

What worried him most now was the increasing menace of armoured cars to which they didn't seem to have a decisive answer.

"I don't like the casualty rate," Rudolf told Heinz. "It's disproportionate to the gains. I don't like that at all."

1000 hours.

That was when Major Chime Dimkpa's convoy rolled into 5 Commando HQ Main.

Colonel Charles Chumah was already on the driveway, waiting for the Major.

The coast was clear for the Colonel. He could now discuss his plans in detail with Major Dimkpa.

He talked, uninterrupted, for about twenty minutes. At the end, he opened the drawer and brought out a sheaf of papers clipped together at the top left hand corner; the revealing messages that Signals had been monitoring for nearly nine hours.

"Read these," he pushed them across the table to Dimkpa.

"Very interesting," Chime said as he read the last page, and passed the papers back. "Are you still sure we don't need more than one battalion of troops, sir?"

"It does depend, I must admit, on what happens to Rudolf in the next twelve hours, Chime," the Colonel answered thoughtfully. "But right now I'm certain we don't need more than a battalion.

"You must bear in mind that I'm anxious to avoid as much bloodshed as possible. If I manage to put a wedge between Rudolf and the bulk of the troops, the rest will be routine."

CHAPTER THIRTY-EIGHT

1100 hours.

The active locations suddenly went dead. It was as if both sides had, by some odd telepathy, agreed on an early lunch-break. Only the columns of smoke from burning depots, fuel plants and warehouses refused to join in the sudden truce.

Captain Amilo Relli leaned back inside a big trench specially dug for him in the rear of his now quiet location around the battered market, and lit a cigarette. He pocketed his lighter and corked the Thermos flask from which he had poured out and drunk two cups of coffee.

Major Derek Tremble crouched over to the river bank under cover of the piles of logs, ripped the red scarf of his Strike Force from his neck and tossed it into the near edge of the river tentatively, almost expecting to draw fire. Nothing happened. He watched the red cloth soak to a dark brown in the muddy water, dived out from behind his cover and retrieved it. He gave the scarf a gentle squeeze, and then curled it back around his throat. He felt cooler.

From his hip pocket, he pulled out a small flask encased in jungle-green cloth, uncorked it and took a long pull at his last mobile supply of whisky. He replaced the flask with a sigh, and lit a cigarette.

Major Dan Marc's forces were now entrenched, strongly he believed, in the city centre, around the roundabout and a large territory of the old school compound. He had not stretched his arm too far beyond this objective, being a professionally cautious man.

He could see the ammo-bearers crouching forwards and backwards to replenish the troops' kits. But he imagined that the enemy would not make a fresh move in the day. They would wait for the cover of dusk. The sun was much too hard.

Up the northern axis, just off Highway A, Major Johann Schmuts was sharing Dan Marc's views.

"I think they've had enough for today," he muttered to himself in a slightly self-congratulatory tone. "Besides, it's a hell of a hot day to start a counter-attack. Phew!"

In the big command bunker over which was built a thick green hut of palm fronds to keep out the sun, he joined Bill Ball for a snack.

On the left flank, far deep in the bush behind the factory, Sergeant Offor heard the leaves rustle in front of him.

He thought at first that it was the wind. He scanned the horizon, but nothing else seemed to be moving. The sun was hard from the sky, the bush was steaming hot and not a tree branch wavered. It couldn't be the wind, he concluded quickly and thumbed his safety catch.

1200 hours.

It was a militarily unholy hour.

But that was when the Federals began what was in effect their real counter-attack.

No artillery or Saracen or Saladin cannon heralded the abrupt end of the sudden lull.

Major Bill Ball and Major Johann Schmuts leapt out of their bunker to meet a volley of fire that sent both men diving into the bush as the chatter of machine-guns filled the air.

Men swarmed around the terrified white men. Their men. They swarmed and stampeded in disarray. In retreat. Soon their most forward trenches were the pursuers' first lines.

Sergeant Offor had taken advantage of the brief forewarning by the rustling bush, and thus was still on his feet, composed and firing. He was spinning and firing into an arc of bush ahead of him. But he, too, was taking cautious backward steps as he fired and spun, as his men stampeded and retreated.

Johann Schmuts and Bill Ball had scrambled frantically to their knees, retrieved their rifles and raced up swiftly to shore up their retreating troops.

"Take up positions right here and fire back, you bastards!" Johann Schmuts yelled through the clangour, hitting a retreating soldier hard on the buttocks with the butt of his rifle. The trooper rubbed his backside, fell to the ground and began to fire fretfully, aimlessly, in response to the order.

One of the trooper's own colleagues, dashing headlong to the safety of the rear, stopped a burst from the trooper's rifle, stiffened, tottered and fell back, his own rifle flying in the air,

The trooper shrieked in anguish. But Johann Schmuts continued to holler.

"Get down and fire back, you bastards!" he roared.

"Fire! Stop there, you bastards! I'll shoot you if you keep running." He transferred his rifle to his left hand, drew his pistol with his right and began to shoot at his own running, un-hearing men.

One of the men Schmuts's pistol struck down was the gallant Sergeant Offor.

The troops all seemed to stop firing at the moment of the cold murder.

Schmuts turned round on them with glaring eyes.

"Fire!" he roared madly, and began firing at them, too.

1300 hours.

The long stretch of pot-holed and dirt-strewn road along the banks of the river was Major Derek Tremble's main axis.

Up to the warehouse on the beach, its roof torn by the withering fire from artillery and mortar guns, and its walls pock-marked with rifle bullets, there was no contact with the opposing forces.

That suited Major Tremble very well. For he was by now the least adventuresome and enthusiastic of the adventurers.

The Major ordered his men to deploy into the trenches around the warehouse once used by the enemy.

With his second-in-command, Captain Ernst Belgar, and two other white officers, Derek Tremble retired to the safety of his rear shelter to smoke and wait.

He hoped and prayed silently that nothing further would happen on the silent axis.

But in his forward line, and unknown to him, curiosity was quietly taking over command of the unit.

The big, battered warehouse just fifty yards from the forward trench was surrounded by cartons, fresh and intact. Even the doors of the warehouse were hanging loose from their broken hinges.

Magnetised by the scene, two volunteers soon began to crouch and crawl towards the warehouse, to the accompaniment of silent prayers from their comrades.

They crept; expectantly, their fingers curled tensely around their triggers.

About ten yards to the warehouse, one of the volunteers picked up a

172

large pebble and tossed it through the broken door. It clanged noisily off the wall, echoing tenfold in the tense stillness of the quiet front.

But nothing happened.

The soldier who threw the stone motioned to his mate with a nod of his head. But the second man still hesitated. The first man shrugged, rose to his feet, tore across to the door of the warehouse, and fell under cover of a pile of cartons.

Still nothing happened.

The daring soldier shrugged again. And his daring soon began to look like a worthwhile hazard when he discovered the cartons were not empty. He could think of nothing that was not there: beer, canned beef, sardines, baked beans and other assorted brands of instant food.

Carefully he put aside his rifle, plucked his bayonet and began to rip open several of the cartons at random.

The beer tasted good. He could not remember when he drank beer last. He grabbed a greedy armful of everything he could before he came out of cover and exhibited his booty to his awe-struck comrades.

It was like an order to charge an enemy on the retreat.

The troops surged forward in one column towards the warehouse, rifles flung away in the sudden, merry pandemonium. Only a few remembered to sling theirs over their shoulders as they descended upon the warehouse and fell to hungrily, thirstily.

From the nearby Federal location, in a block adjacent to the warehouse, a staff sergeant violently snatched a pair of field glasses from his eyes as the hungry men at the bridge of his nose swarmed around like maggots, sickening him. He raised his right arm in the air, stiffly.

"Hungry rebels!" the staff sergeant scoffed.

"Fire!" he hissed, the arm slashing down through the air.

Three Heavy Machine-Guns barked simultaneously. Bottles of beer and cans of beef flew in the air as men shuddered and writhed under the withering hail. Wails and groans filled the warehouse as dead men in the outer ring who took the first impact fell on dying men in front of them.

Over the swelling tide of blood and beer and the mass of ripped, bleeding flesh and canned beef, half a dozen hand grenades hurtled into the warehouse and exploded with tearing impact.

Soon the warehouse was a quiet, smoking crematorium,

By the time Major Derek Tremble, in his rear hideout, had awakened to the fatal assault and reorganised the remnants of his forces to counter-attack the ambushers, the warehouse was already behind the attackers.

1400 hours.

Major Dan Marc's position in the centre of the city became untenable within thirty minutes of the noonday counter-offensive.

Steadily he had retreated to the end of his Oguta road axis; a few hundred yards more he would hit the roundabout point from which his forces had taken off into the city about eight hours previously.

So, to reinforce his striking power and try to match the enemy's flexibility, he had deployed an open-backed Land-Rover mounted with a Heavy Machine-Gun, and put one of his white subordinates, Lieutenant Pierre Coullar, behind the gun.

But the armoured Land-Rover soon returned after a brief brush with the enemy forward lines.

"It's much too open, Dan," Coullar complained, leaping out from behind the gun. "I nearly collected a direct hit from an energar out there," he pointed, wiping the sweat from his leathery face.

"It will be better when night comes."

Marc nodded. "If we last till night, Pierre," he muttered gravely.

"I guess we'll soon be converging out there before dusk." He pointed backwards to the roundabout. "So we better take it easy now, boy. The position doesn't justify any new risks." He lifted his heavy bulk from the bonnet of the Rover and began to stride away.

Dan Marc had gone about thirty feet from the Land-Rover when he stopped abruptly, as if suddenly fore-warned by an inner radar. He groped below his chin for his binoculars and at the same time peered at the top floor of a tall, battered building in the far distance to the left of him.

These damned built-up areas, he cursed silently. I don't like them one bit.

The binoculars didn't make the journey to the bridge of Dan Marc's nose.

The sniper's bullet hit him on the chest between the breasts. His massive frame took the impact with a slight hint of a stagger. He even tried to bring up his rifle. But the second and last bullet threw him sideways.

Pierre Coullar panicked with shock. Charlie Bazooka, just stepping out from behind the armoured Land-Rover to follow his commander, ducked back under the firing and heard the Major mutter something in French.

"The Commander!" Charlie yelled. "The Commander! He has been hit!"

The sniper had thrown aside his rifle now, gripped an HMG and began to fire, halting any attempts to retrieve the dead mercenary.

The shocked Captain was feverishly calling HQ with the bad news.

"SF Marc calling TAC! SF Marc calling! Are you there?"

"Very much so. What's happening in your loc? Over," Rudolf's voice crackled anxiously.

174

"Bad news sir. Terrible news!" Coullar yelled. "The Major's been shot! Over."

The communication ceased for several tense seconds.

"Is it very bad?" the Colonel's voice was now subdued.

"Very bad, sir. He's dead. Shot by a sniper."

"Who's that?"

"Lieutenant Coullar, sir, 2 i/c."

"Listen. You must, repeat must, recover the body at all costs and report back to me. Over and out!"

"Hey, you there!" Coullar called, motioning over some dozen ammo-bearers. "Come here!"

"And you and you, all of you," he told the ammo-bearers. "You get in there, right there, and drag out the Commander's body. Charlie will cover you with the HMG."

The men peered at the body under the shroud of machine-gun fire and hesitated visibly.

"Quick!" Coullar barked, thumbing the pistol on his waist.

Six of the men including Charlie Bazooka, died in the attempt to retrieve Marc's corpse.

1500 hours.

News of the death of Major Dan Marc spread quickly across the location.

"Christ, Dan's dead!" cried Johann Schmuts. "Time to get the hell out of here, Bill."

Captain Amilo Relli slammed the set down with a curse after hearing the news, picked himself and his rifle up from his trench and shook his head.

Dilout wounded. Dan dead. Metzer bitten by a snake. Damned if I'll be the next, Relli swore silently and began to make his way to the safety of the rear-most location as the enemy on his axis continued to advance by leaps.

It was nearly thirty minutes after Captain Relli left that Second Lieutenant Rex Udo discovered that the Relli Strike Force was without a single commander. Only a couple of NCOs and his sharply diminished troops hung on to the crumbling lines.

With little time to find out where his Commander had gone, Rex returned to the side of his men.

But the boys, too, were getting nervous both for want of effective command and from the pressure from the enemy.

Rex distributed the handful of fresh magazines he had collected from Relli's abandoned command post and tried to rally the men for a final, desperate bid to staunch the eroding lines.

Ten minutes later, Lieutenant Rex was still in position, behind his rifle, his ammunition supply vastly increased by the magazines of those dead around him.

Tears blurred his eyes as he surveyed the devastation in his former area of control.

Rex began to hum the 'Song of the Unknown Soldier†', which had been taught them by the Propaganda Directorate:

> My flanks are turned
> My centre gives way
> My position is desperate—
> I attack!
> I find not my of'cer
> I find not a friend,
> I remember my mission—
> I attack!
> I comb through the bush.
> My joints ache me,
> Biafra comes to mind—
> I attack!
> My of'cer stands waving
> My flanks are moving,
> Biafra takes the chase—
> We advance!

He knew well he could not advance.

Rex picked up his rifle and a handful of magazines, and began to move to the rear, too.

Captain Amilo Relli was leaning on a Land-Rover, smoking and watching without expression the pandemonium of retreat to the roundabout from where they had taken off in arms earlier in the morning. It was now the rendezvous of the beaten army.

A convoy of truck-drawn artillery pieces was already clattering down the new road, headed for Nnewi. Another truck laden with wounded and bleeding men was rounding the corner out of the Oguta Road axis of SF Marc.

The first survivors from Derek Tremble's diminished forces were trekking wearily towards the roundabout.

Strike Force Hans had fallen back earlier to the same dismal place, leaving behind a company of their men who were encircled in the post office premises.

Very soon every survivor was in the roundabout. The retreat was complete.

†'Song of the Unknown Soldier' was composed for troops by the Military Publications Unit of the Biafran War Information Bureau.

CHAPTER THIRTY-NINE

1600 hours.

Colonel Jacques Rudolf remained in his caravan as the endless, cheerless reports streamed in.

When all the surviving units had been reported at the roundabout rendezvous he sent a terse order to Johann Schmuts:

REORGANISE AND HOLD THE ROUNDABOUT(.)
AWAIT FURTHER ORDERS(.)

The roundabout, Rudolf knew, was very vital to whatever he decided to do next, as it secured both old and new access routes to his HQ nine miles south.

Defence Operations and State Lodge had been in hourly contact, and Rudolf expected their reaction to the latest development before long.

1700 hours

Colonel Chumah and Major Dimkpa studied their last intercept, Colonel Rudolf's terse order to the roundabout troops, with some bafflement.

"They might try another attack in the night and they might decide to beat a full retreat," the Colonel reasoned without certainty in his voice. "Rudolf is much too shrewd, Chime. By staying at the roundabout, a kind of half-way house, he leaves everyone, including the enemy, guessing. You know, poised to attack and poised to retreat; that sort of situation."

"Hadn't we better risk a move to Ihioma, hoping nothing develops before we get there in the next hour or so?" the Major suggested.

"I've thought about that. I think I'll leave word with the signals chaps to route all messages henceforth to Air HQ, Ihioma."

1800 Hours

As Colonel Chumah, Major Dimkpa and their tiny force of just over a battalion were heading for Ihioma, a stern message was crackling out of the signals tent in Colonel Rudolf's Tactical Headquarters near Onitsha.

FLASH
FM: DEF OPS
TO: COMD 5 CDO
INFO: AHQ TAC(.) DHQ(.) CGS(.)
C-IN-C FOR COMD(.)

UNDERSTAND YOU HAVE LOST ONITSHA TOGETHER WITH NKPOR JUNCTION DESPITE ALL ASSISTANCE GIVEN TO YOU(.) THE LOSS OF ONITSHA PLACES SOUTHERN HINTERLAND ESPECIALLY ULI IN JEOPARDY AND OUR CREDIBILITY IN DOUBT(.) YOU MUST RPT MUST RETAKE ONITSHA WITHIN TWENTYFOUR HOURS AND REPORT BACK TO ME(.) YOU MUST CONCENTRATE EFFORTS(.) LETS NOT HAVE A REPEAT OF ABA AND UGBA JUNCTION(.) ALL ACK(.) ENDS MSG(.)

Colonel Jacques Rudolf read the message without expression, passed it to Kapitan Hans Heinz and began to pace the cabin, arms behind his back.

He stopped in front of Heinz as he finished reading the signal. Heinz looked up at him and nodded gravely.

'Well . . . ?" Heinz asked briefly

"I could have drafted that word for word," Rudolf said. "I knew it was coming."

Rudolf resumed his thoughtful pacing.

"Grave decisions are preceded by hesitation, Hans," he said sagely. "But not too much hesitation," he added.

"I guess I have hesitated enough. We've no choice now. I can't throw the troops back into Onitsha. Hell, no. Not with Dan dead. Our own boys just can't do it. And if we risk it and get beaten back, I know what the next signal from Umuahia will be. So why wait for it?"

Hans Heinz rose slowly from his seat and came face to face with Rudolf. He stopped, put a restraining hand on the Colonel's shoulder, and took a deep breath.

"The best time is always now, Jacques," he sighed. "I think we've done a great deal to avoid having to come to this point. But here we are. We don't want to leave this dusty country feet first, do we?"

"Right, Hans. Get a message to the roundabout, to Johann," Rudolf sounded suddenly businesslike. "Tell him to begin a quiet and orderly withdrawal to the TAC, to here. I'll get Eleven Division to move their men to plug the roundabout."

"Hans," Rudolf called suddenly. "On second thoughts, get the message across by hand. We have entered the critical stage of this business. Discretion is vital for the next couple of hours."

Thus Colonel Chumah's intercept men did not know of the sudden withdrawal of 5 Commando from the roundabout to the TAC HQ.

There was only one way the sword could swing now—southwards.

1930 hours.

Dusk had settled quietly over the Tactical Headquarters when the first convoy of 5 Commando troops pulled into Rudolf's base.

And dusk had settled over the Air Headquarters, too, when Colonel Charles Chumah and his minuscule force arrived at Ihioma.

At Rudolf's Headquarters, a preliminary check had shown some 2,500 men dead or injured and a total of 15 guns destroyed, damaged or captured. Any more casualties and it would have been critical, Rudolf thought.

The meal Rudolf had ordered for the resting troops that evening had been extraordinarily lavish.

Their kit was replenished and fresh uniforms issued to those whose had even the tiniest tear. The *kinkana*, crude, fiery stuff that was three times more potent than ordinary gin, flowed freely from hand to mouth.

It was an unusual, curious refreshment for an army that had just suffered a serious defeat.

Colonel Charles Chumah's first action at Ihioma was to meet with the Chief of Air Staff (COAS), an old friend and a Sandhurst course-mate who had later taken to the wing when the air force was created.

Despite their long-standing amity, the Colonel thought it was too early in his plans to trust him with too much truth. Not that he doubted the integrity of his old friend. But he was sure that the ability to hold a friend's confidence and the strength to endure knowledge of a treasonable intention were two different qualities.

As Chumah had expected, a message from 5 Commando HQ Main was waiting for him. It was the General's dramatic order to Rudolf as monitored by Chumah's intercept men.

He folded the message after reading it, and suppressing his growing excitement, put it in his breast pocket.

The operations at Onitsha, he lied smoothly to the COAS, was entering the critical stage and the reinforcement under his command was going to use the Air HQ as a transit camp for the night.

That was perfectly all right by the air chief.

2000 hours.

A generous meal and several minutes' rest under the cool of the dusk could put even a beaten army in a reasonable frame very soon. The Christian Brothers themselves, now in the know and fully briefed on the implications of Sword Two, were a new breed of eager commanders.

And when the troops heard what Colonel Rudolf had to tell them that evening, the shock of the overwhelming peril the commander disclosed transformed their restful mood into a fresh fighting spirit.

While the General waited for Rudolf's acknowledgement of his message, he had no means of knowing that the mercenary Colonel was preparing to play his last card.

Rudolf's voice was suitably grave.

179

"I have just got an urgent signal from the C-in-C," he waved the piece of paper at the ranks of men in the faint darkness.

"It is not pleasant news, and has nothing to do with our present temporary set-back. We are going to forget Onitsha for now. For right now the airstrip, your only link with the outside world, your lifeline, as the General called it, is seriously threatened!"

A ripple of shock murmured through the lines of men.

Rudolf continued gravely. "Our information says that a small but heavily equipped enemy assault squad is headed right now for the airstrip, after sneaking across the ROB* lines last night.

"They are believed to be trekking through the jungle towards Mgbidi and almost avoided detection. Well, we've detected them now, though not early enough, for they are believed to be already within reach of the southern end of the airstrip. Their objective is to put the airstrip out of action under cover of darkness—tonight!

"The General says to you all, Onitsha is meaningless if the airstrip is endangered. You will proceed to the airstrip immediately, wait for the advancing force, and wipe them out with maximum speed.

"We may yet return to Onitsha to finish our task here, but right now we have to deal with this new threat in a manner that befits a commando force. It is the kind of thing you're trained for, and it is your biggest test so far.

"I'll be right there with you at this grave hour, and I wish you all good luck."

It was the powerful rhetoric of deceit. And it worked.

Johann Schmuts was grinning inwardly, as he ordered the convoy of empty trucks into readiness for the eager troops.

Kapitan Hans Heinz worried over his usual problem of coping with prisoners Michel and Jules. But this time he was relieved that he would not have them in his hands for too long now.

At the head of the long line of trucks and jeeps was Colonel Jacques Rudolf, behind the wheel of an open Land-Rover, and Kapitan Hans Heinz in the passenger seat beside him. An HMG had been mounted on the back of the Land-Rover, with five armed white officers behind the gun.

For once, Colonel Jacques Rudolf, Commander of the 5 Commando Division, was *leading* his men.

2100 hours.

At 5 Commando Main the sleep-starved corporal manning the signals felt the TAC radio suddenly go off the air at fifteen minutes past eight.

That was curious, the corporal thought without any serious suspicion.

*See Glossary

180

He flicked switches, turned and twisted knobs, coaxed and cajoled the set. But not a sound seemed to be coming. Only a vacant bleep-bleep. The corporal shrugged his resignation, bent over the table and tried to get some sleep.

The airstrip was about twenty-five miles south of Rudolf's abandoned Tactical Headquarters on the new, broad and flat highway to Owerri, from which the strip was carved out. On a straight, geographical line across the farmlands, it was less than ten miles from Ihioma, the Head-quarters of the Air Force. But Ihioma town had its back to the airstrip, the town being accessible from the north only by a once-tarred but now decrepit road that actually forked off the new highway at Ihiala, at a point three miles from the airstrip proper.

At exactly the time that Rudolf's convoy passed that battered road that led to Ihioma, and continued on the high-security stretch of three miles that lead to the airstrip, Colonel Chumah was readying himself to get some sleep. For nearly an hour he had had no messages from the 5 Commando intercept man. He felt it was safe to conclude that Rudolf was lying low for an early morning counter-attack on Onitsha.

"Chime, you can stay up a little longer if you are fit," he told his deputy. "But I must get some sleep. I don't know what tomorrow's going to give birth to."

"All right, sir. I've had enough of quiet times down south to last me for a while."

Colonel Rudolf's armed vanguard sped away from the main convoy as soon as he entered the high-security stretch of the airstrip.

The northern tip of the airstrip from which he was approaching was blanketed in darkness and the silence that usually descended on the area soon after dusk and night raids became possible. Rudolf halted the Land-Rover just before the point where the highway widened four-fold on to the runway proper, and hopped to the ground.

"You get down here," he whispered urgently to one of the five white men behind the heavy gun. The man did.

"Now you stay right here. Your job is to halt the trucks when the first one gets here, and get Major Schmuts to take over. We'll be right back."

"Yes, sir!"

He was back behind the steering wheel in a flash, shooting off down the smooth runway. He gunned the motor into higher speed and scanned both sides of the runway. Hans Heinz's face was framed against the left side of the car as he, too, peered hard into the distant bushes.

Midway down the runway, in the faint light from the bright stars in the open clear skies, Rudolf slowed down at Heinz's urging.

To his left, looking past Heinz's face, he, too, could make out the silhouette of the single-storeyed building, now blacked out by darkness and shrouded in palm fronds. A tiny blade of light peeped out from a careless slit in the black-out.

The control tower.

"That's it, Jacques," Heinz muttered. "I think I remember it now."

"Right then. How do we drive up there?"

"No idea. But we don't have to. Just drive up to the edge of the tarmac, get the car facing the building so that the boys can keep it covered. Then we trek across the bush."

Rudolf ordered two men to stay behind the gun, and took two along with Hans Heinz.

"Come on!" Rudolf ordered.

Through the stretch of low bush they waded and soon burst out onto the edge of the fence that enclosed the building, set on a vast, sandy clearing.

Led by Rudolf they walked in a single line along the shelter of the high fence and soon found the driveway that led to the front side of the building, their weapons concealed.

There Rudolf halted, motioned the men into a crouching position, and began to flank right to get to the gate which he knew would be guarded. On to the driveway now, Rudolf and his party rose to their full height and began to stride unhurriedly towards the gate.

"Halt!"

They did.

"Who goes there!"

"Friends," Rudolf said calmly.

"Advance friends to be recognised!"

They did, as a torch-light flashed into their faces.

"What's the pass-word for tonight, friends?" asked the voice behind the torch-light.

God! Rudolf nearly gasped out aloud; but recovered quickly.

"Christian Brothers . . ." he said. "We're the Christian Brothers. Four of us. On surprise checks on the airstrip."

"Oh, the Christian Brothers!" the voice exclaimed happily. "Come in, sir!"

The bar rose heavenwards.

The three guards' rifles lowered.

Rudolf stepped through the gate, sidled to the side of the guard who raised the bar, as if to make way for his comrades following behind him. Heinz followed, but stopped on the other side of the gate too, abreast with the second guard.

The guard who opened the gate was behind Rudolf's two other lieutenants, but his suspicion was long dead and buried.

182

Rudolf cupped a hand to his mouth and cleared his throat. His men got the signal.

One.

Two.

Three.

They broke the guards' necks in one swift strike each using the edge of their open hand like a hatchet. Not a sound escaped from any of the dead men.

"The building!" Rudolf's voice ground with urgency. "You, two of you guard the entrance. Up we go, Hans!"

They drew their pistols.

A control room was second home to former Luftwaffe pilot Kapitan Hans Heinz.

Rudolf herded the three men on duty into one of the several rooms that led out to the large empty parlour that was the control room. He locked the room, went down and brought one of the junior officers to guard the door.

Meanwhile, Hans Heinz had the headphones clamped over his head and everything under control.

Back at the northern end of the runway where the main convoy under Johann Schmuts had been halted, Rudolf stopped his armed Land-Rover and whispered urgently to Johann.

"The control room is secure now. No troubles."

"What next?"

"We move the men into positions, careful how you do it, Johann. Say the enemy has landed at the southern end of the strip, so we take positions up to a point just past the middle of the runway. I expect there will be a lot of civilians down at the southern end and we don't want to get tangled up with them now. Certainly we must avoid contact between our troops and anybody down the other end. For Christ's sake, you must be careful how you deploy them. Then set up the heavy guns. But no firing. Just keep everyone ready but still."

"I get you, Jacques," Johann assured him. "I'll leave the bulk of the men at this end of the strip. . . ."

"That's the idea. They can get busy on digging trenches and so on. Then you can have a Strike Force up the runway, in position, in the bushes of course, say up to three hundred yards to the northern end. Then wait for further orders!"

"It's quite clear, Jacques."

"Good. Now I'll give you thirty minutes and I'll get on to Umuahia. I'm going to love to shock the hell out of the General."

Before Rudolf turned the Land-Rover to return to the control tower building, now to be his command post, Johann Schmuts was already growling out his orders to the ignorant, eager troops.

2210 hours.
  The message that the radio was crackling out at ten minutes past ten in the Defence Operations signals room began to strike terror into the night staff soon after the preliminary opening.

FLASH
FROM: CHRISTIAN BROTHERS
TO: DEF OPS
COMD 5 CDO FOR C-IN-C

ACK YOUR MSG RE ONITSHA(.) REGRET YOUR ORDERS AND IMPLICATIONS UNACCEPTABLE(.) WILL BE SAD TO KNOW YOUR AIRSTRIP FIRMLY IN HANDS OF CHRISTIAN BROTHERS AND TPS OF 5 CDO(.) FIVE THOUSAND STRONG(.) REMEMBER YOU ATTACK AT RISK OF LIVES OF YOUR OWN TPS HERE(.) DEMAND(:) 2 MILLION DOLLARS IN SIGNED CERTIFIED OPEN CHEQUE TERMINAL PAY FOR CHRISTIAN BROTHERS CASHABLE ZURICH(.) WARNING(:) NO TRICKS(.) DEMAND TWO(:) SAFE CONDUCT FOR ALL CHRISTIAN BROTHERS IN FIRST AVAILABLE PLANE(.) AIRCRAFT TO BE RELEASED ONLY AFTER CHEQUE IS CASHED(.) WARNING AGAIN(:) NO TRICKS BY YOUR AGENTS IN EUROPE OR AIRCRAFT WILL BE BLOWN UP(.) AWAIT YOUR RESPONSE(.) MEANWHILE RESERVE RIGHT TO SEIZE ANY AIRCRAFT AND CARGO LANDING ON AIRSTRIP UNTIL DEMANDS MET(.) REGRET INCONVENIENCE(.) ENDS MESSAGE(.)

  Five minutes after the message came through the beam, the Chief of Defence Operations, roused from a fruitless vigil over the long quiet Onitsha front, was on the telephone to the General, breathlessly reading off the startling ultimatum from the Christian Brothers.
  The handset seemed to go dead in his hand as a chilly silence answered from the other end. Then the telephone came alive again.
  "Listen," said the voice, grave, aggrieved and sombre. "This is a most flagrant act of treacherous mutiny, and it should be dealt with accordingly. Our response should be decisive and prompt."
  "Yes, sir," said the Chief of Defence Operations.
  "Where is Colonel Chumah right now? I know he was not engaged in the ill-fated Onitsha Operations. Can you locate him?"

"I should imagine, sir, that he is at 5 Commando HQ Main."

"All right. Take these down."

The Chief of Defence Operations drew a scribbling pad and plucked a ball-point from his pencil rack.

"First priority. You will put an urgent telex message to Lisbon. No aircraft, repeat no aircraft takes off for the airstrip until further notice. They must stop Sao Thome right away."

"Yes, sir," the Chief said, scribbling furiously to keep pace.

"You will mobilise all available manpower with the minimum of delay. You will include practically all units within the neighbouring garrisons and send an urgent signal recalling all units that can be spared from the less active fronts."

"Yes sir."

"You will do everything possible to get in touch with Colonel Chumah immediately. Tell him I wish him to handle the emergency that has developed. Are you following me?"

"Certainly, sir."

"Colonel Chumah is to take immediate command of all the forces you mobilise meanwhile, and henceforth he is to be in overall command of all military formations in the northern territorial command. His first assignment is to proceed without delay to the airstrip and deal with the situation posed by the mercenaries as he deems necessary. Get that clear: as he deems necessary. But," the General paused to emphasise a vital proviso, "but within the limits of reasonable consideration for the lives and security of our own troops apparently being misled by Rudolf and his treacherous gang. Is that quite clear?"

"Perfectly clear, sir."

"One more thing: Under no circumstances whatsoever should Colonel Chumah enter into negotiations or deals with Rudolf. Directly or in-directly. You must emphasise my orders. The whole idea of our continued resistance of a powerful vandal force is defeated if we yield to extortion and blackmail by a miserable band of money-seeking gangsters! This is of the utmost importance."

"I understand, sir."

The voice paused.

"All right. That's all for the moment. I'll call you back if I have any fresh thoughts. But straightaway, get a high priority telex to Lisbon."

"I will do that right away, sir."

2300 hours.

A few minutes after the General issued his orders, Umuahia was awake with frantic midnight activity.

The direct Defence Operations/Air Headquarters radio and telephone network, one of the several pieces of sophisticated communication equipment 'donated' by a French philanthropist who might have been an SDECE* operative, buzzed at 11 p.m. It did not buzz very often or so late these days, since the Air Force was grounded for lack of wings.

The duty Air Staff Officer picked up the receiver hastily, listened for a few seconds and said, "Hold on, sir. I think he is in a room on the ground floor. I'll fetch him in a minute."

"Who's that?" a voice blurred by sleep asked the rattling door.

"Me, sir. Chime." He sounded urgent.

"Chime!" The voice was suddenly awake. "Hang on a second."

Colonel Chumah rose from his bunk in the Chief of Air Staff's guests' quarters and opened the door.

"A call from Umuahia for you, sir," Chime Dimkpa panted, out of breath from a three hundred yards' sprint across the lawns.

"And who's calling at this unearthly hour?"

"I don't know, sir, the ASO* has the call. I didn't wait to find out, sir. I was . . ." Chime Dimkpa hesitated.

"Well, we'll find out in a minute," the Colonel said decisively. He found his slippers beside his bunk in the dark room and stepped out in his billowing night wrappers.

"Def-Ops calling. Where've you been, Charles? I've been calling 5 Codo HQ Main for you all night. What are you doing in Ihioma for Christ's sake?" The Chief of Defence Operations asked.

"Is that why you're calling at this unholy hour? If you must know, I'm in transit," he muttered into the handset.

"Transit? Where on earth to?"

"Don't you know there's a war on, Chief? And that we've had an operation going on at Onitsha? I was getting fed up sitting idly and looking after Colonel Rudolf's empty barracks! Now what are you calling me for? I want to get some sleep."

"Well, Charles, you won't be sitting idle for long now. Who's with you there?"

"Only Chime. Major Dimkpa."

"Charles. There is a terrible crisis of supreme emergency. Take a good hold on yourself and listen carefully."

"I'm on tranquillisers. Go ahead."

The Chief began to read out, first Rudolf's ultimatum, and by the time he got to the General's orders to Colonel Chumah, the Second-in-command of 5 Commando Division was swearing profusely.

"Chief," Chumah's grave voice began to grind as soon as the Chief of Def-Ops had finished. "I want two things."

"One, I want an urgent command directive from the C-in-C to all
*See Glossary

186

service heads and unit commanders for their utmost co-operation. I don't want anyone to think I'm imposing on him. All service heads, I said, because I'm going to need everything I can lay my hands on from all formations."

"That has been done already," the Chief of Def-Ops told him.

"Finally, everything for me should henceforth be directed to Ihioma. Thank you."

He slammed the receiver down.

"It has happened, Chime. The mercenaries have revolted, seized the airstrip with the help of our boys and are demanding two million dollars in ransom or else!"

Chime Dimkpa froze on his feet. They had not reckoned with such an eventuality.

CHAPTER FORTY

0000 HOURS: MIDNIGHT.

The nightly flights from Lisbon to the airstrip usually took sixteen hours. An aircraft would take off from Lisbon in the night and end its first stage on the small secret strip on the Portuguese-controlled island of Sao Thome where it refuelled, waited for the next dusk and began the last stretch to the airstrip where it generally arrived an hour or two after midnight. Barring all accidents and bomber harassments, that was.

Thus by the time the General's order had pattered out of the tele-printer in the small ground-floor room next door to the kitchen at 16 Avenida Torrede de Belem at a little after midnight, gone through the pipeline to the city offices of the agency that ran the clandestine airline, for onward transmission to its operatives in Sao Thome, it was half-past midnight. The first Super Constellation aircraft had long since tilted its tail in the night air more than halfway on its journey to the airstrip.

However, with the usual departure gaps of about sixty-five minutes, a Super Constellation was able to be recalled in mid air, another Constel-lation and a DC-3 belonging to a church organisation were stopped on the ground, saved by a matter of hours from falling into Colonel Rudolf's waiting hands at Uli airstrip.

0100 hours.

On the dark lawns of the Air Headquarters parade ground, Colonel Charles Chumah's rag-tag force stood stiffly to attention.

The 1,100 men of the Ninth Mile Corner from Major Chime Dimkpa's

Brigade had been joined a little earlier by an unarmed motley of Air Force ground-men, Air Headquarters guards, even Air Policemen and conscripts still in the first week of their training. They numbered a hundred and twenty odd. Most were barefoot and bareheaded, and those who weren't, wore tattered canvas shoes brown with mud, and faded peaked khaki caps.

They waited in the chilly midnight air for the Colonel who, now dressed and appropriately armed with a fighting temper, was having a hurried discussion with the startled Chief of Air Staff on the crisis at the airstrip. And, though they did not know it, they were waiting, too, for the vital reinforcement of men and arms from Umuahia.

Cetme Sammy, at the extreme end of the front row, stole his hands behind his back and rubbed his hands together to keep off the cold.

Suddenly, the Major's voice rapped out and Cetme Sammy quickly brought his freezing hands to his sides again.

"Squad! Attention!"

Sammy was glad of the chance to stamp his feet which now no longer felt a part of him.

"As you were!"

"Attention!"

"Stand easy!" It was the Colonel's voice.

Colonel Chumah the 2 i/c! Cetme Sammy almost cried out. When the Major had said they were going on an undisclosed operation as soon as the Colonel had addressed them, Sammy had no idea which Colonel or what operation.

From the tiny pocket of his tattered second-hand swimming trunks, he fished out the neatly folded note from his cousin Captain Michel.

He was filled with gladness now that he had not torn it up in his despair and disconsolation six days previously. Even if it was too late.

"The next few hours will be long and bitter!" the Colonel was saying. "In the next hour or so you'll be joined by troops from Umuahia for one of the most critical operations since this war began.

"I know many of you here; I have fought with many of you. I know you're brave, courageous and gallant men. But your past success will be buried in shame if you fail in tonight's operation. And our setbacks of the past will look like a false alarm in comparison. What you are going in for tonight is, in a way, a sad and regrettable but still necessary operation. You're going to fight some of our own comrades of the 5 Commando Division! They are not our enemy; they are innocent officers and men who have been misled by white mercenaries into a treasonable act. And this is very important: if you can spare their lives without endangering your own, you must do so. Remember they are your comrades in arms. Your enemy is the mercenaries."

188

The contents of Michel's note rang in Cetme Sammy's head as the Colonel paused for breath. Sammy took a hesitant step forward, and froze doubly as he felt the Colonel's tall figure turn towards his direction in the darkness.

"Who's that moving!" the Colonel barked. "Where are you going?" Sammy hesitated and finally rushed out towards the Colonel, the hand with the note outstretched.

"What's that?" asked the Colonel angrily.

"And where's Captain Michel now?" the Colonel asked, after reading the message with the aid of his cigarette lighter.

"I don't know sir. He might be dead now, sir, after what you just said happened."

0200 hours.

The Super Constellation circled the dimly lit airstrip apprehensively and began its most difficult task: taking its bearing for a landing. Ground communication was normal, though the pilot did not give much thought to the foreign accent from the control tower.

"This is Genocide calling!"

"Anabelle still. You're all clear," Hans said confidently. They had lined both sides of the runway, as they remembered it from the night they landed, with hurricane lamps fitted with red globes.

In another ten minutes or so the giant aircraft was bestriding the runway. The whole scene reminded Rudolf of the night of their arrival eleven months before.

The plane was the same Super Constellation, the pilot a different man, a fair-haired, close-cropped, middle-aged gun-runner with a lazy American drawl. He was on his twelfth run to the airstrip.

The seats had been ripped off to make room for cargo. There was only a crew of three: the pilot, his co-pilot and one of the General's agents, a minor official based in Lisbon who took charge of the cargo, and whom Johann Schmuts took away immediately the gangway rolled up to the open door.

Schmuts had mobilised some of the troops and turned them into ground crew. Quickly they began to off-load the massive cargo.

Meanwhile Jacques Rudolf was leaning on the door of the cockpit.

"Well, I hope you had a good flight," he asked the pilot in a rather friendly tone.

"Like hell I did, buddy," the pilot bantered, shifting the earphones from his ears. "Whaddya know, I goddamn near bumped the old ship up there," he pointed a finger backwards. "Guy with the bats was damned scared of something or is new in this job. Not a job for nervous guys, I always told them."

189

"Oh, well, you shouldn't blame him," Rudolf sighed, "we are having a bit of trouble at the moment." He could not add that the guy with the bats had a rifle trained on him by Johann hiding in the shadows.

"You're telling me!" the pilot chuckled. "Say, what in tarnation are you guys doing on the strip, anyhow? Taking a run-out powder or something? Are them Feds closing in on ya?"

"No. We're all right," Rudolf tried a chuckle of his own. "Just getting a couple of things sorted out. Say, you may have to get down a bit and maybe lie low," Rudolf suggested. "You and your mate. The General's orders. While the coast clears."

"What?" the pilot was horrified. "Me stick around while the coast clears? To hell with the coast, bud. Can't see it getting any clearer than it is. I don't wanna be here when the Feds get in. I was in Korea, buddy, and I guess that's OK for a life-time. Besides, I got me a lovely wife and a couple of kids to look after. I'm gonna blow the hell outa here soon as them guys clear the luggage." He replaced the earphones over his head.

"But that's the General's orders. And I think it's in your interest, too," Rudolf insisted, still gently. "There might be an air raid. The last Intruder hasn't been around yet."

"To hell with your General, buddy. I don't take no orders from no goddamn General. I ain't in no General's army. And while we're at it, tell your General to think about calling it quits. He ain't got a dog's chance in hell if you ask me.

"Just let me know when they've got all them stuff down," he added. "Say, you're a nice sorta guy," he continued, now chattily. "Remind me to give you a drink at the Ritz when you get out to Lisbon some day." He winked. "Hank Watson's the name, ship's captain." He extended a handshake.

But what Hank Watson saw was the dark blue steel barrel of Rudolf's automatic pistol.

"You two will get out of your seats quietly and follow me. That's an order. *My* order. I told you there's an emergency. Move!"

"What the . . . !"

"Move, I said!"

Major Johann Schmuts, just through with supervising the evacuation of the crates from the main cabin, joined Rudolf.

"Take them away. To the control tower. Hans will show you the room." Schmuts pulled out his pistol from his waistband and jerked his head sideways for the men to move up.

"Sorry about this business, Hank," Rudolf's voice was suddenly gentle again, "but we can talk it over later. Maybe over that drink at the Ritz, some day."

*   *   *

190

The cargo from the aircraft was massive. Crates and boxes of ammunition, light and heavy; cartons of canned food, liquor, cigarettes, cosmetics and even clothing for the wives and mistresses of high officials and top officers, and several items of the essentials that trickled thus daily into the rebel enclave.

Rudolf calculated there was enough food and ammunition to keep the troops in supply for another day. That would be enough. One more day. The General certainly couldn't hold out for more than 48 hours at the most. Not without the daily flights on which his survival depended; not with two-thirds of his armoury in the hands of the 5 Commando; not with his best fighting forces now on the Colonel's side even if they didn't know it. Rudolf was positive.

"They're safe in there now, Jacques," Johann Schmuts was returning to the aircraft when he met Rudolf on the landing. "A bit crowded now, with that kaffir Michel and the rest. I wish I knew why the hell we're still keeping them around."

"We shan't be for long, Johann," Rudolf promised.

Right at that moment, Colonel Chumah's forces, reinforced by 1,800 men with the guns, rifles and scanty remnants of the armoury from Umuahia, were marching through the tracks, path-ways and by-ways of Ubullu and the other tiny villages bordering the airstrip on the south-east, heading for the highway to Mgbidi at the southern end of the airstrip.

Acting on his hunting dog's instincts, Rudolf began to gear up for a possible confrontation. His determination was now strengthened in no small measure by the aircraft and its crew now in his hands. He wondered whether he should not send a message to the General informing him that, as his earlier signal warned, he had in fact taken possession of one Super Constellation.

0300 hours.

In the trenches now dug on both extreme edges deep inside the bushes that bordered the airstrip, and right up to two-thirds of the strip's mile-long runway, in the reinforced concrete bunkers which served as air raid shelters for the normal ground staff, Rudolf's forces had crouched and waited for four hours.

Tension and anxiety seemed to heat up the trenches and bunkers. The debacle of Onitsha seemed to have been chased several years down memory lane as expectation became the matter of the moment.

At the control tower Jacques Rudolf was reassured to find Sergeant Chiko and his guards firmly in control around the building. He took away Chiko and two other guards. He would need them around for the long critical hours ahead.

Upstairs Kapitan Hans Heinz's head lolled sideways as he began to despair of any further flights coming in for the night.

Secretly Rudolf considered that his gamble had been built on the premise that the General would more willingly pay the ransom than fight his own troops, on his own ground, risking the destruction of his prized airstrip.

But now, as the night wore thin to early dawn, he began to view the imminence of fighting with secret horror.

But he knew that there was no going back now. And so the answer to his doubts was greater, wilder determination built on the lingering belief that he still held the upper hand over the General.

"If fighting breaks out, I will slam him down with heavy artillery and mortar bombardment. That'll take care of the infantry contact you're worried about," he told Hans Heinz. "We'll hit him from arms' length. He can't hold out against that for long, Hans. Not without supplies from his airstrip."

They had reached the armoured Land-Rover now on the edge of the runway at the end of the bush track. The white officer in steel helmet behind the heavy gun lifted his head as Rudolf drew near and motioned to him in the darkness.

"All's still quiet, sir," he whispered. "We just patrolled up to the southern tip of the runway. Not a damn thing in sight."

Rudolf did not welcome that piece of intelligence report. The tension of no war, no peace, so close to the light of dawn, had of course been the subject of his recent reflection.

"Hans," Rudolf turned to Heinz in the darkness. "Where's the stuff and the gin?" He asked, resorting once more to his mother-tongue.

"Johann's got it," Heinz replied.

"Get him to pass the goods round. Let's get the boys in the proper mood. I think time is running out on the General. The first shot may be fired any minute now."

Twenty minutes later the lines of trenches were aglow and the brisk cold night air was tingling with the acrid smell of pencil-thin wraps of hemp. Each man pulled three lungfuls from the wrap, wet and flat at the end from previous drags, sucked in the air through clenched teeth and passed it to his trench-mate.

Quite a few of them, recent initiates, got the push almost as soon as they 'passed on the joint'. A larger number, near-addicts from months of fighting with Rudolf and the Christian Brothers, spent a few minutes of sobriety before their eye-lids began to droop and their trigger fingers began to itch.

There was enough for everyone. And enough of the potent, home-distilled crude gin that preceded the smoke.

In a few minutes their heads began to sing.

The usual furtive trench murmur and mutter became tinged with harsh and threatening bluster. "God save the first man I see in front of my rifle!" said a menacing voice.

"Where are the *Gwodo-gwodo** vandals from Chad?"

"The vandals are cowards! They're afraid to come. They know we shall blast all of them!"

"Let's sing *Enyimba*!† It will annoy the vandals."

"That no work! There is no vandal who can face me now!"

The mercenaries did not need the pep of drugs or drink to stir themselves. The approaching morning and the absence of response from the General, was enough stimulant.

And as the prospect of confrontation became steadily inevitable, the lawless instincts of outlaws on the loose took firm control of a classic opportunity for adventure.

Kapitan Hans Heinz was back at the armoured Land-Rover with Colonel Rudolf as they waited tensely for something to happen.

In the darkness Rudolf's bodyguards paced nervously in the shadows of their masters, scanning the bushes and the silent skies expectantly. It was Chiko who saw the beam of light first and cried.

"Sah! Look!"

The beam of light from behind the rear of the troops split the northern darkness. In the stillness of the night the groan of a distant motor sounded.

Hans Heinz looked up at the light and cursed bitterly, the after-glow throwing his angrily contorted face in relief.

"I'll go and find out, Jacques. It couldn't be our vehicle. Start up that car, Captain!"

CHAPTER FORTY-ONE

0400 HOURS.

Miss Wenda Britta was a tall, twenty-eight-year-old Swedish spinster with blonde hair, blue eyes and a great love for children.

*Gwodo-gwodo – This was a derisory nickname given to some Nigerian soldiers who were believed to be volunteers from the neighbouring Republic of Chad. The men were believed to be over seven-foot tall, had large feet and waddled clumsily like ducks. Hence the onomatopoeic appellation.

†See Glossary

In the three months since she arrived with the very first half a dozen volunteers from the Swedish Red Cross, she had found more than enough employment for her humanitarian pursuits.

With a team of five local nurses and the unskilled hands of a dozen native volunteers, mainly semi-literate teenage girls with no capital to start up the flourishing war-time trade in scarce goods, Wenda Britta had set up a feeding centre for war orphans threatened by malnutrition.

She had chosen to set up the centre at Ihiala, first because it was near to a well-run missionary hospital, and secondly because it was only three miles from the airstrip from which food supplies and drugs trickled in on the nightly flights.

Wenda Britta slept very little. She worked fourteen hours every day and woke up every midnight to get ready to drive up to the nearby airstrip in her white Land-Rover with the bold Red Cross at the sides, to pick up food and drugs for her 'little babies' as she called the swollen-bellied, round-faced and shiny-skinned children under her care.

This night, she had woken up as usual at midnight, dressed up and gone round the ward, a former primary-school classroom, and made sure that the children were all right. She had remembered hearing the sound of only one aircraft about two hours before, had waited for the other flights, and had neither heard the first one take off nor another arrive.

That was strange. She began to worry. The Intruder, she thought, might have been on one of its nightly harassments. The thought depressed her, suddenly robbing her spirit of the buoyancy that normally followed the sound of arriving aircraft and the prospect of fresh food supplies for her little babies.

Wenda Britta had watched MiG jets swoop down to bomb and strafe her centre twice, killing in all six of her helpless little ones. She had, at the beginning, before food began to arrive in reasonable quantity, wept herself sick as she watched the children die from malnutrition at an average of three a day.

But nothing depressed Wenda Britta as much as the prospect of lack of food for her two hundred and one surviving orphans. Any night she failed to collect her usual trickle from the airstrip seemed to her as if starvation and death were creeping back into the centre.

Finally, despairing of any further flights for the night, Wenda roused Ebele, her senior nurse and friend. Maybe there was something for them on the lone flight that had already landed.

Wenda Britta did not hear the harsh curses of the troops crouching tensely behind artillery guns in the bushes as she drove on to the beginning of the northern end of the airstrip.

194

But nearer the tip of the runway, she did notice with quickened heart-beats the unusual convoy of empty supply trucks lined on both sides of the road. She began to slow down.

Ahead of her she could see twin beams of lights tumbling down towards her. She dipped her powerful head-lamps and let her Land-Rover crawl at a timid pace towards the runway.

Wenda Britta wasted no time in jamming on her brakes as Kapitan Hans Heinz's Land-Rover rode into the dim tunnel of her dipped lights. She trembled with fear as she saw not only the white occupants of the Land-Rover but the long black barrel of the HMG nosing heavenwards above the heads of the occupants.

The Swedish spinster's spine dripped with cold fear as Kapitan Hans Heinz's jackboots thudded on to the tarmac, echoing loudly in the emptiness of the quiet night. He strode towards the white Land-Rover, his automatic pistol thrust forward waist high, his face a contorted mask.

"Where the hell do you think you are going, woman?" he demanded, wrenching the door open on the driver's side.

"Please don't shoot!" Wenda Britta shrieked, her hands trembling above her head. Her friend Ebele crossed herself and began to pray silently.

"I say where the bloody hell are you going? Where are you from? Get down! Two of you! Out!" Heinz jerked his head. "Leave the key right there and get down!"

"Oh my God, please don't, don't. We're from the Red Cross, we . . ."

"Shut up, you bitch! Move to the other car!" Hans ordered, prodding Wenda with the gun and jolting the other girl with a booted foot.

He hustled the pair into the back of his own Land-Rover, already cramped from the HMG and the two white officers behind the gun. He went back to the Red Cross car, took away the key and switched off the head-lamps.

"Back to the runway, Miguel," he told the white officer in the driver's seat.

Captain Miguel backed the Land-Rover into the edge of the road, steered it onto the tarmac, minding the row of empty trucks, switched on his head-lamps to full beam and began to drive furiously towards the centre of the airstrip where they had left Jacques Rudolf.

Colonel Charles Chumah was leaning on the wall of the small bungalow that served as arrivals lounge at the southern end of the airstrip. It was about three-quarters of a mile from the spot where Rudolf, now joined by Johann Schmuts, Bill Ball and Amilo Relli, were waiting for Hans Heinz to return from his investigation.

Charles Chumah and his troops had trekked on to the tarmac, the continuing Owerri–Onitsha highway half a mile from the southern end of the airstrip. He had then personally conducted a survey of the neighbourhood and finding no sign of Rudolf and his troops, had led his men finally to occupy and block the southern end of the strip which terminated at the arrivals bungalow.

The civilian staff at the bungalow were, they had told him, still waiting for the Air Force courier. The courier usually gave them the all-clear after military cargo had been off-loaded from each flight and civilians and non-security personnel could drive down the runway to meet any passengers. But the all-clear had not been sounded that night, and, being barred from unauthorised entry onto the runway, they had simply assumed that there was heavy military cargo still being cleared from the lone flight that had arrived some hours before.

Never being one to look for a black goat in pitch darkness, Chumah had withdrawn to the rear, to the bungalow, and waited for dawn. Either dawn or some indication of where the black goat was lurking on the dark airstrip.

Taking his armaments and logistical position into careful consideration, he had told Chime Dimkpa soon after their arrival that insofar as initiative lay with them, they would not provoke a night attack.

"We have to control our fire because of our own men on the other side," he had warned Dimkpa.

Kapitan Hans Heinz's Land-Rover racing down the ramrod-straight tarmac, full beam ahead, gave Colonel Charles Chumah the something he had been hoping for.

From his southern position Chumah saw the twin beams tunnel through the night darkness, just as Heinz had seen Wenda Britta's a few minutes previously.

Chumah started from the wall and instinctively thumbed the hammer of the pistol in his hand.

"Chime!" he called in a voice muffled and urgent. Dimkpa had seen the light too and was already heading for the Colonel. Chumah pointed heavenwards as the Major appeared on his side.

"Look at that!"

"I saw it, sir. I think that's the lamp of a Land-Rover. And it seems to be slowing down," he said, as the head-lamps dipped, shortening the tunnel into a dull glow, and finally went off.

"What do you make the distance, Chime?"

"I would put it at a little less than a mile. That would be about the middle of the runway itself. Somewhere around the area of the control tower, I think on Finger Ten."

"Right." The Colonel put the pistol away in his waistband.

"You're in charge now, Chime," Chumah said suddenly.

The Major turned to Chumah with amazement.

"I'm going back to Air HQ," the Colonel continued. "I'll take Captain Ude along. I have just got an idea. And I need some desperate help from the Air Force. I'll see you in the morning. About 7 a.m. Take care." He patted Dimkpa on the shoulder and was off before the Major could find his tongue.

Colonel Rudolf and his friends were talking in low voices, and did not see the girl Wenda and her friend until Miguel, the Italian Captain, had switched off the head-lights and their eyes became accustomed to the darkness.

Both girls were numb with fright at the sight of the sinister shadows in the darkness smoking from cupped hands like hoodlums from American gangster movies.

" 'Red Cross' she said," Hans mimicked, walking round from the back of the car with Wenda in his vice-like grip.

Jacques Rudolf had never had much use for the Red Cross and the charitable fingers that strayed into military pies. He had even less use for Wenda Britta's midnight humanitarianism.

"Listen, young woman," he began, his tone harsh and unsympathetic, "this place is no longer your Red Cross playground. It's a battlefield! You should have seen the military trucks and machinery down there and turned back."

"I'm sorry we trespassed, please for God's sake . . . I mean, we can still get back to our Land-Rover and leave . . . Oh, I . . ."

"You won't, lady. Not after you have been in here . . . Take them out of my sight, Hans. This will teach the Red Cross to keep to the hospitals."

Rudolf took a long drink from the neck of his bottle, extended it to Amilo Relli and turned away from the night breeze and the pleading girl to light a fresh cigarette.

In the glow from Rudolf's lighter Hans Heinz's face twisted with vicious lust. Like a greedy looter told that he could keep the booty, he grimaced in the darkness and tightened his grip around the terrified girl's wrist.

"Oh, my God, what are you going to do with us?" Wenda groaned helplessly. "Oh, my God, my God . . ."

"Shut up, you!" ordered Heinz, as he led them away.

0500 hours.

Flight-Lieutenant Boma Wari did not know of the emergency that

197

descended upon the airstrip while he was blissfully asleep in the officers' quarters at the far back of the Air HQ compound.

And when he was roused by his batman at 5 a.m. and told that there was an urgent message from the Chief of Air Staff, he had stumbled out of bed, groping for a candle and a box of matches.

It was a long time since he had risen to urgent developments, and the habit of hopping happily out of bed in the middle of the night had almost left him. It started leaving him in fact almost as soon as his last aircraft was shot to pieces in a mad raid with Hans Heinz over a heavily fortified enemy position nearly a year previously.

He shaded the flickering candle flame with one palm while he unfolded the sheet of paper with the other hand.

Soon he was reading the message scribbled in the COAS's own clear, but hurried handwriting.

FROM: BAF* COMD
TO: FL/LT B WARI (TAC)

YOU WILL RIGHTAWAY MOBILISE ALL NEC MANPOWER AND PUT HELICOPTER WORTHY FOR EMERGENCY OPS IMMEDIATELY(.) TECHNICAL PERSONNEL MUST BE DEPLOYED WITH IMMEDIATE EFFECT TO RIGHT ANY DEFECTS IN MACHINE(.) YOU WILL REPORT IMMEDIATELY AFTER TO COL CHUMAH AT COAS OFFICE FOR FURTHER INSTRUCTIONS(.) NOTE THIS IS EXTREME EMERGENCY(.) ENDS(.)

He had not thought it possible that any man in his right senses would want to send another man in the air with a helicopter that had not been airborne for nearly six months. Not even in a situation of 'extreme emergency'.

But in the Air Force the tough little flight-lieutenant had a reputation for being the man for extreme emergencies.

He was a small man of slight build, but with a disproportionate flair for desperate situations. His heart always jumped for joy at a prospect that would make ordinarily stout ones leap through the mouth.

Boma Wari looked at the watch on his wrist. Five minutes since he got the COAS's message. He rose quickly to his feet and began to dress up.

He had flown the first mission, as it were, for the Air Force, a modified DC-3 had been its first combat aircraft.

Now, with the barely serviceable last of the six original helicopters once used for tactical support of hard-pressed ground troops, he was

*See Glossary

going to fly what might well be his last mission. The thought did not dismay him.

CHAPTER FORTY-TWO

0600 HOURS.

Dawn came with slow uneventfulness. Its cool, crisp air and the distant purple light bore no indication that this was a day of bloody decision.

The General had made no move that Colonel Jacques Rudolf could see. And as dawn closed in, Rudolf's fears of an early morning bid by the General began to dissolve with the fast-fading haziness.

The empty ground-floor hall of the control tower had become Rudolf's command post.

The thought of the plane bestriding the runway gave Rudolf a new gust of dawn confidence in the certainty of an escape route. If the gamble began to look like a bad risk, they could always call it off and hop out, he thought.

Johann Schmuts had been thinking of the aircraft on the runway, too.

"Say, Jacques. We ought to do something about that plane out there. Cover it, you know. Just in case there was a raid or something."

Rudolf waved a dismissing hand.

"I don't share your fears, my dear Johann. The enemy wouldn't expect an aircraft to be lying on the rebel runway in broad daylight, would he?"

"They do make occasional daylight attacks on the strip, Jacques. I know that," Schmuts told the Colonel.

Through the crack in the fence Rudolf could see the outline of the huge Constellation hugging the runway beyond the narrow plot of bush. He turned from the window and began to pace the floor thoughtfully.

The prisoners in the room above Rudolf's ground-floor command post had been listening to the muffled screams and groans of a girl for nearly two hours and had finally abandoned their futile curiosity.

Only Captain Michel's mind returned to the greater curiosity of what might be happening outside the building.

Jules sat on the floor in a corner of the room, gratefully smoking the cigarette the Super Constellation co-pilot had offered him a minute back.

Hank Watson, the aircraft's captain, shrugged his broad shoulders in resignation.

In the room adjoining the prisoners', bare but for a few crates that once held radio equipment, Kapitan Hans Heinz struggled for breath. The weary but unyielding blonde girl was half-sitting on the floor and half-leaning on the wall.

He was gaunt and wiry in his nakedness and sweating in the still cold morning.

Her white nurse's coat was lying beneath an untidy pile of Heinz's uniform on top of one of the empty crates. Her torn brassiere hung from one surviving strap over her left shoulder. Her light-blue petticoat was torn.

He trembled and fumbled and panted with a merging of brutal desire and surprise at the girl's strength and resistance.

Wenda Britta's upper arm was an ugly smudge of purple finger-marks. Wild kicking, screaming and stout resistance had succeeded in preserving her panties from the ravaging, feverish fingers of the old Nazi. But the sight of her creamy thighs had fired the lust of the maniac in Hans Heinz.

"I have given you a long enough rope, you bitch!" he wheezed, reaching for her two hands thrust protectively over her groin. He missed one which shot up to his bristly chin and drew a crimson scar on the corner of his mouth.

Wenda Britta was as strong a girl as she was a beautiful blonde.

"Damn you, you bitching bastard!" Heinz cursed in a voice that sounded like air passing through hairy nostrils.

"Now! Or I'll use that gun!" he glared.

The gun!

The mention of the gun, lying among the pile of clothes over the empty crate, caused Wenda's stout heart to tremble. She had put up a masculine fight against the brutal force of Hans Heinz as soon as he had tossed his gun away along with his clothes.

But now, the gun!

Oh God! The gun! She moaned silently, her strength suddenly sapped by mortal fear of the maniac's threat.

"My God! My God, Oh, Oh!" She was moaning ineffectually as Hans Heinz, his eyes aglint with the smile of evil lust about to be assuaged, tore her thighs apart and ripped off the last shreds of Wenda Britta's privacy.

0700 hours.

The lone Federal MiG fighter-bomber swept out of the clear morning sky over the airstrip at seven o'clock that morning.

Colonel Rudolf's commanders exchanged horrified glances as the aircraft's cannon exploded in a resounding staccato over the runway. Rudolf dashed to the window and strained to get a glance at the hostile plane.

200

On the near side of the runway just beyond the bush, Captain Miguel was backing the armoured Land-Rover into the bush, as the white gunners who sat behind the HMG made for the shelter of the nearby trenches.

The plane came, flashing and stuttering, at top speed and low level.

Rudolf smelt the danger. He dashed out through the door, dived into the bush and ran heedlessly to the edge of the runway where the Land-Rover was trying to back out of the line of strafing.

Rudolf fell down beside the Land-Rover, and peered overhead as the MiG drew up above the Constellation.

Rudolf must have seen the first cannon hit the nose of the plane, for he yelled in a terrified voice for Miguel to get back behind the mounted gun and open fire.

But the MiG was gone before Miguel scrambled into position behind the HMG.

It was not gone for long, though. For presently it swept out of the skies again, banked sharply over the tree-tops and regained its bearing directly above the runway once more.

Captain Miguel was right on time this time, chattering away as if both he and the machine had gone crazy. From the remote gun emplacements inside the bushes, the heavier and more effective Bofors were coming up angrily at the MiG. But even the determined Miguel had to give up as the stuttering cannon raked and swept close to the edge of the runway and Rudolf was forced to dive under the Land-Rover.

A volley of cannon spattered the fuselage, shredded the fuel tank and promptly set the huge ship billowing with smoke.

It was a neat precise run that required no follow-up.

When Jacques Rudolf crept out of cover, his normally placid face was a livid mask of fury as he examined the wreckage of the gutted aircraft.

As the Constellation burnt into a black husk of its former, gleaming self, despair began to grope for Jacques Rudolf's heart.

The route of escape that had strengthened his hand inestimably was now irretrievably blocked.

Shaken, Rudolf began to find his way back to the control building.

The brief, brisk raid had caught Hans Heinz literally with his trousers down. Retrieving them with frantic fingers, his recent satisfaction submerged by the horror of the sudden raid, he had raced downstairs in bare feet and flying shirt, the badly bruised and ravaged blonde splayed out wearily behind the closed door.

The Christian Brothers in the ground-floor room wore worried faces when Rudolf entered the ground-floor hall.

"Well?" they asked of no one in particular.

"It could have been worse," Rudolf said in a low voice.

"The runway is not entirely unusable," he went on. "And when the General finds he can't fight with his own men, he will surely radio for a plane from Lisbon or Sao Thome. We mustn't forget that we hadn't reckoned on having a plane thrown into our hands when we started all this." He gestured vaguely.

"So there it is. We better forget we ever had one. It came like that"— he snapped his fingers in the air—"from the sky, and it's gone the way it came, like that." Rudolf sounded subtly firm, pre-empting any scepticism that might be given voice as a result of the recent mishap. The Commander had spoken.

"And so what has my dear Hans been up to with the Red Cross blonde?" Rudolf asked lightly, effortlessly changing the subject and retrieving his bottle of whisky.

Kapitan Heinz gave him a nervous wink and a crooked grin, and went on to repair his dishevelled look; tucking in his flying shirt and patting his tousled hair in place.

It was Major Derek Tremble who first heard the faint noise of the approaching Alouette helicopter.

Colonel Charles Chumah did not return to the airstrip at 7 a.m. as he had promised. The Air HQ Intercept Unit had given him the timely tip-off that a hostile aircraft was monitored on take off from Benin at six-thirty. Chumah had quickly radioed an indefinite postponement to Dimkpa at their southern stronghold. "Don't make any move," he had directed. "I shall be up as soon as the coast is clear." He had emphasised the *up* with a slight inflection of his voice, hoping that Chime would pick up the subtle signal, which he did not.

At 7.30, fifteen minutes after the raid, Intercept had given Colonel Chumah the all-clear.

The helicopter stood like a giant mosquito on the training ground. In the desperate early days of the war they had been used for tactical support operations in a pedestrian manner that belied the jet and technological age.

Armed with HMGs, a tiny handful of troops would nose the gun down through the helicopter's door, and rake their enemy's open trenches with fire from above.

But without spares and battered by anti-aircraft fire to which they had little resistance, the Alouettes had gradually been reduced to ground wreckage in Air Force junk yards.

Only one had survived. It had been covered in tarpaulin and treated to occasional servicing, for a possible emergency, like having to evacuate the General quickly in a moment of danger.

The back seats had been dismantled and an HMG mounted inside, its barrel protruding through the open door.

Flight Lieutenant Boma Wari eased himself into the pilot's seat.

Captain Gideon Ude followed from the open door, pushing the barrel of the gun out of his way.

Colonel Charles Chumah picked up a large cardboard box from the feet of the helicopter, heaved it over to Ude inside the cabin who caught it expertly and stowed it away beneath the pilot's seat, and made way for the Colonel to climb in.

The propeller creaked, revved, whinned and soon became a blurred halo above the tiny cabin.

As the aircraft lifted uncertainly from the ground, the Chief of Air Staff appeared, as if from nowhere, on the training ground, gave the groaning machine a stiff thumbs up and smothered his grave doubts with a nervous smile. He could remember no venture so risky in his whole time as an airman.

The cardboard box contained Colonel Chumah's ammunition for the battle ahead.

It was a peculiar kind of ammunition: over 5,000 sheets of hurriedly cyclostyled quarto-size paper.

"Listen, Bill!" Derek Tremble grabbed at the arm of Major Bill Ball nearest to him. "Do you hear anything?"

Ball inclined his head to the window and strained his ears. Other heads cocked and ears strained. "That sound's like a chopper!" Bill Ball exclaimed.

"Christ!" cried a flustered Johann Schmuts. "Let's get the hell out of here! I'm getting sick and tired of all this!" Johann Schmuts grumbled, not against his commander, but the apparently unremitting harassment.

"Let's get into the trenches," suggested Amilo Relli.

"Wait a moment," Rudolf called, pulling out his pistol. "Johann get the men to open fire. And shoot to kill!"

"Wait a minute, Jacques," Bill Ball put out a restraining hand. "As I said, that sounds like a chopper. It just occurs to me that the General might be sending over a couple of emissaries to talk with us. Surely he wouldn't be attacking in helicopters. Let's get out and have a look first."

How uncommon commonsense could be at times, Rudolf thought, nodding his head in agreement. "That's right, Bill. Let's go!"

"Here we are, now, Boma," Colonel Chumah declared in a low voice, as if afraid the troops below would overhear him.

"Take her closer, and lower now," Chumah directed, gesturing for emphasis. "Hold your fire, Ude."

With the ease of a veteran of bigger machines, Boma Wari nosed the

203

helicopter down to a tilt, reducing altitude by some fifty feet and eased back to a steady course again.

The rolling green bush that bordered the airstrip on the western side leapt up to his face as Chumah peered through his binoculars. The fresh red earth of the open trenches were sharp contours of ridges in the green bushes. Chumah could see the dark forms in the red earth that were the men crouching in wait, now stirring as the strange aircraft flew over their heads. It all happened in under two minutes.

"That's my boy, Boma!" Chumah exclaimed. "Hold her steady on now," he urged, throwing the binoculars from his face.

He reached for the papers in the open carton with both hands, heaved up a stack, flung it through the door and watched the white bombs flutter weightlessly, aimlessly in the air over the trenches.

Two more fistfuls followed in quick succession.

"Now step on her, Boma, and run her down the red lines, like on a strafing run," Chumah ordered, reaching for more papers with both hands as the aged machine groaned to a higher pitch and heaved forward with all her might and Boma Wari's considerable aviation skill.

The helicopter was raiding the far side of the Western trenches when Rudolf and his men ran out through the bush and on to the eastern side of the airstrip. The white papers floating out of the plane must have, for just a brief second, looked like fluttering white flags from peaceful emissaries as the Christian Brothers reached the runway and tried to make sense of this phenomenon.

But Rudolf and his men were soon gaping as brief hope faded into horror. The white flags were not fluttering. They were showering over the low bush in which the commandos were entrenched.

It took a few more horrified seconds before the impact of the unarmed raid permeated Rudolf's incredulous consciousness. Leaflet drops on the troops!

The little group of top commanders around Rudolf were beginning to fret. But Rudolf was trying to instill confidence by defiance. He pulled out his pistol so violently it nearly ripped the band of his trousers. He darted down the middle of the runway to Finger Ten, where Miguel was still gaping with incomprehension at the drama of the creaking helicopter disgorging a skyful of paper.

"Johann!" Rudolf swung round and yelled at his comrades who had failed to follow him. "Amilo! Bill! Derek! All of you get to the guns and get that damned thing down!"

His face was no longer the expressionless mask of the cold schemer. A mixture of fear and rage stood on his face like a dark-red shadow. He looked at his automatic pistol of many years' service, swiftly comprehended its utter futility in the mortal situation prevailing, and tossed it into the bush without sentiment.

Then Rudolf leapt onto the armed Land-Rover and shoved Miguel aside and laid trembling hands on the handle of the HMG. Nervously he swung the barrel towards the sky from where the helicopter was still showering papers upon the troops.

It was a hopelessly long distance from the sky over the far edges of the bush, but the desperate Colonel opened up all the same, an ear drum-piercing burst.

All the HMGs of the 5 Commando, now taken over by agitated Christian Brothers, seemed to open up all around Flight Lieutenant Boma Wari. The chatter filled his ears but he noted with satisfaction that the papers were still cascading below him. He heaved the machine into a shallow bank, and began to dive beneath the raging machine-gun fire.

But the guns were swivelling freely in quick pursuit. He tried zig-zagging as much as the lumbering manoeuvrability of the Alouette would allow, and counted his success in the fact that he had so far avoided a serious hit.

Meanwhile Colonel Chumah carried on with his paper work, steadily showering the bush like dry leaves in the harmattan wind.

They must have covered a reasonable proportion now, Chumah thought. "Now Boma, try getting to the north-easterly direction. We haven't covered that yet."

"The fire seems heaviest there, sir," Boma pointed out, "But we shall try." He began to turn the Alouette full circle.

"Give it your best," Chumah encouraged. "We could endanger the lives of those who haven't got the paper and don't know what the others know. We don't want a three-cornered war!

"And Ude, get ready for action now. Fire hard, but watch out. Not indiscriminate spraying. Pick on the ground gunners if you can spot them. Boma you can go really low now. We'll take the risk." Chumah finished and reached for more stacks of paper with both hands.

Over the northern end of the airstrip, where Rudolf's strong rear base and main body of his troops were concentrated, Boma Wari's ancient Alouette now creaked and groaned. Charles Chumah's leaflets drifted like a hundred paper kites and Gideon Ude's HMG intermittently chattered.

The ground fire also gathered momentum, barking and chattering. But the Alouette held together with amazing stubbornness.

Captain Ude's ears were jammed by the sputter of his own gun, the croaking of the propellers above him, and the stutter of intense firing from below, added to the whines of flying bullets and the richocet of lead against the body of the aircraft.

Colonel Chumah's yells of "Fire!" were lost in the bitter, deafening medley. But Ude was firing without urging, his teeth clenched, his body jammed against the door of the aircraft to support his balance as the plane heaved, ducked, banked and manoeuvred from the terror of the ground firing.

Over the ridge that marked the end of the airstrip at the northern end of the bush, Ude could see clearly, as the helicopter ducked lower and lower, the pink arms against the green bush. He glanced quickly at his ammunition belt. There were still several rounds to go.

Quickly he nosed the gun lower, swivelled the barrel a little to the right of the door and beat out a long sweeping burst that swept a wide arc around the pink targets.

On the ground Captain Henrique Martinez leapt up six clear inches from behind an HMG and dropped still, his face an unrecognisable mess of shredded flesh and blood. Pierre Coullar was already dead from multiple holes in the chest. Over a dozen commandos also sprawled lifeless from the fatal spray. Ude eyed them sadly. I can't help it, he told himself. I can't pick and choose very well from here.

"We can get out of here now, sir," Ude panted. "I think I have got the mercenaries at the end there," he pointed downwards. "And I'm running out of ammo," he added in a sad tone.

After the first ineffectual burst from the east side of the airstrip, Rudolf had got Miguel back behind the steering wheel of the Land-Rover and they were driving up to the northern end of the airstrip as the helicopter was turning for the long lap to Colonel Chumah's southern stronghold.

Thwarted, enraged and nervous, Colonel Rudolf quickly ordered Miguel to turn around just as the helicopter swept out of an arc just above the Land-Rover. The Colonel stopped firing to avoid drawing the plane's fire.

He laid low behind his gun waiting till Boma had cleared the area just over the loading bay and begun the long stretch to the arrivals lounge. Then Rudolf trained the HMG under the tail of the helicopter shouted on Miguel to speed up and began to fire at the escaping Alouette.

"Follow it, Miguel! Move!" he yelled frenziedly.

Captain Miguel followed the plane down the runway, but lost some speed as he skirted the craters dug by the MiG and avoided the black husk of the Constellation on the centre of the runway.

But he closed up as soon as he had navigated the impedimenta and kept to a steady two hundred yards behind the low-flying machine.

A spatter of bullets from Rudolf's HMG swept the body of the Alouette.

Captain Ude flung himself to the right side of the door and swung hi barrel to the left side, nozzle down on the ground below him. But Rudolf's Land-Rover sped down the runway in the shadow of the limping plane.

And when after much straining Ude saw their assailant, it was only the bonnet of the Land-Rover that came into view.

Colonel Rudolf was still firing away, concentrating on the body of the Alouette.

Having fed much into the belly of the helicopter, Miguel, at Rudolf's urging, edged the Land-Rover to the left side of the runway to give Rudolf a clear angle to finish off the plane.

A fierce volley exploded near the door and flung Ude into the corner of the plane, just as he got his first view of the attackers.

But he was up again, desperate to staunch the renewed assault. He angled the gun a little to right, trained it directly on the Land-Rover and began to empty his ammunition belt, yelling for Boma Wari to hurl the creaking Alouette over the last stretch.

But Rudolf came firing again, having ducked the Land-Rover under the shadow of the helicopter once again as soon as Ude bore in on his exposed position. The burst bit hard into the under-belly and tail areas of the fuselage, widening a wound inflicted by earlier bursts.

"Speed it up, Boma!" Ude cried. "We're still under heavy fire and I've no more ammo!"

Captain Ude had hardly turned round when a burst from below knocked him back into the cabin. Another fusillade smashed through into the cabin, sending splinters flying and Chumah and Wari ducking frantically. The Alouette lumbered uncertainly for a brief moment.

Wari quickly recovered to steady his course, but became aware that the little ship was losing both speed and altitude.

"I think we've been hit badly, sir," he announced to Chumah.

"It's none too soon, Boma."

Boma Wari looked back to see what he expected to see: a cloud of black smoke trailing the helicopter.

Chumah, too, looked back. But what caught his eyes was the agonised look of the Captain slumped back inside the cabin.

My God, Ude had been hit! He struggled quickly out of his seat and skipped over the piles of spent ammunition belts to the wounded Captain.

His left upper arm was soaked in blood. Chumah lifted it gingerly and examined it. "Gideon, are you all right?" he asked anxiously. Ude winced and nodded his head. "Just my hand, I think."

Colonel Rudolf had given up the chase as soon as the helicopter began to belch smoke. He knew that another 200 yards would bring him into the gunsights of Chumah's southern stronghold. He hoped the blaze would finish off both the plane and its crew.

Captain Miguel turned the Land-Rover around on the runway, as Rudolf fed a fresh belt into the HMG.

The struggle for his own life, Rudolf knew, was about to begin. In the distance, beyond the black husk of the Super Constellation, he could see no sign of the remaining Christian Brothers, not even of his top commanders.

Gravely, Rudolf ordered Miguel to drive slowly down the airstrip, keeping under cover of the carcass of the burnt aircraft in the middle of the runway.

He did not know what deadly, mutinous exhortation was written on those leaflets, but he did not need to read it to guess, he thought.

CHAPTER FORTY-THREE

THE LEAFLETS HAD brought moments of appropriate uncertainty and indecision rather than quick revelation to many of the troops on whom they fell. The ironic call to revolt against their commanders had an anticlimactic ring in the ears of an army that had been waiting for a clash of clashes with an enemy suicide squad.

GALLANT TROOPS OF THE FIVE COMMANDO DIVISION! THIS IS A SPECIAL MESSAGE FROM YOUR C-IN-C. THE WHITE MERCENARIES WHO HAVE BEEN PARADING AS OUR CHRISTIAN BROTHERS HAVE NOW SHOWN THEMSELVES FOR WHAT THEY ARE: TREACHEROUS ENEMIES OF THE REPUBLIC!
THEY ARE ENEMIES OF THE COUNTRY, YOUR COUNTRY, JUST LIKE THE VANDALS ON OUR TERRITORY! THE MERCENARIES HAVE TRICKED YOU INTO SEIZING YOUR OWN FATHERLAND WHICH YOU HAVE BOUGHT WITH YOUR BLOOD AND SWEAT! WE KNOW YOU ARE INNOCENT VICTIMS OF A TREASONABLE TRICK AND WE FORGIVE YOU UNCONDITIONALLY.
BUT YOU MUST TURN ROUND NOW IN ALL YOUR SUPERIOR NUMBERS AND ARREST ALL THE WHITE ENEMY IN YOUR MIDST. YOU MUST DO THAT IMMEDIATELY YOU FINISH READING THIS MESSAGE! SHOOT THEM IF THEY RESIST ARREST! REMEMBER THE WHITE MEN NOW AMONG YOU ARE AS DANGEROUS AS THE VANDALS!
GALLANT HEROES OF OUR REPUBLIC, ARREST ALL THE

WHITE MEN NOW AND LIBERATE YOUR OWN TERRITORY, YOUR AIRPORT, YOUR ONLY LINK WITH THE OUTSIDE WORLD!

To some of the men, drunk on hemp and nervous from a long wait for the enemy, it sounded like another trick to quell a trick. It might have been a propaganda move by the enemy.

But there at the end of the message was Colonel Charles Chumah's name, rank and signature, a scrawl familiar to the troops of the 5 Commando Division.

In a moment scepticism had begun to yield place to the realisation of the colossal trick, as the troops noticed the Christian Brothers begin to disappear as if on cue.

From one of the rows of trenches now white with leaflets, Second Lieutenant Rex leapt out and waved his men into position on both flanks and began to advance on the runway, his eyes sweeping the bushes for anything that looked pink.

Another junior officer had marshalled the troops on the left flank of the airstrip, rounded up three white captains that had commanded them a few minutes ago, and were prodding them none too gently with the barrels of their rifles.

Soon the troops were linked in a wide arc that covered the width of the airstrip as they advanced to outflank the storeyed building where they guessed the white men had taken armed refuge.

The Christian Brothers, too, had read, eyes wide with fear, the contents of the leaflets dropped on their troops. And their gambling instincts had told them that quick flight was the best route out of immediate massacre by the roused troops.

The unwritten canon of the fraternity of vultures and mercenaries of one-for-all, all-for-one, seemed to melt into a selfish, desperate everyman-for-himself-and-the-devil-take-the-last-man.

Major Derek Tremble did not waste time to surrender, viewing their defeat as a long-awaited victory for the one who survives.

As the troops advanced in two flanks down the tarmac towards the middle of the runway, their fear of a stout mercenary resistance began to peter away, as an increasing number of the former Christian Brothers cowered out from hiding, hands trembling in the air in unconditional surrender.

But Second Lieutenant Rex remained sceptical of the continued absence of the other top commanders and the building that loomed behind green camouflages across the bush.

When his former Commanding Officer, Amilo Relli was ferreted out of the bush where he was hiding in an air-raid bunker, Lieutenant Rex quickly ordered his captors to step aside. He emptied his pistol into the chest of the Italian.

"This one tried to resist arrest," Rex grimaced at the other trembling white soldiers.

At that time Rudolf was still lurking in the shadow of the burnt Constellation about three hundred yards down the middle of the runway.

The burly mercenary crouched behind the HMG in the shadows as the commotion of his advancing, searching, mutinous troops filled his ears.

Coherent thought seemed to desert the artful schemer as he searched fruitlessly for the way out.

The troops hadn't seen his Land-Rover behind the Constellation. Across the stretch of bush he could see the green camouflaged building of the control tower.

A distant commotion from behind caused Rudolf to turn. Right down the southern end were Colonel Chumah's forces marching up towards the middle of the runway! Towards him!

Rudolf needed no further consideration of the net closing in on him now from both ends of the airstrip. Without any warning to Miguel behind the steering wheel, the ex-Commander of the 5 Commando leapt from the Land-Rover on to the runway and broke into a run for the stretch of bush at the edge of the tarmac.

The troops of Lieutenant Rex must have spotted the running figure, for Rudolf quickly drew a rake of small-arms fire that followed his zig-zagging run into the bush.

Below his temple a crimson cut left the painful imprint of a bullet graze, but Rudolf continued to run, broke through the bush and ran for the control tower building.

At the door, Sergeant Chiko and two of Rudolf's bodyguards, innocent loyal guards in their ignorance of the dramatic disclosures on the leaflets, stepped aside and presented arms to their Commander as Rudolf ran up.

But it was not the same Colonel Rudolf that they knew. The usually placid face was an improbable mask of dirt, blood, sweat, desperate terror and fury.

Chiko was nearest to the gate and the first man the Colonel came near to. He did not see the bronzed and blackened hand flash like a matchet. The stocky Sergeant's neck snapped and Rudolf caught the rifle before it could fall, swung round and in the same movement fired point blank into the other two guards.

On the ground-floor he was disappointed not to find Hans and the rest of his henchmen. A bottle of whisky lay untouched on the bench. Rudolf stopped to take one long, last drink. In an instant he was up the staircase.

Rudolf rushed to the second door leading into the main room and raised his rifle to the locks.

The prisoners behind the locked door, nervous with puzzlement and fear, were about as good as deflated balloons when Rudolf's gunfire rattled the door.

Hazy from the darkness of the locked room, Hank Watson's eyes must have had difficulty in focusing. For he spoke, lightly and cheerily, as if he did not see the look on Rudolf's face that spoke louder than the rifle in his trembling hands.

"Well, if it ain't the Colonel!" Hank began. "Say what the goddammed . . ." and stopped abruptly.

"Shut up and get out, all of you!" Rudolf barked, his voice grating against the deadly tension that suddenly rose in the room.

Seven men filed out silently from the building, Michel and Jules, walking abreast, bringing up the rear.

Disappointment twisted the nervous Colonel's face, as he noticed that the white blonde girl was not among his prisoners.

A woman was a most valuable hostage.

He lined all seven of them face to the wall, went over to the door of the first room, and kicked it open with his boots.

Wenda Britta, aching all over with ugly purple bruises now taking on a hue of blue, was huddled by the wall with her friend Ebele who had found her some thirty minutes previously, and given her some water and put her clothes back on her.

"Get out, the two of you!" The weary Wenda staggered up under the unwavering eye of Rudolf's rifle.

With the nine hostages, seven men, three of them white men and two women, shielding him, Colonel Jacques Rudolf descended the steps to meet the troops he was sure were now taking position on the edge of the runway facing the building.

The terrified hostages trod warily out to the front of the house as Rudolf prodded them to the stretch of bush facing the runway.

Colonel Charles Chumah's column from the southern end had not arrived when Rudolf made his guarded appearance.

The sight of the prize object of the hunt caused a moment of blindness and fury. A fierce, brief volley rapidly followed Rudolf's appearance.

To the troops, all white men opposite them were white mercenary enemies.

But the first three men who fell under the hail before anyone could know what was happening, were Hank Watson, his co-pilot and the Frenchman Jules.

The volley caught Rudolf, still behind the women, unprepared. But he ducked instinctively, dragging the Swedish girl down with him.

Two of the three Air Force men were dead, the other badly wounded.

But Captain Michel had dived headlong away from the fallen hostages. He fell on his knees three yards away, and broke into a run before Rudolf could regain his balance behind the blonde hostage and bring his rifle into use.

Colonel Chumah's column arrived in the brief interlude following the fatal volley.

The helicopter had near-crashlanded at the southern end of the runway, and the three had barely cleared out of the cabin when it exploded.

With the troops he had marched down and seen Rex's forces massing on the runway facing the control tower. He had not motored down for fear that his message might not have sunk into the Commandos as quickly as he expected.

Rudolf struggled to his knees and dragged up the white girl. Ebele was trying to crawl back into the building. Rudolf stopped her with a cold gaze and motioned her back.

A disquieting calm followed. Colonel Chumah stood on the runway and eyed the building across the bush patch. There, at the foot of the fence, Rex told the Colonel, was where Rudolf was hiding, armed. The remaining mercenaries, they guessed, must be inside the building or hiding in the surrounding bushes.

Colonel Chumah nodded. He was about to order the troops to begin to flank the building when Rudolf made his move.

He clambered to his feet, dragging Wenda up in front of him, kicked the terrified Ebele up with his boot, and appeared in full view of the massed troops, the girls preceding him.

Chumah saw Rudolf, wretched, cowering behind the shield of helpless women, and held up his hand to restrain fire.

With elaborate deliberation, Charles Chumah began to walk up the edge of the runway. He climbed the parapet that marked the beginning of the stretch of bush and stopped for a few seconds.

With equal deliberation, he raised his rifle high in the air above his head in Rudolf's full view, and dropped it with a thud. He continued to walk towards Rudolf and his hostages.

Both men's eyes, as they confronted each other in the tense quiet of the airstrip, spoke their minds with great eloquence: Colonel Chumah's, cold, raging, and pitiless, bored into Rudolf's panicked and pallid face behind the black girl's shoulder.

"What do you want, Colonel Rudolf?" Chumah's voice was cold with his loathing for the man behind the women. "Safe conduct, I presume?"

Rudolf licked his lips nervously. "Yes," he admitted wretchedly. His voice had lost the commander's tone. "And for those of my men still alive." But his rifle was still nervously poking into the backs of the women hostages.

212

"How many of your men do you think have survived then?"

"I don't know. You've got many of them already."

"And suppose I say no, Colonel Rudolf? Suppose I'm willing to sacrifice these two girls? After all, you've killed, directly or indirectly, more than seven thousand of our boys during the past ten months. Suppose I refuse to make this dirty deal with you?"

"Then I'll shoot you as well as the girls," Rudolf hissed nervously. "I'll shoot you, Chumah, and to hell with what happens afterwards."

"Aren't you talking like the desperate man in a tight corner, Rudolf? What difference does shooting me make? How does my death improve your chances of survival? You know, Rudolf, if you are to live to be a mercenary again, there's one bit of advice you could use. Keep your dirty fingers out of this kind of war. Because you can never understand it.

"For instance, you cannot know that the Biafran Government cannot cough up two million dollars for you, can you? You do not ask for a chair when you see the head of the family sitting on a mat. A desperately poor man cannot submit to blackmail and demands for ransom, Rudolf."

"Then he will submit to death!" Rudolf panted nervously.

"And look, Rudolf. Since you are not a novice in matters of tricks and deceit, maybe it will appeal to you this way. Have you considered that I could give you my word now and take it back when it suits me?

"OK, now," Chumah continued, "so I guarantee you a safe conduct; all right? Now, do you seriously think you can take my word for it? After all the blood you have caused to flow? I suppose like a good mercenary you should know when the risk becomes too much to justify any rewards? You should know when you're in a hopeless position . . . Like now?"

Colonel Chumah spoke in a calm, cold voice that hardly belonged to him.

Rudolf's response was to prod his hostages with the barrel of the rifle.

He guessed that Rudolf's comrades inside and around the building were armed. But he guessed, too, that there could not be more than a dozen of them at the most, all their junior comrades having been rounded up by Second-Lieutenant Rex and his men.

"I think you'd better face up to it that this is the end of the road, Colonel Rudolf. I have no authority to guarantee you anything. That's the prerogative of the C-in-C. But if you insist on safe passage, then I will call your bluff!" he said suddenly sternly.

"And if you try, you'll find that I'm not bluffing. I'll shoot the girls first!" Rudolf countered equally sternly, if still rather nervously.

"And what will it solve? I regret that the girls are involved. But you can go ahead and shoot me. I'm unarmed. But it means that those boys out there on the runway will make sure that none of you gets out alive

213

in the next ten minutes. And what chances do you have of obtaining a safe conduct from the C-in-C when you are dead?

"I'm leaving now, Rudolf. You can shoot me in the back if you choose. But you should hold yourself responsible for what happens next if I do get back to the troops out there." Chumah made to leave, stopped and said, "I'm sorry about the girls, but there is a war on and I'm not submitting to a white mercenary's blackmail! I'll rather have *you* shot first. Good Luck, Colonel Rudolf. I've never seen a man in a more hopeless situation yet refusing to face it." He began walking back to the runway.

One thing had struck Jacques Rudolf silent. *What chances do you have of obtaining a safe conduct from the C-in-C when you are dead*? Colonel Chumah had asked him.

The antenna of his gambler's instinct quickly picked up the vague vibrations of hope. Clearly he did not see why the General should want to spare his life. But neither did he see what the General stood to gain by his death. Executing foreign nationals, even if convicted of a treasonable crime. was hardly good external publicity for man in the General's position, Rudolf calculated.

Well, a good gambler never hesitates to dice with his last franc, he reminded himself.

He decided to make that one last desperate throw of the dice. The gun thudded into the bush. Colonel Chumah, some twelve paces down on his way back to the runway, stopped, as if expecting to be really shot in the back.

The unmistakable voice of silence filled his ears as nothing happened. He turned round slowly to face the unarmed mercenary Commander.

Chumah began to walk back to him.

The General had of course been keeping pace with the progress of the battle for his airstrip. It had been a bitter battle.

Thirty minutes after the last of the surviving mercenaries had been rounded up, and an all-calm radioed to Defence Operations, a flash came through to Chumah.

WE MUST DEMONSTRATE OUR MATURITY AND MAGNA-NIMITY AT THIS REGRETTABLE HOUR.

Colonel Charles Chumah leaned an elbow on the bonnet of the Land-Rover parked in front of the arrivals lounge where Rudolf and the surviving former Christian Brothers were now being held.

He motioned Chime Dimkpa over and gave him the message to read.

"I don't like the word magnanimity in this case, Chime," he said slowly, shaking his head. "Magnanimity is saying to an enemy that his

214

weakness is his strength. That his defeat is his victory. And I doubt that this is fair to Jacques Rudolf and his bloodhounds!"

"So, what do we do then, sir?" Chime Dimkpa asked quietly, and continued: "It is an order . . . and . . . and as I see this business, it may not be too long before we qualify for the vandals' magnanimity. So we might as well do unto Rudolf as we would have our enemy do unto us."

"Alas, it is an order, Chime," the Colonel agreed, leaning up from the car. "And I dare say I'm going to obey it. But sometimes there is more than one way to obey an order. Meanwhile, will you find Lieutenant Uzoh or any officer of the Engineers and tell him to report here immediately." Chumah spoke rapidly; Dimkpa went off like a shot.

The Major returned several minutes later, accompanied by the youthful Lieutenant Uzoh and two sappers. Chris Uzoh had graduated from university with a First Class Honours degree in Chemical Engineering barely three months before war broke out, after a spell with the highly sensitive and top secret Research and Productions squad, Chris Uzoh distinguished himself as a genius with explosives, was soon re-deployed with the Army Engineers Unit where he continued to demonstrate his unequalled skill with bombs, mines and other home-made products of his former RaP* establishment.

Sending off Major Dimkpa on some important-sounding errand, Chumah drew the young Lieutenant aside and began to talk rapidly. "You've got a very crucial assignment, Chris," Major Dimkpa heard the Colonel say. He heard no more as the Colonel fell into intense whisper.

EPILOGUE

THE LAST NIGHT was grimly auspicious, though it had begun inauspiciously. The Intruder aircraft had dropped three bombs, mercifully flung into the bushes under the pressure of intense ground fire, at midnight some two hours before.

The black Mercedes-Benz was, however, absent this night.

Instead three black police vans came.

And they were not parked on the exclusive Finger Eight.

The aircraft that bestrode the runway was another Super Constellation, though. It could easily have been the very one that brought in the
*See Glossary

Christian Brothers nearly twelve months before. But it was not; there was a whole fleet of them in Lisbon.

Captain Michel was at the airstrip, as on the first night.

But so was Colonel Charles Chukwuemeka Chumah. He was now the Commander of the 5 Commando Division. And Major Chime Dimkpa, the second-in-command. And Flight-Lieutenant Boma Wari, now Commandant of the airstrip, though, curiously, for over one hour Wari seemed to have relinquished charge of the airstrip to young Lieutenant Chris Uzoh of the Army Engineers, who politely ordered everyone out of the runway and got quietly busy.

And so was a battalion of commandos armed to their teeth.

They ringed the southern approaches to the airstrip, just beyond the arrivals lounge, Colonel Chumah's former stronghold.

A full company of them surrounded the police vans, all rifles trained on the doors and tail-boards.

Lieutenant Rex, promoted by Chumah soon after the rout of the Christian Brothers, commanded the crack battalion. Through the wire-mesh he saw Kapitan Hans Heinz's face, frowned suddenly and spat on the tarmac.

At the arrivals lounge, Colonel Chumah and his aides waited impatiently for the 'All-Clear' call. They had waited for one hour.

"I wonder what the hell is holding us up."

"Maybe cargo, sir. Heavy stuff and all that."

It came at twenty-five minutes past 2 a.m. The All-Clear.

"Right, then, here we go," called the Colonel. "Chime, you get the Land-Rover. And Boma you tell Rex to move the lorries nearer to the aircraft. Not so fast, so that the guards can keep pace. The only mercenary I can trust is a dead mercenary."

About a hundred yards to the waiting Super Constellation, Lieutenant Rex halted the vans.

The company of guards tensed their fingers round their triggers, all eyes riveted on the vans. The airstrip Commandant had faithfully restated the Colonel's remarks: the only mercenary to be trusted was a dead one. One crack out of the back of that lorry and there would be no passengers for the waiting aircraft. Only corpses. Thirty of them.

Lieutenant Rex went over to the Colonel and saluted.

"Where's Lieutenant Uzoh, Rex?" the Colonel asked anxiously.

"Over there at the aircraft, sir. Here he comes . . ."

"Everything OK, Chris?" the Colonel enquired in a whisper.

"Yes, sir."

And in a louder voice: "Enough room?"

"More than enough, sir."

In the dull glow of the red hurricane lamps that lined the edges of the runway, the drawn, bruised faces of the mercenaries could be seen in grim relief. They all seemed to have aged years over the nights. Wretchedness seemed to be their common denominator.

Jacques Rudolf was still the leader.

He was the first to step down from the Black Maria and the first to go up the ramp into the aircraft.

The rest were all there, following behind him.

All the survivors, that was.

Kapitan Hans Heinz.

Bill Ball.

Johann Schmuts.

Luiz.

Miguel.

Johni, the demolition expert.

Ernest Belgar, though not Pierre Coullar.

O'Casey, the Irishman . . .

And of course, Derek Tremble.

Eight others had been shot out of hand by the Commandos.

Derek Tremble was perhaps the only one who looked forward to departure with the greatest impatience. He was not bowed like the other beaten mercenaries, though he did not show it. His had been a job well done. A delicate under-cover job done without him being uncovered. And he could count the end, wretched as it was, as a resounding victory. For him victory consisted solely in the improbable fact that he was not entering the aircraft feet first.

And there were enough hand-cuffs to go round, too.

No two Brothers were chained together. Each had a pair of hand-cuffs to himself, thanks to the police. Even Miguel, with bandages on both his arms, had them handcuffed behind his back, like the rest.

Just then, as Hans Heinz was about to climb up the gangway, Colonel Charles Chumah gave what appeared to be a most perplexing order. "Release Kapitan Heinz and bring him here."

Chime Dimkpa looked aghast as Lieutenant Uzoh, the only one privy to the Colonel's plans, stepped out of the shadows and freed the hands of the ancient German.

"Hans Heinz," the Colonel began, examining the scrawny face of the aged mercenary. "You are an experienced pilot. You flew both sorties and shuttles in the Congo, so you must be familiar with almost all kinds of aircraft.

"You will fly your comrades-in-arms out in that aircraft," he pointed to the Super Constellation—"to *any* destination of your choice. Our

217

commercial pilots need a rest for now, and in any case the exercise will do you some good after flying a desk at 5 Commando for nearly one year.

"You can say it's our last gesture of magnanimity to you all. On your way!"

Hans Heinz rubbed his wrists furtively and nodded gratefully.

Chumah turned, winked at Uzoh, and carefully ignored an incredulous Dimkpa next to him.

Lieutenant Rex followed the last prisoner up the gangway. Never trust a living mercenary.

As the young man came down the gangway, Colonel Chumah spoke to Chime Dimkpa at last. "There's no need to worry, Chime. We're simply implementing the General's orders to the letter."

"That's all right, sir, but do you mean no one will accompany the mercenaries out?"

"That's what I mean, Chime."

"With all due respect, sir, I think that's a strange decision. Mightn't we be carrying out the General's orders to a ridiculous extent?"

The aircraft's engines were revving full blast. Chumah began to walk back to the command Land-Rover, with Dimkpa at his side. When they reached the car, Chumah planted a foot on the front bumper, turned to Chime Dimkpa and answered his query.

"Don't be a fool, Chime," he began with an admonition. "We are not exactly robots. The luggage compartment of that aircraft is bristling with 200 pounds of Biafra-made *ogbunigwe* chain-mines, wired to a device timed to go off over the Atlantic ocean in precisely two hours from the time the plane leaves here. Our Lieutenant Chris Uzoh saw to that.

"The General can't court-martial us for accidental explosions over the high seas, can he? Come on, let's go and get some sleep."

Colonel Chumah tapped his swagger stick on his right thigh and climbed into the back seat of the command car. Chime Dimkpa gaped for a while at the man, and at the ruthless ingenuity of his friend and commander. In the distance, the aircraft whined furiously.

It was the second night after Colonel Jacques Helmut Rudolf's revolt came to an end.

Another two days later, the 5 Commando Division was disbanded, at Colonel Charles Chumah's suggestion to the General.

The second phase had come to an end.

And the third was beginning.

218

Cover photograph
by Peter Obe
Photo Agency

This superb action-packed thriller centres round 'forty-eight guns', the forty-eight mercenaries who are flown in supposedly to help the Biafrans. As usual the mercenaries are a law unto themselves and their leader, Colonel Rudolf, is ruthless in exploiting the situation to his own advantage. However, when Colonel Chumah is appointed as his second-in-command, the Frenchman finds he has met his match. This intensely captivating tale of war also shows how the mercenary involvement in Angola was a repetition of so much that happened in Biafra.

E D D I E I R O H says of himself:
I was born on banana leaves and partially orphaned at eight. I learnt to pull myself up by my boot-straps. I have been clerk, columnist, critic, correspondent, publisher, and producer—in that order. Trained in the militia I spent the civil war years commanding the War Reports desk in the secessionist War Information Bureau from where I made occasional forays to the battle-fronts, covering the encirclement and recapture of Owerri by the secessionists in the summer of 1969. For a while I served on the research staff of the secessionist Briefs Committee which drafted all major speeches and policy positions. For the past year and a half, I have been writing and producing for Nigeria Television in Enugu.

African Writers Series

An H·E·B Paperback

£1.25 Africa and Caribbean; elsewhere £1.70 net